THE RED WORLD WAR

ARMORED WARRIOR PANZERTER
BOOK 1

T. E. BUTCHER

For my Family

1

"Poncho?" Lieutenant Paul Reiter asked, checklist in his hand. Corporal Mondragon lifted the mud-brown and green sheet. "I see it, Mo." They sat in an old rec room that reeked of cigarette smoke with all the gear the Tharcian Army believed Mondragon needed splayed out on the floor.

"I don't understand why I have to pack half this shit, sir," the younger soldier replied. "It's not like I'm going to get rained on inside a Panzerter."

Reiter shook his head. <$>

"Well, Mo, I can offer you two reasons. The first is that you must leave your Panzerter eventually and it might rain." He pointed to the green-gray jacket and trousers that made their garrison uniforms. "These are only water-resistant, not waterproof, and your crew shirt and pants are neither."

"And the other reason?" Mo asked.

"Because Sergeant Varga will give you the disappointed dad talk when he finds you not following the packing list before he gives one to me about looking the other way," Reiter replied.

The corporal chuckled as he began repacking his ruck.

"You know, I'd rather be yelled at," he said.

Reiter nodded as he stood.

"Same. As soon as you're packed, throw your stuff into your machine," he said. "And Mo?"

"Yes, sir?"

Reiter handed him a worksheet.

"I need you to run PM on your Panzerter and go by the book."

Mo threw up his hands.

"But sir, it hasn't moved. This is our third mobilization drill this month, and the last two drills, we were told to stand down." He sat on his ruck as he tightened it. "Besides, I doubt the gearheads fixed my air-conditioning."

Reiter shook his head.

"Look, let's focus on the task in front of us. It's all we can do."

Mo stood, throwing his bag over his shoulder.

"Hey sir, if I'm a part of history, can that be extra credit?" he asked.

Reiter chuckled.

"If the Union declares war, you and I have bigger concerns than your grades." He patted the younger man on the shoulder as he left. "Now if you'll excuse me, I need to turn in our battle roster."

Memorabilia from the unit's past lined the hallway. Awards for performance, trophies from competitions, and pictures and decorations from the War of 2112 paraded by Reiter as he headed to the conference room. He'd lost himself in the pictures when he bumped into Sergeant Varga.

"Hey, I was looking for you," said the short, stocky master sergeant. "Maintenance is done, we're just waiting on Mo's checklist."

Reiter nodded.

"Have Stanca or Top assigned us anything else for the day?"

His platoon sergeant shook his head and checked his watch.

"Once Mo finishes, we can make a case to Top and the commander to release us by two."

Reiter checked his phone and whistled. It was one in the afternoon.

"So you think we'll get out in an hour?" he asked. Varga twisted his hand in the air like a broken propeller. "I can live with that. We've done this like five times—we should be experts by now."

The older man chuckled.

"Hey sir, I couldn't care less what Stanca says if we can get cold drinks at Mario's in an hour or two."

They finished their tasks in the office and left for the hangar. Two of Fox Company's platoons were Panzerter platoons. On either side of the hangar stood a row of seven Panzerters. Five Panzerters on each side belonged to 2nd and 3rd Platoons; the other four belonged to headquarters. Reiter walked to the left, where his platoon's machines stood.

"Hey sir!" called a voice from above.

Reiter looked up at the nearest catwalk.

"Adamski! How's maintenance going?"

Adamski shrugged.

"Legousi and Mo are up to their elbows in Mo's cockpit, and that's not a euphemism, sir. His air-conditioning is shit." The big sergeant's booming voice echoed in the hangar.

Reiter shook his head as Adamski climbed down so he didn't have to shout.

"Are there any other pressing issues?" the lieutenant asked.

Adamski scratched the back of his head.

"You have a bum searchlight, Varga's machine needs to get jumped off—it might need a new starter solenoid—my defroster fails the bit test, and Legousi had to make a new bailout handle out of parachute cord." Adamski rattled off the laundry list of defects, and Reiter sighed.

"Still? What do mechanics even do?" He ran a hand through his sandy hair. "If anything, we've had more things break than before we started mobilizing."

Adamski shrugged.

"I dunno, boss, it looks like they abused our Mark IVs. They're new machines in name only."

Reiter and Varga piloted the Mark IVs in question. They were slightly bigger than the older Panzerter IIIs the rest of the platoon used, better armored, capable of wielding heavier weapons, and only a couple of kilometers slower.

"Well, they aren't complete write-offs either." He checked his watch. "If we finish maintenance checks, we can leave early," he said to Adamski's amusement.

"Sir, it's afternoon," said the sergeant. "You think we're getting out early?"

Reiter glanced around the hangar for White Platoon.

"Varga is speaking to Top about letting us leave early. Once they're good, I'll talk to the CO and we'll finish for the day."

Adamski shook his head.

"If we're out of here by six, I'll buy the first round of drinks at Mario's," the big sergeant declared, offering his hand.

Reiter grinned as he shook on it.

"I'll remember this, Ski." He left for the commander's office, and 2nd Platoon brushed by him. He didn't know Lieutenant Kress or MSG. Renner, but he knew his own soldiers thought the men were creeps. That all three of Reiter's pilots were attractive women didn't hurt their case. He walked down the short hallway to the commander's office. The door was open, so he stepped inside.

"Ah, Reiter, good, I was about to send for you," the commander said. Captain Stanca stood behind his desk, a map of the Dracul

River Valley stretched behind him. "This could be the real thing. The Union delegation arrived in New Franklin this morning. We'll find out soon enough whether we go to war or avoid it."

Reiter shrugged.

"If we dodge it this time, it will be something else next time. We didn't go to war when they torpedoed our freighter, even though they nuked her. I doubt an accident like the one a couple weeks ago kicks things off."

"Is that your opinion as a soldier or as a history teacher?" Stanca asked.

"My opinion as a man, sir," Reiter replied. "Though, Black Platoon is ready, in case I'm wrong."

Stanca nodded.

"I'm allowing you to dismiss your platoon early because you're done for the day, and it could be the last peaceful night you boys enjoy," the captain finally said. "Don't worry about cleaning the hangar. It'll either be 2nd or the infantry taking care of that, whoever finishes last."

Reiter nodded and returned to the hangar.

His soldiers were standing around Varga, getting a quiet safety brief. He checked his watch. 1:45 P.M.

"Hey gentlemen, who's hungry?" he asked.

───────

REITER THOUGHT THE CLINK OF GLASS MUGS WAS ONE OF THE MOST refreshing sounds on Mars. The five of them sat in a booth at Mario's enjoying cold drinks on Adamski's Krone. Reiter wore a simple black synthetic shirt with a hood. Varga had chosen casual pants and a red polo. The two of them glanced at one of the TVs playing the news.

"Would you rather have fingers the length of legs or legs the length of fingers?" Legousi asked, chuckling when the others shook their heads. The man's dark slicked-back hair and dark eyes contrasted the younger Mo's blond hair and blue eyes as he looked at his mug. They both wore Fox Company hoodies, as did Adamski. Reiter couldn't name the song playing, but the music was festive.

"I'm going to need more beer for this, Gos," Reiter said, nudging him.

"Mo is the little fish; Mo should answer first," Legousi said.

Adamski cut him off.

"Finger-legs I can hide with a wheelchair," said the big man.

Legousi threw up his hands.

"What about when you fuck?" he asked.

Adamski shrugged.

"Then I say, 'hey girl, I got a horrible secret: I have finger-legs.'"

Varga furrowed his brow as he sipped his drink.

"Sex isn't even that big a deal. What about your feet?"

"What do you mean, big sergeant?" Adamski asked as Varga pointed down.

"He said your legs are the length of fingers; he didn't say your feet were different," the older man clarified.

Adamski palmed his forehead.

"I guess I'd have to wear shoes and just say it's a joke," he replied.

Reiter snickered at the thought of Adamski wheeling himself around with a pair of size 17 shoes sitting in front of his waist.

"What about you, big sergeant?"

Varga took a swig of beer.

"Leg-fingers, definitely leg-fingers," he replied.

Adamski's mouth dropped.

"Why?"

They laughed as Varga held up three fingers for emphasis, imagining them scraping the ceiling.

"Well, for one, if my fingers are the length of legs, they're probably as strong as legs, so flicking someone would be the same as kicking them." He made a flicking motion diagonally across the table at Legousi. "Secondly, I could flick Gos from right here in total comfort." They laughed as Varga took another pull from his beer, finishing the glass.

"And the last?" Mo asked.

The older man wiped the foam from his face with his sleeve.

"I'd join a freak show and make more money than soldiering or working construction."

Reiter chuckled with everyone else.

"I don't see why you wouldn't just go to the hospital and get your finger-legs amputated," he said.

Legousi raised an eyebrow.

"Can't do that, sir."

"Why not? I'm thinking outside the box here. You could get cool robotic legs or have regular legs grown for you," Reiter replied.

Gos shook his head.

"That's not the spirit of the prompt, sir," he said.

Reiter glanced at the TV. Howard Mason, the Union's Minister of Foreign Affairs, had arrived in New Franklin. Negotiations would start soon.

"Alright, boys, I got one," Reiter said.

"Well, we're all ears, sir," Adamski replied as a grin stretched across his face.

"Would you rather lose the ability to read or speak?" Reiter asked.

"Read," they all answered immediately and nearly simultaneously.

"Wow, I would give up speaking," Reiter said as he sipped his beer.

"Sir, are you saying you'd never communicate with anyone ever again?" Adamski asked.

Reiter shook his head.

"No, Ski, I could still write things or type them out." He took another swig. "Unless you Neanderthals all can't read."

That brought another round of laughter to their table.

"Who are you texting, Mo?" Legousi asked as he leaned into the younger soldier.

"Who's Amy?" Adamski leaned against his other side. "Oh wait, Amy Steele? Is she in Creepy Kress's platoon?"

Legousi shook his head.

"My guy, don't date army women," he said.

Mo threw his hands up.

"I knew her before she was in! She's in my history class, right, sir?"

Reiter nodded.

"I hope she isn't asking you for help."

Mo shook his head.

"Nah, sir, you got it backwards. I help her in math, though."

Adamski finished his beer.

"How are you sure Steele isn't using you?" the big soldier asked.

Mo rolled his eyes.

"Because she picks up math much faster than I do history." He sipped his beer. "It's not like she was asking me for anything, she was just venting about bringing her poncho and rain gear."

Legousi motioned to Varga and Reiter.

"Sir? Sergeant? Anything to add?" he asked.

They shook their heads.

"As long as they stay professional in the workplace, their personal lives aren't my business like that," Varga said, then he ordered a refill.

"He's not her superior or anything. As long as they aren't breaking any laws or regulations, it doesn't concern me," Reiter added before finishing his beer.

"Okay, just so we're clear, everyone's on their own now unless someone else feels generous," Adamski said.

Legousi raised his half-empty beer.

"Why do you think I'm savoring this one?"

Reiter remembered Stanca's words as they laughed. What if this was one of the last peaceful nights they had?

Legousi caught him looking at the TV. "Think it's another false alarm?"

Reiter shrugged.

"I'd be lying if I said I knew. I know you all hate hearing it, but stay flexible."

Mo shook his head.

"One weekend a month, they said. Two weeks in the summer, they said."

Adamski clapped him on the back.

"Hey, don't forget every flood or tornado in eastern Tharsis."

Varga started his next beer.

"Look gentlemen, it's inconvenient, I get it, but we're getting paid for all this, and it's not really that hard right now."

Reiter nodded and ordered a refill.

"Know what, gents, I got our refills."

Legousi reached across the table and clapped him on the shoulder before finishing his beer.

Adamski and Mo grinned.

"Hell yeah, L-T!" they said together.

A creeping silence descending over Mario's interrupted their laughter. Reiter noticed the music had stopped.

"Excuse me, can someone turn up the TV?" he asked.

They focused on the monitor as the volume rose.

"-Minutes ago, they shot Howard Mason in Delano Plaza," said the news anchor. "The UMR's top diplomat is currently in critical condition. It is unknown what the Union government's response will be at this point in time."

Reiter sighed and stared into his beer.

"Let's enjoy them while we have them, boys. This is the last cold beer we'll get for a while."

The clink of their glasses ended the night on a sober note.

He strode to the edge of the balcony and leaned over the safety railing. Guard Colonel Damian Blake watched as the Panzerter companies below him rushed about. Thirty-two of the most advanced machines in the Union wielding groundbreaking arsenals. Each of the newest model Martian class Panzerters stood as tall as a four-story building. A powerful engine, a 360-degree sensor ring on the head, and thick armor painted in MAG standard double-grays and red told the entire story. The Union had learned from the disastrous War of 2112. The MAGs were evidence of that.

Blake adjusted his large round glasses back onto his narrow face. He wondered if that conflict would have turned out differently had the Mobile Assault Guards existed back then. With a shake of his head, he dismissed that chain of thought and continued to observe the Panzerter companies preparing to muster.

"I thought I would find you up here, Comrade Colonel," said a female voice. Blake looked behind him to the Amazon of a woman that served as his XO. Even for a 3rd generation Mars-woman, she was tall at 192 centimeters.

Blake nodded.

"What's the status of our support elements?" he asked.

Guard Major Meyer got straight down to business. Blake appreciated that.

"Mechanized infantry and scouts are ready to move out," she replied. "The artillery battery and both anti-aircraft platoons are waiting on software updates to install."

Blake frowned.

"Do all the commander units have the proper risk matrices loaded?"

Meyer checked a small tablet in her hand and gave him a thumbs up.

"Have we received word yet?" she asked. Blake shook his head. She leaned over the railing next to him. "I don't understand what they're waiting on."

"Just be patient. We declared war on Roosevelt already. The treaty binds Tharsis to aid them." Blake's words were measured with a precision an architect would appreciate.

Meyer looked down at the ground floor of the massive circular hangar, observing the soldiers there.

"They've grown up in a land surrounded by enemies seeking to undermine them. I bet they can't wait to cut their teeth in battle."

Blake nodded slowly.

"We learned from the War of 2112 that our neighbors seek to dismantle and subjugate us. The *Ave Maria* incident taught us they would do so by underhanded means if possible."

Meyer smirked.

"Bet they never counted on us to strike first," she replied. "We lost the War of 212, but with our new weapons and tactics . . ." Meyer smiled coldly.

"Assemble the officers in the conference room. I need to address them personally," he said.

Meyer saluted and left to perform her duties. Blake remained on the balcony for a moment longer before leaving for the conference room. The room itself was rather spartan, with a central table made from false wood. Within a few minutes of his arrival, all twenty-seven officers of the 12th Armored Battalion sat at the table.

"Ladies and Gentlemen, the question we face tonight is not if, but when Tharsis will declare war in defense of Roosevelt," Blake began. He paced the length of the room.

"Are we going to wait until they attack us again?" one of his officers asked.

Blake shook his head.

"War plans are still being reviewed based on the situation, but I believe we intend to strike first and hard." The young lieutenant who'd spoken looked frustrated. "Be patient, Lieutenant Moore, you'll get your taste of war soon enough." Blake paused. "Speaking of which, none of our soldiers have seen combat outside a simulator."

"With all due respect, Comrade Colonel, what's your point?" another asked.

Blake glanced at the guard captain as he paced.

"My point, Captain Stilwell, is your soldiers are green, and you are green," he replied. "You can sim as much as you want—it will still not prepare you for the real thing."

Stilwell stiffened.

"But we base the simulations on the most realistic models we have available. We have the most advanced weapons of any military on Mars. With all due respect, what is your point?" Stilwell punctuated his words by jabbing his finger on the table.

His XO put a hand on his shoulder.

"I think his point is, we could still die and we'll lose good men and women. Am I correct, Colonel?"

Blake nodded, smiling inside. Sr. Lieutenant Kennedy was a rising star among the ranks.

"Kennedy is correct. War is a nasty chaotic thing, the media expects a quick victory—" He paused and took a seat at the head of the conference table. "I believe we should be a tad more realistic."

Systematically, they eliminated supply and personnel issues. They gave extra equipment to units that were lacking. They sorted pay issues. It was boring, but necessary.

When he finished, Blake returned to the balcony in the hangar. Below, mechanics worked out any last minute kinks while Panzerter crews rehearsed moving in formation.

Meyer reappeared behind him.

"They have given us a rally point," she said.

Blake rose from the railing.

"Then it's coming. Where?"

Meyer stepped up next to him. On her tablet, she pulled up a map of the border.

"Overton Military Airfield, about 15 miles from here," she said.

Blake glanced at the map himself.

"And 60 miles from the border with Tharsis." He ground his teeth. "And the former Gallacian Martian Republic." With a huff, he left the balcony area. "I'm going to check the status of my Martian. If I am needed, I'll be on the hangar floor."

Several flights of stairs later, he strode across the concrete floor of the hangar. The space was divided into thirds for each Panzerter company, with Blake's personal machine standing just in the center.

"Sergeant Drue, what's the status of my Martian?" he asked.

His head mechanic looked nervous.

"Comrade Colonel! Uh, well, your command matrices need to

be reloaded, and your fire control system needs a software update," he replied.

Blake raised an eyebrow.

"They informed me that they'd loaded the matrices. Was there an issue?"

Drue looked about.

"Well, the complete system crashed and needed to be reset"—he looked back at the Martian—"because the command console needed a software update."

Blake took a step forward, forcing Drue back.

"And when was this software update released?"

Drue looked up at him now.

"Last week," the man replied.

Blake took another step forward. Drue was pinned against the Martian's leg, inches from the officer.

"Dereliction of duty is a serious offense, Sergeant," Blake said. "I do not tolerate negligence in my battalion, let alone with the upkeep of my personal machine." He stepped back. "I will speak to Master Sergeant Lee. I expect a different mechanic team by tomorrow. Were there any mechanical issues?" Drue shook his head, and Blake believed him. The hardware was never a problem for the young mechanic.

Blake stepped back to admire his Martian. His own double-gray uniform matched the paint of the rugged Panzerter. Extra antenna for more radio equipment, a command console, and the added cockpit armor marked his Panzerter as a Martian Commander.

"Comrade Colonel!" a young soldier cried as she ran to him across the hangar floor. "They've done it, they've gone and done it!"

Blake set a hand on her shoulder.

"Easy, young comrade, who's done what?" he asked.

She took a few breaths before continuing.

"The Tharcians, they've declared war."

Blake nodded and dismissed the young woman.

"Officers, fall in on me!" he called, stepping on a crate as they ran over. "As many of you already know, Tharsis has declared war. All personnel need to be mounted up and ready to move out in an hour. Now move!"

They scattered to their positions. Pilots rushed into their locker rooms to change into CVC uniforms.

Blake left to do the same. He passed Meyer on his way to his office.

"Have you put out the rally point?" he asked. She nodded. "Good, get the HQ truck ready to move."

Blake's office was next to the conference room. Union interior designers had had their way with it, and it showed in its minimalist furnishings. He opened a locker and removed his Combat Vehicle Crewman uniform. It was a gunmetal gray one-piece with a zipper up the center-front. It had holes for his boots and was woven with flame-retardant material. He wasted no time putting it on.

After changing, he left his office with his helmet in his hand. Now that the hangar doors were opening, a chilly October breeze swept the circular space. As frigid air snatched at him, Blake wished he'd remembered his heavy jacket.

All over the hangar, technicians guided Martians out of their berths and into the dark night. Snow flurries whipped at them— typical for early October in the Union of Martian Republics. Blake climbed up to the catwalk just below the Martian's head. Using the antenna mounts as handholds, he opened the hatch on the Martian's crown and descended into the metal giant.

A short ladder brought him just beneath the Martian's head. As he slumped into the metal-backed chair, he took the Martian through its startup sequence. Engine, sensors, command console, targeting—one by one, his systems came online. The bank of switches, buttons, gauges and monitors in front of him lit up with a soft orange light. The sensor ring treated him to a panoramic view of his surroundings.

Before stepping off, he checked his command matrix. Everything seemed in order. Confident Drue hadn't ruined the expensive system, he grasped his control stick and throttle. A tech on the ground guided him out of the hangar.

Snow danced in the headlights of the tracked vehicles on the ground. Overton's light cast the thick clouds in shades of orange. He moved his Martian to the head of the column. The Martians took both sides of the road, standing two abreast. For a man on the brink of war, Blake's cockpit remained tranquil.

It didn't take them long to move to Overton Military Airfield. As close as they were, they were the second battalion to arrive. The 118th MAG Raider Battalion was already preparing their dropships for battle. He brought his Martian to its knees, then checked behind his seat and sighed. Drue had remembered to put his field bag in the Martian.

After a quick search through his bag, he found his crew jacket. *I have to find Division HQ.* He reclined in his chair, taking in the few precious moments of solitude, then out into the snowy night, he climbed.

The Martians knelt on a tarmac, with their tracked vehicles off to the side. Aircraft hangars lined both sides of the tarmac, which branched off to multiple runways. Blake's eyes focused on a long, low building at the opposite end of the tarmac. The HQ building.

Blake felt a tinge of nostalgia as he entered and walked through the halls. *It's been half a decade since my staff duty years.* After rounding a corner, he ran into the 118th's commander.

"Colonel Druza, I take it the raiders are ready?" he asked.

Druza was broad-shouldered and built. He laughed.

"They are," he replied. "Anything is better than the peace-keeping shit in Lowell by the canal."

Blake nodded.

"I take it your tour was eventful?"

Druza shook his head.

"Here, walk with me. No, it wasn't fucking eventful," the raider officer replied. "Partisan here, partisan there, fucking IED every other-where—it was all horseshit." the Raider officer replied.

"Well, that certainly sounds unpleasant. Has General Nike said anything to you?" Blake asked.

Druza shook his head.

"No, she's in a call with Army Command. She'll brief us when the other bats get here." Druza led him to a lounge room with leather couches, reclining chairs, a refrigerator, and a coffeepot. "Coffee?"

"No thanks, I'm good for now," Blake replied. He watched as the man took a deep whiff of the brewing coffee.

"Beats the hell out of that shit overseas," Druza said.

"Evidently," Blake replied, cringing as Druza loudly sipped his coffee.

"Ah, that's the shit." Druza leaned against the countertop. "I fucking love being home."

"Well, don't get too comfortable. We'll be leaving soon," Blake replied.

Druza grinned.

"Say, Blake, do you have any idea why they picked this airfield to rally?"

Blake folded his arms.

"I have a feeling it's because of your dropships," he replied.

Druza shook his head.

"No, I got word they might try something crazy."

Blake sniffed.

"Are you going to lead me on?" he snapped. "Or will you tell me something useful?"

Druza sipped loudly on his coffee again.

"Ah, there it is. Oh, and they might airdrop your battalion by cargo plane." He continued to sip his coffee as Blake stared. "Just something I heard them throwing around."

"That's utterly ridiculous. No one's dropping Panzerters out of a plane."

2

Paul Reiter pored over the map table with the rest of Fox Company's officers. Just across the Dracul River, Union forces massed on their side of the border.

"That marker means a division. This is a battalion level layout," Lt. Comidus said. The leader of Fox's infantry platoon, he took the lead in setting up the layout.

Reiter showed him a report.

"This indicates a lot of the forward elements carrying jammers, likely for radar, according to scouts," he said.

Comidus took the report and nodded.

"Thanks, Reiter. Kozar, can you mark these elements as having radar jammers?"

The XO got to work quietly, the salt in his peppery hair revealing his age. In contrast, Comidus was a typical infantry officer, fit with good posture. The company's officers stepped back and studied their map overlay.

"It looks like they're readying a defense in depth," Kozar said.

Reiter nodded at the XO's observation.

"If only we could have drones fly over the backend here," Comidus said. "I'd like to know if we're exploiting a gap in their lines or blundering into a meat grinder."

Reiter shook his head.

"I doubt we'll get any intel from drones because of those radar jammers, same with air support, at least in the first wave."

They sat down when Stanca entered the conference room.

"Gentlemen, I have the plan," he said. He walked over to the map layout the other officers had put together. "So the brass think the Union will dig in and fight defensively. They have radar jammers close to the front, most likely to mitigate air support and air recon." He pointed to Mt. Voyager and Mt. Viking to the east. "The boys and girls of 3rd Armored are going to punch through Pine Gap to strike at their rear." Reiter raised his hand. "Yes, Reiter?"

"Are there similar defenses near Pine Gap to what we have here?" he asked.

Stanca shook his head.

"From what I've gathered, they spread them pretty thin over open ground," he answered. "Where was I?" The commander referenced the map.

"Our part of the plan, sir?" Kozar said.

Stanca nodded.

"Thank you, Kozar. Yeah, the rest of 7th Division will stage in advanced positions on our side of the Dracul River," he said. "As a division, we have the central lane. To our right, 51st Infantry is securing our flank, to our left 9th Armored will also be attacking, and to their left, 2nd Mountain will crawl through the Razorbacks."

"So what's our role in this?" Kress asked.

Stanca held up a hand.

"Patience, Kress, I'm getting there. Our brigade will be operating as a quick-reaction force." He traced a line along their section of the map. "The regular army brigades will press forward and force a crossing. If one of them falters or creates a gap, we'll move up and either shore them up or exploit the gap." Stanca looked up at his audience. "That's all I have for now. Tomorrow I want everyone at readiness level one by 0600. Dismissed."

Reiter left the company office and walked towards the barracks area. Under normal circumstances, they'd be here for a range day or annual training. Despite the circumstances, Varga, Adamski, and Legousi were in the smoke shack as usual.

"Hey sir, long day?" Adamski grinned. "I got that frou-frou shampoo if you need to wash the Kress off."

Reiter chuckled. The wooden pavilion reeked of cigarette smoke. While he detested the smell, he didn't mind the company. Speaking of, Mo also sat in the smoke shack, along with the pilots from White Platoon.

"Guys, he's not that creepy, he just thinks he's progressive." Sergeant Bartonova looked away. "It doesn't matter that they've allowed women in combat for as long as we've been a country." She was the oldest of the bunch, as well as the tallest, with almond-colored hair.

Legousi stuffed his smoldering butt into an old soup can next to him before lighting another cigarette.

"But if you ask him, he says the infantry need more women. Would any of you go infantry?"

"No." All the women present answered near simultaneously.

Sergeant Sandic blew smoke in Bartonova's face, much to her annoyance.

"Well, let me see. Sit in a metal box with a bunch of sweaty men"—she raised her hands as if she was weighing something—"or sit in a metal box by myself. Hard choice, really."

Bartonova stood up.

"I'm sorry, I need to go brush my teeth or something. Oh my

God, I can taste it." She walked past the still-standing Reiter as she left.

I probably shouldn't be awkward. I'll sit down. Reiter took a seat next to Varga and leaned forward.

"Ow, don't pinch me!" Mo swatted Corporal Steele's hand.

She wagged a finger at him.

"It's rude to stare, Mo."

"What are you, my mother?"

"Some days."

The other guys laughed.

Sensing Mo's discomfort, Reiter acted fast.

"We have a mission tomorrow." That got the group's interest.

"We as in 3rd or we as in Fox Company?" Adamski waved to the pavilion for emphasis.

"We as in the brigade, though I expect we'll get more company-platoon specific as the day goes on."

Mo held up his hands.

"What's the mission, sir?"

"QRF."

Mo blinked.

"What does that mean?"

Sandic reached over and swatted him.

"Quick Reaction Force. It's like combat fire fighters."

Mo rubbed the back of his head.

"Why'd you hit me?"

"Because you're a corporal. You should know."

Mo shook his head.

Varga stood up and put out his cigarette.

"Alright, gents and ladies, I got a meeting with Top about logistics. I'll see you all later after dinner." He tossed his butt into the overflowing can and left.

"So, I take it we're playing defense," asked Corporal Steele.

Reiter shook his head.

"No, Corporal, we'll be taking the offensive. The brass likely think the War of 2112 scared the Union out of taking the offensive."

"And we're in the back?" asked Mo. "Why are we even here, then?"

"Because things don't always go according to plan, Mo."

Mo slumped back in his seat.

Adamski patted him on the back.

"Don't worry, bud, I'm sure we'll pop your combat cherry soon enough."

Reiter nodded.

"We'll be exploiting openings. This will likely be an offensive war for us."

Sandic took a long drag on her cigarette.

"With all due respect, L-T, can you not be so fucking awkward?"

"MAKE NO MISTAKE, WE WILL STRIKE FIRST." GENERAL LEE struck an imposing figure with her dark skin and well-kept double-gray uniform. "Once we seize the initiative, we must do our utmost to maintain it. We should be advancing at all times." She pulled up a map of the Dracul River Valley for the officers in attendance. Damian Blake made sure he took extensive notes.

"At first glance, we're not in the fight. The other MAG divisions are holding the line at the border, with the 2nd and 3rd Pacifican Infantry divisions in immediate reserve." She smiled. "Colonel Druza, if you may?"

The big man towered over General Lee, herself not a short woman.

"They have issued these bad boys to all forward elements along the Dracul River." The screen changed, showing a cylindrical device in the back of a single-axle trailer. "These are radar jammers, one of the latest innovations of Union engineering. As many of you know, Tharcian strike craft and aerial recon devastated much of our forces." He grinned. "Unfortunately for our cheap capitalist enemies, their drone strike craft and recon drones all rely on radar for navigation." He took his seat, and Lee stepped back up to the front.

"Thank you, Comrade Colonel. These jammers won't affect dropship or airplane crews using a map and compass." She pointed to the area immediately beyond the river. "The 118th Raiders will use their dropships to secure a bridgehead for the rest of the army." Blake had a sinking feeling in his gut. "Meanwhile, the rest of you will be airdropped ahead of Druza's forces and form the spear tip of our thrust. Any questions?"

Blake raised a hand.

"Yes, Comrade General. What's preventing the Tharcians from attacking into Pine Gap and cutting us off?"

The general nodded.

"A reasonable concern. The 3rd Guards Army will attack through Pine Gap themselves. Our combined aim is to get around the defenses of the main border. Anything else?"

"None of my soldiers have airdropped before, let alone at night," said another soldier. "Are we going to practice this?"

"Have they done it in a simulation?" asked the general.

"Well, yes, but this—"

"You have twelve hours. Use them wisely." When she saw no other questions, she dismissed them.

Blake left the conference room and had Meyer on the phone within seconds.

"Meyer, get every soldier in the battalion into a simulator or running airdrop drills. I'm getting the encryption cards, and I'll have them for the comms manager to load when I get back."

"How long should they be training?" asked Meyer.

He checked his watch.

"Give them five hours to train, then they need to bed down for six. That last hour, we will prepare for insertion and board the planes." He terminated his call with Meyer and turned into a secure storage room.

The clerk set his phone down and looked up at Blake. "Unit?" The clerk set their phone down and looked up at him.

"100th MAG Armored."

The clerk walked over to a metal box. He opened the panel and checked a chart.

"Hmm. Alright, here's your master, division-level, battalion-level, company-level, and individual platoons." Three loose encryption cards were followed closely by two bundles of cards.

"Are they marked?"

The clerk nodded.

"Your comms squad know what to do."

Blake left Division HQ and walked over to the hangars his battalion was using. Down the tarmac, transports taxied on the runway. The massive planes had two pairs of wings, one behind the other, with powerful engines. *I really don't like the idea of jumping out of a perfectly good plane.*

The hangar doors were open. Under the gray soup of a sky, he saw soldiers practicing their combat drops. Inside he could see Martians being equipped with drop packs.

He made his way upstairs, meeting his comms chief who stopped and asked,

"Comrade Colonel? Do you have—"

Blake thrust the cards into the younger man's hands.

"You have five hours to get those loaded across the battalion.

After that, you and your people go to bed. We move in twelve hours."

The chief left to round up his people, and Blake headed to the simulator room. To his chagrin, they were all taken. *That's good, I guess—they're training as much as they can.*

Meyer approached with a tablet.

"I'm having them rotate through in platoons as quickly as possible."

Blake nodded.

"That's commendable. I'd want a few rotations myself." He pulled out his meticulous notes. "Are they simulating a night drop?" Meyer nodded. "Good, the planes will take off at 0000. Our drop zone is just north of Neilburg. We're likely to encounter the enemy's reserves, as well as stockpiles, but our primary objectives are this airfield, this road, and these two hills." He marked the objectives on her tablet.

"If we destroy their reserves and supplies, it'll cripple the Tharcians' ability to react." She took another look at Blake's notes. "Not to mention what it would do for our careers."

Blake nodded.

"Indeed, there will definitely be awards and promotions aplenty, especially if we're among the first into the provincial capital." He scowled. "The nerve, to name their provincial capital after that traitor of all people." Pulaski, the provincial capital of the region, sat firmly in the middle of the former Gallacian Martian Republic. It was a real eyesore to the Union soldiers, since they had to see the name of the man who tore Gallacia from their country every time they looked at a map.

There was a hiss, and multiple simulators opened. The salty, meaty smell of his soldiers caused Blake to gag.

Meyer chuckled.

"Too much?"

Blake nodded.

"Comrade Colonel, we didn't know you would be here." Lieutenant Kennedy ducked out of one of the pods as the rest of his company began emerging.

"Where's Stilwell?"

Kennedy shrugged.

"He told me he was reviewing the company's plan in his room."

That's interesting, I haven't distributed company-level objectives yet. Blake put a hand on Kennedy's shoulder.

"Has he shared these with you?" Kennedy shook his head. "Well, your company will be taking the airfield." It would be difficult to drop over an active airfield. Especially if you hadn't practiced combat drops.

Kennedy merely nodded.

"Roger that, Comrade Colonel. I'll inform him after we finish."

Blake raised an eyebrow.

"Oh, you're not done?" he asked.

Kennedy shook his head.

"No, we're just taking a break to use the bathroom, get water, and get a bite," the officer replied.

Blake nodded.

"Well then, Kennedy, while your company takes a break, may I go through a few drops?"

Kennedy waved to the nearest pod.

"Be my guest, Comrade Colonel," he replied.

Blake gagged at the thick stench in the pod. The door closed behind him. Frozen sweat lathered the inside of his sim helmet. Blake cringed. He selected his scenario, and the simulation started. *It can't be worse than the winter of '12.*

BLAKE COULDN'T BELIEVE HOW WRONG HE WAS. HE LOST EVEN HIS thoughts in the drone of the engines. His panoramic cockpit only made him feel worse. He could see the other Panzerters and trucks stacked like sardines. His controls shook from the turbulence the plane experienced. He wished the damn light would turn green already.

Something popped, then several somethings in rapid succession. Flares. The plane was under attack by missiles. Part of Blake wished he could see the missiles. The other half would rather not.

The plane rocked. Had it been hit? No, he would have felt that. He hoped enough of HQ Company made it to effectively organize the battalion. They were with their trucks on a different plane. Instead of HQ Company, Nightmare Company had joined him in the transport plane.

The plane violently lurched. Blake heard a faint beeping. Green flooded his vision. The cargo door dropped away.

"Out, Out, Out!" Blake leaned his machine forward. The walls disappeared, and Mars rushed towards him. Wind noise rose to a fever pitch. Tracers lit up the night sky, and muzzle flashes told him the Tharcians were doing their best to stop the landing. A streaking missile smashed the transport to pieces. The ground approached faster still. He checked his altimeter. 60,000 ft.

The ground fire was walking towards its targets. Blake's stomach tightened. If they damaged the thrusters or parachutes in his drop pack, he wouldn't be able to slow his descent. Flak rounds burst near him. Blake raised the Martian's arms and legs into a fetal position. Hopefully that kept flak out of the cockpit. 45,000 ft.

Not much longer. The closer he got to the surface, the more his machine shook. A Martian to his right burst into flames. Too close. The padding on his chair did nothing. He could feel the stiff metal frame of the chair digging into his back. 32,000 ft. Now.

With a bang and a whoosh, Blake jerked backwards. The violent shaking had stopped. Now he swayed. He disengaged the mag locks and removed his rifle from the drop pack. Carefully, he took aim. A sickly green beam found its mark. That was one flak battery down. Many more to go. More green beams joined the exchange. 18,000ft.

The airfield was in unrestricted view now. Remote weapon stations scythed at the sky. Blake was able to spot quite a few empty missile racks. The airfield centered on two runways oriented in opposite directions. A row of hangars stood near a control tower, several outbuildings, and a terminal.

As he came to treetop height, his thrusters kicked in. When he touched down on solid ground, he ditched his drop pack. He was safe. For a moment. He'd landed on a runway, and he turned his attention on the RWSs. Green beams melted them. He felt as if he was a gardener spraying weeds.

"Any HQ or Nightmare elements, Leviathan 6," he said over the comms. "Rally on my location."

Another RWS blossomed in a shower of sparks. Some were shooting back now. Without the speed of freefall, the flak rounds would not pierce his armor. Something exploded behind him.

A drone had been taxiing on the runway when Martians from Nightmare Company destroyed it.

"Nightmare 5 reporting, Comrade." Kennedy.

Blake continued to mop up the last of the airfield's defenses.

"Where's Nightmare 6?"

Kennedy's response was devoid of emotion.

"Didn't make it."

As Blake had thought.

"Very well, then, 5, Nightmare is yours." When the final RWS crumpled beneath a Martian mace, Blake took a step back to open his command matrix. The system pinged the IFF of every machine belonging to his battalion. At once it informed him of their position and status. "Nightmare 5."

"Roger, Leviathan?"

"Secure our perimeter. Ogre and Malice, take hill 212 and hill 213. From there you will provide covering fire for Predator Company." He pointed to the two nearest Martians. "You two, clear the runways." The Martians sprang to work.

Nightmare was doing their best to avoid the buildings. *I'm going to wait on Druza for that.*

"Blackbeard 6, Leviathan 6. Your birds are clear to land." Blake studied the matrix. Ogre had secured their aim, but Malice was still struggling near hill 213. Predator was getting organized near hill 212. He pinged the matrix for analytics.

Thanks to the matrix, he knew he would take the least casualties if Predator proceeded with securing the road. If he could get some air support, then Predator would suffer nearly no losses.

"Blackbeard 6, Leviathan 6. If your birds have fuel for it, Predator Company could use a gun run."

"Roger, Leviathan, we'll be in contact with them."

Blake heard them long before he saw them. The dropships were squat ugly things. Four VTOL engines carried the fat frame of the union dropships. They came heavily armed as well. A powerful chaingun, multiple rocket pods, and a pair of missile racks were great for clearing landing zones.

As they touched down, raiders poured out of open cargo doors. They wore beige, green, and brown camouflage and wielded the Union standard 8-mm rifle. Systematically, they surged from building to building.

"Leviathan 6, Predator 6."

Blake furrowed his brow. What does he need?

"Go ahead 6." According to his command matrix, Predator Company had the road. *What's their issue?* Then he received an alert on the matrix. Predator had lost vehicles.

"We were able to take the highway without much resistance, but our own dropships strafed us. Casualties follow: two IFVs destroyed, seven soldiers killed, and five wounded. Medevac is on the way."

Blake entered the data into the matrix. It updated its data for Predator Company and also recommended airstrikes farther from troop formations.

Blake ground his teeth. *I didn't even call the airstrike.* Blake guessed he'd have the incident investigated. If Captain Mercer had called an airstrike after the highway was secure, Blake would have the man's head. It wasn't an immediate concern, though.

"All Leviathan elements, set a defensive perimeter, prepare for counterattack."

They held the airfield, the highway that fed it, and the two major terrain features near it. If there would be any major movements of troops, it would come through here. The Tharcians were going to want it back.

Blake smiled as he looked at his command matrix. The Panzerter companies formed a large oval anchored on the hills near the airport. Predator Company pushed out scouts and set ambushes on the highway. *If they want it, they can come take it.*

THUNDER ROUSTED PAUL REITER FROM HIS SLEEP. VOICES BEGAN coming through his door. Footsteps raced across the barracks. Then he realized he wasn't hearing thunder.

"L-T! Wake the fuck up! We're under attack!" Legousi pounded on his door.

"Gos, I'm up! Get everyone to the hangar!" Reiter practically jumped into his combat shirt and pants. He threw his belongings into his rucksack and raced out the door and down the hall. After leaping down stairs, he vaulted out the door.

He heard them now. Airplanes, rare in Tharsis, filled the sky. Tracers swept the sky like searchlights. Missiles rose to meet the invaders. *I better get moving.*

The hangar was across a short field. Reiter ran as fast as his legs could carry him. Soldiers streamed from the barracks to the hangars and motor pools nearby.

Reiter made a beeline for Captain Stanca as soon as he entered the hangar. The older man was on the phone, his ruddy features twisted in pain. He covered the receiver and turned to Reiter.

"Get your platoon spun up; I'll have orders soon."

Reiter nodded and ran onto the hangar floor. Mo caught his eye; the young man was loading 88-mm rounds into magazines for their rifles.

There was a bang overhead. "This piece of shit!" There was a bang overhead. Reiter looked up to see Varga kicking the searchlight on his Panzerter IV.

"Do you still need to be jumped off?"

His platoon sergeant looked down at him.

"Yeah, the fucking mechanics said they fixed it!"

On the hangar floor, Stanca called for all platoon leaders and platoon sergeants.

"Gos, Adamski, can you handle this?" Reiter pointed to Varga's machine.

Legousi ran over. "It just needs to be jumped off, right? With the slave cables?"

"Yeah, get on it." Reiter walked past the two of them, following Varga who was already down the ladder.

Stanca had formed a huddle around himself. In the middle, he held his phone out to show them a map.

"We got word Unis are dropping on Greenwald Regional Airport south of us." He pointed to the airport on the map and circled it with his finger. "If they hold that airport and the surrounding terrain, then they'll choke off our supply lines and reinforcements."

"So we're just going to attack them?" Kress asked.

Stanca nodded.

"Early Company will execute a feint to draw their perimeter out of position east of hill 412. From there we will attack into the gap while Giant Company attacks the other flank. Hussar Company will give close air support and artillery support. Questions?"

Reiter raised his hand.

"Timeline?"

Stanca shook his head.

"You have twenty minutes to get your people out the door."

Reiter nodded, and he and Varga left. He climbed up to the catwalk to see Adamski's entire torso was in Varga's cockpit. Legousi sat in his own with the hatch open.

"Is it jumped off?" Reiter asked.

Adamski pulled himself out.

"No, we need a few more minutes. It might be a bad fuse."

Reiter tapped him on his shoulder.

"Get your shit on: helmet, gloves, armor. You too, Gos." He ran down the catwalk. *Mo, I need to tell him too.* He looked down. "Mo!" The kid stopped with an armload of 88-mm rounds. "Finish that and get your shit on." Reiter ran down to his own machine. His loadout was under his seat, where he normally kept it. As he quickly donned his gear, he kept an eye on his watch. *Come on, big money, no whammies.* He grinned to himself. *Dad said that a lot.* His machine screamed to life as the engine kicked into idle. The system test came back clean.

Mo ran across the catwalk, gasping for breath.

"Everyone has all their ammo but you, sir." He pointed to the seven magazines still on the hangar floor.

"I'll load it; get your shit on." *I'll still need help.* "Adamski."

The sergeant had emerged from his cockpit with his kit on, snap-ping his helmet strap as he did. "Can you give me a hand with my ammo?" They clambered down the ladder.

"Did fucking Mo drop the ball?" Adamski asked.

"No, I told him to get his shit on. They're all loaded—we just need to store them."

They ran across the hangar floor and grabbed the ammo buggy. One by one, they rolled the magazines to a lift and stored them. Once the backpack was full, they loaded the last one into Reiter's rifle. They scrambled back up the ladder. Five minutes left. *Damn, that took way too long.*

The slave cable still ran from Legousi's machine to Varga's. Legousi sat on the edge of his cockpit smoking a cigarette.

"Really, you're taking a fucking smoke break right now?" Reiter yelled.

Legousi showed him his empty pack.

"It's my last one, sir. Besides, Varga's machine isn't holding a charge." He took a drag on his cigarette. "Another minute and we can get it running. We just can't afford to power it down."

Reiter grit his teeth.

"Well, pay attention. As soon as he starts, ditch the cable and get out of the hangar."

Adamski and Mo had already sealed themselves in their cockpits. Reiter ran down the catwalk to his own machine. The hatch sealed behind him.

Claxons blared and yellow lights flashed. The hangar doors crawled open. The catwalk in front of his machine retracted. Reiter walked his machine out of the hangar, rifle at the ready. With its long barrel and pull-up design, it was clear his was a precision weapon. Reiter was glad to see his swords were on board. His chest-mounted machine gun was also ready, the anti-infantry weapon rocking in its ball mount.

Kress's platoon followed out of the hangar, all five of them. Then the command team, except Kozar. For some reason, the XO's Panzerter IV remained in the hangar with Legousi and Varga. *I should have offered my machine and just hopped in a command truck.* Then Reiter heard words that froze his blood.

"Enemy aircraft approaching!"

3

They flew just above treetop height, Union dropships, fast and low. Chainguns blazed. Rockets pummeled the tarmac where the Panzerters stood. Reiter raised his rifle. Two shots. A dropship plummeted from the sky. The rest roared past them.

"Assume anti-aircraft formation!" Stanca didn't waste time with proper radio etiquette.

"We lost Gordos!" someone cried.

The remaining Panzerters formed a circle on the tarmac. Reiter checked on his own platoon. Adamski's machine was belching smoke, and Mo was limping, but seemed otherwise fine. Reiter heard more weapons fire nearby.

"Black 1, head to the motor pool, get Gold Platoon over here," ordered Stanca. "Everyone else, protect the hangar!"

"Fox 6, Black 5 is limping!" said Reiter.

"Then swap your 5 for White's and move!" Stanca replied.

Reiter left with Adamski and Steele in tow, leaving Mo to help defend the hangar. Fort Rainer was in chaos. Fires raged at multiple points. Reiter heard gunfire in the distance. *If I remember correctly, Bravo Motor Pool is across this sector.*

They followed the roads past the rows of barracks buildings and offices. Reiter took point, with Steele behind him. Adamski brought up the rear.

"Gold 1, Black 1, status?" *I hope he's in his track on the radio.* Reiter hailed him again. As they approached the motor pool, they heard the sounds of battle.

"Black 1, we're pinned down in the motor pool." Comidus's reply came back garbled with static. Reiter heard gunfire in the background. "They have anti-tank weapons across the street from us, second floor."

"Drop smoke if you have it. We'll set a base of fire so you can move." Reiter flipped back to the platoon net. "Black 2, White 5, barracks at eleven has hostile dismounts. Set base of fire with me so Gold can move."

"Roger."

Reiter pushed his machine to a run and rounded the corner. He could see the unit firing from the second floor of the barracks. There was a ditch on either side of the road in front of them. On the side in front of the barracks, more unis fired at Gold Platoon. The burning wrecks of two other tracks blocked the way out.

Reiter's machine gun raked the Unionists in their trench. His companions fired burst after burst into the barracks. Reiter stepped forward and kicked the wrecks out of the way for Gold Platoon. The IFVs sped out of the motor pool, tracks screeching as they left.

"Gold 1, we'll follow you out and keep your nose clean."

They hurried back to the Panzerter hangars. The Panzerters eliminated any opposition hiding in buildings or in ditches. In exchange, the IFV's used their autocannons and missiles to keep dropships off the Panzerters. Their combined efforts made reaching the Panzerter hangar relatively easy.

Dropships made a low pass over the rest of Fox Company. Reiter saw their cargo doors open as they strafed the rest of the company. A Panzerter fell. Screams filled the net as missiles chased the dropships.

"Ah, get them off me!" A series of explosions ripped a Panzerter to pieces at its joints. Dismounts.

Reiter rushed to the nearest machine. On its right shoulder, a 3 gleamed in gold. Bartonova.

"White 3, hold still!" Reiter's machine gun roared to life, and he blasted the dismounts off her. Adamski, Steele, and Gold Platoon followed suit, hosing down their allies with small arms caliber rounds.

"All Fox elements, Fort Rainer's defenses are compromised. We need to withdraw," Stanca announced.

Reiter glanced back at the hangar.

"Fox 6, what about my guys in the hangar?"

"What the fuck, they're still in there?" Drones screamed past overhead, no doubt searching for targets. *Good, we'll have air superiority soon.* "Get them out of the hangar!"

Reiter turned back towards the hangar. Desperately, he tried hailing them.

"Black 3 and 4, get out of there!" He heard a distant droning grow louder. "Black 3 and 4!" He saw them standing on the catwalk. The slave cable fell to the floor. They both crawled into Legousi's machine. "3 and 4!" The droning from before became a scream.

"Don't worry, sir, we're on our way out!"

About fucking time.

"Well, hurry up, we're about—"

"Sir, heads up!" Adamski cried.

Reiter turned to see a massive flaming shape fill his vision. He dove left hard and rolled. His head slammed into the headrest, and his restraints cut him. The shape roared. His Panzerter shook. Reiter felt like he'd be sick.

The flaming wreckage of a Union plane smashed into the hangar with a deafening roar.

No way.

"Gos, Varga, are you guys okay?" Reiter felt like he was sinking into his chair. *No fucking way.*

"Black 1, let's go!" Adamski's voice blasted the entire net.

Reiter pulled his machine to its feet. With one last look at the wreckage, he ran after the rest of them. The barbed wire fencing was no obstacle to them. With Fort Rainer behind them, they vanished into the surrounding forest.

I should have said something. I should have spoken to the mechanics myself. I knew that machine had issues. Am I fit to lead if a simple mistake cost me two good soldiers?

"Black 1, BDA," came Stanca's voice over the company net.

Reiter blinked, refocusing on the present. *I won't let that happen again.*

"Black 2, damage report?" He waited for Adamski to respond.

"No critical damage. Armor is breached in a few spots, and my coolant is smoking, but I'm good."

"Black 5?"

"My machine's limping, right knee's damaged, otherwise it's cosmetic."

"You two are sure that's it?"

They both confirmed their report, and Reiter passed it up to Stanca. Their company had lost four Panzerters and an IFV, twelve men in all. Gold and Black Platoons had both lost a platoon sergeant, while White had lost their platoon leader and XO. A devastating day for Fox.

"We'll stop here. Form a perimeter and camouflage your vehicles. After that, I want to see everyone in the middle." Stanca sounded as if he'd aged ten years since he'd asked for the battle damage assessment.

The chilly fall air stung at them. As he walked to the center of the formation, Reiter realized he'd barely slept. Adamski put a hand on his shoulder. In the weak starlight, Bartonova glistened with blood. Reiter thought her injured until he remembered the dismounts that had been on her machine.

Stanca stood in the middle of them and removed his helmet.

"Ladies and gentlemen, today was a shitty day. The Unis kicked our ass. We lost good soldiers, and all of you killed someone for the first time tonight." He made eye contact with each soldier. "But the Unis made a mistake, they brought the fight to our homes, and mark my words"—his voice rose with every word—"if they thought they could march in here, kill our brothers, threaten our families, and not expect a fight, well, they have another fucking think coming!"

The response was quiet, a low "hear-hear" or a nod. But anger hung in the air. Reiter's mouth felt bitter. For him, the war was just beginning.

GUARD COLONEL DAMIAN BLAKE HAD NEVER ENCOUNTERED A problem he couldn't solve given time. South of the airfield lay his next objective: a Tharcian ammo dump. He didn't have the element of surprise. The Tharcians knew he was coming and had favorable terrain. They also had Panzerters, albeit older reserve models. They also had reinforcements on the way. That much he knew.

The terrain between him and his goal was open and flat. Scouts had learned the hard way that the Tharcians had heavy fortifications in the hillside. However, their ordeal yielded detailed information about said fortifications and the surrounding terrain. Beyond the ammo dump was more wooded rugged terrain. The Panzerters could traverse that with ease, but his tracked vehicles would struggle.

Of his forces, Blake knew the Martian was more than a match for any Tharcian Panzerter it encountered. Its mix of survivability, firepower, and speed had proved difficult for the Tharcians to counter. The Martian's laser rifles proved more effective than the ballistic weapons fielded by their opponents.

Single envelopment, that's my best option. Blake pored over the map. The ammo dump sat in a hexagonal structure partially embedded in a hillside. They'd entrenched the north side in the ground but left the south side exposed. A dirt road led back to a major highway. Blake determined enemy reinforcements would use it. So he would use it first.

Before his eyes, his plan developed. Phase 1 would have his artillery bombard the ammo dump relentlessly with smoke. With their big guns blind, Blake's infantry would advance with Ogre Company. Predator would clear the buildings, and Ogre would protect them from Panzerters. Malice and Nightmare would swing wide and follow the highway to the road. There they would serve the dual purpose of cutting off fleeing enemies and stopping reinforcements.

With his plan outlined, Blake briefed his company commanders. None of them had any questions or objections. That troubled Blake. *At least one of them should have had a question or needed something clarified.* He looked over the map again. *I'm confident in my abilities, but there's no way I came up with a perfect plan.*

Despite his reservations, preparations continued. After an hour of maintenance and drilling, they assumed positions for their assault. This time, Blake positioned himself with Ogre Company.

"Are you sure you want to join us, Comrade Colonel?"

Blake pushed his command matrix aside. Captain Wallace's question wasn't a question so much as a formality. The man had known Blake for twelve years—the most dangerous part of any operation was where he'd be.

"Absolutely. I can't ask anything of Ogre Company I wouldn't attempt myself."

The Ogre Martians shifted in his direction, and Blake smiled to himself. *I'll take loyalty points wherever I can get them.*

The thunder of artillery heralded the beginning of the mission. Shells whistled overhead for thirty seconds before Wallace signaled them to advance. The ballistic orchestra blanketed the ammo dump under a curtain of thick black smoke.

The Panzerters accelerated into a run, the IFVs nipping at their heels. They had advanced halfway across the field when the ground exploded. The big guns. They were firing blindly.

Tracers leapt out of the smog in rapid succession. With a scream and a crash, a Martian disappeared in a cloud of metal and smoke. Others stopped, even as shells burst near them.

Blake ground his teeth.

"Advance! Draw maces and prepare for close combat!" He tossed his laser aside. It was useless in the smoke, anyway. From its left shoulder, his Martian drew its collapsible mace.

The other Martians advanced as well. Despite this, Martians still fell. The big guns' fire devoured the Taurus fighting vehicles that advanced on their positions.

The bombardment had ceased, and the smoke was beginning to thin out. Blake rushed forward. His weapon crushed metal. A Tharcian Panzerter stumbled back headless. Blake grinned. He advanced uphill like some kind of fairy tale monster. Wild, savage swings smashed gun emplacements. Other Martians joined him. Without mercy, they hammered the Tharcian Panzerters they encountered until they lay still.

Blake took a step back as his soldiers swept over the ammo

depot. Smoke over the trees told him Nightmare and Malice had found their mark.

"Leviathan 5, Leviathan 6. Mission is complete. Send up recovery and medical assets." Blake checked his command matrix. His company commanders were doing a fine job accounting for casualties, mainly Predator Company. White flares rose from across the ammo dump. It was theirs.

Blake dismounted and pissed. As he walked back over to his kneeling Martian, the command truck rolled up. The squat angular vehicle rode along on six wheels.

Meyer jumped out with her tablet as soon as it parked.

"We already have our next objective. They want us to create a firebase on this ammo dump while identifying bridges and ideal spots for bridge layers."

Blake nodded.

"Have the scouts pushed out?"

"Affirmative."

"Well done. Bridge layers, you say?"

Meyer nodded.

"Although our offensive vehicles are all amphibious and the Panzerters have incredible fording ability, the supply trucks the regular forces provide are not."

Blake looked at her map. To go much farther into Tharcian territory would require crossing the twisting inland river deltas within the Dracul River Valley. *I see, so they made our fighting vehicles with this in mind but not our logistics.*

"Well, it's fine that we wait. Predator Company desperately need reinforcements, and more Martians wouldn't hurt either." He looked across the field. The fighting had scattered mangled wreckage about. Occasionally, the hand or leg of a Martian lay entrenched in the ground. Of the lost boat-shaped Taurus IFVs, no trace remained. Blake shook his head.

"I'll requisition reinforcements as soon as we get long-range communications established."

Blake began walking back to his Martian.

"Thank you, Meyer, and call up engineer assets—we need fortifications and field hangars on the double."

She got back into the command truck, tapping away at her tablet. Blake climbed into his Martian and opened the command matrix.

With every battle, his battalion matrix improved. Its analytics grew more accurate as new data better informed its programs. Blake skimmed through the profiles it had built for each of his commanders. *I know better than to rely purely on the command matrix.* Some commanders he knew had grown over-dependent on the matrix, essentially letting it plan battles for them. *That's not what it's for; it's just another tool.* He pushed it away, and after basking in solitude for a second longer, he keyed up his radio.

———

UNDER THE CHILLY MID-OCTOBER SUN, PAUL REITER SHIVERED. His breath hung in the air as he walked over to his kneeling Panzerter. *I wish I'd said something else to Gos. "Hey, good job, you're an outstanding soldier, you're a pillar of this platoon." But no, Paul, you yelled at him over a fucking cigarette.*

He sat down on his machine's foot. If it fell over and crushed him, he wouldn't care. For a moment, he just embraced the sound of the surrounding woods.

Pine straw rustled behind him.

"Hey, sir, mind if I sit here?"

Reiter shook his head. Adamski walked over and sat against the Panzerter's knee. After lighting a cigarette, they sat there in silence.

"Can I have one of those?"

Reiter hadn't noticed Mo approach them.

Ski puffed smoke at him.

"Since when do you smoke, Mo?"

"Since the other night?"

Adamski waved him over.

"Come sit down here."

Mo took a seat next to Adamski. The older soldier handed him a cigarette and lit it for him. Mo took a drag on the cigarette, an effort that caused him to choke and cough. Adamski chuckled.

"How do you smoke these all the time?" the corporal asked.

"It's an acquired taste."

Reiter shook his head.

"I could never get past the smell," he admitted.

Adamski suddenly laughed.

"I don't know why I thought about this, but remember annual training 2132, when they told Gos a landmine knocked out his Panzerter and he couldn't leave that snowdrift?"

Reiter grinned at the memory.

"And his ass made himself a hot tub. Aw man, the coordinators were pissed. That old fart was like blah blah blah, you fucking Provincial Watch fucks are undisciplined, blah blah blah, and I'm like, what are you talking about?"

Mo furrowed his brow.

"You didn't know he made a hot tub?"

Reiter held up his hands.

"No, I was fifteen kilometers away in a frozen swamp. I did not understand what the old guy was talking about." He and Adamski laughed. "The best part is how he tried to say he was still in uniform."

Adamski held his hands out.

"So he strips off his CVCU to get in his hot tub, right? And the coordinator says he's breaking the exercise rules by being out of uniform, so he goes 'first of all, I'm out of play, and second'"—Adamski and Reiter said the last bit simultaneously—"'I'm wearing my fucking helmet!'"

Reiter slid down his Panzerter's foot as he laughed at Legousi's antics. He lowered his head.

"I wish I'd told them to just abandon Varga's machine and get out."

Adamski shook his head.

"Sir, you know what Varga would say if he heard you saying that?"

Reiter threw up his hands.

"I don't know, you don't really talk to people after they die."

Adamski dumped ashes off the end of his cigarette.

"In classic Master Sergeant Varga fashion, you'd get a disappointed dad talk about feeling sorry for yourself. He'd honestly be more concerned about that than the fact you fucked up."

Reiter smiled and shook his head.

Mo extinguished the cigarette and tossed it away, much to Adamski's chagrin.

"You owe me for that."

Mo shoved him.

"Whatever." He looked down. "You know, when my dad died, my mom said he'd be happier if we remembered the good times instead of being sad he's gone."

Reiter nodded.

"I tell you boys what, let's get through this mess, then we can pour one out to Gos and Varga."

They nodded. A voice behind the Panzerter called out.

"Are we about to move?"

Reiter stood.

"Probably, Ski. Get your machines warmed up. I'll have what we're doing in a few." He walked over to the center of the perimeter. Captain Stanca was there to meet him with Comidus and Renner.

"Well, gentlemen, I got good news and bad news. The bad news is there's the genuine risk of getting surrounded." Stanca's breath hung in the air. "The good news is we've made contact with Early Company." He pulled his hands out of his pockets and opened a map on his phone. "If we can string the battalion back together, we can retake Greenwald Regional Airport."

Reiter raised an eyebrow.

"Has the enemy consolidated their position on the airport?"

Stanca shook his head.

"I doubt it. They've only had a couple hours, tops."

Comidus looked at the map.

"They have dropship support, so they can move and react much faster than us."

Stanca put his phone away.

"Look, it's the only way forward we have. If I hear a better idea, I'll listen."

Reiter glanced at Comidus. *He probably has a bad feeling about this too.*

Reiter walked back to his Panzerter. They would fight again soon. *Who's next, I wonder? Ski, Mo, Me?* He shook his head. *They were people, real people, but I didn't think that once. What does that say about me?*

He climbed into his cockpit.

"Alright, boys, we're going to be moving out soon."

"Where're we going?" Mo asked.

"Good question. Fox 6 wants to link up with Early and the rest of the 230th. Should have a grid soon."

"Are we fighting again?"

Reiter nodded even though Adamski couldn't see him.

"I think so. We have to go south. The frontline's dissolving north of us."

"So much for an offensive war."

"They caught us with our pants down, no doubt, but we're not out of the fight yet." Reiter received the grid and ordered them to move out. They took up the rear, with 2nd Platoon taking point, 1st Platoon behind them, and HQ dispersed throughout.

The heavy woods seemed to drift by. Reiter swung his weapon back and forth. The enemy could be out there anywhere. The sun slunk below the horizon, giving way to cold night. Despite the darkness, Reiter felt safer. His thermals would make enemies much easier to find.

It was nearly dawn before they found Early Company. They helped shore up their perimeter and camouflaged their machines.

"Mo, Ski, get some shuteye. You're going to need it." Reiter undid his restraints and reclined in his chair. *Maybe things will turn around soon.*

His boots clicked smartly on the marble floor. His navy trousers were properly pressed, and his royal blue jacket with red piping had nary a wrinkle, hair, nor imperfection. Field Marshal Ernest Skara seemed to have walked out of a Tharcian Army recruiting poster. His entire war room stood at attention the moment he entered.

"Carry on."

The war room staff returned to work. Four rows of workstations lined the room, each bearing a computer with multiple monitors. A central massive screen displayed a continental map. Markers displayed units as small as individual divisions and their positions.

"Who has my update?"

"Here, sir." A young major approached with a tablet. He first drew the marshal's attention to Gallacia. "Their airborne attack scattered the 7th Armored Division. Now 9th Armored and 2nd Mountain risk being cut off."

"What about 3rd Armored?"

The young man shook his head.

"They met a Union offensive in the Pine Gap and got bogged down."

Skara pointed at the jagged mess on the northern border.

"I assume they have made no progress up north?"

The major shook his head.

"They have multiple salients against us. Every time they create a local breakthrough, they turn it into an operational one."

Skara scanned the map himself.

"Well, War Plan Silver went to complete shit. We're on the back foot now in our own front yard." He looked over at the major. "Major Starnes, did you have a brief prepared on enemy equipment and tactics?"

"Yes sir, would you like to use the briefing room?" Starnes asked as Skara turned to leave.

"Absolutely, I've disrupted the war room staff's day enough."

The officers walked through marble hallways to a smaller room. In the center was a holographic table with a glass top lined with LED lights. A coffee maker stood in the corner next to a water cooler.

"Coffee, sir?"

Skara smiled as he sat at the table. He actually pulled out a notepad and pencil.

"Yes, black please," he said.

Starnes returned with coffee for them. Then he brought up an image of a new Union Panzerter. It was dark gray, with lighter gray sections and red highlights. Its head was saucer-shaped, divided horizontally by a red ring. Its left shoulder was more heavily armored than its right with added segmented armor. Segmented armor skirts covered its knees and upper legs.

"What have we got here?" asked Skara.

"This is the Panzerter their MAG forces have been using, and oh boy is it a bastard," Starnes said. He looked at his tablet as he pulled up more data on the hologram. "Our reporting name is 'tinhat'. This machine is a brute." He displayed an image of a compact rifle with a flared barrel. "They use this beauty, a laser rifle," he continued. "At night or under clouds, a green beam is visible, but not under direct sunlight."

"Damn, it's a perfect ambush weapon," Skara replied.

"Precisely, sir. Fortunately, thermal blooming limits its effective range. We estimate it's only effective out to 2800 meters."

Skara furrowed his brow.

"So it out-ranges the Panzerter V?"

Starnes shook his hands in front of his body.

"Not quite. In semi-auto, their standard rifle is accurate to 3200. The issue is that our Panzerter IVs struggle against them."

Skara looked at the major.

"How so?"

"Our Panzerters can't penetrate their armor until they're well within laser range." He pulled up another image, this time a rod that flared and expanded at the end. "They also carry these collapsible maces for close combat, fantastic at smashing Panzerters or build-ings." He cycled to an image of a dropship.

"Then there are these bastards, assault dropships, capable of close air support and delivering soldiers."

"Another MAG toy?"

Starnes nodded.

"They played a big role in pummeling 7th Armored and Three Corps at large."

Skara rested his chin on his hand.

"They want ground, we'll give them ground in exchange for time." He looked at Starnes. "I will inform Madame President that we need total mobilization. The entire economy needs to re-tune for war." He rose from his seat. "What's the status on our heavy Panzerter projects?"

Starnes checked his tablet.

"Project Tiger is claiming they have an early production type ready, though some of our people have doubts. Project Lowe is in the late prototype stage."

Skara smiled.

"Give them additional resources. We need those units and any advancements they bring on the front-line as soon as possible."

Starnes looked up.

"Permission to speak freely, sir?"

Skara waved to him.

"Granted."

Starnes stiffened himself.

"It would be wiser to focus on fine-tuning the Panzerter V and modernizing the IV and III," he said. "Rushing out experimental Panzerters eats at resources that could be better spent improving what we have and making more Panzerters."

"I like where you're coming from, but we need every unit we can get," Skara replied. "Though, you have given me an idea."

Starnes relaxed slightly.

"And that is, sir?"

Skara's eyes flashed.

"I want developments from Tiger and Lowe to inform a refit package for the Panzerter IV," he said. "That way, we're not wasting resources, as you put it." Skara rose from his chair. "I'm ready to inform our corps and army commanders of the new war plan."

Starnes cleared the hologram.

"Would you like me to prepare orders?" he asked.

Skara folded his arms and faced the map.

"Three Corps is to make the Unionists bleed as they advance through Gallacia," the marshal said. "Olympian reinforcements should be ready for a counterthrust by the beginning of November. As for the Northern Front, 2nd and 3rd Army need to change the way they play defense. Less brick wall, more elastic band." He rubbed his head. "The Unionists prefer a very mobile style of warfare. We need to beat them at their own game."

Starnes looked up as he took notes.

"Anything else you want to say, sir?" he asked.

Skara shrugged.

"I don't think it'll get this bad, but under no circumstances are we to let our spaceports fall," the marshal replied. "We need that supply line open."

Starnes looked up after taking some final notes on his tablet.

"Yes, sir. So to summarize: space for time, weapons development gets a bigger push, keep spaceports open. Did I miss anything, sir?"

Skara shook his head.

"No, that's all, Major Starnes."

The younger man left, and Skara sat. *Damn, feels like the weight of the entire country is on me.* He brought up the image of the tinhat. Skara snarled at the thing. It lacked personality, cultural identity, and most damning of all: soul. Just diligent subservience to its overlords. *Damn godless thing is everything I hate about the Union.*

4

The soldiers impressed Blake with their work. Within 24 hours, they had transformed the ammo dump into a functional forward operating base. Engineers and infantry had erected extensive earthworks on the south side of the base. His two anti-aircraft platoons had put up a vast umbrella of protection for his forces. Mechanics salvaged what they could from the wrecks of both sides' Panzerters.

Even now, Blake looked on as they painted a Tharcian Panzerter in MAG colors. *At this rate, I'll have enough equipment to near full-strength.* He checked his watch. The reinforcements would arrive soon. Young men and women fresh out of advanced training. *Our enlisted personnel aren't the issue. Our officers, on the other hand . . .* Blake shook his head.

It was only the 12th of October, three days since the war started and Blake's forces had been airdropped, and already, he'd lost all of his company commanders. *Stilwell's death was his fault—he should have taken the sims seriously.* Neither Wallace nor Mercer, the CO of Predator Company, had survived the battle for the ammo dump.

Malice's CO, Guard Captain Mau, had been shot down during the airdrop. As far as their performance went, the lot had proved mediocre at best.

Blake sighed. *It's not like their replacements are much better. Beyond Kennedy, none of them have any tactical acumen, battlefield patience, or even charisma.* He heard the dropships coming. *I guess I'll think of a solution later. The reinforcements are here.*

Four dropships approached the firebase. Two of them had their passenger pod swapped for a Taurus IFV. They lowered the vehicles onto the ground on the north side of the firebase. The other two landed and unloaded their passengers. Their mission complete, they departed for the airfield.

New soldiers flocked to the IFVs. Blake had figured most of the fresh blood would be infantry, but it disappointed him to see he only had five new pilots.

With a shake of his head, he approached the new arrivals.

"Welcome to FOB 10. I'm your battalion commander, Guard Colonel Damian Blake." He stood on the edge of one of the old gun emplacements so they would have to look up at him. "I don't know the individual reasons you joined the MAG, and frankly, those are irrelevant to me. What I want you to know is two things." He held up his fingers for emphasis. "You *will* follow my orders, and if you show any talent in any matter, you will be recognized accordingly."

One of the infantryman raised their hand.

"Uh, Comrade Colonel, where do you want these?" He motioned to the two new Taurus IFVs.

Blake pointed to his right.

"Follow the perimeter that way—you'll find the entrance to our motor pool." The infantry mounted up and drove away as Blake descended to the pilots. "I'm going to let all of you know right now, they have killed all of my prior company commanders in action. This war will be far from easy, but there's room for advancement."

"Excuse me, Comrade Colonel, but where are our Panzerters?"

Blake smiled.

"Only some of you will use the new Martian. Others will use captured Tharcian models." He looked over his shoulder. Meyer was walking down the hillside towards them. *Perfect timing. She's perfectly capable of running the battalion if I'm gone.* "Major Meyer will give you your assignments. I expect each and every one of you to push yourselves to succeed."

Blake left them on the hillside for Meyer to address and made his way deep into the former ammo dump. The Tharcian facility had come equipped with a headquarters bunker. *A shame they destroyed their codebooks and hard drives—that would have been a monumental victory.*

Instead he had to make do with access to Tharcian maps. Inside the musty underground room, Blake had them spread across multiple tables. He made himself some coffee and sat down in front of one of the tables.

The Tharcians were no fools. They had recognized the incredible defensive terrain that lay east of Blake's position and had contrived an elaborate web of fortifications, pontoon bridges, and supply dumps around it.

He heard a knock at the door.

"Enter." Meyer walked into the room, followed by Captain Kennedy. *Good, they both made it. I need to develop their own strategic ability fast.* Blake pointed at the maps all around him. "This is our current predicament. What are your thoughts?"

Meyer clung to her tablet as she paced from map to map.

Kennedy gave the largest map a look before walking to Blake.

"How many bridge layers are they bringing up?" he asked.

Meyer shook her head.

"Not nearly enough for this," she said as she tapped away at her tablet. "We have twelve in total. If we bridged every river we encountered, we would run out of bridge layers halfway through."

Kennedy groaned and ran a hand through his hair.

"And with them our supply lines," he finished.

Blake held up three fingers as he sipped his coffee.

"Before I plan, I ask myself three critical questions: what do I know about myself, what do I know about my enemy, and what do I not know about my enemy?" He set his coffee down. "So I'm going to ask you two: what do we know about us?"

Meyer looked at her tablet.

"We're nearly returned to full strength. Logistically we have more artillery shells and surface-to-air missiles than we expected to have." She scrolled down a list. "We have plenty of spare parts, even for foreign machines."

Kennedy folded his arms behind his back and began to pace the room.

"Despite our losses, our soldiers are in high spirits, our veterans are confident in their abilities, and our new bodies are eager to prove themselves." He paused. "That being said, the replacements and the veterans have never fought together. That could lead to communication and cohesion issues. Besides that, we do not know whether the replacements will panic under fire."

Blake nodded. *All good points.*

"So that leads me to ask, what do we know about our enemy?"

Kennedy offered an observation.

"The Panzerters we've encountered have mostly been older models—little threat to a Martian except at close range. That being said, their pilots have proven braver and more skilled than we assumed they'd be, especially considering we've been fighting their second and third strings."

Blake folded his arms.

"We know their expected positions, what parts of the river delta have thick defenses, where they expect to funnel supplies and traverse the rivers." Meyer gave a sideways glance at Kennedy as she listed the cold facts.

Hmm, is someone nervous about their position?

"So you two know what I'm going to ask you next."

They saluted. The second their hands dropped, Meyer flipped through her tablet.

Kennedy looked over one of the maps on the table.

"The units we've encountered are using older equipment. We don't know how we'd fair against a unit with their best tech."

Meyer narrowed her eyes.

"Or they could have spread newer equipment so thin that it doesn't matter."

Kennedy shrugged.

"Either way, it's something we don't know."

Meyer looked back at her tablet, then glanced at the map.

"We don't know how up-to-date this is. They could have more defenses, more supply dumps—hell, they could have far more units than this map displays. We won't know until we've conducted proper recon."

Kennedy nodded.

Alright, I better plan. Blake adjusted his round glasses.

"We can see the areas the enemy is concentrating their strength, but now we need to find patterns that reveal weakness." He pointed to the southern edge of the map. "The right flank is approaching the Olympian border. They're going to face stiff resistance there." He pointed back to their sector. "We need to open up this second front for Army Group Center and Army Group West. This way, Tharsis can be pulled apart quickly."

Kennedy looked confused.

"That's a leap from 'how do we win the next battle.'"

Blake shook his head.

"Because we're officers, it's a vital part of our job to see the bigger picture." He looked at Meyer. "You realized what you didn't know when you looked up from your tablet, you have a good feel for the mechanics of running a battalion, but you've been out of the saddle for a minute." He looked at Kennedy. "Kennedy, you're a natural leader, you've got great tactical sense and combat IQ, but you miss a lot of the admin details." Blake slammed his hand on the table to punctuate his words. "It's possible you two end up leading a battalion by the end of this. Now let's sit down and come up with a battle plan."

PAUL REITER HAD NEVER VISITED ROADSIDE BEFORE. HE'D PASSED through in his car but never visited. *It only took a war to get me to stop here.* His Panzerter knelt in a parking lot along with the rest of 2nd Platoon's machines. Their rifles sat in a partial state of disassembly.

"Man, I just love freezing my ass off," Mo grunted as he and Adamski scrubbed the barrel of his rifle.

Reiter shook his head as he wiped the pieces of the bolt assembly and laid them out on Mo's poncho.

"Mo, your bolt is caked in shit. There're years' worth of gunk here."

The younger soldier shrugged.

"I may have gone overboard."

Adamski chuckled.

"If you stuck to controlled bursts like they trained you, we wouldn't be freezing our asses off doing maintenance."

Reiter threw the dirty towel into a pile.

"Alright gents, let's put this thing back together." They reassembled the bolt carrier. The heavy pieces of the 88-mm rifle required all three of them to lift and reassemble. Reiter stepped back to admire their work. "See now, that wasn't so bad. We'll do it again tomorrow."

Adamski picked up his jacket from an ammo pallet.

"So what is our part in this sweeping counterattack?"

Reiter looked west of them, towards the airfield.

"Well, the spearhead has advanced south towards the river delta and the capital, so the brass thinks the airport is being held by rebuilding units." He pointed back towards Main Street. "We're going to take the main road and attack the airfield from the north-west. From there, the plan is hold until relieved."

Adamski folded his arms.

"They think it's going to be that simple, huh?"

Reiter shook his head and sat on the stock of Mo's rifle.

"Look, as far as we're concerned, the plan will go completely to shit the second shooting starts." He looked back at the main road. A young mother was pulling two little boys along. The boys were gazing up at the Panzerters in awe. *I used to look at them like that too.*

Mo paced around the barrel of his rifle. "All you guys' pessimism is making me hungry. Who's down for soup?" Mo paced around the barrel of his rifle.

Adamski glanced at Reiter.

"I'm down. L-T?"

Reiter sighed.

"Sure, why the hell not?" He stood and followed them down the road to the soup shop.

Adamski clapped him on the back.

"I know things are rough, but you're not an inspiring leader when you're sour all the time."

Reiter raised his hands.

"What do you expect me to do? Lie and bullshit like the other officers?"

Adamski shook his head.

"Not what I meant. I'm just saying throw a little hope or something in when you talk."

Reiter nodded.

"Hope or something, noted."

Mo elbowed him.

"Hey sir, you have all the old brilliant speeches memorized, right?"

Reiter looked at the younger soldier.

"You think I memorized every speech, by every leader, ever?"

Mo shrugged.

"I figured you had an inspiring speech playbook." Adamski held the door for them as they walked into the soup store. The line was up to the door. "Like, in X situation use Y speech by the bulldog guy."

"The bulldog guy?"

Mo nodded.

"Yeah, I think he worked for a king or something, big into cigars, he was a leader during one of those world wars on Earth." He grabbed at his head. "Damn, his name is on the tip of my tongue."

Reiter squinted.

"Are you talking about *Winston Churchill*?"

Mo snapped his fingers.

"Yeah, that guy."

Reiter shook his head.

"Bulldog guy. Maybe I should follow his example and lead while hammered."

Adamski and Mo laughed.

"Uh, sir, unlike him, I think you need your fine motor skills," Adamski said with a grin.

They waded through the line and got their soup.

"A shame they don't have lobster bisque here," said Mo. "Down on the Roma peninsula, they have amazing lobster bisque."

Adamski shrugged.

"Doesn't really make a difference to me, Mo. I was never big on seafood."

Reiter looked up at Mo from his potato soup.

"Get your degree when this is all over and you can have all the lobster bisque you want, Mo."

Adamski glanced at the younger soldier.

"What the hell did that mean? Are you working on a culinary degree?"

Mo shook his head.

"No, Marine Biology. I'm hoping to get a job out east when I graduate. I'm kind of a nerd about fish."

Adamski chuckled.

"Hey man, dream big."

Reiter stared into his soup. *After all this . . . I haven't really thought about it.* He stirred his soup. *Someday, this will end, this war will be over. My pain won't be forever. We won't suffer forever.* Reiter took a bite of soup. *I know what I'm fighting for.*

"So, you intend to sleep with Bartonova and live on the beach?" said Reiter.

Mo froze with his spoon halfway to his mouth.

"That's a little direct, sir, and who told you about that?"

Reiter and Adamski locked eyes.

"Steele did," Reiter replied.

Mo blinked.

"What? When?" he asked.

Adamski patted him on the shoulder.

"She spilled the beans the other day at chow, before we came here," he said.

Mo shook his head.

"That brat, I ought—"

Adamski popped him over the back of the head.

"What are you, a high schooler? Come on, dude, you got the hots for someone, shoot your shot. Just don't be creepy. Right, sir?"

Reiter nodded.

"Yeah, sure."

Adamski looked at him.

"Come on, man, help me out here."

Not exactly my area of expertise. Reiter tented his hands.

"Mo, there's twelve billion people on Mars, 74 billion on Earth, and even more in colony cylinders. Half of them are female. Statistically, there's someone out there who can tolerate you enough to spend their life with you."

Adamski blinked.

Mo dropped his spoon.

"Sir, what the fuck." They laughed. "You're cool, sir, but please don't be my wingman." Mo held up his hand. "As in, like, club wingman. I love you as a Panzerter wingman."

Reiter chuckled. *Laughing is good; it'll keep the rot away.*

"Look, we've been through the wringer already, and this shit show probably isn't even halfway over. If nothing else, I'm glad you two are my platoon."

Mo shook his head.

"Sir, we need to work on your ability to talk before we worry about speeches."

They laughed as they finished their soup, then they walked back to their Panzerters with fullish stomachs and medium spirits. To their surprise, they bumped into Gold Platoon in their parking lot.

That's odd, why aren't they with their Panzerters?

They each carried brooms as if they were weapons. Bartonova, Sandic, and Steele all looked exhausted, while Master Sergant Renner looked annoyed.

"Hey Sergeant Renner, what are you doing in our lot?" Reiter asked.

The man's wrinkled brow gained more creases.

"The last I checked, this was a public lot, Lieutenant. As for what I'm doing, it should be obvious." He motioned to his platoon. "I'm going over our movement techniques and formations, something you should be doing."

Adamski shrugged.

"I mean, our formations are basically the way we walk everywhere. I'm in front or on the left, L-T's in the middle, Mo's on the right or behind us."

Renner's eyes flashed.

"I don't recall asking how to cut corners, *Sergeant.*"

Reiter bit his tongue. *I can't rip into him in front of his soldiers or it will undermine his authority, but if I back down in front of my guys, it hurts mine.*

Reiter cleared his throat.

"Master Sergeant, let's continue this conversation behind my Panzerter."

The older man looked over his shoulder.

"Take five and drink water, and don't you dare let me hear you making small talk with 3rd." He followed Reiter across the lot, behind Reiter's machine. "I'll have you know, I will not have my methods questioned by some second-string Lieutenant. I served in the regular forces for seventeen years before transferring to the watch. What could you possibly know that I don't?"

Careful, Paul, he's one of those guys.

"I'm not questioning your methods or your knowledge." Reiter stepped into Renner's space. "But I'll absolutely question your shit attitude. There's no reason for you to treat your soldiers the way you do and certainly no excuse for you to talk to *mine* that way."

Renner snorted.

"The Unionists won't care about their feelings, why should I? They're only pouting because I'm holding them to a standard. That horny wad Kress let them do whatever the hell they wanted, and like all watchmen and women, they got complacent and lazy."

Reiter steeled himself.

"First of all, that doesn't excuse the way you talk to my soldiers, and second, Bartonova and Sandic tied for top shot their first two years in the unit and didn't lose it until Legousi got a perfect score once."

Renner held up a finger.

"Lieutenant, who are you with your books and your studying to judge me in my decades of experience soldiering?"

Before Reiter could answer, his phone buzzed. It was Stanca.

"Reiter, mount up and head to the main road. I'll give you details on the way."

Reiter nodded.

"Roger, sir." He looked at Renner. "Mount up, but we're not done here." The older man snorted, and they hurried back to the others. "Mount Up!"

"Sandic! Is that another cigarette? I told you not to smoke on duty!"

Reiter tuned him out as he climbed up his Panzerter. Just below the head lay the opening. He entered the clavicle hatch and strapped himself in.

"Black Platoon, give me a radio check." Reiter waited a second before repeating himself.

"Gotcha, Lima Charlie, boss. Man, that guy is a piece of work," Adamski said.

Reiter shook his head.

"Trust me, 2, you don't know the half of it." He checked his gauges. "5, can you hear me okay?"

"Yo, what a dick, uh, 1."

Reiter chuckled. They collected their rifles and chambered a round. They would need cleaning again soon.

BLAKE LOOKED OUT OVER THE TERRAIN. AHEAD OF HIM LAY THE Midway river, the first leg of the Dracul River Delta. The river was actually two rivers that merged and flowed east. *They have the good fording areas covered. No way we'll be able to force a crossing on our own.* He heard dropships behind him and smiled.

Blake had swapped his Ogre Company for Druza's Roc Company for this operation. Druza was currently enjoying Panzerter support in the mountains to the south of him. Blake enjoyed the enhanced mobility of the dropships. They were going to insert raiders behind a suspected Tharcian position while Malice and Predator Company crossed the river in a deeper spot to catch them off guard. In the event things fell apart, he had Nightmare Company in reserve. To his north, 44th Mechanized Battalion was committing to a similar offensive. 8th Armored had crawled through the initial advance and was being rebuilt at the airfield. Elements of the 5th Pacifica Infantry protected them.

"Partisan Battery standing by."

Blake nodded. *They've been bothering me about shooting 'real' rounds since they landed.* Blake smiled as he stood on the shoulder of his Martian. What hair he still had blew in the draft from the dropships flying overhead. The six aircraft reminded him of wolves on the prowl, their bristling weapons racks like bared fangs. *My, my, how things have changed. Father would have been thrilled to have the toys we do.*

Something screamed. One of the dropships fell from the sky, consumed by fire. It crashed into the woods across the river. The others scattered. Flying in a wide line, they raked the forest with chainguns and rockets. Malice and Predator advanced. Concealed positions opened up with cannon fire and machine guns.

Blake donned his helmet.

"Malice 6, Leviathan 6, protect Predator. They're vulnerable when they switch from tracks to propellers."

The Martians pushed forward into the river. Icy water sprayed about as shells landed near them. *I need to get inside my Martian and look at that damn matrix.*

Blake dropped into his seat and swung out the command console. The Panzerter's sensors allowed him to see Martians waist-deep in the river. They slogged forward, occasionally lurching. The Tauruses paddled after, like puppies following their owners.

The Tharcian guns were finding their marks. *We're losing our momentum. If this keeps up, we must break off.*

Blake toggled his radio to division net.

"Overton 6, Leviathan 6, how's your advance?" He didn't have to wait long.

"Leviathan 6, it's almost non-existent. Our tracks and Panzerters keep getting stuck on shit in the river."

Blake wasn't a fan of his response, but if he was to keep his offensive momentum, he had to make something out of this attack.

He switched back to battalion net.

"Roc 1, neutralize the position in front of Predator and Malice." The dropships began circling the Tharcians' position as if it was their prey. They took turns strafing the portion and launching rockets. Surely the Tharcians would be finished here. A distant roar dashed his hopes. "All units, fall back now!"

"Malice 1, we need to recover our troops and—" Roc 1 was engulfed in flames, as were three of his companions.

Drones screamed past, two of them. They came right at Blake. His laser torched one. Its wingmate overshot him, banked, and came around for another pass. Blake pivoted. He had a shot. His beam went wide. Blake was thrown forward. His head cracked his front monitor before he slammed against the right firewall.

Blake tasted blood. His head throbbed. He hoisted himself into his seat and strapped himself in this time. Feeling the ground tremble beneath him, he tried bringing his Martian to its feet. It shook at first but stood up. While its state was far from ideal, it was operational. Blake grinned. *I'm glad this machine is a tough bastard.*

His Martians were retreating. Taurus IFVs came ashore on his side, soldiers clinging to the sides. Both groups fired wildly at the circling drones. *How Tharcian to attack us without putting themselves at risk.* He sighed. *I must answer to General Lee for my failure to advance.*

Artillery picked up. Shells pummeled the opposite bank of the river. The drones—there were five of them now—dove on the artillery battery like a hawk chasing prey. Missiles streaked skyward to intercept. Blake turned towards the bank. *Damn, this entire operation is a wash.*

Then he saw the flares. Green. Objective secure. Blake grinned. Somehow those raider bastards had seized the defenses on the opposite shore.

"Predator, Malice, turn about and reinforce Roc!" Blake pushed his machine forward. As he struggled to stay upright, he met his companies in the field. Limping forward, he raised his Panzerter's fist into the air. Surprisingly, his soldiers rallied. Their spirits renewed, they charged back across the river. The Martians rushed forward firing their lasers, while the IFVs switched to swim mode. Undergrowth burst into flames. Trees split as if struck by lightning.

Blake grinned. *Somehow we salvaged this whole thing.* Then Overton called out to him.

"Leviathan 6, major Tharcian counterattack is heading your way, and a smaller one is hitting our rear. They're going for the airfield!"

"What? *How in the hell did they get behind us?"* Victory was slipping away like water through his fingers. He ground his teeth.

"Leviathan 6, Nightmare 6. I'm moving to reinforce the airfield."

Blake looked at his matrix. The computer proudly displayed its analysis: this wasn't happening. *Helpful.*

"Nightmare, as soon as the line breaks, hammer the Tharcians back through. Roc, recover your men and screen our rear. All other units, fall back and reorient on the airport." Blake pressed his limping machine back to the firebase at full speed. "Malice, vehicle status?"

"Four Martians still operational, all of us left have some damage, and we lost three machines, including the new guy."

Damn, only five Panzerters to help Nightmare.

"Leviathan 5, have the mechanics prepare for emergency maintenance on our Panzerters and IFVs." He looked at his battle map and did some quick math. "Tell them they have five minutes per unit." *By the time we roll out, Nightmare will have been in contact for about a minute.*

"Roger, 6, they'll get it done."

It didn't take them long to return to the firebase. Blake set his engine to standby and climbed out of the Martian's crown.

"Hey, prioritize my leg, don't worry about anything else!"

The mechanics were already hard at work pulling the paneling away from his knee. Now that he had a minute to breathe, Blake looked over his damaged Martian. Crude shells had chewed metal in several places along its left side. Soot smothered his double-gray paint. *Doesn't look like that drone scored a direct hit, probably why it's still able to walk.*

Malice's surviving Martians bore the scars of their assault on the Tharcians' river defenses. Blake noted all of them had mud caked on their lower legs. *If the riverbed is too soft there, then we need to find a new spot to cross.* He glanced back down at his own machine. The mechanics tossed warped and fused magnetic rods and installed new ones.

"One minute!" A crew boss urged the others on with a megaphone while checking a tablet.

The mechanics began re-armoring his knee. Ready to leave, Blake crawled down into his Martian. His head throbbed as he buckled in. *I'll see a medic after this.* He got an all clear from the ground crew and moved out. His artillery came to life. Shells screamed towards distant targets. Blake's Martian still moved stiffly, but better than it had.

"Malice, form up on me," he commanded. "We will countercharge their flank. Predator, follow us into the breach, attack their weak points."

Nightmare was holding steady. It looked like they had absorbed the brunt of the counterattack, but the enemy had a large element swinging wide to strike their flank. *Who's responsible for this? Where did these Tharcians come from? Who dropped the ball?* Blake ground his teeth. *Failure of this magnitude is unacceptable for the MAG.*

"Leviathan 6, we're approaching Hill 213. Do you still want to set a firing line here? Or still countercharge?" Malice 6 asked.

Blake weighed his options.

"We will form a firing line before charging. All units stand by for close combat."

5

P aul Reiter's Panzerter crushed the head of a Union Panzerter as he advanced. They were green-gray, with hooded heads and massive sensor hubs. They used high-caliber rifles and machine guns, similar to them. *Almost a spitting image of the ones from the War of 2112.*

"We got comms with a drone squadron—we'll have air support soon!" Stanca announced.

Reiter grinned. *No dropships to help them this time.* The company formed a wedge. Reiter's platoon took up the right side, Renner's platoon the left, with Captain Stanca and First Sergeant Septimus in the center. Comidus and the infantry followed inside the wedge.

The company commander continued to keep them updated.

"Early Company is taking losses. A reinforcing unit has them tripped up."

Fox Company planned to smash into that unit's flank before taking hill 421 nearby. If it went as well as their initial engagement, they'd have the airport and surrounding area by sundown.

A scream filled the net.

Reiter looked left. Bearing down on them from the south were five Panzerters supported by IFVs. They were unlike the ones they'd fought moments before, rugged and bearing a two-tone gray paint job. MAGs. Missiles streaked from the wood line towards the Martians. Smoke began rising from sections of the wood line that burned.

"Gold Platoon, bound back. Black, absorb the contact!" Stanca's orders were already being enacted by instinct, before the words even broke the net.

Reiter grit his teeth. His rifle came up. Two shots. Center of mass. Both bounced. Reiter took a knee as the treetops near him burst into flames.

He came up. Another shot. This time he struck the side of his target's head. The 88-mm round dug a trench through its saucer-shaped head. The new machine stumbled, but it didn't fall. *Legs.*

Reiter took a knee again.

"Fox 6, their armor's thick!" he cried as he heard rifle fire near him.

"I know! I'm shooting them too!" Stanca replied.

Reiter grit his teeth. The enemy Panzerter advanced closer, crashing through trees and brush.

"We can't win this, 6. We need to fall back!" Comidus spoke sense, even as the enemy Panzerter swung a huge mace wildly. Reiter backpedalled.

His rifle came up again. Another shot, this time into its upper leg. Reiter charged the staggered machine. Forty-five tons of metal crashed into the hapless Unionist, sending it sprawling. *Now's my chance.* Reiter fired two rounds point blank into the Unionist's chest.

Smoke wafted from the stricken machine, and it lay still.

"Black 1, get back!" Adamski cried.

Reiter darted back as another Unionist came crashing through the trees. It made to charge him with its mace, then tracers burned the air between them.

"Sir, now!"

Reiter and Adamski took turns retreating and giving covering fire.

Mo ran past both of them, his weapon gone.

"Where's Fox 6?" Reiter asked.

"Not sure! They were helping us out!" Mo replied.

We need to figure out where everyone else is.

"Any Fox element, respond!" *I hope I'm not shouting into the void.* They lost the pursuing Unionists. A few long moments passed before Reiter got a response.

"This is Fox 7. Break south. We need to regroup with Early Company."

What happened to Early? Turning south, they cautiously made their way through the trees. As the forest began to thin, he glimpsed a silhouette in the brush. His rifle came up.

"Whoa, whoa, whoa! Friendly! Friendly!" The Mark IV emerged from the woods with two more behind it, a pair of Mark IIIs.

Reiter lowered his rifle.

"Who goes there?"

"2nd Platoon, Early Company. Who are you?"

"3rd Platoon, Fox. Good to see you made it. What happened back there?"

They assumed an impromptu formation and moved south.

"The mother-fucking MAGs is what happened. They have much better shit than their regular forces, fucking wrecked our company good." They spread out as the trees thinned.

"Gray paint job, round head?"

"Yeah, those fucks wiped out our whole 3rd Platoon, caught

them in the open with some kind of laser weapon. Thing's a fuckin' nightmare."

Reiter shivered as they entered open ground. He kept his eyes open for any sign of movement. One of the Panzerters behind him exploded. Reiter turned to see its legs still smoldering, its torso blown off and in flames behind them. Mo seized its fallen rifle.

"Contact at 9!" an Early Company pilot cried.

There it was emerging from a crop of trees. A MAG Panzerter.

"Get on line!" Reiter ordered.

The Early Company platoon had four Panzerters now to Reiter's three. They formed up on the left, Reiter's platoon on the right. Reiter's platoon opened fire while Early advanced. Adamski and Mo alternated back and forth with their assault rifles. When one's burst ended, the other's began.

Despite being hammered by shells at long-range, the Unionist stood undaunted. The end of its weapon glowed green. An Early Panzerter fell in a shower of molten metal. *Holy shit, you can't even see it.* The Early Panzerters stopped and opened fire.

"Let's go!" Reiter cried.

They pushed their Panzerters into a run. Reiter's machine jolted him around as it ran as fast as it could across the field. Where Early had run straight at the Unionist, Black Platoon angled right. Another green flash. Another Early Panzerter fell.

"We're not penetrating, we're just pissing him off!" Mo said.

There's no way we can close the distance before he picks us off. They took a knee and opened fire. Three shots and a click. Damn. Reiter reloaded as fast as he could.

"Aim for its weapon!" *That's right, can't shoot us without his rifle.* A different flash. Smoke rose from the Union Panzerter. Good, *fucking got him.* "Early Company, assault through!"

"Roger!" The Early Panzerters fired while moving. The Unionist, trapped in a deadly L, collapsed.

Reiter's platoon ceased fire as the Early Panzerters advanced. The two survivors dumped five rounds each into the MAG Panzerter before Reiter saw the flash of their breast machine guns.

He shook his head.

They shouldn't have done that, but I can't say I blame them. He looked back at the fallen Panzerters behind him. They still burned.

"Fuck, that was just one of them?" Mo sounded despondent. "Fuck, those things can chew through an entire company."

"Lock it up," said Reiter. Let's form back up and head south."

They formed a line. Adamski took point, and Mo brought up the rear. Reiter walked in the center with an Early Panzerter in front of and behind him. *Damn, just one.*

"Under no circumstances are the Tharcians supposed to take the firebase." Damian Blake scowled as he gave the directive. A long caravan of prisoners were being marched into the improvised POW camp near the firebase. He ground his teeth. *They reduced Malice Company to a nub. I can't rely on them for pursuit.* Inside his Panzerter, the command matrix was little help, besides its map.

I can't move Nightmare without leaving the airport vulnerable. I guess I'll take Malice. He looked at their roster. *Ah yes, my formidable company of two Panzerters.* His recon platoon was tracking the enemy approaching from the northwest. *If only I hadn't had those gun positions taken down, they'd be running right into them.* That gave him an idea, though.

"Lamia Battery, I'm sending you a grid. Blanket it with high-explosive and white phosphorus." He switched to division net. "I need all available batteries to fire for effect on the following grid." Back to battalion net. "Malice, who's prepared for combat?"

"I am, Leviathan 6. Malice 4—the other guy's still messed up."

Blake would definitely need to see a dentist if he returned to the rear.

"Well, Malice 4, when this barrage lets up, we will mop up." A flashing light told him they needed him on division net. "One moment, Malice 4." He switched over. "Go for Leviathan 6."

"Leviathan 6, Overton 6. We got word from the airport: General Lee is dead."

Damn.

"Overton 6, I'm sending you a grid. I need any forces you can spare to rally with me there and clear the board."

"Leviathan 6, I've got a couple companies of regular forces coming your way along with my infantry. That should do it."

Blake looked at the matrix's projection of enemy strength and weighed his options. The regular forces used the inferior Terran III but had the numbers to make them more than a match for the Tharcians. With two Martians and infantry support, they could do it.

"Roger, thanks for the help." Blake motioned Malice 4 to follow him, and they left the gate to the firebase. "Get them all on my battalion's freq." He switched back in time to catch Malice 4's question.

"What's the plan, Comrade?"

"It's simple, really. We're going to go in when the barrage lets up and drive them east. By the time we get to hill 213, we'll have completely routed them."

The sound of the artillery was beginning to let up. Two companies of Terran IIIs and an infantry company emerged from the trees. *Perfect, we can do this with what we have.*

Blake divided the group in half. One half would follow him, the other Malice 4. Blake would drive forward while Malice 4 drove into their flank, pushing the enemy southeast. *This might be too easy.* A short section of woodland separated them from the killing fields where the Tharcians lay.

Blake gave Malice 4 some time to move into position.

"Move out!"

His forces moved forward at a brisk pace. The artillery barrage had badly battered the Tharcians. Panzerters lay smashed by shells. Tracked and wheeled vehicles lay in smoldering wrecks. The survivors hardly looked unscathed.

Blake's laser came up. An IFV burst into flames, its turret blown off. The Terrans slogged forward. Their rifles and machine-cannons hammered the Tharcian forces. A wall of shells struck a Panzerter until it fell still. Return fire was sporadic. A shell smashed a Terran's optic near Blake. They surged onward.

We need to keep this momentum up. To the north, Malice 4 was smashing into their flank. Another Terran collapsed. The return fire was beginning to grow stronger. Blake looked off at the dust of the enemy moving. They were heading to hill 213.

"My group, they're heading to hill 213. Cut them off before they seize the high ground!" They picked up their pace. Blake pushed his machine to a run. With his laser ready, he picked off Tharcians at the base of the hill. Return fire grew thicker. It began to rock his machine as he advanced. *They're concentrating their fire. Where are those Terrans?* He glanced back to see he had left them behind. *Shit.*

Blake began zigzagging. He moved as erratically as possible, evading their return fire. His laser flashed here and there. A Tharcian Panzerter exploded at the waist. Another lost an arm, its shoulder completely melted off. Shells streamed past him into the Tharcians. *Good, they're catching up.* Another Panzerter found itself lost in smoke.

The Tharcians' return fire was thinning out again. Blake grinned. *They have the hill but not the numbers to hold it.*

A familiar roar froze his blood.

Drones swung over the hill. A second later, fire washed through Blake's formation. Terrans staggered, wreathed in flames. IFVs swerved to avoid being caught in the attack. Blake grit his teeth. He backpedaled to put himself in the Terrans' formation.

The drones came back. Blake sent one crashing down. The other broke off its attack. More drones came.

"Soldiers of the Union! Rally and take the hill! I'll keep the drones off you!" *If I can keep the drones busy, then the regulars and Malice 4 can take the hill.* Drones began circling overhead. Whenever one banked to make a pass, it earned Blake's wrath. Still more drones came.

Damn Tharcians. This groundbreaking machine made by working men and women tied up by cheap toys. For every drone incinerated by Blake's laser, two more swooped in.

Despite the drones' efforts, Blake's forces reached the base of the hill. They incinerated more drones. Malice 4 had joined the battle, and more Terrans surged towards the hill. The return fire from the Tharcians grew thinner but smarter.

The drones finally broke off their attack. *They could be back soon. Better make the most of this.* Blake charged the hill. The Terrans followed him up. He raised his laser and pulled the trigger.

Suddenly he couldn't see. Blake felt the machine stagger. Unable to keep its balance, it fell. His head slammed back against the wall. His restraints cut into and jerked his shoulders. On the way down, he gnashed his teeth.

Blake blinked. His head throbbed.

As his sight returned, he realized what had happened. His weapon had exploded. The Martian's right hand was a mangled mess of hydraulics and metal. Blake saw a Tharcian crest the hill. *Fuck.* Blake reached for his throttle and control stick. Maybe he could still fight.

"BLACK 1, WE GOT ANOTHER MAG ON US," ADAMSKI WARNED.

Reiter saw him. The MAG had discarded his laser and drawn a mace. As tough as the MAGs were, they had regular forces to worry about. A missile streaked towards a regular. The enemy Panzerter fell, its head smashed.

"Are the support elements clear?" *We can't fight without our cooks, techs, and transports.*

"Not yet, they're still in artillery range!" an Early Company pilot cried.

Reiter lay prone on the center of the hill, most of his Panzerter shielded by the hill itself. To his left, Adamski, Mo, and the last Early Panzerter fought desperately to prevent them from being flanked. To his right, Septimus, Bartonova, and Steele fought a similar fight.

"Shit, I'm out!" said Mo.

Another shot. Another Union Regular fell.

"Mo, fall back. Don't get killed up here."

The MAG lurched forward. Reiter stepped up and back. The mace smashed his rifle into the dirt. None of Reiter's friends could help; they were busy keeping the other enemies suppressed.

If I don't stop this guy, he'll tear us apart.

Cautiously, he drew his Panzerter's sword. The air hissed as the collapsible reinforced ceramic-composite blade vented plasma, giving the weapon a green glow.

You can do this, Paul. Remember your training; remember the clock face.

The MAG swung its mace like a wild animal. The only thing keeping the feral Panzerter at bay was the reach of Reiter's sword. *His legs, go for the joints.* He switched to the offensive, jabbing and slashing at the MAG. It was able to parry him once, twice. Just under the mace head, the weapon glowed orange. *There's my opening!*

His next blow cleaved the head of the mace right off. He lunged again. His sword struck true, severing its leg at the knee. He followed up with his shoulder. The MAG tumbled backward, bouncing and breaking down the hill.

"Black 1, Gold 1. Supporting elements are clear! Get your people out of there!"

Reiter disengaged his sword.

"They're clear! Fall back!" He backpedaled down the slope. The rest of Fox Company followed. Drones roared in from above, cannons blazing. *Good, that will keep them off us.* They'd retreated a few miles south when Comidus hailed them.

"Any Fox element, Gold 1, please respond."

Thank God, we got him on comms.

"Gold 1, Black 1. We got you Lima Charlie. Bring us home."

Comidus sent them a grid, and within a long hour of marching, they found the rest of their company. Or rather, the rest of their battalion. Seven Panzerters, four Iglasio IFVs, two Cstalio missile carriers, and about a dozen breakdown trucks, ambulances, ammo carriers, and comms trucks.

They had made a small camp, with the infantry dismounting and securing the perimeter.

Reiter dismounted his Panzerter and made his way over to Comidus.

"How bad is it?"

Comidus was sitting in the back of one of his IFVs looking at a map. He shook his head.

"Not great, and there's no way to put this gently, but you're in charge now."

Reiter blinked.

"That bad, huh?" Septimus approached the two junior officers.

"In our sad state, we need to make it a priority to rejoin the main body so we can go to the rear and get rebuilt."

Reiter squinted.

"You think they're going to spend resources rebuilding us? We're the provincial watch."

Septimus nodded.

"As unpleasant as it has been, we likely have the most experience fighting the Unionists."

Comidus looked at Reiter.

"As a people, we don't exactly have a great history of fighting defensive wars. If we did, we wouldn't be on Mars. We're going to need to develop new methods of fighting."

Reiter looked at the map.

"While we're doing that, we need to find a place to cross the Dracul. Our Panzerters can ford most of it, but the trucks are going to need a bridge or shallow, slow-moving section." Reiter looked at the other two men. "Right now, our priority is surviving. If we can hurt the enemy along the way, then we will, but we can't be decisively engaged."

Septimus pointed to the map.

"Our best bet is to head south to Pulaski. If the provincial capital hasn't fallen yet, then we'll be able to cross the Midway River there."

"And if it has?" Comidus asked.

Septimus shrugged.

"Then we'll need to find a smaller municipal bridge that can hold our vehicles."

Reiter scratched at his chin.

"Worse comes to worst, we can have the Panzerters ferry them across, but that will be time-consuming, not to mention dangerous." He sighed. "We could easily run into advance Union forces. We need to find ways to counter their weapons."

Comidus nodded.

"I agree. We won't have a drone squadron to bail us out of trouble next time." He pointed to the Cstalios. "We lucked out with these missile carriers, though."

Reiter looked at the vehicle. It looked mostly like the Iglasio IFV, an angular box on tracks. Where the Iglasio had a narrow turret with an autocannon and an AA missile rack, this machine's turret possessed a quad-stack of anti-aircraft missiles and two bulkier launchers on the other side. A medium machine gun sat in a remote weapon station near the front.

"How so?" asked Reiter.

Comidus grinned.

"They have anti-Panzerter missiles. I saw them smash Union Panzerters earlier. The crew said it's a shaped charge stacked on an EMP emitter stacked on another shaped charge."

Reiter whistled.

"So it pierces the armor and releases an EMP inside the Panzerter." Comidus nodded. *That would fry the pilot's brain. I hope the Union didn't think of that.* Reiter whistled. He had a new respect for the missile carriers. "How many do we have?"

"In total? Twenty-four—six per vehicle and twelve in the box still." He stood and stepped out of the vehicle. "Can't rely on them, though. The missile carriers are vulnerable in the open. Great in ambush, though." He looked back at Reiter. "The official name is Oriás-ölő."

Reiter grinned.

"Giant killer, I love it." He looked over at the kneeling Panzerters. "I guess we need to get everyone moving."

Comidus nodded. "I agree, Fox 6."

Reiter shook his head.

"I'll stick with Black 1 for now, *XO.* Now let's get everyone moving. We got a long road trip ahead of us."

DAMIAN BLAKE STRUGGLED TO KEEP HIS EYES OPEN. THE MEDIC shined a penlight into his eyes. The bandages wrapped around his head began to itch.

"It looks like you have a concussion, Comrade Colonel."

Blake stood from the steel chair he sat in. His head throbbed behind his eyes.

"You're going to have to take some time off from frontline combat," said the medic, "two weeks minimum. And minimize screen time, make sure you get plenty of rest."

Blake thanked the medic and left the tent. *No frontline combat, huh? Guess I can't show the flag for the troops.*

The firebase was bustling with activity. Panzerters were being repaired and rearmed with incredible speed. Trucks dropped of reinforcements, ammo, and supplies. *I need to get down to headquarters.*

The dark hallways and soft light in the underground network eased his headache. As soon as he entered the map room, he felt relieved. Few if any screens were down here, just his map tables, a couple banks of computers, and a radio set. The only active screen was Meyer's tablet.

"Meyer, get Kennedy and Wake down here. I want them for planning the next phase of the operation."

Meyer nodded and got to work. Guard Junior Lieutenant Charles Wake, Malice 4, was now the commander of the newly formed Manticore Company. Ogre and Predator Company were now being led by promoted lieutenants. If they showed promise, Blake planned on including them. He'd been studying the map of the next area for a moment when his subordinates entered.

"Good to see you up and about, Comrade Colonel." Wake took a seat at the table across from Blake. Kennedy leaned against the table, while Meyer remained standing. "So what are our orders?"

Blake took a deep breath.

"They have tasked us with seizing the provincial capital of Pulaski, specifically the northern metro area." He pointed to a second map sheet. While the first displayed the area around Pulaski, the second was a map of the city itself.

"That's a big ask from Division," said Wake. "I know we just got plussed up to full strength, but are we sure we'll be able to take our objectives?"

Blake nodded.

"I don't think of us as weakened, but refined. All of our number who couldn't adapt have been purged. Now we have fresh forces and leaders hardened by combat."

Meyer looked at the city map.

"So what are our objectives?"

Blake held up three fingers.

"We need to seize Capital Hill, the City Park, and this bridge over the Midway River." He marked them on his map. "The good news is we need not seize them simultaneously."

Kennedy leaned over.

"Conventional wisdom has us seizing Capital Hill and the Park before moving to the bridge." He looked over at Blake. "Is that the plan?"

Blake shook his head.

"Not quite. We destroyed the Tharcians at Hill 213, but while we were mostly successful, some still got away." He pointed at the bridge over Midway River. "We'll send Ogre and Nightmare to seize the bridge while Predator and Malice—excuse me, Manticore —seize Capital Hill. The two prongs of the attack will meet in City Park." He made eye contact with each of his officers. "Under no circumstances are there to be any Tharcians left in the field."

Wake grinned.

"Understood, Comrade Colonel. Those bootlickers won't know what hit them."

Kennedy furrowed his brow.

"It won't be that easy, Wake, you should know that by now." He pointed to the city map. "There's a lot of narrow side streets and awkward angles, perfect spots for ambushes."

Wake raised an eyebrow.

"That's some mighty defeatist talk there, Comrade Lieutenant. Are you implying we can't beat the class traitors with our current equipment?"

Kennedy shook his head.

"Don't get me wrong, ton for ton, the Martian is a better machine than anything they have, but we have clear weaknesses."

Wake folded his arms.

"Elaborate."

Kennedy grew red.

"Why the hell should I have to explain things you should already know? Besides, you know better than I do about their close-combat abilities."

The younger soldier scowled.

"He got lucky."

Meyer raised an eyebrow.

"How do you know the pilot was a man? We have Tharcian pilots of both genders detained here." Wake scowled. "Anyway, Kennedy is correct: the data we've gathered so far suggests we avoid close combat with the Tharcians for the following reasons." She tapped on her tablet. "Within 600 meters, the Tharcians' weapons can penetrate a Martian's frontal armor. While they have a higher overland speed, the Tharcian machines tend to be more agile. And finally, while great against structures and other vehicles, the mace has proven to be a poor anti-Panzerter weapon."

Kennedy nodded.

"The mace is great for a finishing blow, but it can't parry their thermal swords. In close quarters, you're honestly better off using your fists."

Interesting how the tables have turned. Once rivals, now allies against the new kid. Blake sipped his coffee as they debated courses of action in the city. *We're all loyal to the cause, but Wake is a zealous Unionist. We need to be careful around him lest he bring the Internal Review Service against us.*

Blake set his mug down.

"Enough. I've given you your objectives. Get with Predator and Ogre and develop company-level plans. You're dismissed."

They left him promptly. *They'll be back soon, but until then I'll enjoy the silence.* Blake slouched in his chair. His mind began to drift as he closed his eyes.

Fields full of broken bodies and mangled machines entered his mind's eye. *Three hundred miles of death, no time to bury our dead.* He shook his head. *They're just cowards, kulaks, traitors to the revolution.* Blake ground his teeth. *They fled to Mars because they couldn't protect their homelands; they don't stand a chance.*

"Then how the hell did they get halfway to Foundation?" Blake took a deep breath. *Things are different now. Now they're running, and this time, this time we'll pull them apart.* Blake repeated the thought. As much as he tried, his recent victories didn't wash away the bitterness of twenty years ago.

6

On a typical day, Pulaski was a city moving at half speed. That was not the case today. Cars and people filled the streets. Occasionally, a convoy of military vehicles halted traffic to pass through. Panzerters covered every third block, watching over key intersections and structures.

Paul Reiter found himself in one such building. The terraced structure before him was about ten stories tall. He could see from his spot on the road that the roof was lined with trees and greenery. He entered the beige building's lobby. It was flooded with green-gray uniforms.

Reiter pushed his way forward to the front desk.

"I'm Senior Lieutenant Paul Reiter. I'm looking for Major Strauss."

The attendant at the desk nodded.

"She'll be in room 245 on the second floor."

"Roger, thank you." Reiter pushed his way into a crowded elevator. *It's impressive how they can turn a hotel into Corps Head-quarters.* The elevator dinged, and he disembarked. *245, 245, 245.*

Reiter was almost mumbling it under his breath so he wouldn't forget. Once he found the room, he knocked.

"One second, please!"

Reiter stepped back and waited.

The woman who answered the door was likely in her mid-thirties. Instead of camouflage or green-gray, she wore a black and white fitness uniform. Her dark hair was pulled back into a bun. "Lieutenant Reiter, I was expecting you today."

Reiter nodded.

"You have the orders for my company?"

She looked back into her room/office.

"Wait one second." She closed the door.

Please don't send us into combat, please don't send us back into combat.

Her door swung open again, and this time she was holding a manila folder. "Here, your company is going east to Garden City Technical College. You're going to refit and start rebuilding from there." She handed Reiter the folder.

"How soon can we expect reinforcements?"

She shrugged.

"That depends on where the new bodies are coming from. Your unit is a priority, though. The brass is planning a big counteroffensive to kick them out of Gallacia."

Reiter nodded, thanked the major, and left.

He flipped through the folder as he was walking. A line item made him pause. *Escort civilians to the college?* He reread that part. *Well, it looks like the rest of the company is finding that out now.* Reiter walked over to their staging area.

They staged in the parking lot of Raven Orbital Industries Arena. Their Panzerters knelt, while the Iglasios and Cstalios were parked in a line next to them. Behind the infantry vehicles were a row of buses. *So that's what the civilians are taking.* His soldiers milled about, some talking with civilians. Reiter spotted Mo being harassed by a group of girls while Adamski laughed at him.

Septimus approached him.

"We've heard we're dragging these civilians along with us. Is that the case?"

Reiter nodded.

"Yeah, we're escorting them to the Regional College a few miles from here. We're going to stop there and rebuild. I don't know what they do after that."

Septimus nodded.

"Frankly, sir, it isn't our problem. Our priority is our soldiers and seeing Fox returned to fighting strength."

Reiter looked around.

"It's only a few miles. What do we have to worry about—actually getting attacked?" He checked his watch. "We're going to move out after dark, so let's make sure everyone's tracking."

Septimus nodded, and they split.

The young girls from before were still messing with Mo, but as Reiter approached, he noticed they kinda looked like him.

"Mo, is everything alright?"

Mo looked over at him as he lifted the smallest girl to his hip.

"Oh, it's good, sir. My sisters are part of this civilian convoy." He pointed to the one he was holding. "This one's Izabella, and the twins are Sophie and Zoe. Sisters, this is my boss, Lieutenant Reiter."

Izabella tugged at his ear.

"Javi, where's yours?"

Mo turned around and pointed to his machine.

"It's the one with a big 35 painted on it."

"Why?"

"Because I'm in 3rd Platoon and I'm the fifth machine."

"Why are you five?"

"Because I'm the lowest-ranking member of my platoon."

"Where are three and four?"

Mo grimaced.

"They're in a better place."

"Javi, your robot looks like a piece of junk."

"Yeah, Javi, do you even wash your robot?"

Mo slouched under the twin's verbal assault.

"First of all, it's a Panzerter, not a robot. Secondly, when was I going to wash it when I was in combat?"

Reiter shook his head and walked towards Adamski.

"Have they been giving him the third degree all day?"

Adamski nodded.

"Yeah. Mo said they were staying with Steele's sister when shit hit the fan."

Reiter raised an eyebrow.

"Did something happen to their mom?"

Adamski shrugged. "Yes and no. Her cancer came back, so the church scrounged up money to have it beat for good."

Reiter nodded.

"So I assume they flew her to the capital?"

Adamski shook his head and leaned against his Panzerter's leg.

"From what I heard, they flew her to the coast."

Reiter looked back at the Mondragon siblings.

"Good, I'm glad they got her far from this madness." He checked his watch. "Let's start getting mounted up."

Adamski nodded and began climbing into his machine.

Reiter walked over to Mo and his siblings.

"Sorry, ladies, but your brother is going to have to work here." He clapped Mo on the shoulder. "Mount up."

"That's fine, we like Amy better anyway."

"Well, she needs to work too." The twins pouted, but Reiter

walked down the line with all three sisters in tow. "Steele, Bartonova, mount up!"

The woman they had been talking to ran back up the line towards them.

"Oh, are we leaving soon?" Reiter nodded. "Thank you so much! Come on, kids! Let's get back on the bus!"They scurried off towards the transport.

Reiter walked back towards his machine. He climbed up to the clavicle hatch and entered the cockpit.

"Black 1, all units check in."

"Fox 7 checking in."

"Gold 1 checking in."

"Gold 2 checking in."

"Gold 3 checking in."

"Gold 5 checking in,"

"Gold 6 checking in."

"White 2 checking in,"

"White 3 checking in,"

"White 5 checking in,"

"Black 2 checking in,"

"Black 5 checking in."

"All units up. Fox Company, move out!"

DAMIAN BLAKE COULDN'T REMEMBER THE LAST TIME HE'D WORN his ceremonial uniform. The synthetic double-gray top and pants were tight on his skin. His name sat on one side of his chest, a veritable fruit salad of awards on his other. His shoulder boards were orange with the four silver bars that marked him as a colonel.

He stood ramrod straight as the guard brigadier pinned an Order of the Martian Republic, first class, on his chest. Down the line,

Wake and Kennedy received the same award of a lower class, *for exceptional bravery and leadership in the face of a Tharcian attack.*

The ceremony was being held in a ballroom at the airport. The room had high ceilings and was lit by a grand chandelier. Once the ceremony concluded, they were ushered into the audience for drinks. Bureaucrats and trade union presidents intermingled with MAG and regular army officers.

Parasites. Blake scowled at their guests. *If they weren't so anti-military twenty years ago, we wouldn't be back here fighting for lands that are rightfully ours.*

Blake sipped a water and did his best to avoid union reps.

There was a shout, and a screen began to emerge from the stage. Within moments, the image of Chairman Owens filled the screen. The powerfully built man stood at a podium. Clearly, this was live from the Union capital of Foundation.

"Comrades, we live in trying times. The Tharcians continue to escalate this war, continue to undermine our sovereignty. Their true cowardice was revealed just last evening when they attacked our Jupiter Energy Fleet. They seek to starve us into submission when they can't beat us in open battle." The man gripped his podium and narrowed his eyes. "I say this to every Union citizen: we will rage a relentless fight, and we will not stop until the enemies who surround us have been broken before us." He raised his arms. "Now is the time to stand up for the future of all mankind!"

The room erupted into cheers. Blake was sure the capital was erupting into thunderous applause as well.

He left the hall early. *No need to exchange pleasantries.* He found himself a ride to the firebase, looking over the latest maps while he sat in the back of an armored car. *Hell of a speech tonight by the chairman. Most of the union reps are hopelessly out of touch with reality, but he gets it.* When he arrived at the firebase, he made his way to the war room and was pleasantly surprised to find Meyer already down there.

She strode from map to map with her tablet.

"Did the ceremony go well?"

Blake shrugged.

"It's just more chest candy, nothing special."

Meyer narrowed her eyes.

"When you go before the selection committee for promotion, that 'chest candy' has weight."

He waved her off.

"I've got plenty of medals for bravery. Problem is, they're all from the Tharcian invasion of 2112. Doesn't matter I was just a kid in the cockpit, I smell like defeat to certain higher-ups." He shook his head. "Anyway, what have we got here?"

Meyer gave him a rare smile.

"I've run hundreds of simulations using our current combat data." She pointed to four routes into the city. Each one used a different color string. "Routes green and blue are the safest from ambush and mitigate the parity the Tharcians have in close combat." She pointed to the other two strings: one red, one yellow. "These routes are much more dangerous but allow our forces to reach their objectives expediently enough to warrant the risk."

"And this is just for Capital Hill?"

Meyer nodded.

"We have some data for the bridge assault, but I wanted to get Kennedy's opinion on it before I presented it to you."

Blake nodded. *Good, she feels less threatened and more empowered by a skilled subordinate.*

"Why do you need Kennedy's opinion?"

Meyer looked at the maps.

"It's been a long time since I've been in a Panzerter. Kennedy's a natural warrior. I know what the data says about fording a river, but I haven't *felt* it in a long time."

Blake nodded.

"That's fair. There's nothing wrong with admitting your own faults." He looked at the maps himself. "And you're getting more cockpit time soon."

Meyer blinked.

"Say again, Comrade Colonel?"

Blake shook his head.

"You heard me, Meyer. I'm grounded for the next few weeks. You'll take the Martian Command-type, and I'll ride in the command truck."

"But I don't know how to use the command matrix! Besides, I haven't qualified with a laser rifle this year!"

Blake waved her off.

"The lasers are easy: point and shoot. It's really precise. And don't lead targets; no one is dodging the speed of light." Meyer still looked uncomfortable. "Look, Major, it's like riding a bicycle—you never really unlearn it."

There was a knock at the door. Meyer moved to let Kennedy into the room.

"Figured you two would be down here. Do we have a plan for Pulaski?"

Blake looked at Meyer.

"I actually need your opinion on a few things, Comrade Captain," she said.

Kennedy nodded as she showed him the river routes.

"I like how you left the option open for the Bulls to skirt along the edges of the river," he said, referring to the Taurus IFVs. "They can move like boats, but they're painfully slow while doing so." He looked over the river. "As far as the Panzerters go, we need to be careful in the river. If we step in a muddy part, the machines will sink."

Meyer stepped up to the map.

"I was worried about that. Should we send scouts to check the riverbed?"

Kennedy shook his head. "No, good movement techniques will mitigate the downside of getting stuck."

Blake nodded.

"Meyer is going to see that firsthand. She's taking my Martian out."

Kennedy glanced at her.

"Really?" Meyer nodded. "Would you like to join my company for rehearsals? I know it's been awhile."

Meyer looked relieved.

"That would help, thanks."

Blake smiled to himself. *They're shaping up into a well-oiled machine. I wish we'd had soldiers half as competent as them twenty years ago.* As soon as the thought entered his head, he pushed it away. *If they were around back then, they would have likely been killed in a senseless counterattack.*

THE BUILDINGS AT THE EDGE OF PULASKI LOOMED IN THE DISTANCE. Under the trappings of Tharcian Ecotecture, the major structures were still recognizably Union buildings. *It's so different from home.* Blake's thoughts traveled north to the Cascadian Martian Republic.

Home for the MAG Officer was a former hab dome near Congregation. Like many cities in that region, once the ocean rose and heavy snow began falling, the city dug down until the small dome became a shallow shield for the massive city deep underground.

Returning to the present, riding in the command truck was something else. The seat was less comfortable, but the ride was smoother than his Martian, if less personal. He had a smaller command matrix available to him. *I'd rather not receive contact in this truck. A Panzerter would trash it.* Instead of Blake fighting himself, his command matrix could cycle through each unit's gun cameras.

The truck ground to a halt.

"This is our stop, Comrade Colonel," said the driver. "We don't want to get much closer than this."

Blake thanked the driver and stared at the battle map, his eyes absorbing every detail on the small screen. Ogre and Manticore had assumed their linear urban formation. Meanwhile, Predator and Nightmare were moving to the river, Nightmare in interlocking wedges, and Predator lining up parallel to the river. Meyer was moving with Ogre, positioning herself between both companies.

"Hog-wild, Leviathan 6. Are you on station?" Frequent drone strikes had prompted Division Command to push up their own drone fighters and close air support.

"Roger, 6. We got razorwings and snowbacks on standby."

Blake grinned. *Snowback's a fitting name for the close air support models.* He imagined the wild hogs tearing Tharcians limb from limb, appreciating the thin connection to his home.

Radar returns appeared from the east. Drones. No sooner had they entered the screen than friendly returns from the airfield rushed south to meet them.

Not this time.

"Leviathan 5, status." The urban arm of the attack was rapidly advancing on Capital Hill.

"6, we've encountered minimal resistance. We will reach Capital Hill in three minutes."

Hmm, this is going to easy.

"Hog-wild, can we get snowbacks over Pulaski?"

The coordinator's response was immediate.

"Not without a weapon status."

If I'm not careful, I could have another friendly fire incident.

"Circle the city instead. If 5 needs you, they'll give you the target." *There, that should prevent any mistakes.* He swung his attention back to the bridge group. To his chagrin, they had stopped. A few blips were missing.

"Leviathan 6, Nightmare 6. Our forward platoon has run into armed river boats. They're giving us a bit of trouble."

Blake ground his teeth.

"Nightmare 6, your company is equipped with state-of-the-art laser rifles. How the hell are a few boats giving you trouble?"

"The surf they kick up is dispersing the beams."

Blake ground his teeth to the point he thought he'd chipped a tooth.

"Well, deal with them quick and get to the bridge!" He noticed snowbacks surging towards the urban group. "5, status?" Meyer's group had split into an L-shape oriented on Capital Hill.

"We've encountered stiff resistance around Capital Hill, will report soon."

Blake heard the hammering of weapons fire in the background. *Within the confines of Capital Hill, I'm willing to bet it's a knife fight out there.*

"Leviathan 6, Nightmare 6. They blew the bridge before we could get there."

Blake frantically cycled through gun cams to get to Kennedy's. He caught glimpses of Martians weaving through buildings. Lasers surgically applied to buildings. He saw the river group waist-deep in murky green waters. They swung maces at the attack boats like flyswatters. The boats, as Kennedy had described, kicked up water around most of their hull. Blake was satisfied to see a few burning wrecks.

Then he got a glimpse of it. The broken pieces of the bridge were sinking into the murky waters beneath. *Damn it, that's going to sting.* Blake cycled through gun cams to build a better picture of the situation. *The support beams are relatively intact. Engineers can probably salvage this in a couple days.*

That would still hamper their offensive. Their vehicles were all amphibious, but the supply trucks weren't. Blake held his head in his hands. It began to throb. Then he thought he glimpsed something in the water. Bodies.

Blake snorted. *Serves them right, leaving the Union for what? If the Union is a protective mother, then Tharsis was an absent, if not abusive, father.* He smiled in spite of the situation. *In the grand scheme of things, this prodigal son is coming home whether they want to or not.*

"Nightmare 6, break off and head to the city park. Today is not lost yet." It occurred to him that the boat crews likely knew they weren't surviving their encounter with the MAG forces. Their reckless courage gave him a grudging respect for the Tharcians. Class enemies aside, they had done their job of holding off the MAG.

Those soldiers were probably working class—the bougie bulk of their army doesn't fight like that. Despite his own experiences, Blake never once thought of the Tharcians as defending their home.

He looked back at the map. The urban group was now advancing on the city park from the west, the river group from the east.

This battle is over. The eastern half of Pulaski is ours. Blake relaxed in his seat. He heard a buzzing in his ear.

"Leviathan 6, 5. The remaining Tharcians have surrendered."

Blake nodded to himself. *There're the cowards.*

"I'll send up POW teams immediately." He shook his head as he contacted the battalion's intelligence section. *Were I in their place, I would have fought to the last cook.*

He sat up from his chair and opened the back hatch. As he took a few steps outside, he watched his frosty breath hang in the air. The sun was beginning to sink towards the horizon.

Blake smiled.

"It's about damn time the sun set on Tharsis." With that, he stretched his aching body. *Meyer didn't seem to do too bad. I'll have to let her use my Panzerter more often.*

"Major Starnes, how bad is the Northern Front?" Marshal Skara was on his third cup of coffee and it was only 0530.

The portly man tapped away on a tablet before bringing up an image on the projector in the center of the briefing room.

"After two weeks of intense fighting, the line has stabilized." The map displayed ugly red scars plunging into Tharsis. They were duller than they had been a few days ago, but still deep.

"Why haven't they been able to snap these salients?"

Starnes scratched at the back of his head.

"The common complaint is that a counterattack would spread us too thin."

Skara scowled.

"How much longer before the provincial watch is fully mobilized?"

"Three weeks, and we're already sending up new units."

Skara looked to the Western Front.

"How long until the Olympian counterattack is ready?" He pointed to the sliver of land they still held near the shared border.

"From the latest report, they're sending the XIV, XV, and XVI Legions to the front, but they're still rebuilding."

"I'd like to hold a conference with their commanders, as well as General Basilisk. We need a coordinated operation to defeat the hook coming through Gallacia." Skara looked back over the map. "I want the air fleet to begin massing for a strategic bombing campaign. Prioritize their spaceports and northernmost infrastructure."

Starnes looked over the map.

"So you want to take their space assets off the board, eh?"

Skara nodded.

"I also want more cyberattacks, specifically targeting civilian industry."

Starnes raised an eyebrow.

"That would cross the line. They have banned cyberattacks against civilian industry for over a century."

Skara nodded.

"I understand the risks," he said, "but if they don't get caught, it won't be a problem."

Starnes frowned.

"You say that, but you're going to want to tell General Markos yourself."

"That's fine, Starnes. If you could page him now, that would be ideal. How are our weapons development projects coming?"

Starnes tapped away on his tablet.

"One moment, sir." He brought up a plethora of images on the monitor. "The Lowe research has yielded a number of advances we're working on integrating into our ground forces at large." He focused on the image of a knightly-looking Panzerter with a large shoulder cannon. "The railgun on its shoulder has led to the development of an entire line of magnetic weapons for Panzerters and ground troops."

Skara nodded.

"And the difference in firepower?"

Starnes showed him a multitude of small arms and Panzerter-sized weapons.

"Even the base rifle is projected to have a hundred-and-twenty-percent increase in range and penetration," he replied. "And ammo factories only need to make minor changes."

The projections impressed Skara.

"How soon can we transition to all-magnetic arms?"

Starnes looked nervous.

"If we assume there are no hiccups, six months," he replied.

Skara sighed. *Six months? It'll be a wonder if we still have manpower in six months.*

"Anything else?"

Starnes nodded.

"Our drones will benefit greatly from the thermal-resistant coating being applied to the Lowe." There was a knock at the door. "That must be General Markos. I'll let him in."

Skara remained seated as the major crossed the room and opened the door.

"You wanted to see me, Marshal?" General Markos looked like a man who spent most of his time indoors. His uniform did little to conceal a slight bulge at his stomach. His dark mustache was a little too wide for regulation.

"Yes, I did, General. We need increased cyberattacks against the Union."

The portly man frowned as he sat down.

"I'm afraid that would be difficult, sir. Their cybersecurity is too strong at the moment."

Skara nodded.

"To my knowledge, you've stuck to purely military targets, correct?" The general nodded. "Well, I was thinking of a much softer target."

Markos narrowed his eyes.

"I cannot use cyberattacks against civilian targets. That's banned by the Geneva Convention."

Skara held up a hand.

"First of all, we never signed that convention, and I see no reason for us to be bound by an Earth treaty."

"But what if our actions provoke a response from the Earth Sphere?"

Skara shook his head.

"Brazil and America would be unlikely to condone our actions or even acknowledge any wrongdoing. The SSR is a shell of its former self, and neither China nor Japan's interests are threatened."

"And the North Sea Alliance?"

Skara snorted.

"Markos, it's been over two hundred years since we cared about what any of its member states thought of us." He sighed.

"But if it offends your sensibilities, maybe you can"—he paused, searching for words—"snoop around."

Markos tented his hands.

"What are you thinking?"

Skara motioned to Starnes.

"Major, do you have a graphic for the Union economy?" Starnes worked on his tablet while Skara continued talking. "The Unionist economy is centrally planned, but it's rather robust."

"I can't influence their currency. The exchange rate for the Labor is based on time spent working rather than being backed by a substance or credit."

Skara raised an eyebrow.

"That's interesting. I had no idea. Well, if you know their currency so well, there's no need for me to enlighten you on the trade unions or the Trade Union Congress."

Markos nodded.

"As for its robustness, it nearly collapsed when Roosevelt broke away and Gallacia joined our Republic."

Skara pointed to the graphic.

"Their saving grace was building up their military industrial capacity, but you can't feed people with bullets. With the loss of two regions, they lost access to a vast amount of natural resources. The Union's surface is dependent on space for material resources."

Markos raised a finger.

"They rely entirely on the ocean for foodstuffs. Even inland, their aquaculture is astounding."

Skara thought for a moment.

"Surely, there are more subtle ways to influence the Union war machine, ways that would be hard to notice."

"You're talking small stuff, things that could be attributed to human error: a late shipment of fish, seaweed held in storage just long enough to go bad."

Skara nodded.

"People don't like it when you mess with their food. Shortages could lead to protests and rioting."

"With all due respect, that's speculation, sir."

Skara nodded.

"Still, the effect on morale will be perceivable, and if you're snooping around, say, a bicycle union that makes rifles, maybe you find a backdoor."

Markos's eyes sparked.

"We're walking through a gray area, sir, but I like where we're headed."

Skara smiled. *Give me a month or two, then I might like where we're headed.*

7

Paul Reiter leaned back in his cockpit. After sipping on a canteen, he stared at the forest ahead. His helmet lay to the side of the open hatch. He held the radio to his ear.

"Anyone got eyes on Gold Platoon?"

"Nope."

"Negative."

He sighed. His Panzerter sat in one corner of a large triangle formed by Black Platoon and White Platoon. In the center lay four busloads of refugees, as well as their support vehicles. Reiter stood up and leaned out of the cockpit.

About sixty meters from him, Corporal Steele's Panzerter knelt. A tarp hung over the open cockpit, while mechanics swarmed over the machine. On the ground, Steele worked a barrel brush into her rifle. *Horse, saddle, soldier.* The saying was older than his grandfather, but it was as true today as it was centuries ago.

He slipped back into his cockpit.

"Alright, guys, 1330, sensor sweep." He closed his hatch, and the monitors came to life. Nothing on visual scans. Nothing on thermals. Nothing on ground radar.

"My sector's clear."

"Mine too."

"Same."

Reiter sighed.

"Come on, boys, talk to me. We gotta stay awake here."

Mo responded immediately.

"Sir, this caffeinated chewing gum tastes like feet."

Reiter snorted.

"Then stop chewing it."

"I can't."

Adamski jumped in.

"I think he's addicted to the taste, boss."

Reiter chuckled.

"Mo, is there something you're not telling us?"

Adamski pressed him.

"Yeah, do you suck toes?"

"No!"

Reiter smiled. He knew the question coming next.

"Do you eat ass?"

"No!" Mo's indignation was reaching a fever pitch.

Septimus jumped in.

"You're doing great, Black Platoon. We'll be relieving you in another fifteen."

"Thanks, Top," responded Reiter. "Any word from Gold?"

"Negative. They should be back soon, though."

Reiter leaned back in his chair and yanked a ration bag out from behind him. *They probably have bad news. They left to clear the route hours ago.* Reiter looked at the olive drab bag in his hand. Menu D-3: buffalo macaroni, sweetcorn, bread, Skittles, and trail mix. The pack included apple jelly and electrolyte drink mix.

Adamski's voice sounded in his ear.

"Anyone wanna send a runner? This ration is trying to kill me."

Reiter looked at the Panzerter behind him to his left.

"How so?"

"It came with Reese's cups and peanut butter for my bread. I'm allergic to both."

Oooh.

"Dibs." He was a split second faster than Mo. "I'll send Steele over to grab them. Want some Skittles?"

"Sure, that's a fair trade."

Reiter shook his head. Adamski had no leverage, not with food he couldn't eat.

"Hey, I'll throw in some apple jelly, we'll call it even."

"Damn, boss, you got the buffalo mac, didn't you?" Adamski groaned.

Reiter grinned.

"Yeah, I did. Never understood why it comes with apple jelly, not something I imagine when I think buffalo mac and cheese." He stepped up so that he was standing on the edge of the clavicle hatch. "Hey Steele! Can I borrow you?"

The young soldier walked over from her recently reassembled rifle.

"Yes, sir! What do ya need?"

He tossed her down the Skittles and pouch full of jelly.

"Take that over to Adamski and bring me what he hands you. There's a pack of gum in it for you!"

"Okay!"

Reiter sat down in his cockpit. After cracking open a fresh water bottle, he dumped in the electrolyte mixture. He was still shaking the bottle when Amy clambered up to his cockpit. A pack of Reese's and a pouch of peanut butter fell into his lap.

"Thanks, I suppose I owe you this." He reached between his

seat and the cockpit wall and handed her a pack of gum. "It's water-melon flavored, shouldn't taste bad." She thanked him and left. Now alone in his machine. Reiter began heating up his food. He waited. He ate some. He waited.

He was sipping the salty electrolyte mix when he saw Gold Platoon approaching. *About Time.* With a glance at his watch to see his shift was over, he climbed down to meet the oncoming vehicles. As he passed, he waved to Lieutenant Comidus, who was standing in an open hatch. He stopped his vehicle and climbed out.

"What took your group so long?" Reiter asked.

The infantryman squinted and pointed back in the direction they'd come.

"We can't ford the next branch of the river in the same location. The bridges on the map are out."

Reiter frowned.

"Is there a spot we can ford?"

Comidus waved his hand.

"Two. I found a spot our tracks and trucks can cross, but not the buses."

Reiter glanced back at the civilian transports.

"We can't abandon them."

"And we don't have to. There's a spot where the Panzerters can cross."

Reiter knew what the man was thinking.

"And we can simply carry them across. That would work, but it's risky. The fastest way would be two Panzerters screening while the rest carry a bus."

Comidus glanced back at the center of the formation.

"What if I loan you the missile carriers? That should negate any kind of dropship attack."

"Is that what they're mostly using?"

Comidus nodded.

"I think we're too far forward to see a lot of Panzerters—of their lines, that is."

Reiter shook his head.

"When I was at Frederiksberg, the frontlines always seemed like a solid wall."

Comidus chuckled.

"Instead of this fluid mess? Same. I guess we're in no-man's-land at the moment." He paused. "What year did you graduate?"

"2130? You?"

Comidus grinned.

"2133. We might have had some of the same instructors."

Reiter shook his head.

"They focused a lot on the War of 2112. I think that might be why we're hamstrung now." Comidus waved his hand in the universal gesture for "more or less". "I'll give it six hours. Your people need some rest, and I need to brief our pilots and civilians."

Comidus nodded and left to rejoin his men.

Reiter climbed back into his cockpit.

"Black Platoon, I'm going to brief you on our movement, then you're going to tell White what's up. Meet me in the center—the civilians need to hear this too."

"How much time do we have?" Mo asked.

Reiter checked his watch.

"Five hours and thirty minutes. You can sleep after the brief."

TO BE SURE EVERYONE IN ATTENDANCE COULD HEAR HIM, Lieutenant Paul Reiter climbed up onto a crate of rations. The civilians crowded around him, with Mo and Adamski standing nearby.

"Can I have your attention, please!" He noticed Mo's sisters huddling near him. He held the youngest while the twins stood close. "At 2000, we will move out from here and head east. All vehicles will drive with their headlights off, so watch your speed."

"How am I supposed to see?"

Reiter glanced at an older man in the crowd.

"The Panzerters and missile carriers have cats' eyes on their legs and back. They'll help you follow us at night. Now unfortunately, there's no bridge the buses can cross, so we're improvising."

"Are you seriously going to have us walk?"

Reiter fumbled his words.

"What? No. The Panzerters will ford the river and carry you across."

"Is that safe?"

Reiter held up a hand.

"I'll take questions in a moment. Now, when we begin crossing the river, the bus will stop. At that point you will put on your seat-belts. Then your assigned pilot will lift your bus and cross the river." He looked at Mo. "Water."

"Here." He handed him his electrolyte drink, the one he had half-finished earlier.

"Thanks." He took a swig. "Now, Bus One will be assigned to Sergeant Bartonova, Bus Two Corporal Steele, Bus Three Corporal Mondragon, and Bus Four Sergeant Adamski. Once all vehicles are across the river, we will resume our formation and continue on towards Garden City Tech. Any questions?"

"What if we get dropped?"

Reiter nodded.

"Not an unreasonable question. If you get dropped, remain buckled until you hit the water, then evacuate the bus as if it was flooding."

"Is the Union out there?"

Reiter nodded.

"Our Gold Platoon reported dropship patrols. To counter this, they have loaned us two new Cstalio Missile Carriers. Before anyone crosses the river, First Sergeant Septimus will cross with one of the missile carriers and set up security on the opposite bank." He looked around. "Any other questions?" No one said a word, so he climbed down and the crowd began dispersing.

"You better not drop us, Javi." Sophie prodded her older brother.

"I hope you're not as clumsy in a robot." Zoe grinned as she tugged at his flight suit. Her expression quickly changed to disgust. "Ew, you're all sweaty and nasty!"

"It's not a robot, and you're going to be fine. Now, can one of you take Izzie?"

Zoe also made a disgusted face.

"Ew, gross, she smells like you!"

Izzie pouted.

"Yuck."

Reiter shook his head.

"Mo, get back on your machine, brief Bartonova, and rest until we move."

Mo grinned and put Izzie down.

"Roger that, sir." He jogged away, and his sisters turned towards the buses.

Izzie looked up at Reiter.

"Mr. Lieutenant, are there bad people out there?" She pointed a pudgy hand at the woods.

Reiter knelt down in front of her.

"There are, but don't worry, your brother and the rest of us are going to keep everyone safe."

The little girl smiled at him as she walked with her sisters.

"Thank you, Mr. Lieutenant."

Reiter walked over to the Cstalios. The crews were lying down until they moved again. They slept on the roof, in the crew compartment, and even under the vehicles.

"I hate to bother you all when you're resting," Reiter said, "but I need to talk to whoever's in charge here."

A voice called out from one of the crew compartments.

"That would be Lieutenant Reiter or Comidus, whichever one is around."

Seriously?

"I am Lieutenant Reiter. Who's in charge of these two tracks?" Reiter heard someone swear and scramble in the crew compartment of the track to his left.

A ruddy man in a green-gray shirt and camouflage pants emerged from the Cstalio.

"Sergeant Borowski. I'm the senior VC of the two of us."

Reiter nodded.

"Have you been briefed?"

The other man shrugged.

"They told us we were moving with you lot and the civilians."

"Did they tell you your vehicles were going to get ferried across a river by Panzerters?"

His jaw dropped.

"What? Fuck, no, they didn't!" After a pause, he added, "sir."

Reiter waved him off.

"Relax, and yeah, that's how we're moving your carriers. Rock-paper-scissors the other VC to see who has to get carried across first."

The VC nodded and then walked over to the other track. Reiter returned to his machine. He began to climb up, then remembered Steele.

Opting to tell her in person, he clambered up the side of her kneeling machine. The tarp was pulled back from the cockpit so she could see now.

"Steele, are you tracking the plan?"

She shook her head, and he gave her the rundown.

"So we're carrying the buses across the river?" she asked. Reiter nodded. "I don't think I've even done that in a sim."

"It shouldn't be too bad. Just imagine a cargo container; you've done that." He smiled. "Except there's people inside."

She shook her head.

"Not helping, sir." She relaxed into her chair as he sat at the edge of the cockpit hatch. "Sir, you're older. How would I get a guy to notice me?"

Reiter was taken aback.

"What? I'm not that old! I'm 25!" *She's one of my soldiers now. I need to establish trust.* He cleared his throat. "Well, you're walking around in a 45-ton suit of armor. I'm sure plenty of guys notice you." She frowned, and he gave it another shot. "Is it a specific guy? Or are we talking in general?"

Now it was her turn to look awkward.

"It's Mo, isn't it?"

"Well, yeah."

He nodded. *Was I this awkward as a teenager? And what does this do to unit cohesion? Is she going to take undue risks because of a crush?*

"So, you may not like this answer, but your duty comes first. You two are living through some rough stuff. Naturally, that will create strong bonds. I'm sure a connection can form there." He rose to climb down. *Wow, stiff answer much?* He rose to climb down. Steele stared forlornly at the floor, and he hesitated. "Besides that, guys in general are starving for any positive affirmation. A single compliment could make his whole day. Just don't be weird about it."

She softened as he climbed down. "Thank you, sir."

Yep, good talk. Reiter walked back to his Panzerter. He still had five hours to snooze. *Better make the most of it.*

DESPITE THE CIRCUMSTANCES, BLAKE WAS GLAD TO BE BACK IN THE saddle. His Martian waded through the murky waters with relative ease. That is, until he found a soft patch. He was jerked forward. As he fought the controls, he regained his balance.

After freeing his foot, he scowled at the river.

"Some blue highway. All I see is filthy water over filthy mud."

Nightmare Platoon was currently with him. Ahead of him, the river diverged with one branch continuing east and the other twisting south.

"Leviathan 6, we're going to split up here."

Blake acknowledged Kennedy's choice. "Nightmare 4, stay with me and we'll go east three clicks Nightmare 2, head south the same distance. Update me every click, got it?"

The two groups split, six units headed south, six heading east. Blake opted to follow the east group. *Besides, there's more likely to be a dock this way.* Blake firmly believed if they destroyed enough docks, the attack boats wouldn't be a problem.

The east branch didn't stay east very long. The farther they traveled, the more the river seemed to twist and turn. It splintered into smaller tributaries. Kennedy sent Martians down them in pairs. While the pair looked down the river, the rest of his group would wait on them before continuing. Eventually, they hit a three-way snag in the river.

"11 and 12, take the north branch," ordered Kennedy. "9 and 10, take the east. When you get back, we'll stick our heads down this last branch and then turn around."

Kennedy's proved himself capable so far; he has good instincts.

Blake checked their surroundings. It was just him, Kennedy, and Junior Lieutenant Campos.

"Stay aware of your surroundings, you two. We're still in enemy territory."

The 360-degree sensor array allowed them to look in any direction. Blake could hear it whine and click as he cycled the direction he was looking in. Gray clouds rolled over the horizon. Blake scowled.

"It looks like a storm is coming. That oughta keep drones off us."

Blake didn't share Campos's optimism.

"It also cuts our effective weapons range down, though good on you for being mindful of the weather." Blake caught a movement behind them. "Contact! 6 o'clock!"

An attack boat darted towards them. Autocannon fire peppered his hull. The water near the boat burst into steam. More bursts. The boat weaved through the clouds of steam. Rockets screamed towards Blake. His monitor flickered. *Damn, sensor ring is taking hits.*

The boat sped towards him. He swung a metal fist only to find water. The boat wove circles between them. They did their best to avoid hitting each other. *I thought we had already cleared this section of the river.* Evidently not.

The boat took a turn. Just too wide. Squared to its rear, Blake smiled and fired. The water behind the boat burst into steam. He could glimpse bits of molten metal in it. The boat jerked left. Rather than circling the Martians, it circled the center of them.

Their muzzles glowed green. Each time, the boat sent bits of molten metal into the air. It caught fire. Within moments, it became a flaming wreck. Blake heard the roar of another boat nearby.

"Looks like the Tharcians want another round."

Blake didn't share Kennedy's enthusiasm. The boats were much smaller than the Martians, but the humanoid machines were waist-deep in a river.

The second boat roared into view. Blake found himself immediately beset by autocannon fire. As he drew his mace, he surged forward. His machine suddenly stopped. *Damn it, I'm stuck again.* He swept at the watercraft, but it remained just beyond his reach. The boat returned fire as it swung around behind him.

Blake shielded his head and face with his arms. Shrapnel whizzed around him and stung his left arm. *Damn spalling!* Grinding his teeth, he grasped the control stick and freed himself from the muck.

He brought his mace down hard in the boat's path. The wave it created sent the light craft sprawling on its side. Its propellers uselessly sprayed water about. For a brief second, its underside glowed before the boat exploded in a shower of fire and steam.

"Comrade Colonel, are you alright?" asked Kennedy.

Blake swore as he reached for his medkit, only to find a hole punched through it.

"My medkit's done, and I'm at least going to need bandages."

The rest of their group began returning from their recon. Kennedy's machine approached the colonel's, and he climbed out of his machine and crawled over to Blake's. The younger officer dropped down the crown hatch and lowered a medkit to Blake.

"Need a hand?"

Blake shook his head as he probed his arm to make sure nothing was in there before applying a wrap to it.

"I'm good, Kennedy, but why the hell are boats coming out of paths we cleared?"

The other officer shrugged.

"Maybe we're not clearing them out far enough."

Blake finished applying his wrap.

"Or maybe your soldiers need more motivation."

Kennedy shook his head.

"I doubt it. They're all good MAGs. My only complaint is they're not all Campos."

Blake looked up at him.

"What's so special about her?"

Kennedy grinned.

"She's a tuber and my best soldier by far."

Blake nodded.

"Well, in that case, I'll call division and have more soldiers made for you, and they can all look like her."

Kennedy shrugged.

"She has more kills than I do, or the rest of the company, and in case you forgot, she's our first Panzerter ace as a battalion."

Blake shut his mouth for a moment. *They started that whole mess to erase our population gap. You knew sooner or later you'd have to work with one.* He sighed.

"I'll push it up. Now get back in your machine so we can leave." Kennedy disappeared up the ladder, leaving Blake alone with his thoughts. *Where the hell did those boats come from? And where is the frontline?* His head ached and his arm throbbed. Blake ground his teeth. *I'll need more painkillers when I get back.*

Once everyone had returned, they turned about, heading back up river. They were cautious around every bend and branch. No docks. No positions. No luck. Blake ground his teeth. He hoped his other companies were having better luck.

FIELD MARSHAL SKARA SET THE CYBER WARFARE REPORT BACK ON the table. He sat in his briefing room with General Markos. Rubbing his chin, he looked at the portly man.

"So this is your strategy?"

Markos nodded.

Skara looked back at the report. "I'd like to hear it in your own words, just so I know we're on the same page."

The general blinked.

"Well, sir, we discovered a rather weak link in their information control."

Skara gestured towards the man so as not to waste his own time. "Go on."

Markos relaxed some as he entered his comfort zone.

"Their military information is tightly controlled, but the trade unions reference military information within themselves all the time, mainly with regard to how military projects affect their civil endeavors."

Skara sipped his coffee.

"And this tells you?"

Markos grinned.

"This part was devious on our end. So because of these unprotected communications, we're able to identify who is working on military projects. We also uncovered something else." He picked up the report and flipped to the relevant page. "Some of their communications mention this location."

"Los Estrellas? Where's that?"

Markos sat back down.

"In Spanish, it means city of stars, which leads some of our analysts to believe it's a colony cylinder."

"It doesn't sound like you think that."

Markos shook his head.

"No registered cylinders have that name, and some references included shipyards capable of building capital ships at this location, which is only possible—"

"—on an asteroid, planetoid, moon, or similar body." Skara sighed. "Well, make sure Fleet Admiral Von Braun gets this report.

It could tip the balance of power in space." He looked down at the report. "Anything for us on the ground?"

With a curt nod, Markos looked at his notes.

"We've isolated several prominent unions. Red Steel United manufactures Panzerters, Ironclad Track Works builds armored vehicles, Crimson Sky 411 builds drones, etc." Markos's features brightened. "Within the next month, we should be able to give you technical data on the entire Union surface arsenal. Hell, we might even be able to tell you what their R&D departments are doing."

Skara looked down at the report.

"Will this better enable us to hack their military networks?"

Markos shrugged but bobbed his head in a manner that said he was optimistic.

"That's the end goal, to create an opening for project MAYHEM."

Skara pondered the document.

"Thank you, Markos, I dismiss you. Can you send Starnes back in on your way out?"

Markos saluted and took his leave.

Starnes entered the briefing room with his tablet at the ready.

"I've got troubling news from the front."

Skara groaned.

"Has the Northern Front begun to collapse?"

Starnes sighed.

"Negative." He pulled up a map on the projector. "It's from the knife fight in the Dracul Delta."

Skara raised an eyebrow.

"What is this?"

Starnes pointed to a spot on the map.

"This is Garden City Tech. They're currently housing the Lowe project."

Skara tented his hands and rested his head on them.

"What does that entail, precisely?"

Starnes looked at his tablet.

"It's the hub of all the research relating to the Lowe, and even worse, it's housing an early production model of the Lowe and numerous spare parts." He looked gravely at Marshal Skara. "We can't afford the Union getting their greedy hands on that data or reverse-engineering the machine's tech."

Skara looked at the map. The frontline seemed awfully close.

"We can't afford to abandon that data or the team that created it. Have they been evacuated?"

Starnes shot a concerned look at the marshal.

"We don't have a unit close enough to escort them. Besides that, the Lowe needs to be destroyed or buried."

"Show me the units in that area, down to the company level." Starnes tapped a few things on his tablet, and suddenly the map was nearly flooded with blue boxes. "Ah here, Fox Company, 230th RCT. They're only a hop, skip, and a jump away."

Starnes looked at his tablet.

"230th, 230th, 230th." He paused and looked back at Skara.

"They're more like a big platoon. They're headed to the Garden City Tech campus to rebuild."

"Good, now they have another Panzerter at their disposal."

Starnes's eyes widened.

"You can't be serious, sir. The Lowe has undergone rigorous testing, but it's never been field tested before."

Skara waved him off, as if a simple flick of his wrist could dismiss the man's concerns.

"Then just consider this its field test."

Starnes shook his head.

"Sir, I don't think pilots will want to sortie in a Panzerter they are unfamiliar with that has never been field tested."

Skara's eyes flashed.

"Then we tell the Lowe team only an officer or Senior NCO is allowed to pilot the thing. Also, inform them to make themselves available to Fox Company and provide anything they need." He stood and walked across the room. "In exchange, we will increase our grant to Garden City Tech and offer a better contract to Wallachia Defense. That should grease their gears."

Starnes nodded, taking notes on his tablet.

"Yes, sir, I'll see that it's done."

Skara looked at him.

"And one more thing: don't ever question my judgment again, Major."

Starnes pursed his lips, not taking his eyes off the notes in front of him.

"Yes, sir, I understand." *Good, know your place, worm.*

"Have you scheduled our meeting with the Olympians and the Three Corps commander?"

Starnes handed him the tablet showing the meeting and notes.

"Yes, sir. Your meeting will be next Saturday in Olympian territory. They would like you to review their troops; that conference will last through Monday. You'll be back by Tuesday, and on Wednesday, Madame President has requested a meeting with you in person."

Skara raised an eyebrow.

"Oh?"

Starnes opened the message for the older man.

"Yes, sir, her message shows she would like to discuss uniting the command structure of all Central Alliance forces."

Skara smiled.

"That's interesting. Why is that on next Wednesday?"

"Because of your conference with the Olympians, sir."

Skara sneered.

"See if I can get in this Thursday or Friday. I'd like to have that discussion sooner."

Starnes kept his expression neutral while working.

"Yes, sir, I will contact her office and see what we can work out."

"Good, I will see to it that these conferences are productive. Thank you, Major Starnes, dismissed."

Starnes left the room without another word. Skara pulled up the continental map on the projector. He glanced from Roosevelt, nearly swallowed by the Union, to Olympia being needled by Avalon on the coast, to Tharsis herself. *Supreme Commander of Central Alliance Forces.* A little grandiose, but Skara had to admit, it had a nice ring to it.

8

Paul Reiter looked back and forth as his Panzerter crept forward. Ahead of him, buses and Panzerters alternated as they rolled forward. At the very front of the group, a Cstalio led the way with Septimus right behind it. A similar vehicle tailed Reiter.

"All quiet, just how we like it," the first vehicle said. Reiter relaxed, if only slightly.

"I can barely see a damn thing!" It was the older man from before. *I at least had the courtesy of opening a channel so they could talk to us.*

"Bus 3, just follow the unit in front of you and take it easy. You'll be fine."

His radar began beeping.

"Black 1, White 5. We got unis on air radar, ten clicks out."

Reiter held the throttle and control stick a little tighter.

"Play it cool, everyone. It looks like they're just passing by. Keep this pace and our light discipline, and we'll be okay." He got another transmission on the bus channel.

"If we don't get to this river soon, I'm turning my lights on. I don't want to get into an accident."

Reiter's face burned.

"Bus 3, we're almost there. You will not turn on your lights. We're not out of this yet."

"Listen, pal, I'm not risking our lives in an accident just because you're paranoid."

Damn it, man, I'm trying to keep you all alive!

"Warhorse 11, where are those dropships?" Reiter glanced at his own radar.

"Still on our screen, seven clicks out."

Damn, they'll definitely see us.

"Bus 3, there are enemy aircraft in the area. Do not turn on your lights!" Silence filled the net. In the distance, he could hear the steady drone of the dropships.

"Young man, it's disgusting you'll lie to get your way."

What the fuck, can't you hear them?

"Bus 3, stop now!"

Too late. Bright white light flooded the forest. Most of the convoy was exposed to the night.

"They took a hard left, they're coming right at 9!" Mo called.

Reiter's rifle came up. Four heat signatures. Approaching fast. Missiles raced towards them. He cracked at them with his rifle. The dropships scattered and launched flares. The missiles burst around them.

"Bus 3, turn your lights off!"

The entire convoy opened fire on the dropships. Two failed to evade the wall of shells they faced. The other two sped on. Reiter heard a bang followed by a pop. The bus's lights were shrouded in a thick blanket of smoke.

While reloading, he was cast in a shroud of smoke. *I didn't see any missiles from them. Did someone get hit?* Rockets tore at the surrounding ground.

"I've taken some hits!" Adamski crouched beside him, shielding Bus 4 with his machine. The dropships raced overhead. Missiles left in pursuit.

"They're coming around for another pass!" The Panzerters opened fire again, attempting to break off the dropships' attack run. The bulky ships clipped trees and crashed through brush. *It's like they got demons at the controls.*

The dropships split as they approached the dirt road. Reiter's last shot grazed the roof of the one swinging right. It belched fire and smoke as it limped by. The one on the left swung low. Its cargo bay opened. Reiter raised his rifle.

Mo was quicker. His sword blossomed into existence right in the dropship's path. The aircraft, cleaved neatly in two, crashed in the woods behind them.

The last dropship swung around for a final pass. It didn't fire its weapons. It merely accelerated towards Reiter. A ramming attack. He sighed. Two shots. Both center of mass. The Union craft blossomed in a brilliant explosion.

"Alright, Fox, give me a BDA." He switched to the bus channel. "Bus 3, will you turn off your damn lights?" The lights winked out as the smoke began to dissipate.

"Fox 7, down two magazines, minor hull damage."

"Warhorse 11, both tracks are down to fifty percent on smokescreens and anti-air misses." *So that was you guys.*

"White 3, minor hull damage."

Reiter came back onto the net.

"Okay, just let me know if your fording ability is compromised. We'll do a full BDA after we cross." After receiving negatives across the board, the convoy resumed moving.

"Black 1, Fox 7. That didn't look like a regular patrol."

"Fox 7, how do you figure?"

"The patrols we read about in the reports were pairs of drop-ships. We just fought four."

Adamski joined the conversation.

"Is it possible we just got caught by two patrols bumping into each other?"

Septimus chuckled over the net.

"That would be our luck, but the only other time we saw them move in fours was when one pair escorted another carrying equipment."

Reiter nodded.

"So you think they might have dropped off something nearby?"

"That's my best guess, and from what I've seen so far, their front-line vehicles are all amphibious."

Reiter looked at his radar.

"Warhorse 11, based on the radar data, do you have a guess as to where they came from?"

The infantryman whistled through the comms.

"I'll need to bust out a pencil and some paper, but I can give you a half-decent guesstimate."

"Thanks, 11."

Septimus jumped back onto the net.

"We've reached the river. All units stand by."

Reiter scanned the sky and the surrounding woods. As he did, he looked over occasionally to watch Septimus cross the river with the missile carrier in his hands. "Security set, begin crossing."

One by one, the Panzerters slung their weapons, lifted a bus and waded across the river. Bartonova was the first to cross. As she walked, her machine suddenly lurched forward. Though she stumbled, she didn't fall. She didn't drop the bus either.

"Damnit, be careful everyone," she said. "My machine got stuck. Sorry, Bus 1."

The others were able to cross without issue. Mo even decided to make a point about it.

"Sure it wasn't user error, White 3?"

Septimus cut him off.

"I also had issues getting stuck. It happens regardless of skill, Black 5."

Reiter chuckled. He gingerly lifted the last Cstalio and crossed the river. It vaguely reminded him of being in the pool until he felt his feet beginning to sink. *Septimus and Bartonova are using Panzerter IVs too—maybe it's a weight issue?*

When he emerged on the other side, he set the missile track down.

"Alright, let's move. We still have a couple clicks until we get to the rendezvous point."

They stepped out again. They still had another river to cross, but they'd handle that when they got there.

"Comrade Colonel, we just heard from the Raider Battalion. Guard Colonel Druza died in action while delivering bridge units to a forward base."

Blake scowled. *Of all the ways that crazy bastard could have gone out, that's how he died.*

"Thank you, Sergeant, we dismiss you."

The young man nodded and fled the command tent. Blake sat in solitude for a moment. Just him and the light pitter patter of rain on the roof of the tent. Maps hung from the walls, and a field projector took up the center of the room. Outside the square command tent, long half-cylinder tents provided quarters, a mess hall, and storage for the battalion. An area had even been cleared for a motor pool and field bays for the Panzerters. At the edges of the perimeter stood hastily erected guard towers linked by a chain-link fence. The entire firebase was further protected by its position on an island at the nexus of three rivers.

He heard a knock at the entrance. "Enter."

Kennedy entered the tent, removing his poncho and shaking off the water. *Excuse me, Guard Captain Kennedy.* The younger man pulled out a notebook and pen.

"You got an overlay sheet around here?"

Blake nodded and handed him a blank one from his field desk. The younger man set it over a local map and began referencing his notes.

"You have something for me, Comrade Captain?"

Kennedy nodded as he began marking points on the overlay.

"I believe I've figured out where the boats are coming from, and I have other news for you." He pointed to a town on the map. "Riverside. It was Comrade Druza's objective before he decided to eat a bullet, and"—he looked back at his notes—"likely the site of our next battle."

"How do you figure?" Blake looked at the map himself. Riverside straddled one of the more major branches in the river, one that came from the mountains to the south.

"Based on records in Pulaski, Riverside makes its money off river tours and boat traffic. As a community, they possess plenty of dock space for river patrols and even have a yard to build more of them." He looked up at Blake. "And there's more." He thumbed through his notebook.

"How are they able to operate freely, then? Wouldn't they need more docks?"

Kennedy shrugged.

"More or less. I believe they use caches on the riverbed; that's why we've only encountered a few docks along the delta." Kennedy found his page. "Druza was dropping off bridge layers for us—they found his plan on his computer. He'd land raiders on the southwest side while we used the bridges to cross and attack the north side."

Blake nodded.

"Would have been a splendid plan had they not killed him on his way back."

"That's the other thing: the forces that killed him are likely headed to Riverside."

Blake weighed his options. *If Kennedy's right, that would effectively end the Tharcian guerrilla war on the river delta and probably earn me my star.*

"Let's send the recon platoon that way to check it out. I take it Druza was building up a field base up that way."

Kennedy nodded.

"It's likely defended by raiders, but they don't have any heavy weapons that way. From what I understand, it was in its early stages when Druza kicked the bucket."

Blake looked back at the map.

"If we take Riverside, that will allow us to relieve them, and it will probably lead to the collapse of Tharcian defenses in this region." He looked back at Kennedy. "Inform Major Meyer I want all relevant data on the town to be available."

Kennedy grinned.

"I already caught her on her way to dinner. She provided the records that told me it was a river community. She'll be by later with a map of the town."

Blake looked at his desk before sitting down. *I don't want Kennedy seeing my hands shaking.*

"Kennedy, I would appreciate it if you sent a runner to bring me a hot meal. I just realized I haven't eaten today."

The younger man nodded.

"Of course, Comrade Colonel. I'll make sure they dump a little extra on your plate."

Blake waved him off.

"That's not how it works, Kennedy. Everyone gets an equal portion."

The younger soldier stiffened.

"From each according to his ability, to each according to his needs, and right now you need a whole day's worth of food."

Blake grumbled as Kennedy left, but the pit in his stomach would not be ignored. *How many more risks do I have to take before they see me?* Blake stared at his hands. *I was barely a man then; I did everything I was told.* He clenched his fists. *I didn't fail my country back then; our leaders did.* He grit his teeth and slammed a fist into his desk. *But if I'm a good and capable leader, why is this my ceiling? Why does it seem I can get no higher than this?*

A runner entered with a covered tray. Despite Blake's wishes, it was stuffed to the brim with food. Crawfish, sea rice, spicy trout, and seaweed. As he peeled his crawfish, he thought back to before. *It's a shame they're willing to give anyone this much food. Little do they know, if this war drags on, food will be the first thing to get scarce.* He remembered how much he'd starved back then.

He was still picking at his food when Meyer entered the room. She had a map folded under one arm and a tablet in a case in the other.

"Has Kennedy already been by?" she asked. Blake nodded. "Good. I was able to procure a map of the Riverside Township." She laid the map out across one of his tables. "Until we get better reconnaissance, it looks like there are two main areas: the southwest part on the outside of the river and the northeast on the inside."

Blake glanced at the map as he continued to poke at his food.

"Comrade Major, I apologize, but I'm going to need to lie down."

Meyer looked up in concern.

"Kennedy mentioned you barely ate all day. Are you not feeling well?" She pointed over at his cot behind the desk. "If you need to lie down, go ahead. We can pick this up in the morning."

She left quietly as Blake finished his food. Then he removed his boots and lay in his cot.

The rain, it sounds so peaceful. He closed his eyes. For the first time in a while, he rested.

———

RIVERSIDE WAS A RATHER QUAINT COMMUNITY. AT LEAST, FROM the side of the river Reiter sat on, it was. They had made it with all four buses intact. Now they stood in line and waited to have a hot meal served to them. Rain pattered on his poncho. The Panzerters knelt a short distance away.

"Javi, this jacket is too big!" One of the twins—Reiter didn't know which—practically swam in Mo's rain jacket. The other twin wore his poncho while holding Izabella.

"But are you dry, Zoe?"

His sister pouted.

"That's what I thought." Mo stood in front of Reiter, a windbreaker over his flight suit. He corralled his sisters through the chow line. The mess tent in front of him was in a muddy gulch. Steam wafted out of the shoddy structure.

"Why can't we eat at a restaurant?"

Mo sighed.

"Because all the restaurant workers evacuated. Sophie, don't jump in puddles."

The other twin pouted.

"Why not? Izzie loves it!"

Mo gave her a stern look.

"Because if your feet get wet and cold, it'll hurt really bad."

Adamski nudged Reiter.

"Is it weird for you too?" he whispered.

"Mo sounding like an adult? Yeah, that's new." They stood behind their platoon mate and his siblings as the line waded forward. "After two nights ago, I really don't like the idea of escorting these civilians."

Adamski nodded.

"That dude was asking for trouble. 'Let me shine my bright-ass lights in a war zone.' Gotta be kidding me." He looked back at Mo. "Kid here was about ready to strangle the guy."

"Javi! I got mud all over my nice boots!"

"Then you should have worn shoes you didn't care about."

The line inched closer to the tent. Now people were starting to filter out.

"Remind me when we get up there to mention Gold Platoon," said Reiter. "I don't care who's in line, those guys need to be front-loaded as soon as they get back."

Adamski looked off into the woods.

"Are they out investigating Septimus's hunch?"

Reiter nodded. A gentle breeze whisked through the mess area. Reiter caught a whiff of ham.

"I swear, if it's that cheese pasta that tastes like hot dogs . . ."

Adamski chuckled.

"That's easily the worst meal I've ever had in the army."

Finally, they got to the entrance. A portly soldier stood there in an apron. He tapped a pencil against a clipboard.

"Name?"

Mo rattled off his rank, name, and ID number, and added his sisters' names as well. Adamski and Reiter followed suit.

"Hey, we got a platoon out on a mission right now—"

The soldier cut Reiter off.

"Your first sergeant already told me; we're tracking." He remembered Reiter's rank and stiffened. "Sir."

Reiter chuckled and patted the man on the shoulder. After scooping up a paper tray, they were treated to a slice of ham, some green beans, and mashed potatoes. A small table at the end held drinks, paperwork, and small brownies for dessert.

Once they had their food and drinks, they saw Steele wave them over. She sat with her sister—Giselle—Bartonova, and Septimus. They sat down with them, and Mo popped Izzie onto his knee.

"Gold Platoon hasn't come back from their patrol yet," Reiter informed the first sergeant.

Septimus nodded.

"Even if we don't move against them, knowing that they're there is valuable."

Steele cleared her throat.

"Mo, that was outstanding how you cut that dropship in half."

Reiter cringed. *She could not have sounded more stilted.*

Mo raised an eyebrow as he helped his sister cut her ham.

"Thanks, Steele, I think."

Izzie pointed at Bartonova.

"Who's that?"

"That's Bartonova. She's one of Amy's friends."

Izzie pointed at Septimus.

"Who's that?"

Mo finished cutting her ham.

"He's the first sergeant."

Izzie's eyes grew wide.

"Ever?"

To everyone's shock, Septimus laughed. *I don't think I've ever seen the guy smile but twice.*

"No, young lady, I'm not that old," replied Septimus. Reiter couldn't help but notice there was a certain softness in the older man's voice.

Adamski shrugged.

"Now his dad, on the other hand . . ."

The other adults laughed. Septimus grinned. *Okay, this is kind of weird.*

Bartonova gently slapped him from across the table.

"Behave, Ski."

Adamski snorted.

"Don't tell me what to do."

Reiter nudged him.

"Behave, Ski."

"Yes, sir."

They laughed again.

Suddenly, Septimus's face shifted to a sterner look.

"Gold's back."

Reiter looked at the line to see the absolutely filthy infantrymen trekking into the tent.

Comidus made eye contact with them and got out of line.

"You were right, Top. Bridge layers, a couple engineer vehicles, and an SP gun, all guarded by raiders."

Septimus looked at him without standing.

"Did you take any losses?"

Comidus shook his head.

"No, we did things quietly."

Septimus nodded.

Zoe peered up at the soldier leaning over her.

"You need a shower."

Septimus chuckled again. Comidus glanced down at Zoe before looking at the first sergeant with concern.

"I see," Septimus said with a smile. "Well, get hot chow and a shower. Gold Platoon earned it today."

Comidus hopped back in line, and they finished their food.

As they left the mess tent, Reiter stopped Septimus.

"Are you alright?"

The older man nodded.

"Of course I am, sir."

Reiter shrugged.

"I think tonight was the first time most of us have seen you laugh."

Septimus nodded.

"They remind me of my kids. I haven't seen them in a while, though. They've probably grown."

Reiter looked towards where the Panzerters knelt in the rain.

"I guess it's just odd. We've always seen you as this stern, strong figure."

The older man wagged a finger.

"Now don't mistake my kindness for weakness, sir, but if you must be strong, be strong enough to be gentle."

Reiter wiped his face.

"Is that like a quote from a book or something?"

Septimus shook his head.

"No, it's something my older brother used to say."

"Your older brother Sextus?"

The seasoned soldier looked at him. It could have been the rain in his face, but it was almost like Septimus was smiling.

"I appreciate that you're cultured enough to make that joke, sir." They began walking towards the Panzerters. "And for your information, it was my brother Quintus."

Now it was Reiter's turn to laugh. *What do you know? The man does have a sense of humor.*

DAMIAN BLAKE PORED OVER THE MAP OF RIVERSIDE AS RAIN poured onto his tent. He, Kennedy, Meyer, and Wake all crowded the command tent planning their upcoming operation.

Wake was in the middle of making his point.

"We need to destroy the docks. It denies them to the Tharcians in the unlikely event they retake the town."

Kennedy stood with his arms crossed and his chest out.

"Don't you think it would be more practical to use them ourselves to ferry troops and supplies about? Not to mention, converting surfing patrol boats gives us the advantage in the rivers."

Wake shook his head.

"We have bridge layers; we can make better use of them."

Kennedy shook his head.

"You're suggesting using bridge layers in scenarios we really don't need to when an armed attack boat is safer and faster."

Wake jabbed a finger at him.

"You are undervaluing Union engineering!"

Kennedy narrowed his eyes.

"You want to destroy things for the sake of destroying them. If we controlled this river pre-war, then we'd have patrol craft of our own, but we don't, so we use what we can find."

Major Meyer nodded.

"Kennedy's right, it'd be better to use what we can get our hands on. We're not exactly flush with supplies."

Wake began turning red.

"How could any of you trust Tharcian workers? They're class traitors!"

Meyer narrowed her gaze.

"Keep this up, Comrade, and I'll have you stuffed into one of our captured units."

That seemed to shut Wake up for the moment. Then Blake heard a sound in the rain. The drone of a boat engine. *Shit.*

"We got company!" Blake stepped outside the tent. In the open air, the rain was louder, but so was the noise. "Meyer, tell everyone to mount up."

Meyer, still inside the tent, ran to the microphone for the PA.

"Attention Leviathan Battalion, this is not a drill. Defense, defense, defense! I repeat, this is not a drill. Defense, defense, defense!"

Blake ran as fast as he could across the muddy ground to the field hangar, slipping and sliding the whole way. Kennedy and Wake were hot on his heels. At the hangar, really a glorified motor pool, mechanics ran to the nearest trench while pilots scrambled to mount their vehicles.

Blake nearly slipped a half dozen times climbing the wet surface of his kneeling Martian. Autocannon rounds burned through the air. Pilots were plastered against their machines by the smaller shells. As soon as Blake made it to his hatch, he hopped inside and slammed it shut.

His machine swayed as it was pummeled by shells. Blake rushed through the startup sequence and donned his helmet. His radio squealed to life.

"All units! This is tower three! They have Panz—" Static.

Damn, they're out in force if they brought Panzerters to the fight. Blake raised his Martian to a standing position and drew his rifle. *Laser won't be as good in the rain, better be careful.* He held his laser in his machine's right hand and drew his mace with his left. Feeling a tad more secure, Blake moved in the direction of tower three.

Shells struck tents. The heavier kind used by Panzerters. Blake ground his teeth. There were five of them and probably a half dozen boats. The firebase took up the entirety of the small island in the river. Escape wasn't an option. More Martians rumbled to life.

Green lines disappeared into clouds of steam as they tried to fire their weapons. *Like I thought, rain's dispersing the beam.* Blake rushed the nearest Panzerter. It drew its sword. The blade evaporated the rain it touched. Blake blazed into the river in front of it. The surface erupted into a pillar of vapor.

Eager to press forward, Blake charged and swung his mace. He connected and took his opponent's head clean off. Alarms blared as his Martian was rocked. More return fire. *Nothing critical hit, that's good.*

Blake created another steam screen and backed off onto shore. Another Martian ran past him only to wither under a hail of shells. *At close range they have a slight advantage.*

"Smokehouse 7, Leviathan 6. We need your guns in this fight!" His screen began falling. A Panzerter charged through.

"They'll pick us off in close combat!"

Blake ground his teeth and swung. His mace caught the sword on the tip. The broken pieces of the blade created another steaming cloud.

"We'll keep them off you!" He swung again.

His opponent stepped back. A second late. The Panzerter's head hung at an angle. Its neck sparked wildly. Blake swung downward this time. With a crunch, the Panzerter collapsed into the river, the area below its neck crumpled.

Another Panzerter exploded nearby. Its torso fell into the river as its legs smoldered. Without the element of surprise and most of their advantages, the Tharcians attempted to retreat.

Blake scowled.

"Crush them, leave no survivors!"

Another direct fire volley found its mark. Another Tharcian Panzerter fell. The rain began to let up. Blake fired his laser at a boat. The water craft exploded and disappeared in the black waters. With the enemy Panzerters out of range, he began surveying the damage.

The artillery crews continued to send shot after shot at the Tharcians as sections of the firebase burned. Several Panzerters had new red highlights. Multiple tents lay smashed, and one of their ammo bunkers smoldered.

Blake grit his teeth and slammed a fist against his monitor.

"Leviathan 5, if you can hear me, I want this damage swept away and repairs made immediately!"

Silence. *Please don't be dead, please don't be dead.*

"Leviathan 6, we have damage control teams repairing tents and counting the dead as we speak."

He sighed.

"Do you have a timeline?"

Meyer wasted no time.

"Six hours."

Blake nodded in the comfort of his own machine.

"Meyer, I want you, Wake, and Kennedy in my tent now." He returned his machine to the field hangar. With the towering machine kneeling in the soft ground, he climbed out the hatch. The mechanics were emerging from their trenches and surveying the field. Blake waved them over. "You lot have seven hours to get every machine possible in fighting shape. When I return, I don't want any extra handholds. While you're on that, sort yourselves by whoever has the most time moving these machines around a repair yard. I want every workable machine to have a pilot."

The rain fell harder. Blake liked it as he marched back to his tent. *There's something about the rain; it just makes my resolve stronger.* For a moment, the surrounding scene brought back memories of his first battle. *I'm not that scared young boy anymore; this isn't some politician's war.* He crossed the threshold into the command tent. *This is my war.*

"All of you, what happened just now was completely unacceptable. We got complacent out here in no-man's-land, and they made us pay." He looked to each member of his inner circle.

Meyer looked at the ground. Kennedy met his gaze and a thousand yards past. Wake's eyes screamed for blood.

"So now, we will take Riverside and the whole delta with it in seven hours!"

9

The rain had finally stopped, yet gray clouds still hung overhead. Reiter stood under a tent with a leaky roof. Several pots, pans, and hasty patch jobs fought a losing battle to contain the leaks. *Kinda like we have up to this point.* Along with Septimus, Comidus, and the garrison commander, they looked over a map of the area.

"Gold Platoon had the bridge layers pegged here, possibly a staging area for an attack on Riverside." Reiter pointed to their west. "We can take the road we came in on west and hit their encampment from the south." He shook his head. "The problem is, if Fox leaves to take care of this, it leaves Riverside vulnerable to attack."

Septimus scratched his chin.

"Lieutenant Comidus, what did you say the defenses looked like?"

The younger man checked his notes.

"Besides an SP gun, they don't have anything that will hurt a Panzerter, but the defenders are raiders—they're smart and tough."

Reiter looked at the garrison commander, a Lieutenant Colonel named Kléver.

"How long do you think your forces here can hold off an assault?"

She shrugged.

"It depends on how much warning we get. I have a few hundred men dug in on both sides of the river, and the Special Boat Battalion has a few dozen attack boats and an assault monitor, but we won't have room to maneuver all of them in the river, especially if we're ferrying your civilians."

"What if we split up our forces?" Reiter said.

Septimus looked over at the young officer.

"If we divide our forces, it only weakens us as a unit, especially now."

Reiter held up a hand.

"What if I take some of our Panzerters and a couple of tracks' worth of infantry to attack the staging area?" He pointed towards the river. "I can leave you and Comidus here to beef up the security for the transfer."

Comidus nodded.

"Since you're not worried about Panzerters, we can keep the Cstalios here, and if we can put me and my wingman on a ferry, that's another attack boat right there."

Septimus thought for a moment and nodded.

"I have my reservations, but ultimately it sounds good. Ma'am?"

The garrison commander nodded.

"It's sensible and doesn't put us in too much danger. I'll sign off on it. You're dismissed."

Septimus left to order more supplies, and Comidus to brief his soldiers, so Reiter headed to the repair yard.

The yard wasn't hard to find. All six of their Panzerters knelt in an area about the size of a football field. The Panzerter IVs knelt on one side with the IIIs on the other.

It didn't take Reiter long to find Adamski.

"How are repairs coming?"

Adamski shrugged and pointed at the two machines at the end of the yard.

"Mo and Bartonova's units still got some work to do. Could be some hours before they're ready to go anywhere."

Reiter gasped.

"I thought they both had minor damage!"

Adamski shook his head.

"Bartonova took a drivetrain hit, air intake sucked in a stray round. They have the parts to fix it, but they gotta put on radiation suits to get in there and decon after."

Reiter shook his head.

"And Mo?"

Adamski jerked a thumb back at that unit.

"The suspension issues he's been having hit critical mass. Lucky thing is his ride is getting a brand new set of ankle and knee joints."

Reiter grit his teeth. *Why the hell don't they fix things when it's a problem?*

"If they could have been bothered to do something about it when we said something a year ago—"

Adamski put a hand on his shoulder.

"Hey boss, I said the same thing, and I'm thinking the same thing too. They cost us two good men, but they're all we got right now."

Reiter relaxed, but only a bit.

"How long will repairs take?"

Adamski checked his watch.

"Probably three hours."

Reiter nodded.

"That settles it, then. You're coming with me."

Adamski raised an eyebrow.

"Do we have a mission?"

Reiter looked over towards the front of the gate. Steele sat on the bent knee of her Panzerter, her back arched as she tried to get a picture of the sky.

"Corporal Steele!"

She nearly fell off her perch. Franticly catching herself, she looked his way.

"Yes, sir?"

He motioned her to come down.

"Get your flight suit on. You're coming with us."

"So we do have a mission and we're not taking Mo?" Adamski asked.

Reiter nodded.

"We're going to take some infantry guys. It'll be a walk in the park."

After meeting the rifle squad assigned to the mission, Reiter was able to gather them in the mess tent. He spread the area map and pointed to the Union firebase.

"Is that our objective? We were just there yesterday afternoon." Adamski folded his arms and looked up.

Reiter nodded.

"It's going to be a simple mission. Your two tracks will lead us there. Once we get eyes on, the Panzerters will create a base of fire while the infantry maneuver to flank. We'll smash their equipment and suppress them; you guys assault through."

Adamski blinked.

"Damn, that is simple."

Reiter looked at his watch.

"We'll push out at midnight. The civilians are crossing at 0200 hours, so we should be back in time to assist the others. Any questions?" One of the riflemen raised their hand. "Yes?"

"Sir, that base is defended by raiders. They're some of the toughest soldiers on the surface. Are you sure about directly attacking them?"

Reiter nodded.

"Yeah, not to sound dismissive, but toughness only goes so far against 88-mm shells."

The rifleman nodded.

"That's fair, sir."

Reiter looked around the room. "It's currently 1830—dinner chow is going to be served soon. We'll eat together and then bed down by 2000. At 2300 hours, we'll wake up and make our final preparations. Dismissed."

Chow that night was simple: Gyros, fries, and soda. While they ate, Septimus reported that all three of the Panzerters going out had been totally prepped for combat.

"Is there a way we can mount some sandbags or maybe hang some mirrored plates from our machines?" asked Reiter.

Septimus shrugged.

"Worth looking into if it increases our survivability."

"Hey, instead of riding in tracks, what if we hung cargo nets from your Panzerters and rode in those?" It was the rifleman from before.

Reiter chuckled.

"I'd hope we didn't carry you far like that. You'd get motion sick pretty quick."

The rifleman, Stoker was his name, continued on his tangent.

"Yeah, but what if you, like, grabbed a tinhat, and we climbed onto it?"

Reiter thought about it as he took a bite of his gyro.

"Hey, I see where you're coming from," Adamski said, "kinda like what those raiders did when this shit popped off."

Reiter swallowed.

"Huh, well, anything is worth trying at least once."

BLAKE COULDN'T SEE ANY STARS; THE CLOUDS WERE TOO THICK. The rain had come back for a moment before stopping just as suddenly. *That means IR and thermals will do us no good. I guess we'll have to rely on enhanced imaging.* He glanced over the Martians in the field hangar. Ideally, he'd have thirty-six combat-ready machines with pilots. As it stood, he had twelve, and that depended heavily on borrowing mechanics with experience moving the Martians around.

Feeling droplets of rain on his skin, he marched into the command tent. His anger was still there, smoldering under the surface. All the pilots for the upcoming mission were gathered around the map table. Meyer, Kennedy, and Wake all stood at the forefront, prepared to receive the mission.

He approached the map table and cleared his throat.

"This mission, like any, is wrought with risk." He pointed to the raiders' advanced base. "Wake will take a wingman and link up with the Raiders' forward elements. Because of the weather, we haven't been able to raise them on comms." He pointed to Riverside itself. "Six of you, including Guard Captain Kennedy, will join me in crossing the river and attacking the city from the northeast. Predator Company will attack the other side, along with Guard Lieutenant Wake and his wingman."

Meyer stepped up, helmet under her arm.

"One of you will stay with me and protect this base in the event more Tharcians attack. As soon as the birds are cleared, we will be receiving reinforcements via dropship. We will also be receiving a number of spare parts and additional weapons."

Kennedy moved to speak.

"As many of you have noticed, the laser rifles that come standard are incredible weapons, but rain, fog, and smoke severely limit their effectiveness." He looked around the room. "To remedy this, we're being sent a few containers of regular forces munitions. This is just a stopgap until a kinetic weapon is developed and produced to MAG standards. However, they will not arrive in time for the mission, so be aware of your weapons' limitations."

I'm glad I have capable officers assigned to me. Blake cleared his throat.

"If you feel like this is a suicide run or a poorly informed operation, there's the door, but know that if you walk out there, you'll be shot for treason." Blake straightened his back. "I was there back in 2112 when the Tharcians were right on Foundation's door. None of you were alive then." He looked at Wake. "I know what you've been taught in school—they're class traitors, cowards, kulaks, whatever word your teachers used."

Kennedy moved a crate of rations over so Blake could stand above his audience. He took a swig of his canteen as he stepped up.

"But it's been made clear to each and every one of us that, even on the defensive, the Tharcians know how to put up a fight. If we can take Riverside, we will control the southern part of the delta and be able to break out into the Tharcian plain. Success could end the war by December." He looked around at the gathered pilots. "Speed is key here. We can't afford to let this war drag on while the Tharcians mobilize their economy. If they manage to get the ball rolling, we'll be up to our armpits in Panzerters and shells." He saluted them, his hand palm up just under his left breast. "That's all. Dismissed."

Hardly an inspiring message. Blake stepped down from the crate as they ran to their machines.

Meyer smiled as he passed.

"Where did you learn to give a speech like that?"

Blake snorted.

"Talk for about five minutes or until you think you've said something good. If you do, repeat it every other line. If not, end the speech."

Meyer chuckled as she donned her flight helmet. Blake scowled as he climbed up his Martian to the crown hatch. *So many of these hasty patches. The armor better hold up.*

He opened his command matrix once he got into the cockpit. "Let's see what you say about this."

He entered the available data into the matrix. The system rated his odds at an 84% success rate. *What do you know? A thousand simulations and we come out on top.* Blake wasn't sure how well he trusted the matrix. He tapped the machine on its monitor.

"They built you to help us make faster choices, but part of me wonders if we lost something on the way."

His comms opened up.

"Manticore 6 with Manticore 3. We're headed out."

Blake nodded and watched as the two machines waded into the river. He set his timer for thirty minutes.

"Leviathan 5 with Ogre 2, assuming defensive perimeter."

Blake leaned back in his chair.

"All other elements, we have twenty-nine minutes and counting. If you want to smoke, sleep, eat, or meditate, now's the time to do it." He kept his eyes on the timer ticking down. Rain tapped on his unit intermittently. The gentle sounds allowed him to nod off.

A cold drop interrupted his nap. Squinting at his timer, he saw twelve more minutes. Another cold drop wet his salt and pepper hair.

Damn hatch springs a leak on me now? With a glare at the hatch overhead, he donned his helmet. *I guess the damn seal couldn't hold out for another day.*

In the cramped space, Blake did his best to stretch before strapping in.

"Okay, people, one minute left. Line up at the gate and stand by for departure." Blake waited through the longest minute of his life as he lined up in the center of the six-Panzerter formation. Forty-five seconds. Forty seconds. *It's always so strange how days and weeks are short but minutes and seconds are so long.*

"Nightmare 6 checking in."

"Ogre 6 checking in."

"Nightmare 3 checking in."

"Manticore 5 checking in."

"Ogre 2 checking in."

Blake sighed. *This is it.*

"Taskforce, move out."

They marched east, crossing the river immediately near them. It would have been faster to follow the east branch to Riverside, but Blake didn't want them to be harassed by boats. They were three miles out from their objective when he received an update from Wake.

"Leviathan 6, Manticore 6. We're about to link up with the raiders. We think we see smoke."

Shit.

REITER WAITED WITH HIS PANZERTER IN A KNEELING POSITION, JUST below the tree line. *Any second now.*

"Black 1, Gold 2. A last-second addition, but we got some 60-mm mortars with lum rounds."

Reiter grinned.

"Roger, Gold 2. All mounted elements switch to enhanced imaging."

"Black 1, remind me what lum rounds do again?" Steele asked.

"They're like flash grenades but brighter and mortar-sized," Adamski said. "Did they not teach you that in basic?"

"No, they didn't teach us anything about mortars except don't be hit by them."

Reiter chuckled.

"That's fair enough, White 5." Glancing at his map, he could tell that the infantry were in position. "We'll open fire, then you drop lums and begin your assault."

"Roger, Black 1, waiting on your mark."

Reiter slowly brought his Panzerter to its feet. A hundred meters to his left and right, Adamski and Steele did the same. The firebase was just ahead of them. Camouflage nets hung over the bridge layers, the SP gun, and the tents spread chaotically across an area the size of a baseball diamond.

Reiter set his sights on the SP gun. *That's the biggest threat to us.* The digital zoom was hazy but better than nothing. He could make out the bulky turret and boat-shaped chassis. *3. 2. 1.*

The SP gun's turret rose into the sky. A pillar of fire rose from its body. His teammates unleashed burst after burst from their carbines. They also sprinkled in machine gun fire from their chest mounts. *Sometimes I wish my rifle had full auto.*

The lum rounds ignited high in the air. They washed the battlefield in an eerie white light. *The infantry should be moving soon.*

With more than enough supporting fire, Reiter checked the situation. He scanned the camp with digital zoom. *There they are.*

The infantry looped along. When one group moved, the other gave them covering fire. Occasionally, a machine-gun nest attempted to suppress them. For their trouble, the gunners earned an 88-mm shell.

A tent exploded, and the shockwave swept the trees. His Panzerter shook from the blast. Rising into the air, a mushroom cloud marked the spot of what had once been an ammo dump.

The SP gun was long gone. The bridge layers lay in ruins. Engineer vehicles burned bright in the night. Reiter checked the infantry's progress. They had made it roughly a third of the way through the firebase. *I can't believe it, we're winning.*

As if the world conspired against him, a tree near him burst into sparks and smoke. *Shit.*

"Tinhats at 11 o'clock! 1100 meters!" Steele warned. Sure enough, two Union Panzerters stalked forward.

"Everyone get down!" Reiter took a knee, putting him below the tree line. *We're not on open ground. The woods provide us some protection from their lasers, but we can't blast away at them and expect them to fall.*

"Gold 2, how are you holding up?" Reiter asked.

The rifleman's response came back garbled in static.

"I'd move the tracks to a supporting position, but we'd be sitting ducks against those tinhats."

"How long can you keep going without supporting fire?"

"Not long. They're pretty roughed up, but the tinhats will chew us up easy."

Damn, I have to do something about them.

"Aim for their head or their weapons!"

Reiter came up. Two shots. Back down he fell. To his left, the rattle of Steele's carbine echoed in the night.

Back up again. They were closer. 600 meters. Two more shots. One skewed wide. The other smashed a hand. Back down he went. Adamski fired off a burst to his right. *We can only play wack-a-mole so long.*

Back up. 300 meters. Close enough to penetrate now. Another controlled pair. The tinhat recoiled as it was struck. Its beam swung wildly over his head.

Reiter moved his machine at an angle, putting his opponent between himself and the second tinhat. He fired round after round at the Union machine as it tried to aim its laser with one hand.

Damn. No fuel. No ammo. No oxygen tanks. I've dumped nearly a magazine into this guy and he's still up.

"I'm behind you." Adamski's unit ran to Reiter's left and dove, carbine blasting as he did. His rounds caught the second tinhat as it moved to get a shot on Reiter.

Reiter's screen flashed green before losing any visual to his right. He pushed harder right. *Gotta keep this guy where I can see him.*

Steele rose. Her carbine flashed at the second tinhat. Adamski resumed his own attack. Caught in the crossfire, the Union machine fell in a smoking wreck.

Reiter's opponent wavered. Its sensor ring sparked. Though it still searched for him, the intact arm was slow.

The laser vanished in a shower of sparks and metal. Disarmed, the Unionist machine turned and fled. Reiter raised his weapon for a parting shot. To his disappointment, he heard a buzz. *Empty mag, huh?*

Steele and Adamski gave the fleeing tinhat one last burst before reloading themselves. Reiter surveyed the firebase. He saw raiders still putting up a fight in the northwest corner of the base and gave them a burst from his chest-mounted machine gun.

The small-arms fire died down. He didn't need zoom to know all eyes were on him and his Panzerter. He readied his rifle. His teammates took up either side of him, guns up. *Come on, you're beat, just throw in the towel.*

If the briefings were right, then these guys would fight to the end. They weren't just Mobile Assault Guards, they were raiders—dropship troopers and some of the best soldiers on Mars, perhaps even in the solar system. *And more so than other MAGs, they're fanatics.*

Reiter activated his megaphone.

"Union forces, you're outmatched and abandoned by your comrades. Surrender immediately."

"No way this works, boss."

Reiter couldn't help but feel Adamski was right. He zoomed in to try to read their faces. To his shock, one raider dropped his rifle and raised his hands. Then another, and another.

"Black 1, Gold 2. How are we going to transport these guys?"

Reiter thought for a moment.

"We'll put them under guard in your tracks, if we have room."

"Then where are my guys going to ride?"

Reiter scratched his head before grinning.

"Who was your guy with the cargo net idea?"

The Panzerters knelt so some riflemen could set up their cargo nets while the rest processed their POWs.

In an attempt to get some fresh air, Reiter popped his cockpit. Instead of crisp October air, he was hit with the smell of burnt wires and metal. As he climbed up to get a better look, he saw a flash behind him.

"Sorry, I didn't know my flash was on!" Steele stood in her open cockpit with her phone out.

Reiter looked behind him and groaned. The Unionist's laser had gouged out a good chunk of his Panzerter's head.

"Damn, there goes my air radar, right-side cameras, and my secondary antenna!"

Adamski chuckled.

"You're lucky he didn't hit six feet lower and a little to the left."

Reiter tossed his helmet into his seat and scratched his sweat-slicked scalp. He was about to say something about light discipline to Steele when he heard a burst of static from his radio.

"What's that?" He reached back for his helmet but heard nothing else.

FIELD MARSHAL SKARA HADN'T BEEN TO THE PRESIDENTIAL MANOR in some time. *I was Marshal Lubeck's aide back then.* Now, he stood in his best uniform in the main hall. Before him was a hall that lead to a ballroom, flanked by two curved staircases. The stairs led to a balcony area from which the president received their guests.

Though the space appeared empty save for the occasional manor staffer, Skara could feel a thousand eyes on him. *It's fine. Knowing they're there means they're doing their job.* The doors at the top of the balcony opened.

Her heels clicked sharply as she made her way down the stairs. She wore a rather conservative skirt with a gray coat. Though her black hair was streaked with gray, it reminded Skara of iron.

"Madame President, I'm glad you could find time for me."

President Isabel Reinhardt smiled back at him, her lips veiled in red.

"Well of course I would have time for my top military commander." He saluted sharply for her. "Relax, Marshal. Did your aide tell you what we would be discussing?"

He nodded.

"Of course. He told me we would be taking a more assertive position in the Central Alliance."

"More or less. I also wanted to hear more of the general state of the war from you." She waved to the surrounding hall. "This is hardly the place for such a meeting. Would you mind joining me upstairs? Perhaps we can better discuss the current situation over a few glasses of champagne."

Skara nodded and followed her up.

They walked through the upper hallway, passing paintings of past presidents, relics from the nation-states of Earth.

The president noticed him observing a replica of a Romanian sword.

"You know, it's a shame. For all our grandeur as one of the shining stars of Mars, we hardly have enough history to fill a single museum."

Skara scratched his head.

"There's the Exodus museum. That complex is fairly expansive."

She waved him off.

"Please, most of that history isn't technically ours. It's Austrian, Hungarian, Italian, Czech, Slavic, Croat, Romanian . . . Hell, there's more about the Americans in that museum than Tharcians." They reached the door to the president's personal conference room. "Besides, its main purpose is to remind our people why we can't tolerate the Union."

They entered the conference room. The trapezoid-shaped room held a fireplace on the opposite wall with a wine cabinet on the other. Two rather comfortable chairs rested in the middle, partially turned towards the fireplace.

"Go on, Marshal, take off your coat and stay awhile." The president shed her own coat as she spoke, revealing a white button-up underneath.

Careful not to mess up his ribbon rack or get fingerprints on his brass parts, Skara removed his own coat and placed it over the chair.

As he did so, Reinhardt clicked her way over to the wine cabinet. "Still up for champagne?"

"Shouldn't I be serving you?"

She scoffed.

"Oh please, Skara, you're my guest."

Rather stiffly, Skara sat down in the high-backed chair.

"As it comes to the war, the front is stabilized, the attack from the north has been stopped, and the offensive in the east is stalling." He thanked her when she handed him a glass of champagne. "And depending on what happens in space, it'll be two to four months before we can begin our counteroffensive."

Reinhardt sat in the chair opposite his, carefully crossing her legs. She smiled.

"Unlike the last war, we're taking a more aggressive approach in space. Our spies have been smuggling weapons onto Phobos with the hope of inciting an insurgency." She sipped her champagne. "It doesn't have to work, it just needs to weaken their defenses enough to seize the moon."

Skara nodded.

"A clever strategy. What does the fleet admiral say?"

She shook her head.

"He would rather starve them out by attacking their Jupiter fleet." She held up a hand. "He claims we can't seek a decisive battle right out of the gate, but if that were the case, why would I commission the TNV Franz Ferdinand? Hmm?"

Skara nodded.

"Yes, madame, you have a point."

She nodded.

"Now, this Unified Alliance Command—you're a shoe-in for the position. I've already discussed it with the other leaders, I just need a few things from you."

Skara raised an eyebrow.

"And what would that be?"

The president held up two fingers.

"First, we need a great victory, newsworthy. You may recall multiple MPs from the provinces in the south were against joining the war."

Skara nodded.

"I remember. 'Why get involved with Roosevelt's problems?' and whatnot."

"Precisely. Of course, we must silence them the democratic way, and that is by smashing the Union so badly, the patriotism of others is louder."

Skara sipped his champagne. *This is disgusting.*

"And what would be the other thing?"

The president nodded.

"Yes, of course, the second thing is the postwar situation. I want the Union dissolved."

We're hardly in a position of strength right now. Do you really think after more blood and treasure is spent, we can demand that?

"Well, we can probably secure some territory along the border."

She held up a hand, shaking her head.

"No, Skara, not mere clay grabbing. Dissolved. I want Phobos to become a province and the rest broken up into independent nations. I don't want the Union to ever be strong enough to threaten us ever again."

Skara nodded and sipped on his champagne.

"I will be the loudest advocate for its complete dissolution."

The president smiled again.

"Perfect. I'll make sure you get what you deserve, Marshal—oh, excuse me"—she stood and leaned forward—"Supreme Commander."

The words sent chills through Skara.

The president swayed suddenly before catching herself. "I apologize, there's something I need to attend to. Can you show yourself out?" She hurried out of the room.

Skara sighed and tossed the rest of his champagne into the fire. He stood and began donning his coat, when he noticed the short mirror above the fireplace. *I'm only here because, a century ago, one set of bureaucrats prosecuted a war they were unprepared for and another set took things too far.* He stared at his reflection and shook his head. *In all likelihood, my earthborn grandfather would be disgusted.*

10

M o's Panzerter crouched against an office building. Across the street from him, a Cstalio hid in a parking garage. They were holed up on the north part of Riverside. The river stretched a kilometer between them and the rest of the Panzerters. The attack boats on River Montier had already gone ahead. *Thank God we could get a warning through.*

"Warhorse 12, do you have eyes on?" Mo heard the distant hammering of autocannon fire, as well as exploding ordnance. The rain had receded to a sprinkle.

"Yeah, we got two headed down this street, staggered column."

Mo glanced back towards the other end of the river. *Patrol said six, so four must be on that end.* He hoped his sisters were in a shelter and not on one of the ferries that had launched.

The warning had come in the middle of moving their refugees across the river. As they waited, one ferry was rushing to their end of the river, while the other hung tight.

"How close are they?" Even enclosed in his cockpit, Mo's voice was barely a whisper, as if speaking too loud would summon the Unionists.

"About three blocks away." The Cstalio's commander was whispering. "5, we can take them."

"Not like we have a choice; they're headed our way." Mo took a swig of his canteen to calm his nerves. He could hear them walking now, the echo of their metallic feet on pavement.

"We're going to missile one and drop smoke. When the other comes looking for us, blow his damn head off."

Mo gulped. The control sticks felt slippery in his hands.

"Alright, let's do it."

The Cstalio crept forward, turret swinging sideways. Wicked flames preceded a whoosh. Mo heard a crash followed by a larger one. The Cstalio burned rubber backing into the parking deck. Black smoke flooded the street as a green lance searched for them.

Mo felt the ground shake through his machine. He licked his lips. *Bartonova's out there fighting too, and my sisters are in this battle.* He remembered how the raiders had tried to drop soldiers on him and his siblings. *Not on their lives.*

The tinhat stalked past him. Its laser raked the upper deck of the garage.

Wrong move, pal. His carbine rattled. The tinhat jerked and twisted. At point-blank, the rounds easily pierced its back and head. Flames spouted from the stricken machine as it collapsed.

"Scratch two tinhats. Good shooting, 5!"

Mo sighed and gulped water from his canteen.

"Thanks, Warhorse, but now we need to cross the river to help the others."

"We will not cross with you, not without compromising your ability to fight."

Mo sank in his seat.

"You got any more of those missiles?"

"Two left," the VC said, "but if we have a shot, we'll take it, even across the river."

Mo nodded.

"Got it. Keep an eye out for me as I go to cross." He brought his Panzerter upright and began walking towards the river, the Cstalio tailing him. Across the river, he could make out green lights. His heart sank. As he cleared the surrounding buildings, he began picking up radio traffic from across the river.

"Warhorse 12 is down! Fall back!"

He could make out a Panzerter IV missing an arm and limping, firing wildly at the nearest tinhat.

"White 3, get back here now!" The first sergeant's voice crackled over the net.

Bartonova. Mo surged forward, his Panzerter barely impeded by the mud. A tinhat took aim. Mo fired a wild burst. The tinhat's hand shattered.

Another emerged from the buildings, bearing down on him. *Damn it, I'm barely halfway there.* Something white streaked overhead. The tinhat jerked and twitched. Sparks flew, and static danced over its body before it collapsed into a steaming heap.

"Got your back, 5!" Warhorse 11 cried.

Mo heard a scream over the net. Bartonova's unit crashed to the ground, its legs severed. A tinhat stood over her, mace raised.

Septimus crashed into the Union machine, sword drawn.

"She's bailing out! Give her covering fire!"

Mo blasted at the downed Unionist until a grey fist grabbed his barrel. *Shit.* Mo dropped his weapon and stepped back. He drew his sword, the orange glow reflected in the water.

The tinhat reached for him. Mo stepped back, slashing through the limb. His own swing blinded him to the Unionist's other hand. Suddenly, his vision was shrouded in gray metal. An impact flung him against his restraints before slamming him back into his chair. Sparks flew from his panels.

He attempted to swing his sword, but he felt resistance in the stick. Instead, he twisted the Panzerter's wrist. The tinhat plodded back. Two orange scars adorned its body. Mo held his sword at its face, and it raised its good hand. *What's with the splotchy red paint job? Are they getting lazy?*

Mo looked back to see if Bartonova had gotten clear. Instead, he saw a tinhat pin Septimus's machine beneath its foot before impaling him with his own sword.

Mo's stomach turned to soup.

"Top." He didn't see the gray blur to his right until it was too late. He backpedaled, but was jerked sideways when the mace struck the Panzerter's head. The blow threatened his balance, but Mo found his footing. He lost it when his friend from earlier tackled him from behind. Mo's helmeted head struck both sides of the cockpit.

As spots danced in his vision, he looked around.

Directly in front of him stood the tinhat with Septimius's sword. The one-handed one stood behind him to his right, and the mace-wielder to his left. A light lit up his comms display. *They're hailing me.*

"Tharcian pilot, you are the last one left. We are aware of two civilian ferries nearby. Surrender to be shot, and we will award these civilians with Union citizenship." The soldier addressing him sounded older, possibly a senior officer.

Mo grit his teeth. *Fuck it, maybe I can keep him talking while I think.*

"Union citizenship, huh? Why do I feel like there're more strings attached?"

"Well, they must be reeducated, but yes, full citizens."

Mo looked at the ferry closest to him and used digital zoom.

Zoe and Sophie had never given him a minute of peace since they were born. They always found fresh ways to aggravate him. Now they stood at the edge of the railing, horrified. *Reeducated.*

Mo tightened his grip on the controls. He looked down. The four of them were standing in the river. *The mud.*

"If you keep stalling, we'll be forced to make an example out of them."

Something savage in him roared.

"You won't lay a hand on any of my sisters!" Mo stepped back, drawing his backup sword as he did. "I'll take you all on!"

———

BLAKE PARRIED THE FIRST BLOW. *I COULD HAVE SWORN HE WAS finished. What the hell did he say?* Blake ground his teeth and backed away. His foot snagged. *Damn it, we need to get out of this river.* The Tharcian spun furiously about, slashing and stabbing.

Kennedy attempted to parry a sword, only to lose his mace head. The Tharcian's machine was older; Blake recognized it as groundbreaking in the war of 2112. Blake, Kennedy, and Ogre 6 all tried to attack at once, but the Tharcian used them to confound their attacks.

Blake ground his teeth as his sword caught Ogre 6, his comrade stuck facing away from the Tharcian. Something orange flashed. Blake's machine shuddered, and sparks filled the cockpit. *He threw his sword.* Blake couldn't believe it, but the weapon jutted from his left shoulder.

He scowled. The Tharcian struck the surface of the water. Steam shrouded his movements.

"Fall back," commanded Blake. "He has the advantage in the water. Try to salvage a laser or rifle."

Ogre 6 staggered out of the steam. They didn't make it far. An orange blade burst through Ogre 6, just below its head. The stricken machine collapsed into the river.

Kennedy charged, the hilt of his mace angled like a knife. Blake also lunged forward, attempting to trap the young Tharcian. Instead of staying still, he also lunged forward.

Blake blinked. Alarms went off. His head hit the cockpit wall. He struggled to keep the Martian standing. Blake's damage readout showed he'd lost his left arm.

The Tharcian stood with both swords again. Kennedy advanced with his fists raised.

Blake pushed his Martian forward. The engine revved. It shifted its knees. It didn't move.

He heard another alarm under the critical image alarm. An incessant beeping. *Damn it, I'm stuck.* Blake attempted to free himself.

Kennedy was holding his own against the Tharcian. Every time the Tharcian attacked, he'd interrupt their swing with his arms. Finally, the enemy broke away. Kennedy followed but fell.

Sinking to his hands and knees, it exposed the younger pilot to the enemy.

Damn it, Kennedy. Blake gunned forward, staggering as his feet were pulled free.

The Tharcian saw him coming, forcing Blake to keep moving to avoid getting stuck. *It's just us left.* Blake broke away. *This sword is an excellent weapon, but I'm hardly skilled at using it.*

Kennedy lurched forward, swinging metallic fists.

The Tharcian's sword flashed. An arm spiraled away, disappearing beneath the black waters.

Blake lunged back into the melee.

"Kennedy! Fall back!" His initial blow was parried. He kept moving, but the Tharcian was faster.

"Comrade Colonel! We've got enemy reinforcements incoming! From the west!"

Blake ground his teeth. *So that's what happened to Wake's raiders.*

The Tharcian surged forward. Blake grabbed at its head.

Its swords took his remaining arm off but created an opening. He swung down. A cloud of steam burst from the river between them.

"Kennedy! Fall back, damn it!"

"But Colonel—"

Blake ground his teeth and, for the first time in his career, yelled at a subordinate.

"Damn it, Kennedy! That's an order!" He clashed with the Tharcian again. "I'm a relic of the last war. Wash off the stink of my failures and carry our Union to victory!" This time Kennedy and the Tharcian boy's blades locked, sending sparks everywhere. "Now!"

His command matrix's screen was cracked, but without taking his eyes off his opponent, he could see Kennedy moving away. He disengaged as he felt his feet sink. *Might as well hail that Tharcian again.*

"Are you going to offer surrender terms again?"

Blake snorted. *This kid has some spunk.* Blake moved to keep just out of sword range.

"Young man, how old are you?" He swatted the surface of the water to create another steam screen.

"I'm 19, what's it to you?" The young man came through the screen.

Blake stood prepared for him. He chuckled.

"I was your age in the last war." He disengaged again. *I need to stall them.* "And I fought the very machine you're riding." He parried another blow.

"What's your point, old man?"

Blake stepped back. Something burst in the water near him, and the young Tharcian swore.

"My point? You'll be here in twenty years fighting someone else." He forced the young man back. "That's assuming I let you live now."

An opening.

Blake stabbed at the young man. The Tharcian dodged, rolling to the side. His blade came up through Blake's arm and then his hip.

So this is it, huh? Blake closed his eyes. Overhead, he heard the sword racing down the hatch.

———

KENNEDY PUSHED HIS MACHINE FORWARD. MULTIPLE ALARMS blared. Fuel pressure. Critical damage. Stabilizer damage. His hands shook. *I haven't had a good night's sleep in three weeks.* His eyes were heavy and dry to the point of being painful. Blood dripped down the side of his head under his helmet.

"Any Leviathan element, please respond." They'd damaged his landnav beyond his ability to immediately repair it. "Any Leviathan element, please respond."

This is an unmitigated disaster. For all our advanced technology, for all our training, we still end up stopped.

"Any Leviathan element, please respond!"

"Nightmare 6, Leviathan 5. What's your status?"

"Meyer, my machine is critically damaged and I'm injured. There were no other survivors." The firebase's lights glimmered on his screen.

A few more hours of stumbling and fighting to keep his machine upright and he could see the gate to the firebase. Other Martians supported by IFVs rose to meet him.

"Can you get your machine to the field hangar? We're calling a medevac right now." Meyer's machine assisted him into the hangar.

"If it's alright with you, I'd like to get some sleep."

"Kennedy, we need you to stay awake. A medevac is on the way."

He could hear the dropship approaching. *Perhaps I'll stay awake a little longer.*

———

REITER LOWERED HIS HEAD. THEY STOOD IN THE CITY PARK. IN A bare patch of dirt, they planted a row of rifles, barrel down. Helmets —Tharcian and Union—sat on the stocks. About 24 rifles lined the dirt just off their path.

"It's not the service these men and women deserve, but we're pressed for time," he said. While reviewing his soldiers, he noticed Bartonova had an arm around Mo, her other in a sling. *They're taking Septimus's death pretty hard.*

Just as dawn had broken that morning, a fresh Panzerter company arrived from the east. They shored up Riverside's defenses while Fox prepared to be transported to Garden City. As Reiter left their mid-morning memorial service, a runner informed him that their damaged Panzerters were already on their way to Garden City, along with a few of the recovered tinhats.

By noon, the five of them remaining loaded onto a bus and left. The infantry, comms team, and ordnance carriers had already left in their own vehicles. As the cold October sun filled his vision, Reiter couldn't help but nod off. None of them had slept much, and the night had drained them.

Adamski shook him awake.

"Hey, boss, we're here."

Reiter rubbed his eyes. *Where was here?* He quickly found it to be Garden City, specifically Garden City Tech. He wasn't quite prepared for what he saw.

He'd read about Garden City, even seen pictures and paintings, but that couldn't describe what he felt. Where Pulaski had a few terraces, gardens, or mossy buildings, Garden City blended seamlessly with the surrounding environment. The city's structure didn't intrude on nature here; it amplified it.

The bus took them to a glass dome with a moat around it. *It looks like a repurposed colony dome.* Inside the dome lay several large checkerboard-style buildings. The white "tiles" were walls, while the alternating "tiles" were well-gardened patios with grass and a few trees.

"The dorms are ahead." The bus driver, a sergeant, spoke with a gruff voice. "You'll be staying there. The students evacuated farther east, so you lot will have most of the space to yourselves."

Reiter stood and moved to the front. "What about the rest of our company?"

The bus driver pointed ahead.

"We've already assigned them their rooms, and they're probably sleeping now," he replied. "These dorms max out at 500 students. Your people will have room."

Reiter nodded and returned to his seat.

The bus pulled up to the drop-off area and stopped. They grabbed their rucks and walked inside. The lady at the front desk, a civilian, gave them their room assignments.

"Are you Lieutenant Reiter?" she asked.

Reiter blinked. *It's like I'm walking through a fog.* He massaged his aching neck.

"Oh, yeah, yes, I am."

She handed him a key card.

"Room 305. Go rest up. Your tomorrow doesn't start 'til noon for you."

Reiter raised an eyebrow.

"What do you mean by that?"

"Oh sorry, I'm Lexis, one of the grad students working on the Lowe project. I'm also the dorm manager for this building."

Mo stepped up next to Reiter, Bartonova's bag on his back, his own dragging on the floor.

"When and where is chow?"

Lexis smiled and pulled out her phone.

"We have a 24-hour cafeteria on the second floor. They serve breakfast from 04:30 to 9, lunch is 11:30 to 3, and dinner is 6 to10."

Mo nodded, thanked her, and left to help Bartonova get her bag to her room.

Reiter shook his head.

"What's at noon?"

"Oh right, you have orientation with your regiment's commander, and at six, I will show you around our Panzerter facilities and the Lowe."

Reiter blinked.

"This college has Panzerter facilities? And what's the Lowe?"

She nodded.

"We got a pretty big grant about a year and a half ago to develop a heavy Panzerter. I was working on my thesis and got picked for the project."

Reiter thanked her and left for his room.

It turned out that the open-air hallways in the dorms had grass floors. *They must pay a fortune in landscaping. Do they have janitors or groundskeepers?* He snickered at his own observation. He found his room and entered.

Thankfully, his floor was hardwood, not grass. He kicked off his boots and set his rucksack down. Glass enclosed his shower in a space it shared with his toilet. A computer workstation filled a corner. His bed clung to the floor. When he approached it, he noticed it came with an overhead screen that shifted to the most comfortable view, likely with some kind of eye-tracking tech, so he could lie in bed and watch TV or listen to rain sounds. A modern kitchen with a hamper for his dirty clothes rounded out the room. Drawers that he assumed to be his dresser lay under the bed.

He walked over to the bed. They'd arranged gray pillows at the head. Towels of all sizes lay at the foot of the bed. Curiously, there was a note with a captain's rank included. Reiter stared at the three six-pointed bronze stars arranged in a triangle before reading the note.

Captain Reiter,

␣You've more than earned this with all you and Fox Company have been through. *T*here're fresh uniforms and socks in the drawers. *A*fter you've rest*ed* and recovered, I'll see you in person tomorrow.

Colonel Hawke."

Reiter heard a knock at his door. "Come in."

Adamski walked into his room.

"Did you know about this?" he asked.

"About what?" Reiter replied.

Adamski held up a patch with three silver stars framed by a gold border. A master sergeant rank.

Reiter shook his head.

"I think it's the regimental commander because I got promoted too and he left a note."

Adamski shook his head.

"I thought I would get out before I saw master sergeant."

"Well, congratulations, I guess." Reiter looked towards the patio. "Maybe it's because that's the lowest rank you can be while acting as first sergeant."

Adamski shook his head.

"I'm not ready to be Varga, let alone Septimus."

Reiter put a hand on his shoulder.

"You don't have to be, Master Sergeant Adamski."

Adamski stared at him through red eyes before grinning.

"Sounds like something a captain would say."

KENNEDY FELT LIKE HE WAS FLOATING. ALL HE COULD SEE WAS THE river. *Am I being born again? Did I die and get reincarnated into another tuber?* He felt cool but dry, like he was in a refrigerator, but his feet couldn't feel the ground. The river. He could still see the sword piercing Blake's crown hatch. *How did things go so wrong?*

His eyes opened. He was floating in some kind of cool, clear liquid. He could see shadows moving beyond his vision. *I'm being recycled!*

"No!" His fist pounded the wall of a container. His breath was ragged, but he realized he was wearing a mask over his mouth and nose. He grasped at the hose it connected to. *Why bother with my air if they're recycling me?* He heard a sound nearby. Speakers were built into the tank.

"Please calm down, Comrade Captain. We wouldn't want you damaging this expensive equipment."

Kennedy noted his surroundings. He was in some kind of tank filled with a thick, transparent fluid. The internal lighting of the tank blinded him to the outside, but the way they called him "Comrade" told him he was among his own people.

"Where am I? I thought I was going to a field hospital."

"You're at MAG central headquarters, New Gallacia, formerly Greenwald Regional Airport." The man—he sounded like a man, anyway—paused. "But perhaps you mean your glass enclosure?" Kennedy nodded. "You're in one of our state-of-the-art recovery tanks, this model specifically built to treat your kind."

"How so?" Kennedy felt the shadow grin.

"Well, in the week since you've been here, we've extended your lifespan by a year, cleared plates from your brain, and undone the operation that kept you sterile."

"I thought that wouldn't happen until after I completed my service."

"Comrade Captain, you've seen some of the thickest fighting any MAG has seen. We figured, while we were poking around your body, it was the least we could do."

"Who are you?"

A dark man wearing glasses and a MAG uniform filled the screen.

"I'm Guard Colonel Chaney, chapter head of Congaree and commander of the R&D division."

That explains the experimental medical tech.

"I take it you've heard the combat reports from the front."

Chaney nodded.

"I have. I protested the Martian being solely equipped with a laser rifle and mace. Mark my words, Comrade Captain, we will avenge your company."

"How soon will I be able to return to the front?" Kennedy asked.

"At least two weeks," Chaney replied. "One for you to fully recover and another for you to train in your new Panzerter."

"New Panzerter?"

An image popped up next to Chaney. It looked like a Martian had hit the gym. The head was smaller and rounder, the 360-degree sensor ring cut to 180 degrees, while the back of the head possessed additional armored plates. A shoulder cannon hung over its left arm.

"We based this design on combat reports from the Martian and data we received from our own spies. The Tharcians are working on a heavy Panzerter, so we intend to beat them at their own game."

"It took a year of training for me to master the Martian. How can I possibly master this machine in two weeks?" Then he felt a brace on his head.

"Ah, so you noticed our virtual interface assistant. It uses your subconscious to inform your conscious. For medical, it helps you recover from nasty emotional and mental experiences while you sleep. For training purposes, it allows us to put you under and run a whole year's worth of sim time through your subconscious. By the time you step in the Jupiter's cockpit, it will be like riding a bike."

"Riding a bike, huh?" Kennedy gazed at the model. "So, I can reproduce—what's my service incentive now?"

Chaney smiled.

"Full citizenship. You may join any trade union you like and hold office, as well as vote in elections."

Kennedy laughed.

"Is there something amusing, Comrade?"

"I have to survive first," he said. "The brass is banking on that, aren't they?" He grinned. "I know you're playing me, but I'm in."

Chaney raised an eyebrow.

"You think I'm being duplicitous and yet you're agreeing with me?"

"You're leaving out details, but that's too good to pass up." His eyes were growing heavy. "This war has taught me two things: it's going worse than you expected, to the point where you feel you need every tuber you can get." *Damn mouth is getting dry. I wonder if I can drink this stuff.* "And if you'll offer that to me, you'll offer it to any tuber with promise."

"What's the other thing?"

"I'm the best Union pilot alive," he said, "but even I'm ineffective without a talented team." He fixated on where he believed Chaney to be. "I want to pick my new company."

Chaney nodded.

"We'll take care of it. As a double-ace pilot and commander, you have a lot of discretion."

Ten kills—was it really that many? He blinked slowly.

"I'll be going back to sleep soon, but I have two more questions."

"Yes, you must sleep for your training and recovery, but we can answer your questions."

We? He either has a big ego, or he's with someone.

"What happened to the 10th Armored Battalion after the Battle for Riverside?"

"They withdrew a day after you were evacuated—the entire division did. The 25th Armored Rifles division took their spot on the line. Your second question?"

"I've figured out your tells, so I'll know if you're bullshitting me, but what's the real origin of tubers?"

Chaney blinked. No answer.

He's pretending he didn't hear me. "I said, how were tubers created and why? I know the medical center stuff is bullshit." *Shit, my eyes are getting heavy. They must have put me to sleep.*

"That answer will be given to you in due time. Sweet dreams, Comrade Captain."

As the shadow faded, Kennedy drifted to sleep.

11

Reiter wiped the sweat from his brow. His canteen lay empty on the cockpit floor along with several drained water bottles. He reached for another packet of nutrient paste before realizing he had none left.

"Hey French," he called, "I need a beverage and snacks before I drop again."

He looked around the new cockpit. It was far more streamlined than the Panzerter IV's. Most of the critical information was projected onto the main monitor, with backup mechanical gauges in case those systems were damaged. A targeting computer hung from the ceiling just behind his head. *That must be for the railgun.*

"Yeah, give me a second. Collect your trash—I don't want you dirtying up the Lowe."

Reiter collected his trash, careful not to smear the remnants of nutrient paste on any surfaces. He opened his hatch. Rather than the monitor and ceiling over him moving away, a section of the ceiling receded slightly, revealing a ladder. A cover closed on the main monitor, and French appeared at the cockpit opening with a trash bag.

"These controls are sensitive. Can we tune them?" Reiter talked as he stuffed trash into the bag.

French shook his head. The lanky mechanic sported an impeccably thick mustache.

"That's how it's supposed to go. The Lowe moves with your inputs instead of reacting to them."

"Well, it's a hell of a thing to get used to." Reiter handed him his canteen.

"Can you top me off?" French took the container from him. Reiter glanced at some blank spaces in the cockpit. "Hey, what are these? It looks unfinished here."

French lowered his head into the cockpit.

"Oh, that's futureproofing. Say down the line they want to make a commander's version or mount a weapons platform that doesn't exist yet. The Lowe has more hard points and cockpit space for such systems."

Reiter nodded.

"That makes sense," he said. "Well, I better get back at it." He lowered himself into his seat and strapped in.

"Ready to go another round, boss?" Adamski asked.

"What's the matter, Ski? No more round count?"

The other soldier chuckled.

"Nah, I lost count a while ago."

They all had new Panzerters. Well, Reiter had a new Panzerter; the others had a Panzerter new to them. Since someone had tagged them with the Lowe, a Panzerter IV was freed up for Steele. After replacing the cockpit, Mo inherited Septimus's old machine. However, the Panzerter IVs served as the building blocks for new variants of the chassis.

With parts from the recovered tinhats, their units were being refurbished by the Lowe team into what Lexis had christened the Panzerter IV-M, the "M" standing for Modern. The new machines used the tinhats' engines to increase their power to weight ratio considerably. Since aspects of the Union's laser weaponry eluded them, they resigned themselves to outfitting Fox Company with ballistic weapons.

"Okay, since you guys won last round, I'll pick the terrain," Reiter said. To the Lowe team, Reiter fighting sim battles against the rest of the Fox Company pilots was the best way for all involved to learn the ins and outs of their new machines. Reiter selected his desired environment from the menu.

"Northern Arcadia? I'm going to freeze my ass off!" Mo griped.

Reiter grinned.

"I'm tiring of the four of you hiding behind cover, and I figured we need to prepare to fight in the snow."

"That's on the Roosevelt border. Like, if we got there, it'd be like cutting hair until we reach the stomach," Steele said.

After five brief minutes, the simulation ended.

"Alright, everyone, let's get out and stretch our legs for a bit. We've been at this for hours." Reiter climbed out into the light of the hangar. He arched his back and stretched his legs. *The others should be on the sim deck.* The new model Panzerter IVs were still undergoing their refit process in the hangar. He turned and looked at the Lowe.

The Panzerter VII was slightly taller than the other machines. Instead of the dull browns and greens of most Tharcian Panzerters, the Lowe was painted black. French had told him it was a version of the thermal dampener painted on warships safe for the atmosphere. French claimed that between the coating and advanced armor composition, the Unionists' lasers would do little to the Lowe.

As he looked up at the machine, Reiter thought it looked rather knightly. He smiled to himself. *Thousands of years ago, our ances-tors looked like this when they defended their homes.*

French walked down the catwalk and tossed Reiter's canteen to him.

"I like the aesthetic; it's a wonderful touch." He pointed to the railgun slung over the right shoulder. "That thing kinda blows it, though."

French glanced at the railgun as Reiter took a swig.

"It may not be aesthetically pleasing, but it brings the firepower of a battleship to surface combat." He lit a cigarette. "Come to think of it, our new tech primarily comes from adapting technologies we use in space for surface combat." He held his free hand in front of him while his other held a cigarette. "Just imagine a few years from now, a Lowe with twin-mounted railguns, one over each shoulder."

Reiter shook his head.

"At that point, you're just adapting a cruiser turret into a back-pack." He looked over to the empty spaces around the hangar. "So, what are the odds we can fill this hangar with Lowes?"

The engineer blew smoke into the air.

"It'll take the folks at the plant months to retool for production. We still have a few kinks to work out before mass production is possible." He gazed at the Lowe in its berth. "I assume everyone will want one after seeing what Fox can do."

Reiter nodded.

"Well, it's a good thought, anyway." Briefly, Reiter pictured the hangar loaded wall to wall with similar machines. *Yeah, a good thought.* He climbed back into the cockpit. *Time for another round.*

Snow fell all around Kennedy. *I'm southwest of Foundation. If we can't stop them here, they will threaten the capi-*

tal. His machine moved much quicker than the surrounding units in the sim. Their movements were stiff and haphazard, their weapons crude ballistics. *Original model Terrans—they were relics even back then.*

Kennedy knew where and when he was. Founder's Gate, December 21, 2112. He'd never seen this place with his own eyes, and he was born the following year, but he'd seen it many times in his mind's eye. In the stories told by Guard Colonel Blake. *I wonder if a version of him is out here.*

The system used his brain for additional processing power, so it was possible his impression of a younger Blake could surface.

"Tharcians are coming down Highway One!" a voice in the sim cried.

Kennedy ran that way, several Terrans stumbling after him. *I need to slow down, otherwise I'll outrun my support.* He slowed his pace to a crawl, the Terrans still struggling to keep up with him.

A nearby Panzerter exploded, its body smashed to nothing. *Artillery.*

"Scatter, don't bunch up." He didn't know if the Terrans could listen to him, but he'd try.

The Tharcians came over the hill. Panzerter IIIs. Kennedy grinned. In this era, they were groundbreaking. In his time, he'd beaten them like a drum. His grin wavered. *Mostly.*

They opened up with their rifles. Kennedy's armor was too thick for them at this range, but the Terrans were torn apart. Kennedy engaged his shoulder cannon. 155-mm shells smashed the Tharcian Panzerters, but more came.

Kennedy grit his teeth. He sent more shells their way. Despite him bringing artillery-level firepower to the fight, more Panzerters stalked forward. *If I catch an enormous volume of fire, my armor won't matter.*

"Fall back! To the Rodriguez-Martinez line!" Kennedy dumped

a wall of smoke shells in front of the Tharcians before he broke off his own attack. Once again, he long overtook the Terrans.

Just like the history books, a set of trench lines several miles long stretched from northwest to southeast. *This was the last line between Foundation and the Tharcians.*

Kennedy guided his machine into a Panzerter-sized trench. The Terrans near him took a knee and leveled their submachine guns over the infantry before them. *That last attack was the Journeyman offensive, meaning . . .* He grit his teeth. *Their next attack will break this line, and the Union will surrender.*

He'd always imagined that last attack coming immediately, crushing the old army and rushing towards Foundation. *I can't change history, not in this simulation.* Snow fell gently in front of and around their machines. *This is a test, a no-win scenario in a target-rich environment.*

He sat in his trench, waiting. And waiting and waiting. *Do I go over the top? Rush the Tharcians so they only attack in drips and drabs? Or do I stand my ground and unload on them with every weapon I have?* He looked behind him. Foundation was somewhere beyond this trench line.

He heard a sound like a rushing train. Artillery. Shells pounded the trench. The Jupiter weathered the storm of steel, but the Terrans and infantry did not. After an eternity, the artillery ceased. Terrans lay smashed in the pits. Men lay twisted in the trench line ahead of him. At best, there were maybe twenty survivors.

He could see them now. They came across the plain. The Panzerters advanced in wide, angular formations. Kennedy hammered them with his shoulder cannon, and as they came into range, he added his laser. *Their hips—that's where they store their ammo.*

His laser lanced out, bisecting Panzerters in a fiery explosion. Sporadic reinforcements jumped into the larger trench or ran across rope bridges into the infantry trench ahead of him. Armored

Personnel Carriers raced forward behind the Panzerters bearing down on the trench. Kennedy pummeled them with cannon fire but soon found he had depleted its ammo. *Damn ballistics needing to be fed constantly.*

He picked off Panzerters and APCs with his laser, but they kept coming. Despite the faster charging cycle, he felt like it wasn't nearly fast enough.

A thunderous sound shook the sky behind him. Kennedy turned and looked up. White flares. The Union had surrendered. The purpose of the scenario suddenly became clear to him. *Never Again.*

Kennedy opened his eyes. He was back in the tank, surrounded by the strange aloe water. He felt oddly relaxed and cool, the best he'd felt in years.

"Comrade Captain, it's good to see you awake." Guard Colonel Chaney's image floated on the glass of the monitor.

"Is this my wake-up call? I'd kind of like to snooze."

The older man chuckled.

"I'm afraid the next time you close your eyes, it will be in a proper bed. Time for you to leave the tank."

"Aw man, and I was getting so good at being a fish," Kennedy said. "All I need is a plant, maybe a tiny shipwreck."

Chaney grinned.

"Well, we're glad that your sense of humor survived your experiences."

The liquid drained from the tank. Kennedy's legs shook, as he hadn't stood on them in some time. He gasped as he removed the breathing mask from his face. *Real air, how I missed you.*

The glass receded, and he staggered forward. Two men approached and draped him in a soft robe. After covering himself, he looked up to see Chaney in person. Wire-frame glasses hung on the lanky man's sharp face. His dark skin blended with the rough colors of his garrison uniform.

"Comrade Colonel, speaking of that proper bed, where are my quarters?"

The man approached and offered his hand. Kennedy shook it cautiously.

"I'll have an aide show you to your quarters. We have fresh uniforms and other effects for you there." He waved around the room. Tanks lined the walls, many still occupied. "This is our primary medical bay. Though we've only been here for a month, we've furnished this facility extensively to meet the MAGs' needs."

Kennedy nodded.

"So, where do we begin?"

REITER BLINKED. HE COULDN'T BELIEVE HIS EYES. HE SAW THE soldiers getting off the bus and shedding their winter coats in the warm dome.

"Ski, let's call the colonel and get some answers," he said. "There's supposed to be seven of them."

Adamski looked at the tablet he was holding.

"Well, let's do roll call and find out." He stalked towards the meandering group under the dorm's overhang. "Fall in!" The soldiers scrambled to create a formation in front of their bags. "When I call your name, sound off. Private Ernest Merlin?"

A thin young man with large round glasses answered. "Here, Sergeant."

"Private First Class Lenuta Unger?"

"Here, Sergeant," a dark young woman said.

"Private Vass Si-lizard?"

"Szilard, Sergeant," replied a ruddy boy.

"What the fuck, Szilard," Adamski said. "How old are you?"

"Seventeen, Sergeant."

Adamski looked back at Reiter.

"Ever get that feeling you're on one of those hidden camera shows?"

Reiter chuckled.

"Keep going, Ski."

Regaining his composure, Adamski looked at the tablet.

"Private First Class Stasiak?"

"AWOL, Sergeant," Unger answered.

"What? Where did he go?"

"His girlfriend convinced him to run away with her instead of go die in the war. She was one of those."

Adamski shook his head.

"Thank you for saying something, Unger. Trust me, I know the type." He looked down at the tablet again.

"Private Julia Zoromska?"

"Here, Sergeant," a short auburn-haired girl answered.

"Private Akecheta Smith?"

"Here, Sergeant."

Adamski raised an eyebrow.

"First Nation immigrant?"

"Roger, Sergeant."

He nodded.

"Since there's only five of you here, I assume Private Noah Schwartz is AWOL?"

"Yes, Sergeant," they rattled off in unison.

Adamski sighed.

"You'll all pick up your bags and head in to the front desk. The woman in there has your room assignments, and she will show you around the campus later. Reiter walked up to his side. "I'm Master Sergeant Adamski, your acting first sergeant in Fox Company." Reiter walked up to his side. "This is Captain Reiter, your company commander."

"Good morning, ladies and gentlemen. Welcome to Fox Company. While my NCOs might not be that much older than you lot, you will treat them with the respect their rank entitles them to. If there's a problem, you'll deal with Sergeant Ski here. Every one of them has seen the enemy and lived. Now we're going to get out of your hair for the rest of the day. All of you will report at 0600 hours. Dismissed."

The new soldiers filed in. They chattered eagerly amongst themselves.

Adamski leaned over to Reiter.

"Boss, they're kids. None of them are drinking age. Hell, two of them are a year from voting!"

Reiter nodded.

"But that was our roster?" Adamski showed him the tablet. Every single name was on their list. Reiter shook his head. "Then it's no mistake. We got a bunch of kids."

"Maybe the veterans are heading to the Northern Front? And Early Company is probably getting loads of veteran soldiers because the Union killed them down to a man."

Reiter sighed. Adamski had a point. Other units would likely need veterans more than Fox, as they had five experienced pilots and most of their infantry intact.

"Yeah, you're probably right. Guess we got to get these kids up to speed. Are their machines even in?"

Adamski shook his head.

"No, I don't believe so. They're supposed to be getting Mark IVs, though."

Reiter looked up. Rain poured onto the segmented glass dome, its inner surface coated in moisture.

"Ready to get lunch?"

Adamski nodded, and they walked back inside. They wore field uniforms: an olive drab jacket and pants with black boots. Their sleeves were rolled to their elbows to deal with the relative heat in the dome. The replacements snapped to attention as they walked in.

"Carry on," said Reiter.

They went up to the second floor, to the cafeteria. After ordering their food, they sat with the other pilots and waited. Reiter had given them the day off, so they wore civilian clothes, mainly shorts, tank tops, and sandals.

"How'd reception go?" Bartonova asked.

Adamski shook his head.

"They gave us an incomplete gaggle of kids."

Reiter nodded.

"Yeah, one ran off with his girlfriend and the other we don't even know what happened, they were just like, 'yep, he's AWOL.' I just don't get it." He looked at Mo. "You're in the Provincial Watch or Regular Army. When your country goes to war, what the hell do you think happens?"

Mo held up his hands.

"Hey sir, don't look at me. I already answered the call." He took a bite of his burger.

Adamski lowered his head.

"I swear, I need a damn cigarette."

Bartonova shrugged.

"Why not go outside, then?"

"Because I can't smoke in the dome, and it's raining outside."

"Oh yeah, that would make it hard."

Reiter chuckled as the cook brought out their food.

"About the kids—we need them combat-ready. Establish their baseline knowledge and build from there."

Mo held up his hands.

"Do we really got to talk about this at lunch?"

Reiter shot him a glare that silenced him.

"Yes, we do, otherwise one of them or one of us gets killed. I know we're getting fancy new machines, but that doesn't make the tinhats any less dangerous." The rest of the pilots looked unnerved, and he relaxed a bit. "Granted, if we're on edge all the time, we might blow a vein."

Adamski put a hand on his shoulder.

"You checked your blood pressure, boss?"

They laughed.

Reiter looked from Mo to Steele.

"I hate to drop this on you two, but you'll be acting platoon sergeants for a while."

Steele dropped her potato, and Mo nearly choked on his drink.

"What?" Steele's eyes seemed to double in size.

"What about Bartonova?" an incredulous Mo asked.

Reiter gestured to her.

"Would you do the honors?"

She grinned.

"One weapon we're being given is a 155-mm Sniper rifle. I'm the only one qualified to use it, so I'm our company sniper."

Reiter nodded.

"She's a company-level asset." He grinned. "Don't worry, me and Adamski will be with you. See you in Ski's room at 1900."

"What's at 1900?" Mo asked.

"The platoon draft."

———

Skara swaggered into the room as if it was his, Major Starnes close behind him. The elegant meeting area before him was fully furnished. Four comfortable chairs were arranged around a marble table with a built-in projector. Marble walls and silk upholstery amplified the soft lighting. Tasteful red and white colors adorned the entire room.

The three legates stood near their chairs. Valious, commander of IX Legion, Comodre, commander of the X Legion, and Virilus, commander of the XI Legion, were all present.

Skara took his seat as Starnes pulled up the map of Gallacia on the projector.

"Gentlemen, I'm glad we were able to meet today. I apologize for the need to reschedule—there was an incident with our space forces that required my attention."

Valious raised a hand.

"It's no matter. We had to reschedule as well due to Avalon's encroachment on our shores."

Skara nodded.

"Yes, I heard. Were they able to damage anything of importance?"

Two of them looked blank until Virilus spoke up.

"One of our major spaceports was severely damaged. Our flow of materials from the stars has been dampened, though our manufactories at Lagrange 7 remain fully operational."

One of the other commanders, Comodre, cleared his throat.

"I apologize for him speaking out of turn. Now then, shall we begin what we planned to do?"

Skara nodded. Attendants poured wine for them as they hashed out details.

"I regret that my Three Corps commander can't be here today," said Skara. "He is indisposed." Indisposed as in dead, killed in a dropship attack a week prior. "Before we form an operational plan, I'm going to need the Olympian strategy. Give me the big picture."

Comodre nodded.

"Ah yes, our overall strategy. Well, across multiple fronts, we engage the enemy in battle, intending to overcome them in their entirety."

Starnes raised an eyebrow.

Skara chuckled.

"Don't we all want that? Now I need your strategy, your war plan, if you will?" He looked at Starnes.

Comodre waved his arms in a grand gesture.

"Well, of course! We seek breakthroughs were we can find them and exploit them for maximum effect by prioritizing the front."

Skara smiled and nodded. His patience was getting thin.

"So which fronts are a priority?"

"Well, all of them, of course!"

Skara could feel his blood pressure rising. *If my own Corps commanders acted this ignorantly, I'd have them thrown out on their heads.*

Comodre stood.

"Excuse me, I think the wine isn't agreeing with me." He left in a hurry, his ridiculous cape fluttering behind him.

Skara shifted his gaze to Valious. He left after Comodre without a word. Starnes, Virilus, and Skara remained.

"I believe his mistress is having a medical emergency," the youngest commander said.

Skara scowled. *No use keeping up pretenses now.*

"Well, thank you for your time. I think my aide and I will be on our way," he said.

"Your assumption about our command is correct, Marshal Skara," Virilus said.

Skara paused.

"Go on."

The young legate continued.

"Our General Staff is a joke. They believe the Union will be easily defeated and any battlefield failure is the fault of the men on the ground." He shook his head. "Their grand strategy is armies just battering each other until one keels over."

"Hardly a grand strategy," Skara agreed.

"So if I might be bold, what is the Tharcian war plan? I ask so we might be as clay to our friends."

Skara raised an eyebrow.

"Awfully forward for the junior of these three legates."

"That's true, but if the Supreme Commander of Central Alliance Forces wishes to create a marshal-type position for Olympia, his word would go a long way towards ensuring that promotion."

Skara nodded.

"You're undercutting not only your two seniors here but also your General Staff," he said. His expression softened. "If such incompetence didn't surround you, it would offend me much more."

"So, Marshal, your strategy?"

Skara sat and turned to Starnes.

"Major Starnes, take one of these chairs and pull up the continental map for our friend here."

Starnes obliged him.

The continent unfolded before them. Jagged red scars covered Tharsis's northern border and westernmost province. Roosevelt was nary a sliver on the map. Union and Avalonian tendrils reached into Olympia herself.

"As you can see, Tharsis is besieged on two fronts. We've stalled them on the northern border, and we're bleeding them as they attempt to advance through Gallacia." He looked over to the younger commander. "Our strategy is to push them back through Gallacia and out the other end. Once Gallacia has been liberated, we will launch a major counteroffensive through the Pacifica Gap, with smaller offensives along our northern border."

Virilus nodded.

"In that case, we will support your operations in Gallacia. If we contribute to your Gap offensive, then that frees up more forces to attack along the northern border." He looked over to his own country's northern border. "As for us, we will lock them in a stalemate up north until our Gap offensive is ready, then launch our own broad offensive to free Roosevelt."

Skara smiled.

"Yes, the strain from defending all fronts will drain their resources to the point of breaking," he said.

The younger commander smiled impishly.

"To further compound this, we should coordinate this offensive with some grand naval action."

Wait, Von Braun's plan and the president's desire . . . I can kill two birds with one stone because of this man.

"Our own fleet admiral has enacted a plan of resource attrition, attacking their freighters and mining sites, hoping to whittle down their ability to defend themselves."

"They could launch a joint attack on Phobos or a similar target," Virilus suggested.

I think I found a marshal for the Olympians.

12

Reiter stood on his patio. Below him, Mo was training his platoon. Or at least trying to. They walked around the driveway holding brooms as if they were rifles. Mo was leading them through formations to the best of his ability.

"He's not doing bad," Adamski said. The other soldier was standing on his own balcony, also watching the proceedings.

Reiter shook his head.

"He's definitely rough around the edges." Glancing at Adamski, he continued. "Do you think you can help him out?"

Adamski shook his head.

"I'm still feeling out my new position myself. Leading a platoon is more your area."

Reiter sighed.

"You're right, I should probably talk to him." He looked back at the junior pilots.

Mo threw his broom on the ground and yelled at Unger.

"I don't care what Master Sergeant fuck-a-bucket said at your stupid school! This is how we do things here!"

Reiter shook his head and pulled out his phone. *Do I call him or send a text?* Deciding calling would be more effective, Reiter rang Mo's number.

The younger soldier answered quickly.

"Yes, sir?"

"Give Unger and Smith fifteen and come up to my room, time now." Reiter did his best to sound stern as opposed to angry.

"Yes, sir, I'll be right up." Mo waved to his team and set his broom against a wall.

Reiter left the balcony and walked back into his room. *What should I say to him? He should be a senior wingman, but now he's leading a platoon.* Reiter shook his head. *No, Mo should be studying for finals and finding a job on the coast, but the Union had to have their damn war.*

He walked over to his bag. Reaching into the bottom, he removed the book he was looking for. Mo knocked at his door.

"Come in." Reiter shook the dust off the lamented pages of the spiral-bound book he held.

"You wanted to see me, sir?"

Reiter folded his hands behind his back and popped his spine.

"You're a busy man, so I'll make this quick," he said with a grunt. "Your soldiers need to learn fast, but you need to step up too." He handed him the spiral-bound book.

"The Training and Employment of a Panzerter Platoon?" Mo held the book at arm's length. "Is there going to be a test?"

Reiter chuckled and leaned over Mo's shoulder.

"Yeah, combat. That book contains all the technical knowledge you must have to lead your team."

Mo thumbed through its thick pages.

"So, this is it?" he asked.

"Not exactly. Your leadership ability needs to improve, but that isn't something you can grow by reading alone."

Mo exhaled sharply.

"Not gonna lie, they test my patience sometimes," he said.

Reiter smiled slowly.

"Trust me, I understand your frustration." He thought back to his earlier years as a platoon leader. "You know, Kozar once told me, 'Don't yell. Raise your voice, but don't scream.'"

Mo paused.

"Why'd he say that?"

Reiter waved his hand in front of him.

"He said screaming makes you look unhinged. Be stern and only raise your voice occasionally. That will strengthen your authority."

Mo nodded slowly as it all came to him.

"So if I control myself, I'll control the situation?"

Reiter patted the younger soldier on the shoulder.

"Now you're getting it," he said.

Mo looked through the manual again.

"Thanks for lending this to me, sir. I appreciate it."

"Anytime, and if you need to talk, my door is always open."

Mo left, and Reiter slouched onto his bed. *Well, that went better than I thought.* He checked his watch. 1500. *And just like that, my off day is gone.* Reiter did his best to relax. He read, watched TV, and napped, limiting his contact with other people. He just needed to let his people-meter recharge.

The next day, Reiter got breakfast with everyone else. It wasn't mandated they eat together, it just happened that way.

"How did training go yesterday?" he asked.

Steele looked at her glass of milk.

"I gave my team a written test to gauge their technical knowledge, then filled in the gaps," she said.

Reiter raised an eyebrow.

"How did they do?"

Steele grimaced and glanced at her soldiers.

"Not terrible considering they were military prep cadets."

Reiter nodded and looked at Mo. The other corporal swallowed the bacon he was chewing.

"We rehearsed movement techniques and formations," he said. "Fundamentals, fundamentals, fundamentals. They need to perfect small things."

Reiter grinned.

"So that was your broom drills yesterday?"

Mo paused with a wad of French toast inches from his mouth. He pointed at one of his young soldiers and barked, "Smith, where are you in a line formation?"

The young man snapped to attention while sitting. "I take point, sir."

Reiter chuckled.

"Relax, Smith, we're at breakfast," he said. Unger raised her hand. "You're not in class, Unger. If you have a question, ask."

"Why does our platoon have three people and Steele's has four?"

Reiter glanced up at her.

"Because your classmates went AWOL," he replied. "But Corporal Mo is an ace, so he counts as two pilots."

Unger and Smith looked at him in awe.

Mo paused with a bite of waffle on his fork.

"What? Three tinhats are coming at you, you're the only friendly left standing, and there's a boat loaded with civilians, including your three younger sisters—what do you do?" Now all the replacements looked at Mo.

"I'm trying to eat here, guys."

The others laughed. Reiter glanced at his watch. *In a week, we're going back to the front.*

From the briefings he'd been to, Colonel Hawke had explained that the units would work in a sword and shield manner. Three divisions would form the frontline and hold their positions. The two other divisions, including his, would attack from behind the frontline. Whenever they seized an objective they could hold, the "shield" divisions would advance to hold the ground they had taken.

"Boss, Merlin had a question," Adamski said, breaking him from his thoughts.

"Oh, yes, Merlin, what was that?"

The younger man adjusted his glasses.

"What are the tinhats like, sir?"

Reiter shook his head and smiled.

"So, we're retreating in the face of this counterattack just south of the border, and one comes over this hill . . ."

───────

"YOU HEARD ME CORRECTLY," KENNEDY SAID. HE AND CHANEY sat across from each other in one of the many lounge areas at the new MAG headquarters, each in an ergonomic leather chair, before a stone fireplace with a monitor overhead.

Chaney blinked.

"Well, I'm going to make some calls and—"

"You heard me, Comrade. I want to personally select my company, and I want all the candidates to be tubers."

Chaney nodded.

"I'll make all the calls, then."

"I'd even like to pull from the regular armies. I know a lot of tubers join the MAG, but some still join their home republic's army." Kennedy stroked his chin. "I also want the recent version of the Martian to fill my ranks."

Chaney scowled.

"The Martian Trooper is meant for the Republican armies. We will receive an upgraded version of the current model later."

Kennedy shook his head.

"When you said the Trooper could wield ballistic weapons or lasers, you had me. I want the firepower of the lasers but the reliability of ballistics. I want flexibility, with our loadouts being mission-based."

Chaney listened and jotted down a few notes.

"You have a point there. I could make the argument that you're field-testing a more flexible doctrine, with our company-level units having access to a variety of assets to fit many mission criteria."

Kennedy smiled.

"I like that. Mission, terrain, and climate should dictate the loadouts, not the unit profile. How soon will I have a personnel pool to choose from?"

"I can get you a list within the hour, a pool of at least a hundred," Chaney said.

"I want the ones with the best service record at the top—aces, combat vets, soldiers that test well—divided into officers and enlisted."

Chaney smiled, sending a message on his tablet before reclining in his chair. He held a glass of whiskey in one hand.

"Do you smoke, Comrade Kennedy?" he asked. The ace shook his head. Chaney lit a pipe and visibly relaxed. "Do you know what I appreciate about the MAG?"

Kennedy smiled as he sipped his own whiskey.

"No, but I have a feeling you're about to tell me."

Chaney grinned.

"We're the only meritocracy in the Union. The trade unions—whether they're a research union or a trade union—they don't care about the quality of work. You go in, do your work, collect your labors for the day, and leave." He took a few puffs on his pipe. "You can submit all the research proposals and papers you want, but your effort and your work isn't recognized."

"Careful there, Comrade, you're starting to sound like a Tharcian Capitalist," Kennedy said.

Chaney merely clapped his hands.

"But see, you're a living example of my point. You're a tuber, but you're also an officer, and an ace at that!" He shook his head. "Kennedy, what would you be in, say, a fishing union?"

Kennedy thought about it for a second. *Frozen waves, crab cages, and fishing nets . . . Sounds thrilling, but not my style.*

"I'd probably be a fisherman," he said. "But to cede your point, that's probably all I'd ever be, and I couldn't even reproduce."

Chaney grinned.

"The way I see it, the Mobile Assault Guards serve two purposes: to give the Union a national army and to serve as a release valve."

Kennedy nodded.

"So instead of pressure generated by those who would stifle under the Unionist system, say building up and creating another Gallacia or Roosevelt, they are given a space to excel and relieve the pressure."

"But also the true believers, the die-hard Unionists, they join too, and instead of becoming a heavy-handed and inflexible community leader—"

"—they become a MAG and work just as hard as the dissenters, with the sense of fraternity preventing a rebellion from the force."

Chaney nodded at Kennedy's observation.

"It really is a clever bit of social engineering." He laughed.

"What's so funny, Comrade?" Kennedy sipped his whiskey as Chaney regained his composure.

"The irony is, whatever bureaucrat came up with the Mobile Assault Guards got eight labors for showing up."

Kennedy grinned.

Chaney's tablet pinged. "Your officer candidates pool is ready." He handed his tablet over to Kennedy.

If he included those in the regular army, he had about a hundred and seven candidates. He scrolled through the list of names.

"Are they sorted by merit?" Chaney nodded. Kennedy showed him the top name. "This guy here, James Ballard, Peninsular Republican army, twelve kills in a Terran III, and he's still a sergeant."

Chaney shook his head.

"He's probably being held in that position because of his birth."

Kennedy grit his teeth.

"He'll already be proficient with kinetics. Invite him to MAG." He marked his name on the list and looked at the next one down. Not liking their personality profile, he continued scrolling. "Her."

Chaney looked at his selection and nodded as he read.

"MAG, new lieutenant, six kills in a Martian on the Western Front, excellent performance reviews." He looked at Kennedy. "Good choices. I'll make the necessary calls." Chaney rose and left, leaving Kennedy alone with his whiskey and the fire.

I wonder where we'll be sent. We're getting awful close to the Olympian border, and they've been quiet so far. Kennedy didn't like that. It meant they were up to something. *Besides, we could return to the Western Front. Riverside is still in Tharcian hands.* He glanced over to one of the nearby windows. Snow flitted about, not sticking yet.

We could wait until the rivers freeze. That would negate the Tharcians' advantage. Kennedy tightened his grip on the whiskey glass. *That way we won't have those damn boats harassing us.* The gray skies outside reminded him of the Battle at Founder's Pass. Or rather, his simulation of it.

Chaney's voice jarred Kennedy out of his reverie. "You know, if the weather reports are to be believed, we're in for another harsh winter. Your enlisted pool is ready, Comrade Kennedy."

Kennedy nodded and accepted the tablet as Chaney sat.

"Yeah, let's get on this."

———

MO STALKED DOWN THE HALLWAY, BROOM AT THE READY. WITH THE grass beneath his feet, he felt like he was playing outside as a kid again. Except he was training his soldiers.

"Unger, how many paces do you check your six?" he asked.

"Every third step, Corporal."

"Good. Smith, where are you looking?"

"Nine to three, Corporal."

Mo grinned. *It's all coming together.* Somewhere out there, an enemy lurked.

"Unger, if I go down, are you going to trip over me?" The young woman backed up from him. "If you can't see the feet of the Panzerter in front of you, you're too close." They approached a T-intersection in the hallway.

"Intersection ahead, branch right, checking branch," Smith said as he swung his broom down the hallway.

"Bang!" Bartonova lay prone with a dry mop.

"Contact! Sergeant! Four doors down!" Smith cried as he darted forward. The junior soldier took cover behind the opposite corner, raising his broom and shouting "bang."

Mo came up on his own corner and began saying "bang" himself. He couldn't help but smile. They may have looked ridiculous, but this was how he had learned his movement formations and tactics. Along with Legousi, Adamski, Varga, and the L-T. *Excuse me, Captain.*

"Alright, I think you guys got me," Bartonova said with a smile.

Mo's own smile broke into a grin.

"Smith, you're getting good at being point man. Unger, don't think I forgot about you. You're showing great discipline pulling rear security." Mo found himself on the receiving end of Bartonova's smile. "I think that's it for today. Report time is 0600 hours. You'll be receiving your Panzerters."

"Really!" Unger was practically beaming.

Mo nodded and steadied his voice. *I need to come across more serious.*

"Yeah, we'll be undertaking missions out of here soon, and combat is the actual test."

Smith smiled.

"I'll do my best, Corporal."

"Yeah, me too," Unger agreed.

Mo couldn't help but smile again. Between Bartonova looking at him and his soldier's motivation, it was inevitable.

"Well, I can't ask anything more of you. Now hit the showers. You two earned it."

They scampered away, smiling and giddy.

"Well, look at you sounding like an NCO." Bartonova walked over to him, leaning on her mop.

Mo grinned, but he was nervous. *She's so beautiful—why is she talking to me?* None of the girls in his hometown looked like Bartonova. *That's because she's a woman.* Until they started mobilizing what seemed like an eternity ago, he had only seen her from a distance and talked to her in passing.

"Well, I've heard a lot of them talk," he said. "I'm not nearly old enough to appear fatherly, so I'm trying for cool older brother like Ski or Legousi." Mentioning the dead man caused them both to look down.

Bartonova sighed and sat down against her door.

"We've lost so many good people since the war started," she said.

Mo nodded and sat next to her.

"Yeah." *Yeah? That's it? That's all I'm going to say?* Mo thought about Legousi teasing him at the restaurant. *You should remember your dead friends, not try to pick up your senior.*

"Mo, I'm sorry about Riverside," Bartonova said, breaking Mo's train of thought.

"What?"

"I'm sorry. I fucked up and got Top killed, and that nearly got you killed in front of your sisters." She wasn't crying, but her voice suddenly got watery.

Mo put his hand on her shoulder.

"Hey, Septimus is at peace now." She looked over at him. "Besides, my dork sisters ended up with front row seats to see how badass their big brother is." Mo flexed his arms and grinned, but he wavered. Just thinking about that night, the fear, the exhaustion, the desperation . . . He shook his head. Some parts he'd rather not relive.

"Are you okay?" Bartonova asked. Mo gestured "more or less" to her. "What's bothering you?"

"That night, the enemy commander hailed me." Mo deflated slightly. "He said he was my age in the last war, and he told me, if they didn't win, I'd be back fighting some Union kid in twenty years."

Bartonova turned to him.

"I call bullshit. Besides, you'll be retired by then."

He looked at her.

"You don't know what I'm about."

"You don't seem like a lifer."

Mo nodded.

"Alright, you got me." He raised his hands in mock surrender.

"As soon as I'm out of school, I want to get a job with THOR and move to the coast."

Bartonova squinted at him.

"I never took you for a scientific type."

Mo shrugged.

"What can I say? I'm a nerd for fish." He rose to his feet. "Well, I better shower. It's late."

Bartonova smiled at him.

"Good night, Mo."

"Good night, Bartonova." Mo was giddy as he made his way back to his room. *My first genuine conversation with her, just the two of us, I can't believe it!* After a hot shower and a clean set of clothes, he felt fresh. Mo leaped into his bed, letting his back settle in the soft but firm mattress.

He stared at the ceiling. *I'm going to have to lead Smith and Unger into battle soon. I wonder what kind of leader I will be out there.*

"Room, set lights to three." In response to his verbal command, the overhead lights blinked out while the floor lights dimmed so he wouldn't trip. *Is the frontline really stable? Are we going to wake up to shells destroying this dome?* Mo shook his head, pushing the fearful thoughts out. *I need to clear my head.*

He grabbed the projector remote and opened the menu. He had all the main streaming services available, and a few other ones too.

"Let's see, documentaries, nature . . . Oh, look what we have here." Much to Mo's delight, a rather old documentary was available for viewing. *For free.* Mo selected *Blue Planet IV: Two Worlds.*

I remember watching this with my mom. It's half the reason I think they're so cool. As coral reefs blossomed to life before him, Mo found the narrator's soothing voice putting him to sleep. *It's okay. It's not like I don't already know every word.*

"THE FIRST MAJOR CLASH BETWEEN FLEETS OCCURRED YESTERDAY morning in Saturn's gravity well," said the reporter.

Reiter sat in the media room with Adamski and Comidus. He leaned back in his chair as the reporter went on.

"A Union taskforce led by the Panzerter carrier *Ceres* met a Tharcian force led by the Heavy Cruiser *Salt Lake City*. The Union forces are believed to have been en route to attack a Rooseveltian Mining Colony near Titan."

Reiter shook his head.

"I wish I could shake the hand of the guy who thought of using Panzerters as space weapons," he said. "If I remember correctly, it was the Japanese, and the first Panzerter carrier was just a cruiser with a frame for them to hold."

Comidus raised an eyebrow.

"So wait, you're saying that Panzerters in space just hold on to the carriers?"

Reiter held up his hand.

"No, not in 2135. Modern carriers are more complex."

"Did you ever think about doing that?"

"What? Being a naval pilot?" Reiter shook his head. "I could never do space, and it requires an entirely distinct skillset. Where Panzerters on the surface are large metal infantry, space models are like attack boats, combat divers, and boarding parties all in one."

Comidus nodded.

"I could never do space either. I don't like hanging out in a tin can surrounded by hard vacuum and radiation." He shook his head. "Definitely not for me."

Adamski leaned forward.

"I always wondered what it would be like to live in a colony."

Reiter shrugged.

"It depends on the colony, I guess. An ark would probably give you the best quality of life, but good luck affording to move there."

"Check it out, boss: I live through this, retire early in fifteen years, and by then have enough saved up to move to an ark and live in luxury retirement."

Reiter thought about the proposal. Luxurious housing, all the amenities of a major city, with the added benefit of being off-limits to weapons and protected by international law. The thought of living in luxury, free from the effects of war, was appealing.

Of course, free from war is relative. If an ark is cut off from trade, food shortages and rationing are still a thing. Reiter shook his head. Those people could easily suffer too.

"Sorry to shift gears kinda suddenly," he said, "but it's easy for us to forget this war is being fought in space."

Comidus nodded.

"My old man used to say, if you knew where to point a telescope, you could see the space battles through it."

Reiter cocked his head.

"Really?"

Comidus nodded.

"Yeah, he said you could see railgun fire and torpedoes and even the occasional ship exploding." He slouched into his seat. "Hell, on a clear night, you can see torpedoes, but they look like shooting stars."

Reiter nodded. The news suddenly flashed again.

"And we have breaking news! As of 6:30 P.M. East Mariner Time, the ark-class colony *Isle of March* was destroyed during a battle in Lagrange 7."

"Hey, turn it up!" Adamski said.

Reiter fumbled for the remote.

"The initial reports claim the HMS *Alfred the Great* careened out of control after its primary thrusters were disabled. The battleship, over a kilometer long, broke through one of the solar arrays and smashed the glass beneath. The dead and missing are still being counted."

"Jesus," Comidus whispered.

Adamski pulled out his phone.

"Grand Carnival, right?"

Reiter nodded.

"Ski, what are you doing?"

Ski typed something on his phone.

"I'm searching the population of Grand Carnival."

"The news said casualties were still being counted," Reiter said.

Adamski shook his head.

"Boss, no warning, no time for shelters or lifeboats, atmosphere venting . . ." He shook his head. "No way anyone is living through that." He turned his phone around to show Reiter. "Three point five million people."

Reiter shivered. Suddenly, ark colonies didn't seem so safe.

They stayed in the media center. Before long, the other members of Fox Company began trickling in, asking if they had heard what happened to The Isle of March. They watched in horror as the number on their screens climbed towards 3.5 million.

The Olympian prime minister gave a statement.

The man unequivocally blamed Avalon and by extension the Union of Martian Republics. While he pounded the war drums, the scrolling bar at the bottom claimed that the king of Avalon was giving his own statement blaming the Olympians themselves for putting their own people in harm's way. When Reiter pointed it out to the room, Adamski shook his head.

"That's utter bullshit. Why was their fleet at Lagrange 7? The only thing there is Olympian colonies. What did the Avalon forces plan on doing if the Olympian fleet wasn't there?"

A dark thought crossed Reiter's mind.

"You don't think they'd attempt a colony drop, do you?"

Adamski began to answer, but he paused. The color drained from his face.

"As much as the Union are bastards, I doubt they'd be the ones to get desperate enough to commit war crimes. Avalon, on the other hand . . ." He looked down at the ground. "Their population isn't nearly as big as ours, Olympia's, or the Union's. If losses get bad enough and they can't use their fleet, they just might."

Comidus shook his head.

"I don't think so. A colony drop has so many factors that could go wrong. It's just as likely you screw up and drop a colony on a neutral country and bring them into the fight against you, and that's assuming you don't screw up and damage your own country."

Reiter sat up a little more.

"He has a point. The only attempted colony drop in history was done with an incomplete colony, the United States was in a different hemisphere than the People's Republic of China, and the US and Japan had such a massive edge in space, there was little the PRC could do to stop it." He thought of a map and the situation in space. "Avalon has a slight edge in space power over us, Olympia, and Roosevelt. They would have to seize a colony—not an easy task—force its orbit to decay, and assume the home fleets of the entire Central Alliance don't band together to shoot it to pieces. Hell, I can see neutral fleets, even the fucking Union, jumping in to stop that."

Comidus nodded.

"Yeah, and assuming they succeed, they'll get a ton of backlash from the Earth sphere."

Adamski remained unconvinced.

"After the US dropped a colony, World War Four ended. If Avalon got desperate enough to do that, our war would be over."

Reiter didn't want to think about it, but suddenly the sky overhead seemed a lot more hostile.

13

Kennedy strode into the town hall, his two lieutenants behind him. *So, I've been attached to a regular forces battalion. Let's see how this goes.* He was directed to the former mayor's office to meet with Citizen Colonel Heywood. He knocked at the door and waited.

"Enter," said a gravelly voice.

Kennedy entered a wood-paneled hexagonal office. A topographic map of the area hung on a wall to his left, and a massive Union flag was draped from a panel flanked by two windows. In front of the flag was a wooden desk sporting a smaller flag of the Pacifican Martian Republic.

If this is all genuine wood in a small-fry bureaucrat's office, it really shows the excess of the wealthy Tharcians.

Colonel Heywood stood in front of the map on the wall.

"You must be the MAG attachment," he said.

Kennedy nodded and saluted the man.

"Guard Captain Declan Kennedy and Reaper Company, reporting for duty."

The colonel's eyes narrowed as he saluted back.

"Are you here to undermine my authority? Tell me how to run my battalion?" he asked.

Kennedy shook his head.

"No, Comrade, I'm a team player. Any advice I offer is merely a suggestion. You know your battalion far better than I do."

Heywood nodded but seemed unconvinced.

"Well, if you're here to advise me, then advise me." He turned to the map behind him. "Where should I slot your company on the line?"

Kennedy approached the map. The 121st Battalion had four Panzerter companies counting Kennedy's, two infantry companies, and an assortment of support companies. Heywood had his three other Panzerter companies spaced out along his section of the defensive line with his infantry companies filling the gaps manning defensive positions.

"How long have your forces been holding these positions?" Kennedy asked.

"Since we advanced this far, so right around when Pulaski fell."

Referencing the map, Kennedy pointed to an area just behind the frontline.

"Your people have been used to these positions and likely feel good having people they know on their flanks, so it would be best if we're held in immediate reserve. If there's a break anywhere or a portion of the line thinning out, we can absorb the contact while the line unit regroups. "In addition, we can protect your soft assets like air defenses, resupply, and artillery."

Heywood studied the position on the map and sighed.

"I almost hate to admit it, but that idea is solid. I'd hate to have one of my units tear up everything to make room for you." He glanced back at Kennedy and the lieutenants. "Your fancy MAG Panzerters will not be hangar queens, will they?"

Kennedy shook his head.

"My personal machine is experimental, but we've had few if any issues so far. The Martian troopers the rest of my company ride are rugged and dependable machines. In fact, they will eventually replace the Terran IIIs your pilots currently ride."

That got Heywood's attention.

"Is that so?" He looked back at the map. "Interesting."

"Do we have a timeline for future Olympian attacks?" Kennedy asked.

Heywood shook his head.

"Not really. Intel has been saying 'sometime this week' for three weeks."

"Great, that will breed complacency." Kennedy looked towards the easternmost portion of the map. "Soon, the surface of the rivers in the delta will freeze and the Tharcians will lose their advantage. If they want a counteroffensive, they'll do it while they can use their boats."

"And if they commit to that, a pincer attack is probably coming." Heywood finished the thought.

"From what I heard from up north, the Olympians are skilled fighters as far as the individual soldier goes, but as tacticians and strategists, they're rather unimaginative," Kennedy said.

Heywood tapped on the map markers depicting the Olympian forces.

"They have three legions across the border from us."

"Mountains on either side. They don't have a lot of space to maneuver. The enemy's most likely course of action is to form a line and launch a frontal attack supported by air and mobile artillery," Kennedy observed.

Heywood nodded.

"The good news is, it gives us plenty of time to plot target reference points, build up our defenses, and dig in." He pointed to the infantry positions. "We have layered trenches, heavy direct-fire guns and missiles for Panzerters, multiple machine gun nests, and rocket batteries for infantry and light vehicles. My intent is that they funnel forces into our Panzerters, who will mop up the leftovers."

Kennedy studied the positions.

"Obstacles?"

Heywood traced his finger along the map as he went over their prepared defenses.

"We got track traps, Panzerter pits, anti-personnel, anti-tank, and anti-Panzerter mines, wire, the works."

Kennedy whistled.

"Looks like the Olympians are in for a hell of a fight when they attack."

Heywood agreed.

"We've got drone and satellite recon and underground radar. When they're coming, we'll know."

Kennedy saluted and, when it was returned, dropped it and held out his hand.

"Comrade Colonel, thank you for getting me up to speed. You've been far more accommodating than you had to be, and I sincerely appreciate it."

Heywood hesitated before shaking his hand.

"Kennedy, you're not what I expected when I was told a MAG captain and his company would be attached to us. Our dealings with the MAGs in peacetime were less than stellar, and I'm glad you're different."

Kennedy and his entourage left the town hall and made their way towards their machines. He smiled as the rush of cold air hit him.

"So, Ballard, Fletcher, what did you think of Heywood?"

Fletcher snorted.

"He's a bootlicker. He should have asked us if we needed anything the second he saw double-gray."

Ballard shrugged.

"That's harsh, Fletcher," he said. "He seemed like a guy just trying to make the best of his situation."

Fletcher pouted.

"You're only saying that because you used to wear those ugly mud-colored uniforms," she replied.

Ballard shrugged.

"You know, Comrade Captain, it's ironic how a diehard Unionist looks down on a working man."

Kennedy shook his head.

"Enough, both of you. I fully expect nothing but professionalism when dealing with the regulars, especially Heywood."

They arrived at the holding area their Panzerters waited in. The Jupiter gleamed under the late October sun, its gold and black paint shining. *My personal colors.* Ballard's Martian stood to the Jupiter's right, its bottom half in MAG colors, its top in Cascadian camouflage. Fletcher's stood to the Jupiter's left, painted in the colors of the Union flag.

"Now then," said Kennedy, "let's win this war, one battle at a time."

———

CAPTAIN REITER AND MASTER SERGEANT ADAMSKI ENTERED THE office and came to attention. At one point, it had been the college president's, but now it belonged to Colonel Hawke. He'd made minimal changes, save for the black and gold Tharcian flag that hung on a sidewall.

"Captain Reiter and Sergeant Adamski, reporting combat ready status, sir!"

The older man smiled.

"Relax, gentlemen. Now take a seat. Let's get down to business."

Reiter and Adamski sat in the two high-backed chairs across from the man. *It feels like I got called to the principal's office.*

"Here's your mission," said the colonel. "I take it you've already heard our regiment will be taking the fight back to the enemy?"

They nodded.

"How will we accomplish that, sir?" Reiter asked.

Hawke smiled and pulled up a map of the region on a projector.

"The battle lines are solidified. We think the Unionists are going to hold out until the rivers freeze. Once we've lost our ability to use attack boats, they'll resume their offensive." He dotted the map with unit positions as small as regiments. Reiter could trace a rough line along both sides. "I'm tasking Fox Company with reconnoitering the defenses near Floodgate. I don't care how you do it, but come back with as much information as possible. Dismissed."

Reiter and Adamski returned to their rooms. The administrative center wasn't far from the dorm dome. Their breath hung in the air as they walked back.

"Not a lot of parameters, huh?" Reiter said.

Adamski nodded.

"I guess that's something we got to come up with," he replied.

Reiter scratched his chin with a gloved hand. *We can't let the Lowe fall into enemy hands. Besides, I don't want to overplay my hand.* The dome looked over them as they approached.

"Let's talk to Comidus, he's a lot more familiar with recon than we are."

"Yeah, good idea, boss."

They stripped off their overcoats as they entered the dorm dome.

After changing into more comfortable clothes, Reiter knocked on Comidus's door.

"Good evening, Reiter, need me for something?" the infantryman asked.

Reiter held up a notebook he'd been carrying and wiggled it in front of the other man.

"We need you to help plan a recon mission," he said. "Can you meet me and Adamski in the conference room in thirty minutes?"

Comidus nodded.

After leaving him in his quarters, Reiter went to the conference room. He activated the projector through one of the work terminals. *I should be able to access that map data the colonel pulled up.* Once he was logged in, he browsed through the common files available to him until he found the map he was looking for. He had just put it on the projector when Comidus and Adamski walked in.

"Is this the area we're reconnoitering?" Comidus asked. Reiter confirmed with his notes before giving a thumbs up. "Since we have their general positions, the colonel must want tactics, techniques, and procedures."

Reiter looked up at the other officer.

"What would you recommend?" he asked.

"What would I recommend?" Comidus leaned over the table and looked at the map. "A recon-in-force. The infantry set up observation and listening posts, and the Panzerters attack, raid-style, fast and hard."

Adamski tapped on the suspected enemy positions.

"So while the Panzerters test their defenses, the infantry observe. Nice." He looked over to Reiter, who shook his head.

"I don't want to reveal the Lowe's existence yet, so I'm going to hang back with Bartonova and provide supporting fire."

Comidus grimaced before nodding.

"I get that. At best, the enemy thinks we're using a new sniper rifle and are none the wiser," he said.

Reiter waved a hand over the map.

"I like that aspect of the plan, but now we need to consider our positions and terrain." He zoomed in on Floodgate. It sat at a vital fork in the river, one branch running north-south, the other branching off slightly southwest from west.

Comidus pored over the map, his brow furrowed.

"We got the best terrain to set up LPs and OPs on the south shore of this river, opposite the city," he said.

Adamski clicked his tongue and leaned forward.

"In that case, we'll stage on the east shore of this branch. When we initiate contact, you'll have a front-row seat."

Reiter looked over the map himself.

"There's some high ground just behind your staging area. Bartonova and I can provide supporting fire from there."

Adamski looked at the map and folded his arms.

"Yeah, that looks good. Do you think we're ready to brief Mo, Steele, and Bartonova?"

Reiter shot him a thumbs up, and Adamski left to get the two platoon leaders.

"It's going to be interesting shooting the railgun live," Reiter said.

Comidus grinned.

"You do not understand how bad I want railguns on my tracks," he said. "That would be a game changer."

Reiter took a seat and tried to pop his back.

"Hopefully, they'll have more of these magnetic weapons soon. They're already working on magnetic rifles. I would imagine magnetic vehicle weapons aren't far behind."

Mo, Steele, Bartonova, and Adamski entered the room. Reiter briefed them on the mission.

"So, whose group do you want taking point?" Mo asked.

Adamski scratched his chin.

"I'm not sure," he said. "Let's rehearse it a few times either way and see what we're most comfortable with."

Reiter nodded.

"Yeah, it's good for the two teams to rehearse together, especially since this is the first mission for a lot of us in new positions," he said.

Bartonova elbowed him.

"Guess you're going to be my wingman, sir."

Reiter grinned.

"Don't get too used to it. I'll deploy with you until I feel comfortable revealing the existence of the Lowe to the enemy," he replied. "Comidus, do you need me to brief Gold Platoon?"

Comidus shook his head.

"I should be able to brief them myself. Besides, there are a lot of infantry-specific pieces I need to go over with my squad leaders." He looked back at the map. "That being said, I'd like my people to rehearse with yours."

Adamski whistled.

"A company-level rehearsal—that's almost unheard of," he said.

Reiter leaned back in his chair and folded his arms.

"Mo, we're going to need brooms, mops, and everything remotely rifle-like for the company," he said.

Mo grinned and saluted.

"Yes, sir!"

"STEADY, REAPERS, WE STILL HAVEN'T RECEIVED THE SIGNAL." Kennedy steeled himself. The artillery behind him had been firing on all cylinders in a fierce battlefield orchestra. His company was dispersed along three dug-in positions, four Panzerters each. Kennedy and both of his lieutenants each led a wing of his company. His enhanced forward sensors fed him a lot of information about the battle in front of him.

Dust and grit floated like fog over the ground ahead. The infantry positions might as well have been invisible for all the smoke and grit they created. Even in his cockpit, Kennedy caught a metallic whiff of gunpowder.

"Reaper 6! Denali Company needs to fall back!"

The company directly ahead of us, how convenient.

"Roger, Redwood 6. Reaper Company, forward!" The Jupiter struggled at first to leave the trench. Kennedy cursed its excessive weight, but it climbed out. Trailing behind the Martian Troopers, he supported them with his shoulder cannon as he closed the distance.

Denali Company staggered past them. Terrans were missing limbs or weapons. A few crawled past, their main cameras smashed. One fell onto its back, a spear dug into its hip.

The Olympian Panzerters reminded Kennedy of an ancient warrior. Each one carried a large rectangular shield in their left hand. In their right, the ones he could see carried bladed weapons similar to the Tharcians, except their swords were shorter and they carried spear weapons. One stood over the fallen Terran, its spear raised for a killing blow.

Kennedy fired his cannon. Direct hit. The Olympian staggered back, smoke pouring from the cavity in its chest. His second shot took its head off.

"Fall back, Comrade!" he ordered. "The Reapers are here!"

The Troopers closed to rifle-range. They unleashed burst after burst into Olympian machines. The Olympians closed their formation. Creating a shield wall, they held their ground. *They all have melee weapons. The next wave will probably have ranged weapons at first.*

The Olympians formed a tortoise shell with their shields and advanced into the oncoming fire. Their shields withered but held. *Shields are too thick for rifles, need to try something else.*

Kennedy hammered away with his shoulder cannon. Olympians staggered and fell. The fallen created gaps the Martians exploited. Within minutes, they had whittled them down.

With no immediate threats, Kennedy took the initiative.

"Occupy Denali's old positions! Improve them as quickly as you can!" Kennedy himself had to widen a position to fit the Jupiter.

The Martian Troopers improved their positions and switched to fresh magazines. They had an alternative model 100-mm rifle with an underslung laser. While not as powerful as a dedicated laser rifle, it was a devastating close-range weapon.

Kennedy's own laser rifle was an improved model, with a faster cycle time and a new firing mode. He checked his cannon ammo. 40%. *Shit.*

"Redwood 6, what's Denali's status?" he asked.

The colonel came back quickly.

"They're out of the fight," he said. "Unless they can get more machines."

"That bad, huh?" Kennedy scanned the horizon. He could see another wave of Olympians. Their white armor stood out among the smoke and dirt of the battle. "Do we have any air assets free?"

"We have a CAS flight on station."

"How about the artillery, do they have smoke rounds?"

When Heywood came back over the net, he sounded resigned.

"I can hear the gears turning all the way back here. What are you thinking?"

Kennedy licked his lips.

"We've got five company-sized Panzerter elements crossing no-man's-land with infantry support. We hit the flanks from the air and use smoke to screen the other companies' movement, infantry force them down our fatal funnel, and supporting Panzerter companies break off a platoon and envelop them." Kennedy spoke about a mile a minute.

"Well, it beats the hell out of sitting and watching them approach us," Heywood replied. "It will take me a few minutes to put all of that together."

What the hell? Isn't it just an entry in his command matrix?

"Roger." Kennedy began picking off Olympians with his shoulder cannon as they entered range. Their Panzerters marched inexorably on, their infantry rolling behind them.

The Martians began taking shots where they could. At long-range, however, the rounds either missed or glanced off Olympian shields. At about 1500 meters, they paused. Kennedy could now see the Olympians. Their Panzerters formed a three-by-three box with presumably the commander behind the box. The front rank took a knee behind their shields.

"Recoilless rifles!" Kennedy called.

The two ranks behind the front row held recoilless rifles, one firing left-handed, the other right. Shells smashed bunkers. Terrans crumpled. A Martian Trooper fell, its head gone.

Kennedy's machine rocked. The Jupiter's armor held. He returned fire with his cannon. Another volley savaged their lines. *Any day now.*

Drones swooped low, blasting away with missiles and chain-guns. Their sudden intervention killed the Olympians' momentum. The infantry positions roared to life as smoke blossomed in front of the Panzerters on the flanks. *Now's our chance.*

The Olympians began grouping together, following the fatal funnel. Artillery and heavy-weapons fire on their flanks hemmed them in. The MAGs unleashed withering fire on their opponents. At full automatic, their rifles pummeled the Olympians' shields to scrap.

We had our hiccups, but we're going to triumph.

Kennedy switched his laser to strobe. Instead of a long exposure, his emitter simply closed between high-power pulses. He swung the laser back and forth. Olympians fell in droves. Orange scars covered them.

Despite the losses, despite the intense fire, the Olympians marched on. *They may try their damndest to kill me, but damn I have to respect their bravery and discipline.*

The Olympians entered melee range with the Reapers. Kennedy ducked a spear lunging at him. Drawing his mace, he fended off the encroaching Olympians. The Jupiter moved smoothly in the melee, its torso and arms fluid. *It feels more like an extension of my body than a machine I'm commanding.* The Olympians repelled their attacks as best as their stiff Panzerters could.

After a few minutes of intense melee, the last few Olympians threw down their weapons. Surrounded, they surrendered.

Kennedy breathed a sigh of relief. *I'm glad they saw reason. Last stands are a waste of lives.*

"Redwood 6, the plan was successful. What do you want to do about our prisoners?"

Reiter looked through the sights of his targeting computer. As he lifted the scope slightly, he glanced at the map unfolded in his lap. Taking a knotted length of bootlace, he traced his position to the spot he was looking at.

"Bartonova, I'm going to set my zero to five thousand meters," he said.

"Where did you get that number, 6?" she asked.

Reiter grinned.

"I have a knotted bootlace and a map. The knots correspond to kilometers on the map."

The two Panzerters were posted up on a small hill overlooking Floodgate. Bartonova's machine was mostly prone, her massive 155-mm sniper rifle taking up most of the ridge. Reiter's machine leaned over the ridge, bracing for the recoil of the railgun.

"Alrighty then, I'll adjust my sights too," she said.

Once the shooting started, they'd activate their laser rangefinders, but to lase the enemy now would give away their position.

Reiter unbuckled his restraints and stretched.

"And now we wait," he muttered to himself. *This is honestly the hardest part, knowing any minute we're seconds away from bad things happening.*

"Fox 6, Gold 1. We're in position."

Reiter looked south of the town. From his vantage point, he could see faint lines in the grass where Gold Platoon had walked.

"I got you, Gold 1. Maintain radio silence." He twisted sideways, using magnets to hang his map on a blank space in his cockpit. *That'll do for now.* He placed magnet markers on the rough position of his infantrymen. Unable to find gold, he simply used yellow magnets.

"Fox 6, Fox 7. Both teams are staged and ready to go." Adamski's group hung just outside the range of Union patrols.

"Roger, 7. Stand by for initiation by fires." Reiter pulled down his targeting computer. Floodgate wasn't enormous, maybe seven blocks with a small dock area and only a couple of four-story buildings. Two companies guarded it. One Panzerter, one infantry.

"I got six IFVs patrolling the perimeter, with six Panzerters posted up on street corners," Bartonova said.

Reiter himself could see six more Panzerters kneeling in a

parking lot. *Probably their night shift. There's probably more IFVs inside the city.*

"Prioritize the Cyclops—they're weaker than tinhats, but still deadlier than the IFVs." *If I target the offline Panzerters, I can stop them from escalating the fight, but that doesn't reduce the threat from the ones already active.*

"Roger. I got the far side, at 1130."

Reiter saw the target in question. *If I hit their reserves, they'll think they're being attacked from the opposite direction of our actual attack.* He furrowed his brow. *Careful now. If we get too big-brained, it could come back to bite us.* It was a calculated risk.

"Roger, I'm targeting their reserves." *We're here for information, but the priority is survival.* "All units stand by for opening fire."

He sighted in his target. A kneeling Panzerter with two more slightly behind it. *If I line up this shot, I can destroy all three.* He squeezed the trigger.

The Lowe kicked hard. The Cyclops's head shattered. Its comrades remained intact. *Shot must have bounced.*

After a second of delay, Bartonova's target fell in a smoking wreck. *Shot high.* Adjusting his sights, he focused on the next target. The engine roared, the railgun humming as its capacitors recharged.

Another kick. Now two Cyclopes keeled over headless. Beeping nabbed his attention. The barrel had to cool besides recharging. Bartonova had downed another Cyclops on the far end.

"My weapon's down. It's all you for a minute, Bartonova." He looked over at the river. Adamski's group advanced in a double wedge. The Cyclopes and IFVs they encountered were surprised. However, they quickly sorted themselves out.

"6, Gold 1. We got what we need. We're withdrawing."

"Roger, Gold 1. Fox 7, hold the enemy until Gold is clear."

Adamski's group continued to exchange fire from cover. They were taking hits, but nothing critical for the moment.

The IFVs raced away past his position.

Alright, now we break contact.

"Fox 7, break contact. We'll cover you." The railgun had cooled off, so he took aim at a cluster of infantry in a building and fired.

The entire bottom floor vanished in a shower of debris and dust. The second floor rose into the air a few feet before slamming back into the ground and crumbling. Reiter blinked in surprise. *Holy shit, that was awesome.*

"6, 7. We've completely broken contact, and we're on our way to RP Clarke."

Reiter shoved his targeting computer back into the housing. The railgun folded back over his shoulder.

"Roger, 7. We'll see you there. Let's get out of here, Valkyrie." Bartonova had chosen the call sign herself. Apparently they were angelic female warriors that escorted fallen soldiers to heaven. Her new position involved power coming from on high.

After a thirty-minute walk in their Panzerters, they met in a clearing behind their own line.

"Alright, I want BDAs. Once we're up, we'll head home." Reiter knelt his machine and opened his hatch. A handy grip attached to a spool of cable lay in a secure hatch at the lip of the cockpit. He set it down and descended to the ground, the spool unwinding as he lowered himself.

"Well, aren't you fancy, sir!" Bartonova called as she climbed down.

Reiter smiled as his feet touched the ground.

"Hey, you can't use this if you don't have decent grip strength!" he replied. The Panzerters formed a rough circle, with the IFVs forming a smaller one in the center.

"Hey, boss, Steele and Mo are going to bring you the BDAs for their teams," Adamski said as he approached the center, stretching. "Hot damn, I could use a cigarette."

"Hey, Top, my driver has smokes if you're down some!" Comidus said from atop his Iglasio.

Adamski walked towards him and was surprised to have the lieutenant throw an entire pack at him.

"What the hell, sir?"

Comidus waved him off.

"Markos has a whole carton of them, he's good."

Adamski chuckled and pulled out his lighter.

Reiter looked around. All the tracks had returned. Their Panz-erters had been in a fight, but their pilots were in *high spirits. Considering everything, that was a successful mission.*

14

"So you open this menu and it will give you all the analytics regarding the situation on the map." Kennedy leaned over Heywood's shoulder as he showed him the command matrix.

"And this helps me how?" the older soldier asked.

Kennedy opened the menu and showed him the numbers.

"So typically, you receive information and have to weigh it against what you know, while also remembering all the relevant data," he replied.

Heywood frowned as he looked at the screen.

"So, how does it get these numbers?"

Kennedy took a step back.

"The system runs 10,000 simulations a second based on the information you've entered, so the analytics only get more accurate with time." He pointed to the numbers. "It remembers all the information for you and gives weights to your choices. All you need to do is enter the data and determine what risks are worth it."

Heywood folded his arms.

"It seems like it's easy for a leader to become over-reliant on these analytics," he said.

Kennedy nodded.

"When they train us on using these, they remind us constantly to not just pick the safest option every time. If nothing else, it makes battle tracking significantly easier."

Heywood leaned over in his chair.

"So, this mission, you have a plan?"

Kennedy walked around to the map that hung on the wall. He pointed to the Olympians' position.

"I would like to hit Olympian supplies. If we can damage their ability to continue fighting, we can speed up their eventual defeat on this front."

Heywood stroked his chin.

"I'm listening," he said.

Kennedy circled a section of the line.

"First, we need to let them know we bite back. So far, we've only played defense."

Heywood held up a hand.

"I would like to remind you that our stance here is defensive. We may not advance on the enemy."

Kennedy gripped his pencil a little tighter.

"That mindset has created complacency in the Olympians," he said. "They launch an attack every six hours along at least two sectors, with no unit attacking twice in the same twenty-four-hour window."

Heywood waved him off.

"I'm aware of this, Comrade Captain. Their attacks have become predictable but have allowed Higher to shift resources around to blunt them."

Kennedy held up a finger.

"It has also given us a clear window into when certain units are vulnerable." He pointed to the cohort directly across from them. "This unit and its adjacent units attacked us a day ago. Soon, they will attack the Booker Battalion to our west. As soon as their attack ceases, they'll be vulnerable while they refit."

Heywood scowled.

"Are you proposing we create a salient in the center of the enemy line? We'd be destroyed the second they counterattacked."

Kennedy shook his head.

"No, I'm proposing a raid. While they refit, second-line personnel will be at the front." He pointed to their own lines. "I propose taking a couple platoons of infantry to capture these second-line personnel, and to protect them, I will go myself with a detachment of three machines."

Heywood scratched at his chin.

"We captured a half dozen pilots after the last battle, not one of them has yielded us any information we didn't already know, and didn't you open this conversation talking about supplies?"

Kennedy folded his arms behind his back.

"The pilots are soldiers first," he said. "Why memorize where an ammo dump is when all the ammo they need is brought to them?"

"So you think if we capture support personnel, we can get good intel out of them?"

Kennedy gave him a quick north-south with his head.

"I believe they won't have nearly the same SERE training as warfighters," he replied. "They'll know more information and break easily. Heywood looked at the matrix again. We don't even need to send infantry or Panzerters, we just need their location so artillery or bombers can attack them."

Heywood looked at the matrix again and sighed.

"I can't authorize your mission with the forces you asked for.

Cut it to a couple of squads of infantry and just yourself and a wingman."

Kennedy clenched his jaw but didn't protest.

"Roger, Comrade, I can make that work," he said. *If nothing else, it'll be easier to move with fewer personnel.*

"In that case, this operation has my full authorization. Good luck, Comrade Captain," Heywood said. "I'll inform my infantry companies and have personnel selected for you."

Kennedy saluted.

"Roger. I'll get things done." He left the man's office and made his way to the Panzerter hangar that serviced his machines. The Jupiter gleamed in the white light, its gold and black armor shimmering brightly. The damage from the previous battle had already been repaired. *Compared to the Martians, the Jupiter looks like it owns a gym membership.*

"Comrade Captain, how was your briefing with Colonel Heywood!" Fletcher ran to greet him, Ballard trudging behind her.

Kennedy sighed.

"It went. My mission was authorized but with half the personnel I requested."

Fletcher pouted.

"How dare he? Is he trying to enable our reactionary enemies?"

Kennedy glanced at Ballard.

"I take it you haven't gotten her to talk normally?"

Ballard shrugged.

"I tried telling her to dial it back. She accused me of enabling class traitors."

Fletcher stuck her tongue out at him.

"And you're a misogynist!"

Ballard shrugged again, holding up his hands.

Kennedy sighed.

"Fletcher, let's talk about the way you address others. I know you're passionate about fighting the good fight, but not everyone here wants to talk about Unionism all the time." He looked over at Ballard. "In fact, most like to gripe about their current situation."

She folded her arms.

"I don't see why I need to change my behavior to cater to others."

"Then why should you expect others to cater to you?"

She blinked.

"Because I'm a MAG officer and they aren't."

Kennedy grinned.

"So you're asserting your class privilege?"

Her jaw dropped and her face went red.

Kennedy pointed to a group of soldiers looking up at a Martian Trooper. "Here, try talking to those guys. Just walk up to the group and say, 'man, this is bullshit, am I right?' And you can't say 'class traitor' or 'reactionary.'"

She huffed and stamped off towards the group.

Ballard stood next to him.

"She was from the far Northern Front, right?"

Kennedy leaned back and nodded.

"They sent most of the crusader types up there. It's like a holy war to them, reclaiming Roosevelt."

"And here?" Ballard asked.

Kennedy looked down.

"They tended to pick leaders who had a personal vendetta against Tharsis, leaders like my former commander." Kennedy looked south. "Enough of this. I have an operation to prepare for."

———

PAUL REITER LEANED OVER THE PROJECTION BEFORE THEM. THE map displayed an island in the center of the largest branch of the river. The island's position made it the centerpiece of the Unionist's line in the region. It was also the regiment's ultimate target.

"So as you can see here, our last target in this thrust is this firebase, codenamed Objective Mauler," he said. "We've got a lot of ground to cover between here and Mauler."

Comidus, Bartonova, the infantry's acting platoon sergeant Decimus, and Adamski all huddled around the map with him.

"It looks like we got seven miles of rough terrain and river crossings to get to Mauler," Comidus said. "For now, the rivers are an asset for us with attack boats and other river-borne assets, but that'll change once the rivers freeze."

Reiter nodded. Even as they spoke, more attack boats were being built, as well as larger assault barges. *If we can get the barges down the river, then that firebase won't be defensible.*

"Our next objective will be upriver of Riverside," Reiter said. "We're going to secure a route for the assault barges to attack Mauler, but we'll accomplish several smaller objectives before the attack, all of which will make the assault on Mauler much easier."

He pointed to the town they had probed the previous day. Floodgate was held by Union regulars and not the elite units Fox had previously faced. They had also been shaken by the probing attack.

"Floodgate is our objective again, but this time we're going to take the town," Reiter said. He pointed to the branches of the river. "Think of the river delta as a highway Floodgate sits on an important junction on our path to Objective Mauler."

Comidus looked over the map and pointed.

"Now we need to lay out our plan of attack," he said. "Once we take Floodgate, the defensive line will move to hold the new position, so we only need to hold the town for roughly six hours."

Adamski leaned over the table, a lit cigarette in his hand.

"We did considerable damage to the town in the last battle. We want the riverfront intact, if not the entire town." He dumped his ashes into an empty energy drink can. "Boss, do you think you and Bartonova can draw them out of the city?"

Reiter scratched at his chin.

"I don't want to read too much into their intent," he said, "but if we attack them from long-range, the way I see it, they have two choices: rush out to root us out, or dig in and get shot." He shook his head. "I don't like option two; it forces us to destroy chunks of the city."

Comidus looked concerned.

"If they figured out where you two were shooting from, then they've probably got it marked for artillery," he said. "That and we haven't seen their dropships in a while."

As she looked at the map, Bartonova traced a line from Floodgate to just past where Gold Platoon had staged their OPs the previous day.

"You guys had a pretty excellent line of sight through here, right, Lieutenant Comidus?" she asked.

The infantryman wiggled his hand in the universal gesture for "more or less."

"Yeah, we could see most of the town from there."

Reiter raised an eyebrow.

"What do you got, Bartonova?" he asked.

She tapped on a position past the OP area.

"We'll have a good line of sight through here. We can lay down supporting fire and force them to confront us."

Reiter tapped his upper lip.

"And if we force them into this open ground, the two teams can ambush them," he said. "Once their Panzerters are out of commission, we can attack the town in a pincer with Gold Platoon." He looked around the table. "Are there any objections to this plan?" They all shook their heads. "Are we sure?"

"I just have one question," Comidus said. "Do we have a spot to cross the river?"

Reiter looked at the map and shrugged.

"I got nothing. All I can say is find a place to ford it."

"I don't like that at all," Comidus replied. "The nearest place to ford the river could be miles upstream,"

Reiter massaged his temples. *He has a point. It would be best for him and his people to be carried across the river, but what about our ambush?*

He leaned over the map before swatting himself on the head. *I have more assets than just what's in my company.*

"I can't believe I didn't think of this sooner, but we have Bravo Battery from the 56th Artillery regiment providing fire support." He pointed to the former OPs on the map. "We can bracket this for an artillery barrage. While the big guns do the heavy lifting, the maneuver group crosses with Gold Platoon."

Comidus smirked.

"I like this version better. We're vulnerable during the crossing, but it should be quick," he said.

After tying up any last-minute logistical concerns, Reiter determined they would attack in two days.

"One last order of business: we'll form a triangle once we've secured the town. Myself, Comidus, and Adamski will take up the corners, with units dispersed along the edges."

Adamski raised a hand.

"What if Bartonova took your spot and you stood in the center?" he said. "That way, you and the Lowe are protected while being able to reinforce any section of the perimeter."

Reiter scratched his head.

"Yeah, I can't argue with that. Anyone got anything else?" Everyone shook their head. "Dismissed."

Reiter left the conference room and returned to his own quarters. He took his time in the shower, letting the warm water wash over him. After changing into his evening clothes, he lay back in his desk chair. He spun himself back and forth for a moment before reaching for his book.

He'd borrowed it from the school library. *The Dark Below* was a horror novel, centered on the demise of a seafloor mining crew. Reiter had always feared Earth's Oceans, despite having never been to Earth. They were so vast and still very much unexplored. Through the words on paper, he was able to let his mind go somewhere else. Somewhere he wasn't responsible for every death.

THE JUPITER STALKED FORWARD, CROSSING THE SCARRED landscape that lay between Union lines and the Olympian border. Three hundred meters to Kennedy's left was a Martian Trooper. Six hundred meters to his right, two squads of Pacifican regulars crawled through ditches and under barbed wire. The stars hung in the sky, numerous and beautiful.

I'd appreciate the ocean hanging over my head more if I wasn't in the middle of a raid. He'd insisted on strict radio silence. It wasn't because the Olympians stood any chance of breaking their encryption, but rather the radio waves could be easily detected and triangulated.

A light flashed three times in his direction. The regulars were in position and ready to attack. It was up to him now to initiate fires. He took aim with his shoulder cannon.

Instead of Panzerters and infantry in prepared positions recuperating from an offensive, Kennedy saw rows of tents, stacks of crates, and men smoking in the open. *Did we get lost?* Then it clicked for him. He'd beaten the Olympians back to their line, passed it, and arrived in their rear area.

He focused his cannon on the nearest cluster of tents. The Jupiter buckled. The Olympians never heard the shell. Tents were thrown everywhere. Kennedy heard his comrades' rifle chatter nearby. He switched his laser to strobe.

Green light danced through the encampment. An ammo cache went up in a mushroom cloud. The ground shook. Tents burst into flames.

This isn't a battle. A Panzerter under repair collapsed in a molten heap. *This is a slaughter.*

An Olympian Panzerter escaped its bay. It staggered forward, one of its ankles not repaired. Its shield arm was missing, and its other arm held a gladius.

It charged, gladius held high. Kennedy's laser worked like a surgical knife. The Olympian lost its good arm. Then its head. It swayed, its balance lost with its mass. A last burst. Center of mass.

The Olympian's heart glowed orange, then blossomed. Suddenly, it became the sun. His cameras blacked out to protect his eyes. An alarm blared. Radiation. *Shit.* Kennedy's CBRN system kicked in. The air became stale and stuffy in his cockpit.

"First and Third Squads, fall back. The radiation will cook you if you don't get away now!"

The infantry's response was garbled and filled with static, probably due to the radiation in the air.

"Roger, Reaper. We got what we came for; we're already on our way back."

Kennedy grinned in his cockpit. *This couldn't have gone better!*

"Roger, we'll mop up here and head back." He and his wingman, Bournival, walked through the area, destroying anything that looked intact. Comms arrays melted. They smashed radar equipment. Fuel burned. They destroyed dropships attempting to take off.

The pair began crossing the sea of flames when the infantry called back.

"Reaper, you got Panzerters headed your way; they're booking it."

Kennedy's grin wavered.

"How many?"

"You've got six, including a nasty-looking one we haven't seen before."

A new model? I hope it's not something comparable to the Jupiter.

"Thank you, gents. I'll see you on the other side." Kennedy killed the channel, lest the infantry be found. "Bournival, we've got six coming our way. I'll establish fire; you maneuver." The plan made sense. His wingman's Martian Trooper was far more mobile than the heavy Jupiter.

"Roger, Comrade!"

Kennedy saw them crest a low hill. Six, just like the riflemen said. Five were of the type that they had fought the previous day. The sixth one was new. It used a similar chassis to the others, but it carried no shield. Instead, it wielded some kind of heavy weapon.

Kennedy fired his shoulder cannon. An old model collapsed. Bournival opened up with his rifle. Both added their lasers to the mix. *We need to keep this up. At long-range, we have the advantage.*

Then the new model opened fire. So many tracers filled the air that it looked like a single twinkling red line. Kennedy watched in horror as they walked onto Bournival. The flashing light of the tracers illuminated the Martian's death.

Kennedy took a shot. The Olympians shielded their comrade. He charged. The laser whistled down their numbers. The new model opened fire again. This time targeting him.

The Jupiter rocked and groaned. Kennedy's head rattled against his chair from the impacts. He fired his laser wildly. The impacts lessened.

The Olympian attempted to use its weapon one-handed. Its other arm hung from the weapon. Shells still struck Kennedy, but they were bearable now.

He steadied himself and fired. Green light dissected the Olympian machine. Molten metal splattered on the ground. The Olympian collapsed in a smoldering wreck.

He surveyed the battlefield. Bournival's machine lay broken and scattered. Kennedy walked towards the downed machine looking for its pilot, but found nothing. His own Panzerter had taken an absolute pummeling. His shoulder cannon was offline and his armor breached in several places.

Dawn was coming when he limped back past his own lines. He informed the tech teams his machine would need decontaminating along with himself. After a chemical shower and a radiation screening, Heywood summoned him to his office.

"You need me, Comrade Colonel?"

Heywood nodded.

"Sit down, Kennedy. We'll be here a minute," he said. Kennedy stared at the open chair in the office and nodded. His eyes hurt. "We were able to get a lot of good intel out of your raid, and from what I hear, better."

"Yeah, it turns out we blundered into one of their rear areas by mistake," Kennedy replied. "We didn't let it go to waste."

Heywood nodded.

"That you did, but you've also set a dangerous precedent."

Kennedy furrowed his brow.

"I don't follow, Comrade Colonel," he said.

Heywood's jaw tightened.

"I'm willing to bet you didn't see the markings, because it was dark, but you destroyed their field surgical hospital," the older man said.

Through all his fatigue, all his soreness, Kennedy's stomach turned to ice. He opened his mouth to speak, but no words came. All he could do was look at his hands.

"I-I had no idea." *I'm a war criminal.*

Heywood sighed.

"When I heard, I was prepared to have you relieved, but your superiors had other ideas." He rose from his desk and approached Kennedy, who flinched when the older man jerked the Guard Captain rank off his shoulder. Then Heywood slapped a new rank in its place.

I don't want to look down. I'm probably a private now.

Kennedy glanced at his sleeve. A Guard Major rank hung on the velcro strap. Kennedy's mouth dropped. He looked at Heywood. Unable to speak, he simply mouthed, "Why?"

"Your superiors made a good argument. You've done more to hurt the Olympian war effort than anyone else." He walked past his desk to the window. "Besides, we got their encryption library. Soon their communications will be open to us." Without looking back, Heywood dismissed him.

Kennedy made it to the stairwell before grabbing the railing. He couldn't tell if his legs shook from fatigue or horror. *Well, the gloves are off now. The wounded are no longer off-limits.* Kennedy looked at his hands. All he could see were the hands of a murderer.

THE LOWE CROUCHED IN A COPSE OF TREES ACROSS FROM Floodgate. Reiter propped the Lowe on its arms, forming a tripod with them and its bent legs. He had set the 88-mm rifle on the ground in front of him.

"Alright, Valkyrie, I'm about to set my range," he said. He lowered his targeting computer and sighted in on the nearest building. Turning to his map, he pulled his handy bootlace from its magnet clamp and measured the distance. "I'm calling it 3,600 meters."

"Roger, 6, adjusting sights," she replied.

Reiter looked back at his map.

"Bravo 6, are your guns sighted in?"

"Roger, Fox 6, we're standing by for fire mission." They had used the coordinates from Gold Platoon's OPs and LPs to orient the guns of Bravo Battery. Now a large part of the field was bracketed for an artillery barrage. Reiter unbuckled his restraints and waited.

"Fox 6, Fox 7," Adamski said. "We're in position and prepared to cross the river north of the city."

Good, everything is coming together so far.

"Roger, 7, we're about to initiate," Reiter replied. He buckled himself back in, having learned his lesson before, and pulled his targeting computer down. Their probing attack had reduced the enemy's numbers to six Panzerters. Three patrolled the perimeter, while three more knelt in parking lots around town.

"Valkyrie, got your target?" he asked.

"The one on the west end." Her Panzerter lay prone about 300 meters to his left.

"Roger. I'll get this guy closest to us." He zoomed in on his target. Bringing his crosshairs down, he centered on the Cyclops's pelvis. *We can probably get some decent spare parts out of this.*

The Panzerter's knees swung inward. The Unionist collapsed on its face. Across town, another Cyclops fell without its head. The hornet's nest had been kicked.

IFVs raced out of town and began crossing the field. The last standing Cyclops took cover and returned fire. Bartonova began picking off IFVs while Reiter waited for the railgun to recharge. *Just a little more time. We need the Cyclopes to come out here.*

Reiter fired again. An IFV vanished in a shower of smoke and metal. *That was excessive. I should save the railgun for Panzerters.*

The other Cyclopes were active now, making their way towards him and Bartonova.

"Hold your fire, Valkyrie."

The Cyclopes advanced with IFVs roaming ahead of them. They crossed into the field.

Reiter let them get halfway across.

"Bravo 6, fire for effect." He heard the rolling thunder of the guns in the distance. Shells fell like rain in the field. IFVs were cast about. The Cyclopes fell under the weight of the fire. When the storm of steel subsided, not one Unionist remained standing.

"Fox 7, you're clear to seize Floodgate," Reiter said. He unbuckled his restraints and stretched. *Now it's all on the others.* He patted the cockpit wall. "We're not going to be able to keep you secret for much longer."

After a few brief firefights, Gold Platoon and the Panzerter teams had secured Floodgate. Attack boats arrived from Riverside. Some pulled into the docks, but others followed the forks to conduct recon.

Reiter strapped in and brought the Lowe to a standing position. Retrieving his rifle, he and Bartonova walked over to town. His position secure, Reiter surveyed his surroundings.

"Fox 6, this is PB-26. You've got Unionist reinforcements bearing down on you from west-southwest."

Reiter grit his teeth.

"Roger, 26, thanks for the heads up." He switched back to his company channel. "We got Unis headed our way. Everyone buckle up." He reoriented his forces on the threat. "White Platoon, we'll fall in and support you. Fox 7, go with Black Platoon and flank them."

He saw them moving through the trees. Ten gray tinhats supported by two dropships. *Damn, elite forces.* Reiter took a knee and readied the railgun.

The dropships swooped low, unleashing missiles. White Platoon returned fire, along with Bartonova. Reiter took aim at the nearest tinhat. His first shot tore the unit's legs off. The railgun vented heat and began recharging.

Nearby, Merlin's machine collapsed, its knee a molten glob.

"What was that?" the young soldier cried.

"Stay in your machine and play dead!" Reiter replied. He picked another target and fired. Another tinhat fell, a gaping hole in its lower torso. *Those lasers will wreck this weapon, and I don't know if we could replace it.* Cautiously, he stowed the railgun.

Szilard's Panzerter collapsed in a screech of metal. Smoke poured from the machine as it burned. *Damn it.* Reiter slid his shield off its mount on his left shoulder and into his hand. Rifle in hand, he emerged from cover.

A dropship fell past him in a ball of fire. Reiter opened up on the advancing tinhats. His burst jammed an arm on one. It swung toward him, laser ready. Its laser pulsed, but the Lowe was unaffected. No damage registered.

A predatory grin bloomed on Reiter's face.

"You guys just walked all over us." He dropped his rifle and drew his sword. A metallic blade extended before being bathed in a blue light. He charged the nearest tinhat. "At first we could barely stop you."

The tinhat fired again. Its invisible beam struck his shield. No damage. It raised its hand in an attempt to stop him. The sword cleaved through its forearm and the entire unit behind it, head to groin.

"By day five, you'd killed a whole platoon." He rushed another tinhat. This one drew a mace. It made no difference; the gray machine was too slow to parry his blows. "How does it feel, Unis?"

Reiter turned towards another. Green flashed. Reiter's shield hand melted as he pulled back for a swing. His sword went through the tinhat's shoulder before it went through the top of its head. "How does it feel to be on the receiving end!"

The remaining tinhats fled. They were hammered by fire from Black Platoon as they ran. As his blood cooled, Reiter checked his company. Merlin was wounded, but it was nothing major. No one could raise Szilard on the net. He feared the worst for the young man.

Removing his helmet, he put his head in his hands.

Where did all that come from? It occurred to Reiter that he hadn't really had time to grieve, to process all the losses up to now. Legousi, Varga, Stanca, Gordos, Septimus, the platoon from Early Company. *I'd known these people for years, and it makes me wonder, how did they do it?* He picked up his helmet and stared into the reflection in his visor. *More importantly, how will I do it?*

15

K ennedy stood at attention with his company. The recently repaired Jupiter stood proudly behind him. Its gold and black paint gleamed under the late autumn sun. He waited patiently in front of his company as Heywood approached him.

"For incredible valor, cunning, and perseverance in the face of the enemy, the chairman of the Union of Martian Republics has recognized Guard Major Declan Kennedy as worthy of the Order of the Republics, First Class." Heywood's XO read the order while Heywood himself clipped the medal to Kennedy's collar.

"You know what this means now, Comrade Major," he said.

Kennedy nodded subtly. *It's either win or die. If we lose the war and I'm alive, I'll be tried as a war criminal.*

He saluted Heywood as he stepped back. The older man returned his salute and turned around.

After the ceremony, Kennedy met Heywood in his office. He'd already reviewed the bounty of information they had gained from the captives the infantryman took. He couldn't help but notice the dirty look the XO gave him as he passed him on the stairs.

Shaking it off, he entered Heywood's office.

"You needed to see me, Comrade Colonel?"

The man rotated in his chair.

"Yeah, as much as it pains me to admit it, your recommendation makes the most sense out of those of my sub-commanders."

Kennedy blinked.

"What did they recommend?" he asked.

Heywood waved him off.

"They don't think we need to change our stance. They all believe that the Olympians will stick to their pattern."

"You disagree?"

Heywood nodded.

"I do. Your little escapade disrupted their pattern, and they know your Panzerter's section of the line, so yeah, I believe we're due for a massive counterattack." He relaxed into his chair. "And since you're not part of the groupthink, I'd like you to assist in planning our defense."

Kennedy nodded.

"I see. Guard Colonel Chaney told me we received some more equipment. Have we?" he asked.

The corners of Heywood's mouth turned up slightly in his best imitation of a smile.

"That is correct. Our old Terran IIIs are off to the scrapheap. Our mere regulars are now piloting the same Martian Troopers as your lot." He pulled out a small tablet. "We also have flash mines, flamethrowers, even a few man-portable chemlasers."

Kennedy walked over to the map.

"How long do we have until they can attack our sector again?"

"At best, 24 hours."

Kennedy pointed out in front of their lines.

"They'll attack in the middle of the night. We need those flash mines planted and a skirmish line set up ahead of our own."

Heywood looked up from his chair.

"Your Panzerters have searchlights, correct?" Kennedy nodded. "I want all our pilots to flash them before attacking, disrupt their night vision." Heywood shook his head. "Those Onager units are nasty."

"We'll have to deal with them from the air. I got lucky against the one I saw, but the best way to deal with them I can think of would be sending drone after drone to attack them."

Heywood sighed and stood.

"I don't know if we'll be able to get enough drone coverage to sustain that," he said. "It'd be more practical to identify them and try to destroy them with artillery." He looked at the map. "Or just combine the two, use artillery and air to pick off those problematic units."

Kennedy traced a finger along the angle of attack.

"I assume we're going to try to drive them into the infantry positions?"

Heywood shot a glance upward and gave an affirmative.

Kennedy looked back at the map. The image of a man covered in bandages came to the forefront of his mind. "Their pattern may be broken in another sense."

"How do you figure?"

Kennedy pointed to the area he'd raided.

"We not only destroyed a field hospital, but their surgical unit." He spread his hands. "They may be eager for revenge, but they may not be able to launch an attack on account of a lot more of their wounded ending up dying."

Heywood shrugged.

"Well, we'll plus up our security tonight and see what happens." The commander turned towards Kennedy and waved him off. "You're dismissed, Major."

Kennedy walked out of the building as quickly as possible and headed to his barracks to brief his company.

Snow flurries danced by him as he walked. He stopped to watch. Born in the gray sky above, the individual flakes joined together and drifted toward the ground. They couldn't stay there; the ground was too warm for them to stand, and they perished.

Someone said no two flakes are alike. He looked at his hands. *I wonder if there's another tuber that looks like me.* Kennedy didn't often think about the circumstances of his birth. It was . . . uncomfortable. He folded his hands together and continued walking.

I wonder if they recycle, if at some point in time, there was another tuber who looked just like me, had the same experiences. A flurry stung his cheeks before melting. *I wonder if I'll die the same way they did.*

He caught a glimpse of himself in the reflection of a storefront window. *I wonder who my gene donors are. Do I look like them? Sound like them? How many were there?*

He walked into the barracks. After finding Ballard in the rec room, he asked him to round up the company. As his subordinate sauntered off, Kennedy couldn't help but observe his features. *Do we look like siblings? Do we share donors? If we do, how many?*

He shook his head and waited in the rec room. *I can't dwell on all that. I need to keep my head clear.* Soon, all of his soldiers had gathered in the rec room. *Enough existential nonsense; time to be a leader.*

"We have reason to believe an Olympian counterattack is going to hit us in the middle of the night," he said. "I want all of you to bed down right now and set your alarms for nightfall. We'll be on standby all night. Any questions?" A pilot raised her hand. "Yes?"

"Does this have anything to do with last night's raid?" she asked.

Kennedy nodded.

"We believe so. Now go get some shut eye. Dismissed."

As the pilots left for bed, an image crossed Kennedy's mind: a pile of bodies, all identical to his. Kennedy shuddered. He wasn't sure if he was going to be able to sleep at all.

REITER SANK INTO HIS MAKESHIFT HAMMOCK. THE OLD STORAGE room attached to the GCT hangars served as a makeshift ready room. A whiteboard hung on the wall with their names, Panzerters, and operational status. All of Fox Company's pilots occupied the room. They were on standby in case something happened.

Reiter held his book in his hand. In the corner across from him, Smith, Mo, Adamski, and Merlin played Spades. Closer to where Reiter was lying, Unger and Bartonova worked on a puzzle. Steele was out picking up their lunch.

"Merlin, what the hell? Why would you cut me?" Mo asked.

The younger soldier raised his hands.

"What do you mean? I played the best card I had!"

"We already won that hand," Mo said as he grabbed the cards. "You wasted a spade we might need later." Adamski and Smith snickered. Seconds later, Reiter heard moans from Mo and Merlin. "Merlin, you're letting team M down."

Adamski confidently took the hand.

"I hope you're not gambling down there, gents," Reiter said.

"None of that down here, boss, only good clean fun," Adamski replied. "At least if you're on team Smoker's Teeth." He high-fived Smith.

Reiter shook his head and returned to his book. He quickly became lost in the ocean of his mind, the words of his soldiers blending together outside of his notice. Completely immersed in his book, he didn't hear Steele return.

"Sir, sir." His mind imagined rocking waves when she pushed on his hammock. "Excuse me, sir."

Reiter glanced over to see the top half of Steele's face peering at him.

"Oh, sorry, Steele. You have food?"

She nodded and handed him a white box.

"Stuffed peppers, roast potato, and steamed broccoli."

Reiter took his paperware and drink from her. She had picked up a citrus energy drink for him in addition to his food. He sat up slightly so he wouldn't spill anything.

"Thank you, Steele," he said.

Everyone began echoing him as Steele went around delivering their food. She plopped down on a hammock near his side of the room. The guys went back to playing Spades, and the room grew quiet as everyone ate and resumed what they had been doing.

A klaxon went off. Reiter shoved his box onto a shelf near him and rolled out of the hammock. The ready room erupted into chaos. He threw on his boots and laced them. The Spades game ground to a halt.

"Go, go, go!" Adamski hollered as they rushed out of the ready room, grabbing their helmets off the rack.

They flooded into the hangar. Reiter, Bartonova, and Black Platoon broke left while Adamski and White Platoon ran right. Mechanics ran about on the hangar floor below them.

Reiter swung into the Lowe. Throwing himself into his seat, he whipped his restraints on. He clipped his helmet with one hand while running through his startup sequence with the other. His gauges lit up, and his monster came to life.

The gangway in front of him receded. A mechanic on the floor waved two glowing rods. He guided Reiter out of his berth, onto the main road out of the dome.

Reiter opened the radio net.

"Fox Company, check in."

"Fox 7, checking in." Adamski fell in behind him.

"Valkyrie, checking in." Bartonova fell in on Reiter's 7 o'clock.

"Gold 1, all tracks are up."

"White 1, checking in." Steele fell in behind Adamski.

"White 2, checking in." Merlin offset himself from Steele and fell in behind her.

"White 5, checking in." Zorro fell in directly behind Steele, but farther back than Merlin.

"Black 1, checking in." *It's still weird hearing Mo use my old call sign.* Mo fell in ahead of Bartonova.

"Black 2, checking in." Unger positioned herself in front of Reiter but gave Mo some room.

"Black 5, checking in." Smith took point.

The tracks rolled by. An IFV placed itself behind each Panzerter, with the missile carriers being split between the two teams. Comidus's vehicle fell in between Reiter and Adamski.

"Shepherd 6, Fox 6. Fox Company is up, ready for orders." Now they waited. Reiter tightened his grip on the control sticks. He could hear his pulse in his head.

"Roger, Fox 6. Stand by."

Reiter exhaled slowly. *Great, more waiting.* Now that they were operating out of GCT, this felt different. Before, combat was something that happened to them. Little warning, little anticipation. Retreating in Panzerters felt hardly different from driving Panzerters around, which he'd done a weekend a month and half a month in the summer.

But things were different now. They were headed into battle. Into the unknown. It was no longer something that happened to them as much as something they did to others. He bounced his leg nervously and tightened his grip.

Shit, I got to ease this tension somehow. "How are we doing, everyone?" he asked the company.

"I need to pee," Merlin cried.

He heard Steele groan into the radio.

"Why didn't you go before now?" she asked.

"Because I pounded an energy drink on my way out the door!" he replied.

"You got a bottle handy, kid?" Adamski asked. "Because it sounds like you're going to have to piss in a bottle."

"I don't have an empty one handy!" Merlin cried. Reiter shook his head.

"Well, the simple thing would be to pop your hatch, dump one out, then pee," Mo said.

"Just please close your hatch before you pee," Unger said.

"What are you saying? You're in front of me! Just keep your eyes forward!" Merlin's voice sounded distant and airy. Silence fell over the net for a moment. Then Merlin came back on. "Thanks To-er-Fox 7."

Adamski chuckled.

"Don't mention it, kid. Just throw that bottle out when we get back, otherwise your cockpit will reek," he said.

"You didn't even need to pee in a bottle. You could have just popped the hatch and done your business," Comidus added. "All of nature's our urinal!"

"With all due respect, Gold 1, I don't believe White 2 is coordinated enough to do his business and not either piss all over his machine or fall out," Smith said.

Laughter filled the net until the regiment came back to Reiter.

"Stand down, Fox. Early Company has this."

Reiter sighed.

"Roger, I got you, Lima Charlie." He switched back to his company net. "Pack it in, people. We're back on standby."

MARSHAL SKARA CLENCHED HIS FISTS AS HE STARED AT THE MAP IN front of him. The Olympians had met the Union in battle and failed to move them. The Northern Front sat unmoving, and III Corps crawled forward in the west. He had integrated what was left of the Roosevelt General Staff into his own organization, though the government-in-exile's forces did little to augment his position on the surface.

"Starnes, remind me the next time I meet with Madame President that we need more allies," he said.

The major adjusted his glasses.

"Well, sir, the Central Alliance would make a lot less sense as a name if, say, Lowell or Tsushima joined our cause."

Skara shook his head.

"We need to dogpile the Union. If we don't get more allies, the Union will just manufacture more soldiers!" he spat. He looked back at the map. "Especially the First Nation and Plata—we need them to get involved."

Starnes made a few notes on his pad. Then he changed the image. Now the projector displayed a column of separate line graphs. Some had two lines. One said "Steel mined" and "Steel available for production," with the bottom axis titled "Days since the war started."

"Von Braun's plan to starve the Union seems to be working," Starnes said. "If this drags on, they won't be able to manufacture enough weapons to go with their dolls."

Skara looked through the charts. Occasionally he touched one to get a better look.

"So, they're going to get desperate to win the war too," he said.

The accident with Isle of March crossed his mind. *What if we evacuated an older colony, one in disrepair, and deorbited it on a course for Foundation?* At first, Skara believed they had to do it before the Union did it to them. Ultimately, he dismissed the idea, though the thought of Foundation flattened by a massive cylinder tickled him. *Besides the international relations toll, they still have to live on the surface, just like we do.*

"Oh and you might want to see this, sir." Starnes slid his tablet into his hands.

Skara narrowed his eyes.

"What am I looking at? An asteroid?"

Starnes pulled up the image on the projector. Now Skara could make out docks and other facilities.

"This is a celestial object that was moved into the Martian gravity well, large enough that it's creating a new set of LaGrange points," Starnes explained. "Avalon moved it into the system recently, but it looks like they've been building on it for a long time."

Skara nodded.

"So the Boreal pact just keeps moving shit into our gravity well so they have more moons?" He looked back at Starnes. "It sounds like they're worried about losing Phobos to me." He looked back at the image. "This doesn't change our policy: Union first."

Starnes tapped on his tablet.

"Well, speaking on the subject of the Union . . ."

Skara was treated to a raging inferno. He saw shapes moving through the flames. A burning tarp with a red cross on it fluttered past his view.

"This footage is from the X Legion nerve center," said Starnes. "A Union raid turned into a massacre."

Skara grimaced.

"How bad is it?" he asked.

Starnes paused the footage. A chart replaced it on the projector.

"Forty-five hundred dead, twenty-seven hundred wounded,

according to the latest estimates, including Comodre," he said. "And a lot of those wounded will end up dying. That field hospital included the surgical center for the entire front."

Skara sat down.

"So this is what they've come to, huh? Committing war crimes? I'm honestly tempted to authorize attacks on their hospitals ourselves, but I have a better idea." He leaned back in his seat and folded his arms.

"And that is, sir?" Starnes asked.

Skara grinned.

"We can publish this footage, use it as propaganda. It'll silence the anti-war crowd and drive recruitments," he said. "That'll give our manpower pool quite a boost."

Starnes thought about it and nodded.

"On top of that, our diplomats can probably leverage this to force neutral countries to stop trading with the Union or Avalon." Starnes glanced at his tablet. "You were going to meet with the Olympian leadership out west two weekends from now. Would you like me to move that up?"

Skara nodded.

"Yes, I would. We need to execute this pincer before our rivers freeze and we lose our advantage in the west," he said. "It'll be a pain, but I may be able to give overall command of the front to Virilus."

Starnes moved a few meetings around.

"Madame President is addressing Congress on Thursday. She's requested you to be present."

Skara nodded and raised his hand.

"Tell her I'll be there. I'm always willing to make time for the president," the marshal said. "I need to talk to her about getting more allies, anyway." Skara paused. "Starnes, get Markos in here, time now."

"You need him for something, sir?" Starnes asked.

Skara nodded.

"I need him for a diplomatic mission."

Nervously, Starnes paged the commander of the cyber division.

Within minutes, the overweight man was in Skara's war room.

"You asked to meet with me, Marshal?"

Skara motioned for him to sit down.

"I did, in fact. How much access do you have to the Union's networks?"

"Well, if we're looking at surface systems, forty-five percent, but overall access is about twelve percent."

Skara rubbed his chin.

"Do you have access to their war plans?" he asked.

"More or less," Markos replied. "We got their plans pertaining to us as well as a few neutral countries."

"Good, I want those countries and the plans for them," Skara said.

"What do you want with that information?" Markos asked.

Slowly, a predatory smile spread across Skara's features.

"Well, that's easy. I want it doctored up, made to look like their next move after beating our little republic will be to gobble up smaller countries," he explained. "It's not like we're lying, more like we're only telling half the truth."

KENNEDY RECLINED IN A CAMP CHAIR. HIS JUPITER SAT IN A Panzerter-sized foxhole, currently under repair. The Olympian attack had been vicious but short-lived. Both infantry companies were scrambling to repair their earthworks and fortifications. The Panzerter companies had been hammered pretty bad as well, but the introduction of the Martian Trooper kept losses low. *Red Steel Union is certainly going to be making a killing.*

Both of Kennedy's lieutenants sat near him, while a fire burned in the middle of their circle of chairs.

Fletcher scowled at Ballard as he puffed on a cigarette.

"You know those are bad for you," she said.

Ballard shrugged.

"It keeps me relaxed, and it keeps my insides warm." He took another long drag while Fletcher frowned.

"They're taking years off your life," she went on.

Ballard gave her a sad look.

"Do you really think any of us have a chance at a long lifespan? War notwithstanding." He tapped ashes onto the ground. "Even assuming I survive this, it's not like I'm going to live happily ever after."

Fletcher's face went red.

"Then why bother? Why join the Mobile Guards if you don't plan on enjoying life afterwards?" she asked.

Ballard blew smoke into the cold air.

"I joined simply because Comrade Major asked me too. All I've ever done is what I've been told." He flicked his cigarette to the side. The orange butt landed in wet mud. "Let me guess, you joined for reproductive rights? Or was it the right to vote?"

Fletcher faltered a bit.

"I'm-I'm not the one we're talking about," she said. She looked over to Kennedy. "Comrade Major, why did you join the guards?"

Kennedy opened his eyes and looked up.

"Well, I'm a Panzerter-class pilot template, so it was either MAG or the regular forces." He looked into the fire. "I figured if I was going to serve in an army, I might as well make it worth my while."

Fletcher straightened up a bit.

"And has it been worth it?" she asked.

Kennedy stared into the fire. It was probably just his imagination, but the burning papers reminded him of the burning hospital tents. He shrugged.

"It depends. Chaney sweetened the deal for me even more, but ever since that raid went awry, I've noticed our wounded a lot more than I used to."

Fletcher shook her head.

"Honestly, I can't believe that bothers you. They promoted you and gave you an award—what more could you want?"

Kennedy waved her off.

"I inadvertently made it okay for them to target our wounded, our field hospitals, our medical frigates in space. My actions have serious implications that go beyond this theater."

Ballard quickly intervened.

"You said Chaney sweetened the deal for you—what did you mean?" he asked.

Kennedy relaxed a bit.

"While I was healing, they undid the operation that sterilized me. To keep me loyal to the cause, they extended the right to hold office when I complete my service." Both the lieutenants' eyes went wide.

"What? That's historic! Revolutionary even!" Fletcher said.

Ballard eyed him a little more warily.

"Were you ever an ambitious individual?" he asked. Kennedy shook his head. "Then, what would you even do with that power?"

Kennedy shrugged.

"I have no idea, to be honest," he said.

To his surprise, Ballard laughed. It was dry and humorless.

Fletcher scowled.

"What's so funny?" she asked.

Ballard clapped.

"Do you not see it?" He motioned to Kennedy. "They offered political power to a tuber who will either not live to use it or choose not to use it!" His words stung, but they forced Kennedy to reflect on his life.

The only decision I've made for myself was the choice to be more comfortable later. He gazed into the fire, his thoughts far from his subordinates' squabbling. *All the choices I've made besides that were just me doing my job.* He folded his hands together. *Do I have a will of my own? Am I even an individual? Or just one of many?*

"Ballard, your cigarettes help you relax?" Kennedy finally said. His subordinates looked surprised.

"Yeah, they help. Do you want one?" Ballard asked.

Kennedy nodded, and the man handed him a long, thin cigarette. He leaned over, and Ballard gave him a light.

Fletcher shook her head.

"You disgust me," she spat at Ballard.

The man shrugged.

"It's not like I'll live long past this war, assuming I survive this war," he said as he lit another cigarette. Kennedy sharply inhaled the smoke, only to have a coughing fit. "You need to take it into your lungs, Comrade. You're holding it in your throat."

"You're so gross," Fletcher said.

Ballard shook his head.

"You've got plenty of life to live, Fletcher," he said. "You wouldn't get it."

Kennedy held his cigarette in one hand while he stared into the fire. *Ballard's right, she wouldn't get it.*

"Fletcher, why are you such a hardcore Unionist?" Kennedy asked.

Fletcher looked shocked.

"Well, why wouldn't I be?" she asked. "Unionism enabled my existence, *our existences,* in fact. We owe everything to Unionism."

Kennedy shook his head.

"You owe your existence to the *Union*, specifically the republic you came from," he said. "But then again, is our existence unique?"

Fletcher blinked, her mouth slightly ajar.

"What do you mean?" she asked.

Kennedy took another drag on his cigarette.

"You're you, but are you the first you? Are you even the only you?" he asked. "They made all of us once; they can make all of us again." He tossed his cigarette butt into the fire. "We're all aces— who's saying our performance wouldn't merit our DNA being copied? Why bother making new pilots when they can just keep making us over and over?"

Fletcher brought her legs to her chest and shuddered. Ballard's eyes went wide. Kennedy rested his head in his hands. *Was I maybe too harsh?* They sat in silence for a moment.

"You can change it, Comrade," Fletcher said.

Kennedy looked up at her.

"Say again?"

Fletcher curled up tighter.

"You can change things, make us equal to normal people."

Kennedy stared into the fire.

"Should I, though? Or should I stop the creation of tubers entirely?"

Fletcher scowled.

"That would make the Union no better than Tharsis. We're illegal there, remember?"

Kennedy looked at his hands. He didn't know if he wanted to follow that train of thought. Not yet, anyway.

16

"We're making excellent progress, but we're starting to run out of time," Reiter said as he and Adamski walked through the hangar. Repairs from their most recent battle were underway. For all its incredible durability, even the Lowe had taken considerable damage in the last engagement. Reiter sighed. *With even a moderate amount of damage, this thing takes forever to get repaired.*

"It's not all bad, we've actually done a decent job knocking the Union around." Adamski looked at his own machine receiving a new hand. "We've come a long way from just running away from them." He put a hand on Reiter's shoulder. "You're not failing, boss."

"Why do you say that? Ski, the enemy still occupies our homes!"

The other man shook his head.

"My parents got out, Mo's family got out, we've saved so many lives so far," he said. "The location may be in enemy hands, but the people that live there are safe."

Reiter nodded.

"You know, it's crazy sometimes to think how everything got out of control so fast," he said. "We stood up for mobilization so many times, I thought it was another false alarm."

"I know what you mean. We heard the same bullshit all the time. It was all too easy to let it go in one ear and out the other," Adamski said. "I didn't honestly think it would happen."

Reiter looked up at the Lowe.

"I honestly never thought of myself as a soldier. I went to the academy because it was free, and joining the Provincial Watch, well, that allowed me to control my own life," he admitted. "And then this shit pops off . . ."

"And you're suddenly in charge," Adamski finished. "Man, anyone would feel overwhelmed. Hell, who would have thought we'd lose our entire command team in a couple weeks?"

Reiter sighed and stared at the Lowe.

"It doesn't feel real—none of this does. We went from aging units in various states of disrepair to, well, this." He gestured up at the looming Panzerter in the bay. The machine's knightly visage seemed like it was always on guard. *Always ready, always there.* Reiter smiled when he thought of the Watch's motto.

"Level with me. Do you ever get imposter syndrome?" Adamski asked.

Reiter smiled.

"All the time, and I'm sure the other old hats do more or less as well." He pointed up at the Lowe's head. "You know, Ski, something's been bothering me. Why did they make it look like that?"

Adamski shrugged.

"You got me. Psychological impact? Better ballistic shaping?" He shrugged. "I mean, ancient knights wore armor like that for a reason. You know we can just ask the Lowe team, right?"

Reiter shrugged.

"I'm content speculating," he said. They sat quietly for a moment, the only sound the racket of tools and torches making repairs. "Szilard's father sent me a message."

Adamski raised an eyebrow.

"He did? That's the first I heard of a 'we regret to inform you' letter getting a reply. What did his old man say?"

Reiter hung his head.

"He wasn't angry. He didn't come across as anything I expected." He raised his hands. "The guy just sounded disappointed. He didn't yell, he was just . . ." Reiter shook his head.

Adamski patted him on the back.

"He can hardly be mad at you. The General Staff are the ones who asked for cadet volunteers, and Congress authorized it."

"I know, but Szilard specifically was my responsibility."

"The enemy killed him," Adamski said. "Do you think at some point we can blame enemy action for why our people die?"

"But if I did something different, if I did something better—"

"Boss, I got a lot of respect for you, but honestly it's dumb to agonize over every loss and blame yourself," Adamski said. "The enemy's out there trying to *kill* us."

Reiter shrugged and nodded.

"Well, I will not say you're wrong, Ski."

"If it helps you, put up pictures of our fallen in your cockpit. That way you can remind yourself of everything they took from us."

"I don't put things up besides our map, because I don't have a force tracker."

"Well, I have a bunch of pinups in my cockpit. I think you can make room."

Reiter shrugged.

"I guess I need to go print some pictures, then." He looked up at the Lowe. The towering metal giant loomed over them in the hangar. "And you know what, I have a spot for them in mind."

The hangar PA buzzed.

"Captain Reiter to the war room, please. Captain Reiter to the war room, please."

Reiter sighed.

"I guess I'll get around to it later," he said as he left. Reiter walked back to the cab dome containing the dorms. Gray clouds hung overhead as he walked through the chill air. His cheeks stung from the cold. The weather turned his mind towards their current operation.

We need to do more, faster. If the rivers freeze, we lose the boats and our advantage over the Union. But will it matter? The thought cut to his core faster than the freezing wind. *This will not be a quick war. It's not like we're going to win back our homes and stop there. Higher is going to want to drive into the Union so they can hit them with a harsher treaty.*

Reiter clenched his teeth. *But that would mean they learned nothing from 2112. If the Union can't stand the treaty, it'll lead to another war in twenty years.* A chill ran through him, but it had nothing to do with the wind.

Our politicians might not realize that, but I'm certain the Union does. Reiter chased the thought, much as it bothered him. *They know if the war ends, a treaty will just make Tharsis resentful.* He froze outside the door to the hab dome. *So the only way to prevent another war would be for them to dismantle Tharsis.*

He'd been teaching history long enough to recognize the pattern. *Our own people fled to this world after being dominated by a superpower not unlike the Union. Our ancestors swore to never let that happen again.* He looked at the ground beneath his feet. *This war isn't about politics; it's about our survival as a culture.*

"I DON'T THINK WE WILL BE NEEDED HERE MUCH LONGER," Kennedy said. He sat on a gangway overlooking their Panzerters with Ballard. Both of them smoked.

"What makes you think that?" the older man asked.

"Because their losses since that hospital attack have been atrocious. They haven't been able to maintain any offensive momentum since their surgical center was destroyed."

Ballard took a drag on his cigarette.

"You sound glad, almost relieved," he said.

"Does it concern you?" Kennedy asked.

Ballard nodded.

"It concerns me quite a bit. Don't get me wrong, I'd rather you didn't agonize over it at every waking moment, but I'm also glad you're not celebrating it, Comrade."

"I've been thinking, actually. I think we're too nice about the way we fight," Kennedy said before taking a drag on his cigarette. "If we didn't do things like that, like destroy hospitals or target civilians, then wars wouldn't drag on like they do."

"How do you figure?" Ballard asked.

"Look at the Olympians: one hospital gone and they can barely fight anymore. If we just did that right out the gate, we'd be having this conversation on the shores of the Mariner Sea or on the slopes of Olympos Mons," Kennedy said.

"Or we'd be having this conversation in Foundation before we hung," Ballard said. "If the gloves were off for both of us, there'd be nothing stopping them from doing it to us."

Kennedy sighed and let loose a cloud of smoke.

"Tharsis wouldn't give us the dignity of a hanging. They'd have a boot on our necks and a bullet in our heads," he said. "We're not even human to them, anyway."

"And if we just go around committing atrocity after atrocity, war crime after war crime, then we'll have justified their perception," Ballard countered.

"It doesn't matter what we do; that's all they will think of us," Kennedy said.

Ballard took a long drag on his cigarette before slowly releasing the smoke.

"What about our people? What will they think if we go around doing these things?" he asked.

"Would they even know?"

"If we acted like that and lost?" Ballard asked. "Yes, they definitely would. We'd be held up as examples of why you shouldn't allow artificial people to be made."

"They would say we shouldn't exist anyway," Kennedy said.

"I know that, but there's a nuance you're missing," Ballard said. "'Don't make artificial people' is radically different from 'don't make artificial people because you'll make soldiers that become monsters.'"

Kennedy sighed and puffed out smoke.

"We're already monsters to them," he said.

Ballard leaned back, smoke leaking out his mouth.

"But our people don't need to see us that way."

"Who do you mean when you say 'our people?' Other tubers? Other Unionists? Or do you mean natural-born Unionists?" Kennedy asked.

Ballard simply looked away.

"I was married once," he said.

Kennedy paused. *That's a hell of a shift in conversation.*

"What did she do?" he asked.

"She was a poet, and as you can probably gather, she was a natural."

"That's legal?"

Ballard nodded.

"Because her job lacked political power and I was in the army. Anyway, she got pregnant at 17 and had a daughter. Little thing was two years old when we got married."

Kennedy blinked.

"What happened?"

Ballard threw his cigarette butt aside.

"She was asked to go on an 'inspiration cruise'—it's something literature unions do now and again—but this time, they collided with a Tharcian cruiser. No survivors." He lit himself another cigarette.

"What about your daughter?" Kennedy asked.

Ballard stared up at his Panzerter.

"The courts took her from me," he finally said. "They said that, as a tuber, I had no claim to custody while she had a biological family that were still alive. In a sense, I lied to Fletcher the other night."

Kennedy raised an eyebrow.

"How so?" he asked.

"When I got the offer to join the MAG, I joined because I thought, if I had reproductive rights, I could fight for custody of her again." He looked right at Kennedy. "You have a good head on your shoulders for the most part, but I'm not following you to the gates of hell." He looked back at his machine. "If we are gone and defeated, I'd like her to remember me as a good man. If that's the only thing I leave behind, then I'm content."

Kennedy clenched his fist before relaxing. *I could send him to another unit, but he's one of our best.* He pushed the thought away and confronted Ballard's argument directly. He had to admit, going around crushing soft targets like hospitals might win the war quickly, but it would create resentment among the powers in question. *And unless we dismantle their country entirely, it will create the same circumstances that led to this war.*

"I'll concede your point, Ballard," he finally said. "We have to win this war, but we have to do so honorably and completely. As for your daughter, I will talk to Colonel Chaney about it. Maybe we can get you some face-to-face time or something."

Ballard's eyes went wide.

"You can do that?"

Kennedy shrugged.

"Colonel Chaney has powerful connections, a way of getting things done," he replied. "I'm just going to need something from you."

"What's that?" he asked nervously.

Kennedy grinned.

"Be my conscience. No more burning hospitals or other abhorrent attacks. If I make a questionable decision, then I want you to let me know."

Ballard chuckled.

"I guess that makes me a regular Jiminy Cricket," he said.

"A what?" Kennedy asked.

Ballard shook his head.

"Nothing, just a character from a fairy tale my wife used to tell our daughter," he said, then he chuckled. "Funny thing is, Jiminy Cricket was asked by this fairy to be the conscience for a puppet that came to life."

"A puppet that came to life," Kennedy said, grinning. The irony wasn't lost on him.

"But here's the kicker: guess what this little boy puppet wanted more than anything else?"

"What did he want?"

"To be a real boy!"

Kennedy and Ballard fell back onto the catwalk, their cackling echoing into the empty hangar.

SKARA RECLINED IN HIS CHAIR, THE GENTLE ROCKING OF THE airship nearly putting him to sleep. Nearly.

"Starnes, what's the status of our counterattack out west?" he asked his aide.

The younger man sat near him on a leather couch. The heating unit in the room was concealed behind a projection of a fireplace. The light of the false flames cast Starnes in grim shadows.

"Not as well as we hoped," he said. "They're gaining ground, but slowly.

I fear the Union is preparing for a grand counterattack."

Skara raised an eyebrow.

"Where do we think this will happen?" he asked.

Starnes looked down at his tablet.

"Our best guess is they'll try to break out of the Dracul River Delta," he replied. "And if that happens, our northern front will be facing an exposed flank."

Skara sighed.

"We need more allies, competent allies. The Olympians have only been able to stall the Union. Roosevelt has been barely a doormat for them. If only our allies weren't incompetent!" he exclaimed.

Starnes looked at the fire.

"Well, sir, be sure to bring that up with the Olympians in this conference." Skara scoffed. "Though to be fair, their weaknesses seem to be organizational more than anything else."

That last statement piqued Skara's interest.

"Go on," he said.

Starnes continued.

"Well, from what we've observed so far, the Olympians have a very romanticized view of war. Unit commanders plan battles by what will win them and their unit the most glory, in some cases at the expense of supporting units." He pulled up a time-lapse map of the Union. "Most of their major defeats can be traced to two things: unit commanders biting off more than they can chew or neglecting to guard against certain less-than-honorable activities simply because they wouldn't do them."

"Ahh, activities like savaging hospitals with Panzerters," Skara said. "Well, let's hope that incident teaches them a lesson." He rested his head in his hands. "I have a number of reforms I want them to undertake, namely their strict adherence to military districts, but I worry whether the Olympians will be able to rally quickly enough. The Union is cutting them deep."

"Well, they need to reform. We were able to carry the day in the last war, but that may have allowed the Olympians' own development to stagnate," Starnes said.

"What other news do you have, Major?" Skara asked. "I can see it in your face, there's more going on."

Starnes nodded.

"There is, but it's concerning Avalon and space," he said. "Intelligence believes, if the war goes poorly enough, they'll leave the surface of Mars altogether." He pulled up an image of an asteroid. "It's the object they moved into the gravity well. They're calling it Camelot."

"Well, that's good news, isn't it? They aren't exactly helping the Union much on the surface, anyway," Skara said, but he felt there was more to the situation.

"If they completely evacuate the island they live on for space, they take away their only weakness and replace it with strength," Starnes said.

"How would they gain a strength?" Skara asked.

"If they become an entirely spacefaring people, their fleet suddenly becomes their sole resource focus, and there's nothing stopping them from using orbital bombardments or even colony drops against us," Starnes explained.

Skara stood and walked to the window. He was treated to a view of the snowcapped peaks of rugged Olympia. Flurries whipped past the window as the airship made its way to the Olympian capital. Briefly he imagined a host of O'Neill cylinders descending through the clouds.

"I will not allow the home we have built here to be wiped out by Avalon or subjugated by the Union," he finally said. He turned towards Starnes. "Have the cyber department scour their spaceport servers. Cripple Avalon's ability to move information or people off the surface. They won't have the chance to ravage our world from the heavens."

Starnes nodded and went to work on his tablet.

"I'll definitely let them know. We're getting a message from the Olympians. They want to know what to expect from your meeting with them."

Skara looked back out the window.

"We'll talk about reforms they'll be making to their command structure and doctrine and revising our overall strategy for beating the Union," he said.

"You're revising our strategy?" Starnes asked.

Skara nodded.

"I am. I thought we could stall for time until we won the war in space, but I was wrong. We need to strike a decisive blow against the Union and strike hard." He glanced back at Starnes. "Can you pull up a map of the continent?"

Starnes handed him a map on his tablet.

"What do you have in mind, sir?" he asked.

Skara grinned.

"We're going to use amphibious elements to raid their coastline, specifically smashing ports and air defenses. Once we have softened them, we'll assemble the air fleets and sick them on Foundation."

"That's a bit of a gamble, sir. How many airships to you intend to commit?" Starnes asked.

"All of them. There will be losses, but if we convince the Union leadership they're under threat, it could force them to seek terms. Not that they'll ever agree to our terms, but it buys us time to attack Avalon proper."

"Excuse me if this sounds stupid, sir, but what exactly does that accomplish?" Starnes asked.

"If we take the Avalonian royal family hostage, we can force the lot of them to surrender, allowing us to focus entirely on the Union," Skara said. "And just in case that fails, we have diplomats trying to pull other nations into this war. If the First Nation, Lowell, Kanto, or Plata can come into this conflict, it will shift the balance of power further in our favor."

"So, is that what you're going to tell the Olympians?" Starnes asked.

"Not exactly. I'll tell them to focus on retaking Roosevelt while we use reserves to retake Gallacia," Skara replied. "No need to put all our cards on the table."

Starnes lowered his tablet and looked at Skara.

"I don't understand, sir, why throw our ally to the wolves?" he asked.

Skara didn't look back.

"It's simple. Madame President wants us to have a commanding influence on surrender terms, no matter the cost."

MO'S PANZERTER IV WADED THROUGH THE RIVER, WATER splashing around his hips. Smith's machine waded ahead of him, and Unger followed. Attack boats sped by while a barge carried two IFVs after them. He checked his map and saw his objective was near.

Captain Reiter had split the company up to strike multiple weak points in the Union line. Mo's objective, a communications bunker, was just one of about a half dozen poorly defended sections along the Union line. Reiter believed they were pulling back forces for a major offensive, but Mo wasn't sure. *This entire thing could be a trap.*

"Black 1, PB-11. We've sighted the objective. You've got two Panzerters, tinhats."

Mo grit his teeth.

"Roger. Keep your distance and keep them off balance. We're right behind you," he said. "Black, guns up. Tinhats are tough. Aim for their heads and weapons, and use the river." He received acknowledgments from both his wingmates and pushed his Panzerter forward.

They've never fought tinhats before, only in simulations. He saw the patrol boats ahead. They zigged and zagged, the surrounding water bursting into steam. *These are the best of the Union's machines and soldiers. We can't afford to not take them seriously.*

A patrol boat burst into flames, and he saw them.

Two tinhats. Both that same two-tone gray color scheme. Smith fired a burst at the nearest tinhat. The shots glanced off the machine's shoulder armor. Black Platoon engaged the Unionists to the best of their ability. The battle quickly grew stale. The improved armor of his team could withstand frontal hits unless the lasers struck a joint. They faced a similar struggle as most of their rounds failed to penetrate the tinhats' armor.

This isn't sustainable. Mo's mind raced for a solution. They only had so much ammo, and the tinhats didn't have that problem. *I have to change the math here.* He remembered a trick from the Riverside battle, something he'd done instinctively then.

"Cover me for two seconds!" Mo shouted into the net. He drew his sword.

"You're going to rush into hand to hand?" Unger cried.

"Watch and learn!" Mo replied. Igniting the orange blade, he flicked his wrist. The tip danced across the surface of the water in front of all three of them. A fierce wall of steam rose in front of them.

"Damn it, I can't see them!" Smith said. "What the hell, Corporal?"

"Take a step back and wait," he replied. Mo stood with his sword drawn while the others stepped back. *Any second now.*

Sure enough, a tinhat charged through the steam. It swung its mace about like a wild animal. *Going through the cloud must have fogged the cameras.* Mo twirled about with his sword, gracefully severing arms. His wingmates poured rounds into the tinhat. At close range, The 88-mm armor-piercing rounds punched smoking holes in the Unionist's armor.

The gray machine staggered and collapsed. The steam was beginning to abate. Mo grit his teeth, ready for another fight, but the tinhat was gone.

"Damn, where'd he go?" Mo asked.

"I don't know," Smith replied. "Why didn't he shoot us?"

"He couldn't, the steam would scatter his beam," Mo said. "Gold 3 and 5, what's your status?"

"Black 1, we see the bunker as well as the adjoining comm tower, but we have company."

"Let me guess, a tinhat?" he asked.

"Roger, our vehicles are camouflaged and engines are shut-off, but if he looks hard enough, he'll find us."

"Can your dismounts take the bunker without the tracks

supporting them?" Mo asked. He waved his team to follow him, and they proceeded in an arrow formation with Mo at the tip. Though most of the trees in the region kept their leaves, some were skeletons by now. These gaps gave him pockets where he could see a little farther than otherwise.

"We think they can swing it, but this tinhat catches them, they're done." Mo bit his lip.

If they kick off dismounts, we cut our losses in case one group gets compromised.

"Do it; we'll take care of the tinhat," Mo finally said. He fired a burst from his rifle into the air.

"What are you doing?" Unger asked.

"Getting his attention," Mo replied.

"But that tinhat will have the drop on us!" Smith whispered, as if that made up for his 47-ton walking war machine crashing through the forest.

Mo chuckled to himself.

"We can take a few hits. Besides, we—" Branches bursting into flames cut Mo off. Smith's machine staggered and fell backwards, the young man crying out as his Panzerter crashed to the forest floor. "Smith, are you okay!"

"Yeah, I was just startled. I think I can still—"

"Play dead!" Mo ordered. After following the line of flaming branches, he fired at their origin. "You'll know what to do!" Unger joined him in his blind fire. After a few bursts in that direction, the tinhat emerged from the thick trees.

The gray machine's red ring glowed at them. Branches near Mo exploded. Mo returned fire, backing away as he did. Unger followed him. Eager to press its advantage, the tinhat pursued them.

The Unionist pressed forward. It crashed through trees and brush. Its laser blazed wildly. Neither Mo nor Unger took a long enough exposure to seriously damage them, but Mo was all too aware a thousand cuts could kill them too. *Come on. Follow us just a little more.*

Smith's rifle rattled. The tinhat stumbled. Smoke poured from between its legs and its back. A second burst. The tinhat keeled over in a smoking heap. Mo sighed.

"I can't believe that worked! That was amazing, Corporal!" Smith exclaimed.

Mo grinned in his cockpit. He felt like Jello as his body released the tension he'd held.

"See, kids, you can trust me. It's like I know what I'm doing," he said. "Gold element, status?"

"We've knocked down the tower, and the bunker is ours. We have some injuries, but no dead."

Mo smiled. *Honestly, this went as well as it could have. Those pilots were probably green.* Mo thought about the way they'd reacted. *Yeah, veterans wouldn't have fallen for either of those tricks.*

"Smith, get up. Gold will get back on the barge, and we'll head home," Mo said. "You both did good today. Once we get back, Smith, remind me to have a kill marker painted on your hull."

As they turned back towards Garden City, Mo reflected on the implications of the firefight. *If they've got green pilots at the front, they're either running low on veterans or they're saving them for something.* Mo sighed. *It's too early for them to be running out of veterans; we've barely been at war a month.* He resigned himself to bringing it up with Reiter when he got back, but as it stood, he had enough on his plate.

17

K ennedy had never set foot in the war room before today. Come to think of it, he didn't think anyone had. Now though, Kennedy sat with the other company commanders in the wood-paneled room. A projection table in the center of the room displayed a top map of the immediate area.

Colonel Heywood paced around the map.

"Comrades, we've received intel that the Olympians are marshaling for a major offensive," he said. As icons representing units appeared on the map, he began walking his officers through the Olympian plan. "They are committing the entire legion to the west to attack the 2nd Pacifican Guards. Higher command is allowing this to happen."

One of the other officers raised a hand.

"Comrade Colonel, how did we get ahold of these plans?" she asked.

Heywood gestured towards Kennedy.

"It was actually Kennedy's raid that gave us an Olympian

encryption key. MAG's cyber-arm not only beat their encryption, but their ability to generate encryptions."

"Comrade Colonel, why are we allowing them to follow their plans?" another commander asked.

"Because we've set a trap," Heywood said. He pointed to the Olympian units' march across the plain to engage the guards division. "The 2nd will engage in a bit and hold strategy while other divisions roll into the Olympians flanks and envelop them."

"Will we be participating in this flanking attack?" another commander asked.

"No," Heywood said curtly. "Our Panzerter companies, along with reserves pulled from all across the front, will attack into the gap the Olympians leave in their own lines. They will hit their rear areas and roll up their line."

"The same as the Olympians are trying to do to us," Kennedy said.

Heywood nodded.

"Exactly. Do unto others before they do unto you," the older man said. "Major Kennedy will be our battalion's representative and field commander. You have"—he checked his watch—"48 hours to prepare your soldiers. Dismissed."

Kennedy stood to leave, but the other two Panzerter commanders approached him. He'd seen the two men in passing but never interacted with them.

Guard Captain Michaels, Commander of Ibex Company, spoke first.

"So, Comrade Major, do you have a specific plan for how you want us to move?" he asked.

"Well, you're putting me on the spot here, but I would put Ibex up front, Reaper in the middle, and Hellion in the rear," Kennedy replied.

Guard Captain Jayard, Hellion's commander, raised an eyebrow.

"Are you trying to protect yourself? That's heroic," he said.

Kennedy frowned.

"If you must know, that formation would be best because I can support anyone with the Jupiter's shoulder cannon if we need it," he said. "It's easy to forget, but I'm essentially lugging an artillery piece into battle."

The other commanders seemed a bit peeved.

"It's honestly amazing how you got ahold of an experimental unit like the Jupiter. How did that happen?" Michaels asked.

"An ace in the MAG has benefits, and I'm a double-ace," Kennedy said.

"That seems rather bourgeoisie. Are you sure you're a dedicated Unionist?" Jayard sneered.

"I am. The MAG just recognizes that I'm much better at killing class enemies than you," Kennedy sneered back. *So what if they think it's elitist? I was the one with my life on the line in that brutal first wave.* "Say, have either of you jumped out of a plane in a Panzerter?" They both shook their heads. "Good. I have. I think we're done here. See you in thirty-six hours."

Kennedy left the two of them standing there in the war room. *Fuck 'em, I'm not out here for them, anyway.* He shook his head. *They probably have me figured as a tuber. My whole damn company is, so it wouldn't be a stretch.* Snow began nipping at his cheeks.

Kennedy took a deep breath. The frosty air felt like needles in his lungs. It also grounded him. *What am I even out here fighting for?* The question had been dogging him for a while.

Kennedy looked at the gray clouds hanging overhead. *Ballard is out here fighting for the right to his daughter. Fletcher wants to bring honor to our people. But me?* He looked at his hands. *I've always been more competent than ambitious my entire life, merely doing what I was best at the entire time.*

Slowly, he clenched his fists. *I don't think they meant to, but the brass gave me an ambition.* Political power. From what he understood, politics required as much cunning and strategy as being an officer, if not more. *I can build a better Mars for tubers, hell, for all people.*

Kennedy walked into the field hangar. Snow was beginning to accumulate on the cold composite surface of the Jupiter. He looked up at the gold and black machine, an armored warrior cast in humanity's image.

His lieutenants approached him.

"Comrade Major, do we have orders?" Fletcher asked. She was getting restless from the lull in action. Ballard followed behind her, a lit cigarette in his hand.

"We do," Kennedy said as he pulled out his own pack of cigarettes. 'We're going to be part of a huge counterattack that could utterly destroy the Olympian forces in this area."

"That sounds awfully grand. How do they think they're going pull it off?" Ballard asked.

Kennedy grinned.

"They've been using broken Olympian codes to intercept their plans, codes they were able to break because of our actions. We're going to trap an entire legion and counterattack into the gap." He looked back up at the Jupiter. "And I think we'll be able to break the Olympians back on this front."

"Oh, if we're not needed on this front, do you think we'll be sent to fight the Tharcians?" Fletcher asked.

Kennedy shrugged.

"I don't know. I honestly don't know what Command will decide after this battle." He got a light from Ballard and took a long drag.

"I mean, this sounds great and all, but we know plans go to shit the minute shooting starts. How will this be any different?" Ballard asked.

Kennedy blew a cloud of smoke that hung in the air for a moment.

"That's the trick, Ballard, turning the chaos to our favor." *And from that chaos, I'll make a better future, for all mankind.*

GUARD COLONEL CHANEY STRODE DOWN THE IMMACULATE hallway. Today was going to be a good day. Or so he kept telling himself. He entered a sculpted marble room centered on a round wooden table. *It feels like forever since I've been here.*

Gathered around the table were some of the most powerful men in the Union Military, nay the Union itself. At the North Pole sat the Guards Marshal, commander over all surface forces. Opposite him sat the admiral of the Republican Fleets, the man who commanded the space arm of the Union military. Chaney seated himself near the equator, next to his own counterpart in the fleet. After an attendant handed out refreshments, they began their meeting.

"The first thing we need to address, comrades," the ARF began, "is the conduct of this war, wouldn't you say, Comrade Marshal?"

The other man sighed.

"Ground combat is an ugly, personal affair, Comrade Admiral, but if you must bring up honorable conduct, I must ask why the Tharcians are claiming we're targeting colonies?" he responded.

"Those were accidents," the admiral said.

"As we accidentally destroyed several enemy medical centers. Though, like our incidents, I'm sure we can regret the destruction yet appreciate the results," the marshal said. "That doesn't change the fact that we'd like to expand conscription into our own colonies. If we restrict our recruitment to the surface, it will hamstring our manpower in the long run."

The admiral held his head in his hands.

"Masterson, what's the status of our space elevator to Phobos?" he asked.

The man next to Chaney stiffened.

"Comrade Colonel, it will be ready in another week to start moving people and materials," Masterson replied. "Within six months, it will be operating at full capacity,"

Chaney tried not to scowl. *I almost had control of that project too, if it wasn't for favoritism.*

"As soon as the space elevator is finished, we will allow you to extend conscription to the colonies, starting with Phobos and the Phobian Archipelago," the admiral said. As he spoke, an image of the space elevator was projected onto the table. The elevator extended into the south pole of the moon from the surface of the planet. The Lagrange point beyond it, Lagrange 2, was dotted with O'Neill cylinders.

"Have you adequately defended it? I've always said that this structure is too vulnerable to attacks from space and the surface," the marshal said.

Masterson nodded.

"I've lined the outer part with point defenses, as well as rail-guns and laser batteries. The surface portion has drone bays, though not all of them are filled, and most of the heavier weapons are offline," he said. "However, most of the point defenses are up."

"See to it that it is properly defended. If the elevator is destroyed, it would be apocalyptic to those living on most of the surface and even into the capital," the marshal exclaimed. The projection changed to show the affected area and projected casualties if the elevator was destroyed.

"I have a solution, but I will need more backing for one of my projects," Chaney finally said. Now the dozen or so admirals and generals looked directly at him.

"Do you have something to add, Comrade Chaney?" the admiral asked.

Chaney nodded.

"I do, Comrade Admiral. I've been working on particle-beam weapons with the intent of eventually phasing out our laser weapons on the ground," he said. "Although, I'll have warship-ready versions ready before I have anything for our Panzerters."

"He's bluffing," Masterson said. "Our department's particle weapon project got nowhere. There's no way of maintaining a stable electromagnetic field outside of the weapon barrel!"

Chaney smiled coyly.

"There is if you're not incompetent," he said.

"Enough," the marshal said. "Comrade Chaney, I'm not familiar with these particle-beam weapons. Perhaps you could explain them?"

Chaney nodded.

"In layman's terms, a particle-beam weapon works in a manner not dissimilar to a railgun," he said. As he spoke, the projection changed to an image of three barrels. "A railgun uses magnets to accelerate a super-heavy payload to high velocities. Due to issues with power supply and air resistance, this has remained a space-borne weapon." The projection demonstrated the operation of a railgun.

"So how exactly is a particle-beam weapon different?" the admiral asked.

The projection shifted to the prototype Chaney was currently working with.

"A particle-beam weapon uses essentially the same principle, but instead of a super-dense payload, the weapon accelerates charged and compressed particles along a track. This allows for a weapon with incredible amounts of thermal and kinetic energy, to the extent no amount of armor or thermal coating can block it."

"What Comrade Chaney is neglecting to tell you is that the particles will scatter once they leave the track," Masterson said. "It's the reason our project never got off the ground."

"Your project only used individual particles. We used a chain of five, where every particle bound to the adjacent particles repelled each other, so that once the string leaves the barrel, it's constantly accelerating itself with its own magnetic field," Chaney said.

The projection shifted to demonstrate the power of a particle-beam weapon. Warships fired on each other, with Tharcian vessels being smashed apart by the beams. The projection shifted to Panzerters on the ground. Jupiter units fired shoulder-mounted particle cannons that utterly destroyed the opposition.

"Well, it certainly makes an entertaining projection, but what are your limitations? What has held your project back?" the marshal asked.

Chaney sighed.

"For starters, funding. We simply lack labors to keep paying scientists and engineers to devote more time to it," he said. "That and power supply. We need to refine how power is supplied to the weapon system. For that reason, it will probably be ready for battleships and heavy cruisers first."

Both of the authorities seemed appeased by the idea.

"I couldn't help but notice you used your new heavy Panzerter design to demonstrate the ground version. That was no accident, am I correct?" the marshal asked.

"No, Comrade Marshal, it wasn't. I intended the Jupiter to eventually mount particle weapons of its own, so I futureproofed it," he said.

"You'll need some help from our weapons division to work it with warship weapon mounts, so we can allocate labors and personnel to you," the admiral said.

"I can't spare any personnel to aid the ground forces R&D," Masterson sneered.

"You will, Comrade Masterson, and they will come from your weapons department," the admiral said. "They should have plenty of time, since you're occupied with the space elevator."

"We will also double your quarterly funding," the marshal said. "Make these weapons a priority, but don't neglect Panzerter development."

Chaney smiled.

"Yes, comrades, I won't let you down," he said. *And just like that, everything swings my way.*

"I SWEAR I HAVE A LOVE-HATE RELATIONSHIP WITH BEING HELD IN reserve," Reiter said into the net. He sat in the Lowe's cockpit, overlooking a hilly stretch of terrain. To his left hung a map of the area; on his right were the pictures of their fallen. He was unbuckled in his seat and trying to recline.

"I get that," Bartonova replied. "On the one hand, we're not in any immediate risk. On the other, we're just sitting here in our Panzerters."

"You guys got it lucky," Comidus said. "I have to smell a dozen sweaty assholes in here."

"No one said you had to smell their assholes, Gold 1, that's all you," Adamski replied. Laughter filled the net.

"Very funny, Fox 7, real comedian," Comidus grumbled.

"Thanks, I'm here 'til Thursday," Adamski replied.

Reiter glanced at the map. He stood in a copse of trees with Bartonova, Adamski, and Comidus's IFV. To his 10 o'clock lay Black platoon, with White platoon hanging out at his 2 o'clock. *Mo was pretty set that he encountered green pilots the other day. I doubt the Union is running into any shortage of capable pilots.* He narrowed his eyes and gazed across the horizon. *So where are they?*

With another look at his map, he checked their distance to Objective Mauler. *Fifteen miles from us, ten miles from the front-line, so they can see it, most likely.* Reiter frowned when he noticed a small town on his map, near Objective Mauler. *I hope those people evacuated. I'd hate for civilians to risk getting caught up in the fighting.*

"Listen up, there's a town near Objective Mauler on the map. I don't know if any civilians are still there, but we're going to do our best to avoid civilian casualties," he said. He received a chorus of acknowledgments and sank back into his chair. *How many people lost their homes because of the Union? How many lost their lives?* As far as Reiter was concerned, it was hard to hold the moral high ground while trying to conquer people.

"All points, Black 1. We're getting radar returns from the south-west," Mo said.

Reiter strapped himself in.

"Friendlies?" he asked.

"Unknown," Mo replied.

He was just a goofy kid with a crush and mediocre grades at the beginning of the month. It's a shame he's had to become who he is.

"ETA 'til visual contact?" Adamski asked.

"Any minute. We got four inbound, diamond formation," Mo replied.

The returns suddenly appeared on Reiter's own radar. The signatures matched Union dropships.

"We've got inbound raiders," he said. "Watch out for their cargo doors—they might drop troops." He could hear his heartbeat in the back of his head, and his body tightened. *Here it comes.*

They came over the tree line. Four dropships, their ugly frames bristling with weapons. They fired rockets and chainguns into Black Platoon. Unger fell, her unit's head leaking smoke.

Adamski fired burst after burst while Reiter brought the railgun online. *I'll take them all out at once.* Adamski found his mark, bringing down the rightmost dropship. Bartonova fired her sniper rifle. The dropship buckled but didn't fall.

The railgun hummed as the capacitors charged. *I don't necessarily need a direct hit; a near miss should bring them down.* His fire-control system presented a firing solution. Reiter pulled the trigger.

The Lowe pitched hard backwards. Reiter fought for balance. *Damnit! I didn't set my feet!* He stayed upright. The dropship Bartonova had damaged careened out of control.

The remaining dropships scattered. Missiles from the IFVs and MCVs raced after them. The dropships spun, wove, and dropped flares. White added their guns to the fight. Caught in the crossfire from White, Black, and Gold, the last two dropships plummeted from the sky.

"Gold 1, have your people secure the crash sites. We don't want any surprises. Panzerter teams, send a unit to help mop up." Reiter sighed and relaxed in his seat. "Damage reports?"

"Black 2 is going to need a new head entirely, in addition to other smaller repairs," Mo replied. Reiter saw Mo's Panzerter guiding the stricken machine as if it was a blind man.

"Fox 6, we've got a squad in contact with some survivors," Comidus said. "They're exchanging fire right now."

"Roger, keep me updated," Reiter replied. He called the regiment and gave them a brief battle report. Informing them he'd keep them updated, he checked back with Gold Platoon.

"Two dead, three injured on our end. We've got five prisoners, no other survivors," Comidus said.

"Roger, recover what we can from these dropships. We might

find something worthwhile in the wreckage," Reiter said. Armor plating could be melted down and reused. Electronic components could be saved, cleaned, and reused. Hell, an intact radio could yield codes or be reverse-engineered to determine how it encrypted its signals.

For a brief moment, he appreciated the utter pragmatism of his people. *Well, nearly two centuries of either Soviet overlords or interplanetary colonization will do that to a culture*, he thought.

After giving his last report to the regiment, he was told to return to Garden City. The line ahead of them solidified. There would be no more advancing today. Frustrated, he informed his company.

"Seriously? At this rate, we'll get back to our homes by March," Bartonova protested.

Reiter shook his head.

"It's not my call, but I will admit it's weird they keep telling us we're running out of time, only to crawl forward."

"It's almost like they want to drag this shit out," Mo said.

Reiter couldn't tell him he was wrong. *They have a point. Since the line's stiffened, there's been little movement from us, the Union, or anybody.*

"Part of me is wondering if both sides are training more troops to throw into the blender," Adamski said. "The only justifiable reason I see to move forward like we have been is to limit our own casualties."

"That's a good point," Reiter said. "Who knows how many provincial watch units are rushing through mobilization right now?" *They were quick to send us cadets in their last year of military prep —that's telling me the scarcity is formal training, not necessarily people.* Reiter thought of the scale of a few rounds of the draft and shuddered. The entire Tharcian military numbered around 300,000,000, a drop in the bucket next to the total Tharcian population of 12 billion people. He shuddered. *A war on that scale . . . It's unthinkable.*

———

"That's the signal! Let's go!" Kennedy cried as he brought the Jupiter up to speed. The Panzerters around him surged forward, crossing over hills and through trees. Soon, they encountered the cratered and torn ground of no-man's-land. He heard a buzz in the sky and looked up.

Drones filled the sky like a swarm of locusts. He could see some CAS drones banking west towards the trapped legion, but many more surged forward. Even farther above, air-supremacy drones raced forward to clear the skies for the Union.

"They're going to sing songs about today," Fletcher said softly.

Kennedy grinned.

"I don't know about that, but I would like someone handsome to play me in the movie," he said. That got a few chuckles on the net.

"That seems deceptive, Comrade Major," Ballard said.

A few pilots, including Kennedy himself, guffawed into the radio. *He actually made a joke? Someone write this day down.*

Drones in the distance exploded or launched missiles, making the swarm look all the more like a rising thundercloud.

Speaking of thunder, artillery rumbled in the distance. No doubt they were pounding the legion trapped to their northwest. Kennedy pitied the Olympians stuck there. Almost.

They're in my way, he thought. *They're all in my way. This isn't just about serving the war anymore. Every day, I'm a little closer. Every day, my vision becomes clearer. A better future is right there.*

The Jupiter pounded onward, centered on the forward-most group of Panzerters. In his mind, Kennedy felt like their solar system neighbor. Like the planet his machine was named for, the important things were closer to him. The less important ones, namely the other company commanders, were farther.

He turned on a private channel.

"All Reaper elements, we were created for days like today," Kennedy began. "They may have stamped us with a number, taken things from our bodies, used us to fight their wars, but we are tomorrow!" He raised the Jupiter's mace high. "Now is the time we stand up for the future! Now is the time we lead the way to tomorrow! For the Union!" The Reapers echoed him and doubled their pace.

"Enemy Panzerters!" Tracers tore into the ranks of Ibex Company. The regulars returned fire. They fought valiantly but couldn't hold. Kennedy swung his company to flank the attacking element. Ten Legionnaires. Two Onagers.

Kennedy took aim with his shoulder cannon as MAGs rushed past him. An Onager collapsed. A shell took its head. The other turned to fire on him but was met with laser fire from the underslung lasers.

"Eliminate them quickly. We can't let them stall us, and we can't let them report our position!" Kennedy ordered. He took another shot, this time at a Legionnaire. It fell in a shattered wreck. *I need to get the other Onager, otherwise it will tear us apart.*

Kennedy took aim, but the Onager hid inside the square the Legionnaires formed. *Damn, he'll be back.* Kennedy unleashed the shoulder cannon on the Legionnaires, supported by his laser. He blew a hole in their formation. His comrades exploited the gap.

"Keep moving! Go around them!" Kennedy said. They surged past the Legionnaires' square. Follow-on units were engaging the Olympians as well. Another group of Olympians crested a hill in front of them, only to be blasted by a CAS drone.

The battle devolved into a blur. Kennedy found himself losing track of things in all the running and blasting. The Olympians had never organized a large-scale counterattack, merely advancing in drips and drabs. *It's like they don't know the scale of what's coming.*

Their loss was his gain, as far as Kennedy figured. Closer and closer they advanced. More and more Olympians came. The machines they faced were in various states of disrepair or battle-damaged. Finally, they crested the last hill.

To their surprise, a machine they hadn't yet encountered waited for them. It was larger and more heavily armored than the Legionnaire. Instead of a large spear, it wielded an odd rifle in one hand. It saluted Kennedy before clanging its rifle on its shield. An honor guard of Legionnaires behind it did the same.

That must be the Centurion. Kennedy fired his shoulder rifle. The round clanged off a shield. The Centurion raised its rifle.

A stream of fire erupted from the barrel. It crossed the ground in front of him, igniting it. *Napalm.* Kennedy fired his laser to little effect.

Smoke is already blocking the beam. Kennedy waved for the two platoons of his company to go around the flames and attack the flanks. *I'll take care of the Centurion.* He folded the shoulder cannon down and drew his mace. He kicked dirt onto the fire in front of him and advanced.

Kennedy couldn't see through the smoke. No thermals. No ground radar. Nothing. Instinctively, he lunged forward and swung his mace.

The weapon crunched against a shield. *Found him.* Kennedy advanced, each blow flowing into the next. The Centurion blocked every attack, crouching behind his shield.

At first, the shield held up, but soon every blow bent it a little more out of shape. *He can't keep this up indefinitely.* Using his size to advantage, Kennedy began swinging with the Jupiter's entire body. Finally, Kennedy knocked the shield away. Instead of staggering, the Centurion used the moment to spin away and raise its rifle.

Kennedy's monitor filled with flames before going dark. Multiple alarms sounded as systems began overheating. Internals were melting. *It's like I'm in a furnace.* Kennedy's mouth felt like cotton.

He forced the Jupiter to the side and rolled. His helmeted head slammed against the sides of the cockpit. His stomach twisted in knots, and he threw up in his mouth a bit. The Jupiter settled on its back.

Within moments of restarting the sensors, Kennedy's monitors came back to life. The Centurion stood over him, sword drawn. He had seconds to dodge left as the super-heated blade plunged into the mud next to him. He grabbed the Centurion's leg and rolled again.

Kennedy whipped about in his cockpit but was able to stand his machine from a prone position. As he found his footing, so did his opponent. The Centurion brandished his sword.

Kennedy got into a fighting crouch.

"You're a cunning warrior, Olympian pilot, but you're in my way." They charged each other. The Centurion lunged, sword pointed at his cockpit. Kennedy caught the blade in his palm. The super-heated blade became trapped in his elbow. *I got you.*

Kennedy raised his mace and smashed the Centurion's head. After two blows, the elaborate head of the machine crumpled and fell away. Another blow caved in the base of its neck. The Centurion . . . set a hand on his shoulder.

Kennedy swung again. He felt the cockpit give in. The Centurion let go of its sword. It slumped to the ground with a resounding crunch.

What the hell was that? A last-ditch effort to save himself? No, that doesn't seem right.

Dawn was beginning to break over the horizon. Kennedy saw his comrades ravaging the Olympian rear areas.

As he took it all in, the surrounding devastation grounded him. *This legion will probably surrender soon, and we'll be able to roll the rest of the line.* Kennedy smiled as he looked over the fallen Centurion. *You fought well, and ultimately you probably wanted the same thing I do.* He looked out over the ruins of the Olympians' rear areas. *I'll build a better Mars, then all of this will be history.*

18

R eiter hadn't thought about his home since the fighting started. Not the single bedroom house he lived in near the school, but his home. Where his mother was buried. Where he would normally spend Christmas with his siblings and father. Home wasn't in immediate danger, not yet. His father's house was on the southern coast, near the Mariner gulf.

"Hey sir? Do you have a minute?" Steele called from the stairs behind him.

Her voice yanked Reiter out of the sea of his thoughts. He was lying in a hammock in the rec room of the dorm building.

"Yeah, what's up?" he said as he sat up slightly. *How long have I been up here staring at the foggy dome?*

Steele sat across from him in another hammock. Her feet just barely grazed the ground as she did.

"I don't know if I can keep doing this," she said, her voice cracking.

Uh oh.

"Can't do what exactly? I'm not big on the pronoun game," he replied.

Steele's eyes watered and she waved her hands.

"I can't lead these kids to their deaths. I didn't sign up for that!" She sobbed now, the tears coming uncontrollably. "I just wanted to be a primary school teacher!"

Reiter sat there and let her cry. *I'm going to have to put the "strong enough to be gentle" thing into practice.*

"Tell me everything," he said. "Start at the beginning."

"I'm not cut out for this. Renner never taught me shit, Sandic made me do every stupid detail and task, and Bartonova let her," Steele wailed. "I wasn't learning, I wasn't being mentored!" *That explains why we graded better than them every time we went through annual training or pre-mobilization.*

"What kind of platoon was Kress running?" he asked.

Steele's face somehow became redder.

"That fucking pervert. He'd get me out of doing things only to try to grope me in his office. I told Stanca, and he didn't believe me." Steele took a breath and collected herself. "Septimus believed me, but every time he brought it up, Stanca killed the investigation, and the bullying by Sandic just got worse."

"I . . . I had no idea," Reiter said.

Steele took a deep breath.

"I got away from that. Kress died the first night, Renner, Sandic." She shook her head. "But they didn't prepare me for this, they didn't do their job, and that poor Szilard boy had to pay for it." She sagged into another sobbing fit. "He should have been worried about homework or taking a pretty girl skating, but no, he fought in a war he had no business being in, and now he's dead because I don't know how to lead."

They sat there in silence for a time.

She tried getting her breathing under control.

"I'm sorry," she said quietly.

Reiter shook his head.

"There's nothing to be sorry for," he replied. "We're at war, Steele; the enemy is going to have a say too." Twisting towards her, he propped his head on his hands. "I'm sorry I wasn't around to support you when you needed it, but we're a different Fox company now. Be the NCO you need to be to ensure it doesn't happen again."

He stood and stretched. "There's nothing I can say that will undo the harm that's been done to you, but you are a capable leader, you just don't see it yet." He turned to the stairs and saw Mo standing there slack-jawed.

"Amy." Mo took a step forward and paused, looking at Reiter. He nodded, and Mo stepped up to Amy and embraced her. Reiter left them on the roof and headed back inside.

"About time she said something," Bartonova said just inside the door.

Reiter's stomach tightened, but he remained calm.

"You knew what Kress was doing to her?" he asked.

Bartonova nodded.

"He did it to all of us. Sandic had her own way of coping, I had mine," she said.

Reiter realized he'd never seen Bartonova wear short sleeves.

"What happened to the two of you is unacceptable, but I assure you, we are nothing like Kress."

"I know," she replied. "All the time you and I have spent on overwatch together told me that."

Reiter glanced upstairs.

"Let's give those two some space. I think they need some alone time. He's lived next door to her since they were six, and he had no idea."

Bartonova nodded.

"She's had all of that bottled up this whole time. It was going to blow at some point."

"She needs a healthier way to deal with trauma," Reiter replied. "And you do too, while we're on it."

Bartonova smiled.

"I haven't needed to do that in a while, sir," she said.

"Good, let's keep it that way," he said. They walked into the cafeteria. "In the mood for dinner?"

Bartonova nodded. As they sat with their food, she raised her eyebrows and squinted.

"You know, sir, I know the rest of old Fox fairly well, except you," she said.

Reiter shrugged as he ate his salad.

"What's there to know? I'm just a boring history TA."

Bartonova didn't look convinced.

"So, where's your family from?"

"Curiosity Bay," he replied.

She smiled.

"No way, my grandmother had a summer home out there."

Reiter smiled.

"What part?" he asked.

"Asimov street."

"Really?" Bartonova nodded, and he smiled.

"My parent's house is on Bradbury lane, a block away from the pier."

Bartonova's eyes went wide. "No way! And you're, what, in your mid-twenties?"

"25."

"Wow, so every summer we're only a block away from each other," she said, shaking her head.

"I wish I took advantage of it when I was a kid, but I was too scared of the ocean," Reiter admitted.

Bartonova paused.

"Shut up, sir."

"What? I saw too many deep sea horror movies as a young kid, and it freaked me out. Like a six-year-old can differentiate Earth's and Mar's oceans. Hell, back on Earth, they've still barely explored that mess."

"So let me get this straight: you're scared of a body of water on a planet you've never been to," she said with an incredulous look.

Reiter shrugged.

"I was an impressionable kid," he replied. "And never going there adds to the mystique."

"So how did you react when Mo told you he wanted to study the ocean?" she asked.

"Well, in my head I was like 'good on you, send me pictures, have at it,' but I just told him that was admirable and to work hard."

She snickered.

"Oh my God, you're such a dad," she said.

Reiter simply smiled. *One day, maybe.*

KENNEDY WATCHED REAPER COMPANY'S PANZERTERS AS THE technicians prepped them for transport. They were no longer needed. The strung-out Olympians had fled for miles before reforming on the other side of the Amazon Pass. The new battle line allowed for a smaller front the regular forces could hold.

"I've been told you're heading back east," Heywood said. The older man walked down the catwalk in the field hangar to join him.

"North or west of Tharsis?" Kennedy asked.

Heywood shook his head.

"Hard to say, but if I was a betting man, I'd put money on staying in Gallacia," he replied.

Kennedy nodded.

"I wonder if I'll rejoin my old outfit. They've probably been completely rebuilt by now." He looked down at the Jupiter. "Hopefully, we're going to be seeing a lot more of these. Guard Colonel Chaney has plenty of combat data to work with now."

Heywood nodded.

"The Martian Troopers already made a tremendous difference," he replied. "I can hardly imagine what some Jupiters of our own would do. I admit, I was hardly warm to the idea of a MAG company being attached to us, but your people have cast doubt on a lot of the horror stories I've heard."

Kennedy nodded curtly.

"I'm glad we're able to exceed your expectations," he replied. Standing up, he turned and saluted the older man. "I'm afraid I must take my leave now. We've got a long bus ride ahead of us."

Heywood nodded and saluted him.

"I serve the Union of Mars," he said.

Kennedy returned the salute and greeting and left the battalion commander on the walkway. *I'm actually amazed he knew the MAG motto. Not many people outside the organization do.* The motto was an affirmation, a reminder of their organization's end-goal. *A United Mars.*

The rest of Reaper Company had dutifully packed their bags and stood lined up by the platoon at the bus depot. Each pilot carried a duffel bag in one hand and their ruck on their back. He met Ballard and Fletcher by his things.

"Did Heywood talk to you?" Ballard asked. Kennedy nodded. "Did he have anything to say or just empty platitudes?"

"He was grateful for the material support, and we definitely earned his respect," Kennedy answered.

Fletcher frowned.

"We're better soldiers by birth and training. We should already have the respect of a citizen colonel," she said.

Kennedy shook his head.

"That attitude is why you haven't been promoted. You need to play nice with others," he said.

Fletcher frowned.

"I would play nicer if I wasn't surrounded by incompetent idiots for most of my career!" she exclaimed. "Present company excluded, of course," she quickly added.

The bus came, and they boarded. Being a company of twelve people, everyone was able to get their own seat and some space to spare.

Kennedy sat in a seat across the aisle from Fletcher. Ballard sat two rows behind him and racked out. Kennedy tried leaning his seat back. He tried lying across both seats. He even tried leaning back and propping his legs up, but nothing allowed him to be comfortable enough to sleep.

As he struggled to get situated, he noticed Fletcher staring out the window.

"You know, you never answered my question way back when," he said.

"Say again, Comrade?" she asked.

Kennedy was pretty sure she'd heard him.

"You never gave me an answer when I asked you why you joined the MAG," he said.

She looked back out the window.

"I'm not sure I'm comfortable talking about it in front of the entire company," she said.

Kennedy looked back down the bus. Everyone else was fast asleep.

"Yeah, the entire sleeping company, got it," he said.

They were quiet for a moment, then she suddenly spoke up.

"I'm a hypocrite," she said.

"And that's why you joined the MAG?" he asked.

She shook her head.

"No, but the reason I joined makes me one," she said. "Unionism grants everyone equality. I've been saying it for years, but I joined so I could have a baby." She shook her head as she continued. "I don't have reproductive rights at all, no one in our company does, but we're equal to civilians, right?"

Kennedy shrugged.

"I mean, we all get paid the same," he began, but a glare shut him down.

"If a natural-born woman gets pregnant, she can just get an abortion at the hospital, but if I want to get pregnant, no matter how hard I try, I can't," she said. Her eyes glistened in the afternoon light. "It's . . . it's . . . it's . . ."

"I won't judge you for whatever you're trying to say," Kennedy said.

"It's not fair," she said weakly and looked out the window. "I can't believe I said that."

I have an opportunity to earn her loyalty forever. Her skill and devotion make her an incredible ally.

"Fletcher," he said softly, "I hear your pain, and you have my word that once this war is over, I will use my power to build a better world, for all the people of Mars."

She continued to look out the window.

"You will?" she asked.

Kennedy nodded.

"They gave the opportunity because they don't believe I'll take it," he said. "Before the fighting started, I wouldn't have, but war has a way of changing people." He sat against the window and put his feet up. "Although, I'm prompted to ask another question."

"What's that?" she asked.

"Have you thought about who the father would be? Have you thought about living situations? Would you get pregnant with a needle? Or the old-fashioned way?"

"I want a smart man. I'd love if my child was able to be a doctor, architect, or an orbital engineer," she said. "I hope that they would never have to be a soldier. I don't want my children to fight for the right to exist."

"And how many do you want?" Kennedy asked.

"The more the merrier," she said. "I want a house filled with love."

He grinned and folded his arms.

"Chaney. Man's an engineering genius and also not opposed to kids." Fletcher blushed and looked away. "Fine, maybe not Chaney. He's old for you, anyway. Don't worry, you'll find Mr. Right."

Kennedy looked out the bus's windshield. The Dracul River Delta stretched before them.

"You have worthy goals," he finally said, "and I will do my utmost to help you." *And just like that, she's in my pocket.*

THE LOWE TOOK COVER BEHIND A SQUAT BUILDING. *HERE WE ARE, back in Riverside, repelling yet another attack.* Reiter's machine wielded an assault rifle in one hand. His other hand carried his shield. *Any minute now.*

"All points, how we doing?" he asked. *Got to break the monotony somehow.*

"I'd be a lot better if we weren't here again," Mo said.

Reiter nodded in the cockpit.

He was looking at the hill he'd crested three weeks ago, coming towards his current position. When he came over the hill, he'd found his first sergeant dead and the other half of his force in tatters. *Not today. We're ready for the bastards today.*

"We got movement at 1230!" cried Merlin.

Reiter set his sights on the area Merlin had pointed out. *Is it just the kid getting spooked?* No, he saw them crest the hills. Two-tone gray paint jobs and round heads left no doubt. MAGs.

"They look like they got regular rifles with some kind of grenade launcher," Adamski said.

Reiter furrowed his brow.

"Hold your fire until they attempt to cross the river. Don't give away your position unless absolutely necessary."

The tinhats stalked forward. Their weapons swung back and forth, searching for targets. *Looks like about six of them—a recon in force, maybe?*

"Their lead unit is approaching the river," Bartonova said.

"I'll initiate contact," Reiter said. "Bartonova, pick a target. I've got their leader." He edged his machine just out from cover. Lying in a prone position, he swung the railgun forward. He lowered his targeting computer and took aim.

The lead tinhat waded into the river. The dark water lapped at its hips and masked the heat from its legs. The air in Reiter's cockpit grew still. All he could hear was the sound of his breathing, his heartbeat, and the click of the targeting computer. The tinhat swung his way.

A burst of rifle fire pinged off the rightmost tinhat. The Union machine twisted and returned fire. *Damn it.* The lead tinhat swung sideways and unleashed a burst of its own. Reiter pulled the trigger.

The lead tinhat fell forward. Debris blossomed out of its back. The other tinhats perked up. Another stumbled when a high-caliber shell took its head off.

Fire poured from the northeast side of the river. The exposed tinhats withered under the relentless attacks but returned fire. Their shells pummeled the Lowe's armor, rattling Reiter in his chair. He brought the Lowe to its feet and returned fire.

Caught in the open, the Unionists began falling back. *Thank the Lord we don't have to fight them close in.* A stream of shells struck his arm. His armor held until a shell struck his elbow, shattering it. The Lowe's severed forearm fell to the street.

Reiter shrank behind cover. With his shield raised, he stared at the severed limb. *Damn it, I got careless. How long will it take to fix this thing? Can they fix the Lowe?* Suddenly, piloting an experimental Panzerter seemed much less appealing.

A green flash snared his attention. He heard a crash to his right. Unger swore into the radio.

"Those aren't grenade launchers, they're lasers!" Mo said.

Reiter grit his teeth. He fired again as he swung out from cover. A tinhat spun around, its arm ripped away by immense kinetic force. Staggering, the tinhat limped away, its stump sparking.

Reiter listened. No more shots rang out. The tinhats had retreated beyond the hill. Frontline forces beyond were waiting for them closer to the actual front. He sighed and put away his targeting computer.

"BDAs? And Valkyrie, I'm going to need your help in a second. Could you head this way?" he said. Bartonova's machine meandered over to his position. "Could you rack my shield for me so I can pick up my arm?"

"They were able to damage the Lowe?" she asked with alarm.

"Yeah, well, the joint, but I do need to be more careful about exposing myself to enemy fire," he replied.

Gingerly, Bartonova returned his shield to the rack. It felt shameful to recover his arm. Reiter's head swam. It was as if he was damaged instead of the Lowe. The Panzerter was still invincible, but he wasn't.

"Black is up. Unger took a hit from a laser, but she can still walk. All of us will need armor patching," Mo said.

Reiter nodded.

"Who opened fire? I was going to initiate contact with the railgun."

"That was Merlin. His comms are wrecked, and his entire head is going to need replacing, but otherwise we all just need armor patching," Steele answered.

Reiter shook his head.

"Make sure you discipline him when we get back. A mistake like that is unacceptable," he said. "Gold Platoon, come up and assist the garrison forces in sweeping for debris."

"Roger, Fox 6, we'll scrounge up what we can," Comidus replied. As the Panzerters filed out of Riverside for the march back to Garden City, the IFVs disembarked their troops. As the Panzerters left town, the infantry rolled in.

Reiter took another look at his severed arm.

It looked like the shell had struck a seam in the armor. Hitting at just the right angle, the fat round had split the seam and shattered the joint underneath. Subsystems had already cut the power from the shoulder down. *Good, in my old machine I would have had to flip open the circuit board and cut power myself.*

"French and the other techs are going to kill me," Reiter said.

"Well, it's just the joint, right?" Adamski asked. "That's not too bad. It's not like the railgun was destroyed."

Reiter nodded.

"Let's just hope the joint isn't overly complex or hard to otherwise repair," he said.

"Well, did you take any other big hits?" Adamski asked.

"Yeah, a few, mostly non-penetrating hits. Nothing vital got hit," Reiter replied. "Except, of course, the catastrophic hit to the elbow."

Adamski whistled sharply into the net.

"Damn, the durability of that thing is insane," he said. "If only we had a few hundred of those."

"Yeah," Reiter replied. "The shitty thing is, by the time we got a hundred of these, its durability would probably mean a lot less." He stared at the severed arm. *If it doesn't already.*

———

SKARA RECLINED IN THE LAVISH CHAIR. *RANK INDEED HAS ITS privileges.* Yet another meeting with the Olympians after another disastrous loss. *If only we had competent allies.* However, there were benefits to the Olympians' ineptness. While the Union had pummeled Olympian forces back into their own lands, the Tharcians advanced, threatening to cut off the Unionists in southwest Gallacia.

We've only just tapped the surface of our potential. If enough people get drafted and I lead us to victory, it'll give me a big enough voter pace to run for president when this is all over. Skara smiled at the thought. *The Isolationists and pacifists wouldn't stand a chance.* He had just begun to sip his whiskey when Major Starnes walked in.

"Sir, I've just received the latest report from the air fleet. They've taken heavy losses round the clock over Foundation," he said. "Our estimates state that our rate of loss over replacement will climb to fifty percent in two months."

Skara nodded slowly.

"Yes, those are acceptable losses," he said.

"Acceptable, sir? Each bombardment airship has a crew of a thousand, and each drone carrier has a crew of a hundred. At these rates, we won't have an air fleet this time next year!"

"Major, what have I said about questioning me?" Skara asked.

"You should know your place by now."

"My place," Starnes began, "is to aid you. Your place is to win this damn war."

Skara emptied his glass. Setting it firmly on the table next to him, he rose.

"Are you insinuating, Major, that I am not interested in winning this war?" he asked.

"No, not right now, anyway," Starnes said. "But you have ulterior motives. You're not interested in winning this war quickly."

Skara grit his teeth.

"What makes you think we could win this war quickly?"

"Because we did it before. We beat the Union in two months twenty years ago," Starnes replied.

"And you know what that got us, Major Starnes? Complacency, organizational rot, budget cuts!" Skara said. "It took us ten years to justify the Panzerter IV contract. All the while, the fleet was in an arms race with the Union, an arms race, I will remind you, we lost!" He was shouting now, his fists balled in rage.

"So what, you want to drag out this war to justify our budget?" Starnes asked. "That's absurd! You said our war goal was the dismantling of the UMR. How do we justify a large standing army with no immediate enemies?"

Skara grinned.

"Because if the Union citizens feel cheated, they will start an insurgency, or the MAG will. Either way, we will continue to get favorable contracts and budgets," he said.

Starnes slouched at the news. His eyes went wide, and he ran a hand through his hair.

"Are you saying that you're willing to essentially drag this war out forever if it protects our budget?"

Skara's eyes flashed.

"I need not justify myself to some upstart major," he said.

"Speaking of which, you're relieved of duty. You'll be lucky if I don't have you demoted and sent to the bulwark."

Starnes sighed.

"I believed for a long time you were a better man, Marshal," he said sadly.

"Major, I always have been and always will be your better," Skara said.

"No, you're not. At the end of the day, you're just a politician wearing a soldier costume," Starnes replied.

"How dare you disrespect me, you insolent, insubordinate—"

Starnes drew a handgun, cutting Skara off.

"What are you doing, soldier?"

"I'm cutting off a diseased branch. It's clear to me now the biggest obstacle to victory isn't the Union," Starnes said. "It's you."

He's not going to shoot me. No way. He hasn't seen a range in years. Besides, security is on the way.

"You don't have the balls to shoot me," Skara sneered. "I may be a politician in uniform, as you say, but you are a mere paper pusher, a desk jock."

Starnes flicked the safety off.

"You're no hero, Captain Starnes, only a traitor."

The airship suddenly groaned and lurched.

Skara was unable to prevent his head from smashing into the false fireplace. The screen spider-webbed, and the image distorted. Starnes slouched against the wall. The gun lay on the floor between them.

Klaxons blared. The airship was under attack. *I need a parachute; I need to escape.* Skara got to his feet, only to fall again when the airship rocked. Something brushed his hand. The gun. He suddenly felt lighter. *We're falling.*

Seizing the gun, he looked for a place to brace himself. The chair slid against the opposite wall. He crawled towards the window, heading for the handrails. Another jolt and he lost the gun.

He was starting to slide towards the rear of the airship as it dove towards the surface. *It's going to be fine; I'll live through this and come out a hero.* He grabbed the solid bar between the upper and lower windows. *It's better than nothing.*

Over the sound of the rushing air outside, he heard a click and laughed.

"Starnes, you bastard, you aren't going to kill me," he said.

Starnes clung to an open closet door, the pistol aimed at Skara.

"You're a bureaucrat, a paper pusher. You don't have the will to shoot another man."

The portly aide looked tired.

"You're right, Marshal Skara, I don't," he said.

Two shots. Both struck the windows. They spider-webbed before shattering. Cold air grabbed at Skara like clawed hands. He struggled to maintain his grip as the metal railing became icy. His leg slipped under the railing. *No, No, No.*

A shot whizzed past him. Then another. *That stupid, fucking, bastard Starnes.* A shot grazed the railing. It vibrated, and his hand slipped.

Skara's arm groaned briefly. He made one last-ditch effort to pull himself back inside. Then his arm gave out, and he fell. Cold air seized him in its grasp.

So this is it, huh? Skara took in the sight of the gray world around him. Gray sky. Gray surface. It was all just murky soup. The airship dove towards the ground, and so did he. *Well, so be it. They didn't deserve my genius, anyway.*

19

R eiter hovered over the projection on the table. The frontline was less than five miles from Objective Mauler, and they had been assigned a wing in the attack. The regiment was tasked with taking the southern section of Mauler. In support of this, Fox would take the heights and provide a base of fire for the rest of the regiment.

His eyes drifted to the small town he'd noticed before. Its name was Wayside, and it was right next to the heights they were supposed to take. He sighed. *None of this is ever simple.*

"Comidus, I want Gold Platoon to sweep this town ahead of us," Reiter said. "Clear out any enemies and inform any civilians to evacuate."

Comidus nodded. He, along with the other leaders of Fox Company, sat around the projection table as well.

"That might slow down our offensive momentum. Are you sure, sir?"

Reiter nodded.

"I want no surprises, no accidental civilian deaths, either," he replied. As he looked at the faces of everyone around him, he continued. "This upcoming battle is going to be unlike anything we've faced before. It's not just going to be us out there. There's a lot of moving parts, so it's important we do ours."

"How are we planning on doing this?" Mo asked. He pointed to their company objective. "It looks like we just take some high ground near Mauler and unload on them."

Reiter wagged a finger.

"Not quite. Gold's going to go in first and recon the area like I just detailed." The projector changed as he spoke, showing units moving along the plan. "White and Black Platoons will follow and eliminate hard targets before they set security. Gold will establish screens to the west and north." He noted their perimeter around the heights. "Headquarters element will set up on the heights and provide supporting fire for other companies moving on Mauler. Any questions?"

Steele raised a hand.

"What'll we do if we get counterattacked?"

"Excellent question," Adamski said. "Most likely we'll come under attack by dropships. They're tough, highly mobile, and capable of taking on Panzerters. Adamski said. The good news is, our newer Panzerters can take some hits from them, and Gold Platoon has a stupid amount of anti-aircraft missiles."

Reiter nodded.

"More than likely, they'll send dropships to harass us so we stop shooting Mauler," he said, "and they'll withdraw if they think they'll go down. The most dangerous thing they could do is send a company of Panzerters supported by dropships to attack us. However, we think that's unlikely."

"Why?" Mo asked.

"Zoom out," Reiter said. The projection zoomed out to show multiple smaller lines of attack along with the push for Mauler.

"Besides reducing reinforcements for Mauler, they're going to stretch themselves thin all along the front."

Mo nodded and whistled.

"All this to take a single forward base?" he asked.

"Mauler sits on a strategic point," Adamski explained. "If it falls, it exposes the Union's entire rear to raids by attack boats and insurgency fueled by weapons shipments, and we have a base to launch an attack back towards the old border."

"Okay, I think I understand now," Mo said.

Reiter slapped his forehead.

"That reminds me, we're getting some additional firepower from GC Tech." He pulled up an image of a long tubular weapon. "Steele, Adamski, and Mo are all going to carry these into battle in addition to their rifles. They're bazookas with four-round magazines."

Adamski grinned.

"Damn, 200-mm shells? Those bitches will punch right through them!"

Reiter nodded.

"We've come a long way from barely being able to hurt them," he said. Someone knocked on their door. "Enter."

Merlin opened the door with a folder and storage drive in his hands.

"Some guys from HHC dropped this off. They said it was the latest intel report." He adjusted his glasses and handed his materials to Reiter, who loaded the drive and thumbed through the folder.

Oh no, that's not good at all.

"You guys know how bad news comes in threes?" he said. His leaders groaned. "Merlin, you might want to stick around and hear this."

Adamski stood and walked over to Reiter.

"What's the damage?" he asked. Reiter showed him the files before handing him the folder. "Lord help us."

Reiter turned back to the table and changed the projection.

"So our first piece of bad news is, it looks like the Union regulars are getting tinhats, or at least a version of them, and like we saw the other day, they're using ballistic weapons." The projector switched to an image of the regular tinhats.

"What are the other two things?" Steele asked.

Reiter slumped a little.

"There's not a lot of information available. It's more rumor than anything else, actually," he said. "But our intel believes the Union are fielding a new heavy Panzerter, roughly comparable to the Lowe."

"Ooooh shit," Mo said. "Do you think it has a railgun?"

"How many do they have?" Steele asked.

Reiter raised his hands.

"Let's relax a little. If it's comparable to the Lowe, I would wager they have maybe one operational. Unless they back-engineered it, it's likely an early prototype," he said. "And a bit of good news I also forgot, MAVAG got a manufactory going on the Mariner coast. As soon as the first production Lowe rolls off the line, we'll be receiving it."

"I call dibs," Adamski said, getting a laugh out of the room. His smile withered rather quickly. "Well, I guess we have to mention the worst news now."

Reiter nodded and sighed.

"We've received reports that the Union will launch an attack inside the window for our own attack," he said.

"What does that have to do with our attack?" Mo asked.

"If we're busy fending off an attack, it could stop us from launching our own before the rivers freeze," Reiter explained.

"Oh," Mo said quietly.

Reiter scanned the room.

"Are there any other questions?" he asked. When he saw no hands, he dismissed them.

As they filed out of the room, Reiter pulled up the projection of the Union's heavy Panzerter. He studied the image and sat down. *It looks like the bastard child of the Lowe and a tinhat.* The thought angered him.

So either there's a spy in the Lowe team, the Union's hacked their files, or both. He spun the image around so he could better take it in. *Is that black paint? Or the heat-resistant coating of the Lowe? Not that it matters—I don't use thermal weapons.* He didn't think it was likely, but he imagined this thing going toe-to-toe with the Lowe.

———

"Good evening, Comrade Major," called a familiar feminine voice.

Kennedy grinned as he walked towards the massive tent before him. Snow batted at his head, but the ground refused to allow it to stay.

As he crossed the wet gravel, he smiled and shook hands with the woman who greeted him.

"Ah, Comrade Lieutenant Colonel Meyer, it's good to see you empowered," he said.

Meyer grinned back at him.

"After our battalion fended off multiple attacks with limited resources, they had no choice but to promote me." She waved her hands at everything around her. "And now we're able to support all of this. I didn't think it would have been possible three weeks ago!" The retreating sun cast the clouds above with a blueish-gray haze.

Kennedy sighed, gently releasing a foggy breath.

"And yet the Tharcians draw closer."

Slowly, a smile spread across the battalion commander's face.

"And yet they haven't done anything we haven't expected," she said. "They've taken mostly minor footholds, while we saved our veteran pilots for Operation Scour."

Kennedy looked east.

"Excuse me for not having overwhelming confidence, but based on the warning order, there's a lot of moving parts involved," he said. "That doesn't exactly fill me with confidence." He took out a pack of cigarettes and lit one.

Meyer raised an eyebrow.

"I didn't know you smoked," she said.

He shrugged.

"I picked it up on the Olympian Front" He took a drag on his cigarette and relaxed as he released the smoke.

"I had no idea it was that rough," Meyer said.

"It got weirdly existential at times," he admitted. "I never thought about things like purpose or future until I got down there." He heard a click and noticed Meyer lighting her own cigarette.

"What?" she said. "I had four Panzerters against an entire regiment. I'll smoke if I want to." After her first drag, she looked at him. "You're a tuber, though, right?"

"Yeah, what of it?" Kennedy asked.

"What would prompt you to think about your purpose or future?" she asked. "I thought it was all laid out for you."

He fumbled with the cigarette in his hand before answering.

"I used to think that too."

"Well?" she asked. "What changed?"

Kennedy took another drag on his cigarette.

"You know that guy in charge of R&D? Guard Colonel Chaney?" She nodded. "He undid my sterilization procedure."

Instead of shock, Meyer reacted with mild surprise.

"Why are you here, then?" she asked. "Why aren't you hip-deep in some civilian of your preference?"

Kennedy kicked at the wet gravel at his feet.

"They offered me more than the right to vote," he said. "They're giving me the right to hold office when I complete my service."

Meyer slipped into a coughing fit when he said that. Blinking through her wet eyes, she shook her head.

"That's fucked up," she replied.

Kennedy raised an eyebrow. *Am I crazy or does it sound like she knows more than she's letting on.*

"Why do you say that?" he asked.

"They offered Wake the same thing, even gave him an experimental Panzerter," she replied.

Kennedy's eyes went wide.

"They gave him a Jupiter?"

"They gave you one of those too, huh?" She wrinkled her nose in disgust. "Your point of contact is Chaney too, I presume?"

"I need to contact him," Kennedy said.

"I'll contact him. You and Wake are both my soldiers, so I'll take care of the issue," she said. "Besides, you're my XO. I can't have you going off on a Guard Colonel, even if he's a shady egghead."

Kennedy relaxed. A little.

"So, executive officer, huh?" he asked.

Meyer nodded.

"You think if I have a competent guard major, I'd be content for him to be a mere company commander?" she asked.

Ignoring the rhetorical question, he asked a question of his own.

"Who's going to take over Reaper?"

"You are, until a clear successor becomes apparent or you're promoted to a rank that prevents us from justifying you leading a company," she said.

Kennedy puffed on his cigarette. The next step up for him would be a battalion command, like Meyer's. *Makes sense. I'm getting as high as I can get while being in the field.*

"As of right now, I don't have a clear successor," he said. "Both my lieutenants are good, but Ballard lacks initiative while Fletcher lacks maturity."

"Then, that's something we'll work on now that you're back in a proper MAG battalion," Meyer replied. She took a long drag on her cigarette. "So, what would you do with the ability to hold office?"

Kennedy shrugged.

"I want to build a better Mars. I think the Union would be stronger if we blurred the lines between tubers and naturals. We have so many resources in space." He waved his arms at the sky. "Imagine how much we could improve our lives if we used them more efficiently, or if we didn't have to compete with Tharsis or even Avalon."

Meyer nodded.

"You know, I think the problem is Tharsis using up resources way too fast." She tapped a wet gravel stone with her foot. "There's only so much water in the solar system, and you know they use excessive amounts of it."

"Well, yeah, we'd have to regulate water usage, but I'm sure we can get experts to figure out the perfect amount of water for everyone, and food too." Kennedy scratched at the back of his head. "And I'm sure we'll be able to integrate former Tharcians as well."

Meyer's eyes narrowed.

"Probably not going to be a good idea, Comrade," she said. "The old Soviet Union tried giving them all the rights of Soviet citizens." She dropped her cigarette butt and stamped it out. Gesturing in the general direction of Tharsis, she continued. "*That's* what ended up happening. Now the SSR is a shell of its former self and the Tharcians are here."

"You're telling me this why?" Kennedy asked.

"Because you won't be able to trust the Tharcians. They're shifty, superstitious class traitors," she answered. "I'm not even a hardcore Unionist, but even I can see the Tharcians don't have or want any place in it."

Kennedy nodded and stared off at the gray clouds.

I had no idea about any of that. Guess I need to learn my own history before I go trying to make it. He kicked a gravel stone. *I know basic facts, but I need a deeper understanding of things before my time.* With a sigh, he dropped his cigarette and stamped it out.

"LOOK ALIVE, PEOPLE," REITER SAID AS THEIR PANZERTERS crossed into rolling hills south of Garden City. The remains of a colossal airship bent over the nearest hill. The wreck disappeared into fog beyond his sight. Debris littered the fields.

"Alright, let's get our perimeter set," Adamski said.

Reiter approached the hull. Lady Sofia. Though the lettering on the hull was warped and disfigured, he could make out the name of the airship. *The supreme commander was aboard.*

"Gold Platoon, status?" he asked. Snow flurried about the Panzerter's head.

"We're just beginning our sweep for survivors," Comidus replied. "We're going to figure out how many decks are intact and where survivors are most likely located."

Reiter nodded.

"Roger, keep me updated," he said. *This isn't a military vessel, it's a luxury liner.* He brought the Lowe back and paced the wreck. *Did someone tip off the Union?* He began examining the engines, the ones he could see, at least.

"Think they knew he was aboard?" Bartonova asked. She stood by with him, in case the infantry needed something moved.

"I was wondering that myself," he said. "This obviously isn't a freighter, so they would have known they were committing a war crime." They hadn't known Field Marshal Ernest Skara was aboard the vessel until they'd stepped off to come here. Six hours prior, he'd been informed of a downed airship south of Garden City.

"We've cleared the lowest deck," Comidus said. "Trust me, you guys don't want to come in here."

Reiter shook his head. Hours passed. He scrounged around the debris field, looking for any sign of survivors.

"Status?" he asked after the sun began its descent below the horizon.

"We're about to cut through a bulkhead into the main dining room. At least, that's what the map says is on the other side here," Comidus replied.

"I recommend you hurry. It's already getting dark out here," Reiter said. "I'd like us to be well rested before the big offensive." Silence hung in the darkening air.

"We got something," Comidus said. Reiter perked up. "We can hear voices on the other side as we're cutting."

Bartonova's unit stepped around the broken nose of the airship and waved him over.

"Hey, 6, you should come look at this," she said.

Reiter followed her around to the port side of the fallen vessel. She pointed up to a set of pylons jutting out of the upper edge of the hull.

"What am I looking at, Valkyrie?" he asked.

"Those are engine mounts, and they're too high to have been sheared off," she said. "An airship can remain aloft without them, but it won't be able to turn or fly as fast."

"So they disabled her first," Reiter nodded. "Is that a standard tactic? Like, if it was a freighter, would they have disabled it so they could tow it?"

Bartonova pointed to a gaping hole in the top of the bow.

"Not in this case. That's where the helium cells are stored in the bow. If they're destroyed, an airship will crash." She began tracing lines from the sky into the hole. "Yeah, and with that angle of attack, they would have seen the lights of the dining hall and the ballroom."

"So no way they mistook this for a freighter?" he asked.

"No, none," she replied.

"Hey 6, we got survivors: ten women, six children, four men," Comidus said. "We're going to need some help to extract them."

"Praise God," Reiter said. "What do you guys need?"

After a brief pause, Comidus came back.

"So two of the kids can't walk out of here, and there's no elevator or anything to move them."

"Where are you guys?" Reiter asked.

"Main dining hall, upper deck," Comidus replied.

Reiter walked over to the damaged section. Turning on his floodlights, he saw an elevated area of the surface capped by a gleaming glass dome.

"What if I cut through the hull?" Reiter asked.

"With your sword?" Comidus asked. "Probably a bad idea. You can't see in here, and if the walls are completely compromised, the transparent steel above us will give and rain shattered glass on us."

"Noted," Reiter said. "What if I worked slowly? Cut a space just big enough for my hand to reach in and get the passengers?"

"That might work," Comidus replied. "Line up on the center of the dome and cut a space for you to stick your hand through. I'll let you know if you're coming too far."

"Roger," Reiter replied. He reached into his shield and grasped the hilt of his sword. He yanked it free of its holster, and it crackled to life. Bathed in its blue glow, he angled the blade at the hull, one hand gripping the hilt, the other guiding it.

Gingerly, he sank the blade into the skin of the airship. Sparks spewed from the hull as the blade sank in.

"That's good, 6," Comidus said.

Carefully, he brought the blade over in a small arc.

"Alright, get everyone away from the opening," Reiter said.

As soon as he got the all-clear from Comidus, he slowly pushed his left hand into the section. The plates he cut were easily displaced. Unable to see inside, he turned his wrist up and opened his hand.

"Come in a little closer," Comidus asked. Reiter inserted the arm almost to the elbow. "That's good."

"Got it, let me know when they're ready," Reiter replied. He stood there, arm awkwardly inserted into the airship.

"They're set. I got two of my guys with them," Comidus said.

"Roger, lifting now," Reiter replied. Bracing himself with his sword arm, he withdrew his arm from the dining hall. Released into the harsh glare of his floodlights, the kids covered their eyes. As if he held Christmas ornaments, Reiter lowered his hand to the ground. The riflemen assisted the children out of his hand.

Once on the ground, they gawked at the metal giant towering in the darkness. An IFV came around the corner, ready to tend to their needs. After five hours of rescue operations, Reiter dismounted to confer with Comidus and Adamski, taking his maps with him.

"We've got too many people to carry them all back with our tracks," Comidus said.

Reiter spread his map across the hood of the nearest track. Turning on a small red light, he showed them their position.

"Can you fit all the survivors on tracks?" Reiter asked.

Comidus nodded.

"You're not going to make my boys walk, are you?"

Reiter shook his head.

"No, they're going to ride in cargo nets attached to the Panzert-ers," he said. "Now let's get to work."

KENNEDY STALKED FORWARD. THE JUPITER'S FOOT STUCK FAST. Yanking it free brought back memories of the attack at Riverside. *Things are different now. We're working around our weaknesses, while they still have theirs.*

Ahead of his forces lay a shallow section of this leg of the river. This area was called Black Moor, and in the dark of the night, it seemed a fitting name. Skeletal trees scraped at their armor, creating haunting wails throughout the low hills. Clouds blotted out most of the stars, save for a scant few clusters.

Beyond the stretch of river lay a fortified Tharcian gun position. *I'm pretty sure it's right across from here.* Kennedy's plan was fairly straightforward. Leave a platoon across from the guns, then take another platoon around behind the position to flank it.

"Alright, fires element set?" Kennedy asked.

"Roger, Comrade, standing by," Fletcher said.

"Roger, flanking platoon, let's move out," Kennedy said.

Ballard confirmed, and five Martian Troopers followed him south. Kennedy continually referenced his command matrix, if only to keep track of their positions. *Damn satellite reception is spotty as hell.*

They split into two groups. Two troopers followed Ballard while two others followed Kennedy himself. They kept about a half a click between the two groups as they approached a deeper section of the river. His machine waded in, the black water lapping at his torso. Occasionally, a chunk of ice struck him. *You're running out of time, Tharcians.*

Somewhere ahead of him, artillery rumbled. *Shit, were we spotted?* Kennedy pushed his machine into high gear, its treaded feet tearing up the riverbed. Water poured down his sides as he heard the shells rush overhead like a passing train. And burst in the distance.

Kennedy relaxed, slightly. Slowing his pace, he checked the command matrix again. *Alright, now we just turn east and, in another klick, north.* They had only moved a few hundred meters when guns thundered behind them. *Must be answering that Tharcian battery.* Kennedy grinned. *Fuck 'em.*

The familiar train sound took on a higher pitch. One Kennedy knew all too well.

"Incoming!" he hollered into the radio.

The Jupiter and its escorts broke into a run. The scream of the shells grew louder. The Trooper to his right, Kopperud, staggered. A shell struck his leg. Then he fell, several others striking his back.

His Martian suddenly disappeared in a pulse of blue. Kopperud's dying light burnt the trees around him and turned scant snow to steam. It also gave away their position.

"Shit, Reaper 2, our approach is compromised, we're double-timing to our position," Kennedy said. "Reaper 6, begin your attack run. We'll meet you there." As the Jupiter ran, he checked his matrix. Based on the analytics, Fletcher's group would only last two minutes before they were completely destroyed. On their shortest route at max speed, they'd make it in one minute, forty-five seconds.

"Flankers, double-time and follow me!" Kennedy zig-zagged the Jupiter as he ran towards their target. The other soldiers with him did likewise. Bigger guns struggled to get a fix on them, and smaller guns only scored glancing hits. Between having his head smashed against the wall by sudden turns, he looked at his matrix.

One minute until they reached their objective. Forty-five

seconds until Fletcher's element was destroyed. They were already down two units with another damaged. *We're cutting this shit close.*

As gun positions revealed themselves, his laser stabbed out at them. Ghostly green light lanced into bunkers. Magazines exploded. Gun barrels melted. Unable to hold them back, Kennedy's element was able to break through the screen.

The Tharcians had Fletcher's element against the ropes, but they weren't down yet. They clung to the lower slopes of the hills like a bulldog to a toy. Fletcher herself wielded a rifle in each hand, making up for their reduced numbers. Kennedy added the shoulder cannon to the fray and advanced.

Quickly setting his laser to strobe, he tore apart bunker after bunker. Something flashed near the Jupiter's head, followed by a series of dull thuds. Then he was blind for a moment. His vision returned. To his right, a squad of infantry perched in a barren tree. Several of them held rocket launchers.

Cute. He drew his mace and shattered the upper portion of the tree, soldiers and all. Then he caught movement on the Jupiter. *Shit.* He dove and rolled. Sirens blared all across his HUD.

"Aw, get them off me!" One of Ballard's wingmen ran about. Infantry clung to him.

"Hold still!" Ensuring his laser was set to strobe, Kennedy systematically picked the men off his comrade.

"Thank you, Comrade! I—" He was cut off when several small explosions raced across his Panzerter. Then his ammo cooked off. The Martian Trooper collapsed in a catastrophic display.

Kennedy opened his mouth to say something, but his own machine was rocked by explosions. *Damn it, they had satchel charges.*

He fought for balance. So far, his ammo was okay, but he didn't know if the enemy had secondary charges. The Jupiter jerked as if a giant mule had kicked it. Kennedy's head slammed against his chair as his Panzerter was knocked on its back. He looked at the damage readout.

The satchel charges had ravaged him, but the Jupiter's thick armor prevented damage to anything vital. The chest armor had been very nearly penetrated but just barely held against a Tharcian howitzer. *This is our chance.* Slamming a switch to his left, smoke poured out of the Jupiter from several areas. If one didn't look closely, it looked like his engine had caught fire.

The smoke wafted between the remaining gun positions and his forces. *That should give them a few seconds to regroup. From there, it's either fall back or assault through.* He turned to the remaining gun positions. Only one contained heavy guns; the rest were clearly meant for autocannons. *They don't stand a chance if that thing gets the drop on them.*

The dots on his map formed a wedge and advanced on the last positions. *Damn, they're persistent, if nothing else.* He turned his attention back to the heavy guns. *Just like that Centurion, you're in my way.* As the rest of the Reapers advanced, Kennedy nudged his laser towards the heavy guns.

The smaller positions opened fire. Their stray shots nearly blinded him, but most just bounced off his hull with a dull ring. The Reapers would pass him any second. *Now or never.*

The strobing light of his laser sent the heavy gun skyward. The shockwave from its exploding magazine knocked multiple systems offline. Briefly, the night was illuminated by an expanding orange mushroom. The autocannons were silenced.

When the ringing stopped, he rolled his Panzerter onto its stomach and stood. The gun positions were destroyed. Reaper Company was now seven Panzerters in various states of disrepair, but they stood on the first parcel of land the Union had taken since the invasion stopped.

"Comrades, for those of you who are new, welcome to Tharsis,"
he said.

20

"So, you kept the survivors alive for a week?" Mo asked. He poured coffee for the portly major across from him. *Not that I'm used to overweight majors, but I thought that was a Provincial Watch thing.*

Major Starnes nodded.

"Yeah, I did. None of them had any survival skills whatsoever. Luckily, I remembered enough from SERE training to pull through."

"You had SERE training, sir?" Mo asked. "No offense, but I thought you were a desk jock."

Starnes shrugged.

"None taken. I'm an Intelligence officer. We're all given SERE training in the event we're captured so we can escape." He poured another cup for Steele, who sat next to him, and set the empty pot in the center of the table.

"Sorry if our coffee is a little black for your liking," Mo said. "We've been short on cream and sugar."

Starnes waved him off.

"I was an operations officer in an infantry regiment before I was the marshal's aide. Trust me, I'm no stranger to black coffee." They chuckled at that.

"So, what was the marshal like?" Steele asked. "Captain Reiter is the highest-ranking officer I've been around long-term, and he's kind of boring at times."

"Reiter's bookish and stiff, but I wouldn't call him boring, necessarily," Mo said.

Starnes shook his head.

"Honestly, I would have taken a boring officer over the marshal," he said. "He was a career politician, one who happened to wear a uniform." He sighed. "I apologize. I'm not going to get into the politics of the General Staff. Tell me about your commander instead."

"Well, what do you want to know?" Mo asked. "And why?"

"I'll be working closely with the man for the time being, and I want to know what he's like," Starnes replied. Mo scratched at his head. "Mo, was it? You seem to know him better. What kind of man is he?"

"Well, he was my L-T when this shit show started," Mo replied. "He's also the TA for our Tharcian History class in college. He was thrown into his position because we lost a lot of good people, but he's good." Mo threw up his hands. "If I say much more, it'll sound cliché. You'll just see for yourself, sir."

Starnes nodded.

"That's fair," the man replied.

Why do I get battered wife vibes from this guy?

"So, what will you be doing, Major?" Steele asked.

Starnes sipped his coffee before replying.

"Your regimental commander has commandeered my services as an operations officer. He's been looking for officers to fill these rolls." He took another swig of coffee. "Apparently the Union has a whole computer system dedicated to relaying tactical information."

"Then why aren't we using that ourselves?" Steele asked. Mo nodded.

Starnes set his coffee down.

"Well, for starters, a guy with a map, notepad, calculator, and a radio is harder to hack, isn't vulnerable to cyber warfare, and is, in some ways, more reliable," he replied.

"That's fair," Mo said. "But doesn't that create a conflict of interest with Captain Reiter?"

Starnes shook his head.

"Your commander makes the hard choices. I just give him the numbers or update him on the big picture," he replied. "Just think of me as a computer that's a major."

Mo nodded.

"Okay, I think I understand," he said. He finished his coffee and left the cafeteria. He was about to head to his room when Steele called out to him.

"Hey Mo, do you have a minute?" she asked.

"Sure, what's going on?" he asked. "Walk with me." He strode down the hall with the shorter woman at his side.

"So, how does your team get ready for battle?" she asked. "I go over our plans multiple times, but I feel like I'm missing something."

"So you want to know why we walk around as if we're Panzerters with brooms in our hands like a bunch of weirdos," he replied, "but you're being polite about it."

She blushed briefly.

"I didn't *say* it looked weird."

"But you did the same thing with Renner," he said. "It's called a walkthrough."

She blinked.

"I thought he was doing that to punish us for something or whatever."

Mo shrugged.

"To the extent you guys were doing it, yeah," he replied. "And he wasn't running you through a mission, just random formations, if I remember right?" She shrugged. "Well, first we go over the plan on paper. Once we've established the plan, we walk through it with brooms representing weapons."

"Why do you do that, though?" she asked.

"It helps with muzzle discipline and to keep their attention where it's needed," he replied. "It seems bizarre, but it helps. After a few broom runs, we go to the sims if we have time, but lately we haven't."

She shook her head.

"Where did you get the idea?" she asked.

Mo hung his head slightly.

"It was Sergeant Varga's bread and butter," he replied. "He always did whatever he could to teach us, make sure we understood everything we were being trained to do." He shook his head. "He always told us, 'know how to do the job of the next guy up, in case something terrible happens.'"

Steele took his hand.

"Mo, are you going to be okay?" she asked.

Am I okay? Why am I like this? She went through hell because of her leadership. And here I am just sad.

"Yeah, yeah, Amy, I'm going to be fine," he replied.

She smiled.

"It feels like forever since I've heard my first name."

"It was kinda weird saying it," he replied. *I haven't heard mine since my sisters got sent east.* "I wonder if my sisters were able to find Mom."

"I can call Erika and find out," Steele offered.

Mo nodded.

"Yeah, that'd be great." They got quiet for a moment.

"You were close to Varga?" she asked.

He nodded.

"Closer than most. He's the closest thing I've had to a father in thirteen years. Third Platoon in general was pretty tightknit." He reached his door and faced her. "I'm sorry your platoon wasn't like that."

"Maybe someday I'll know what that's like," she said, avoiding eye contact.

Mo folded her into a warm hug.

"I'm going to lie down, but call me if you need anything," he said.

After going into his room, Mo collapsed onto his bed. Turning on a nature doc, he relaxed. *I've been pining for the opportunity to talk to Bartonova since I got to the unit, but now that I talk to her whenever I want, Amy's had me feeling some kind of way. Leave it to a war to make me figure my life out.*

———

KENNEDY SURVEYED THE SCENE BEFORE HIM. THE THARCIANS HAD seemingly left a gap in their lines. Not a particularly large one, maybe three kilometers wide at most. Nevertheless, the flats before him presented an opportunity.

Flooding removed most of the trees and brush, leaving little cover for Panzerters. *If I were a betting man, I'd say they had artillery or big guns zeroed on that area.* The flats terminated roughly four clicks away from him into a low hill. *Really, they'd only have a few, if any, target reference points.*

He made a few estimates on their ground speed. *They're probably ready for an attack straight through, but what about a flanking attack?* Kennedy pictured the adjacent company setting a base of fire while they attacked through the flank. *Wait, what if both companies to my flank attack and I flank the weaker one?*

"Leviathan 6, Reaper 6."

"Go ahead, Reaper," Meyer replied. Kennedy walked her through the basics of his plan. "Roger, sounds good. I'll have Sandman and Goblin cause a fuss down there."

Kennedy relaxed for a second.

"Heads up, Reapers. Friendly elements on our flank are going to open fire on the Tharcians in front of them. I'll engage the weaker one, and we'll destroy them." He received a chorus of confirmations. *Good, now we're all on the same sheet of music.*

The Reapers had been reinforced to ten machines, his Jupiter, his two lieutenants, and seven other pilots. Three machines led by Fletcher formed a triangle in front of him, three more formed a diamond with him at the tip, and Ballard brought up the rear with two machines in another triangle.

The Panzerters on either side of them opened fire. Heavy shells and high-intensity lasers tore into bunkers and brush. Kennedy patiently observed the response from both sides of the gap. The right side reacted immediately, but the left was slower despite being shot first.

"Heads up, we're going left," Kennedy said.

The Panzerters surged forward. Ballard's wingman went down, struck by a high-velocity shell. It collapsed without its head. *Damn it, a concealed big gun? No, the angle is too high. Sniper.*

Kennedy faced a choice: press on or fall back? "Continue to advance, lay down covering fire!"

The Reapers blasted away as they advanced. Kennedy added his shoulder cannon to the suppressive fire. One of his wingmen staggered, smoke leaking out its torso. A second shell struck its spare mags, and it burst into flames. Still, they advanced.

Kennedy swung them left as they came online. Weapons fire arced toward them. *Enemy Panzerters.* As Kennedy pushed his element forward, the Tharcians advanced on them. Kennedy's shoulder cannon and strobe laser tore through their armor, but his comrades began reporting penetrating hits from Tharcian Panzerters.

We're caught in a counterassault. If we don't get into the woods, the snipers will pick us off. I need support, or my company is going to get massacred. Kennedy cleaved through a Panzerter's head. The unit spun away and fell.

"Leviathan 6, we're caught in the open without support!" Kennedy cried.

"Hang tight, Reaper 6, help is on the way," Meyer replied.

Hang tight? Does she fucking want us to get killed? A swarm of dropships raced overhead. Drones screamed past them and launched missiles at targets on the ground while drawing anti-aircraft fire. The pressure let up on them.

Still, they were locked in close quarters with Tharcian Panzerters. Fletcher's machine danced around a charging Tharcian. Its sword just missing her, she fired her laser into its back. It collapsed in a burning wreck. She staggered as a stream of shells struck her machine. Another Tharcian had her dead to rights.

It was promptly blasted to scrap by Kennedy's shoulder cannon. More shells struck him, rattling his teeth. His armor held, though, and he downed another Tharcian. Only for yet another to rush him with a sword. He caught the blade with his free hand, letting it penetrate up to his elbow.

"Hold him right there," said a familiar voice. Kennedy barely understood Wake over the wail of alarms as systems in his arm failed. So he was surprised when the Tharcian's head disappeared in a shower of sparks and metal. Not wasting the opening, Kennedy poured shot after shot from his laser into the headless Panzerter. Its sword deactivated as it collapsed.

The Tharcians faced a counterassault of their own now. *A counter-counterassault, I guess.* Wake's forces attacked along the seam between the gun positions and the Tharcians in the gap. Unsupported by their snipers and facing twice the amount of MAGs as they thought they would, the Tharcians attempted to withdraw back to their positions.

Reaper and Wake's Manticore Company gave chase. They destroyed forward-facing guns as they went. Having routed the Tharcians in the immediate area, Goblin Company advanced to help hold the salient Wake and Kennedy had created. Meyer informed them regular forces would arrive soon to hold the new front.

"Well, Comrade, this takes me way back," Wake said.

Kennedy took a moment to examine the other Jupiter. Wake's machine had a few minor differences. His shoulder cannon possessed a different muzzle brake, and the head had a different antenna arrangement. Other than that and the red and gray paint job, the Jupiters were twins.

"Yeah, we didn't have machines like these back then, though," Kennedy replied.

Wake laughed.

"We would have sent the class traitors running back then if we had these," he replied, flexing his machine's hand. "They wouldn't have stood a chance."

From what I can tell, he's still merely an attack dog, an unthinking, unquestionably loyal brute. What did they see in him?

"You wouldn't happen to have some spare parts lying around, would you?" Kennedy asked. He raised his ruined hand and forearm.

Wake laughed.

"Yeah, between the two of us, I don't think we need to worry about spare parts. We should be the only ones getting them," he replied.

Kennedy nodded. Unless both machines were nearly totaled, they would have enough parts to fix whatever was wrong with them.

The dropships returned, fewer, but likely victorious. Kennedy smiled as snow drifted past him.

"THIS IS CONCERNING, TO SAY THE LEAST," STARNES SAID. REITER shook his head.

"You can say that again," Adamski replied. "It's a damn near fucking disaster."

Reiter set a hand on his shoulder.

"Easy, old friend, but Major Starnes is indeed correct." What had started as a trap for the Unionists turned into a disaster when the Unionists managed to turn the flank of an entire six-kilometer stretch of defensive lines. Gunboats and drones still harassed the Union as they tried to consolidate their new positions.

"Then why the hell are they still insisting we're going to attack Mauler when our northern flank is nearly compromised?" Mo asked.

Steele nodded.

"I don't want to get cut off in the middle of an attack," she said.

Reiter raised his hand.

"It's actually a better plan than you would think," he said. "Attacking your enemy's rear or homeland usually forces them to pull back and do nothing but defend themselves."

Starnes shifted the projection to display the tactical situation around Mauler.

"Mind you, this could all change at a moment's notice, especially since we're QRF for this sector," he said. "But otherwise our plans remain the same."

Comidus folded his arms.

"There's been a lot more reports of those MAG forces in the theatre," he said. "We fought them during the initial stages of the invasion, but the new soldiers haven't had that much experience against them."

"Black tangled with them the other day," Mo said, looking at Reiter. "I might be reading too much into it, but they fell for tricks that they had been starting to wise up to when we previously fought them."

Starnes raised an eyebrow.

"Tricks such as?"

"Sticking your sword in water to create steam and block their lasers, playing dead, that kind of thing, sir," Mo said. "They reeked of green forces, and personally, I don't think we're killing them nearly fast enough to cause a pilot shortage."

Starnes nodded.

"Trust me, you're right, we haven't," he said. "Which leaves us with the implication you just made."

"They're holding their veterans in reserve," Reiter said. *They're consolidating veteran pilots while we shove kids into Panzerters, at least on this front.* He looked from Mo to Steele and back. *They're definitely not green anymore. Hell, they're training each other now.*

"You got something, boss?" Adamski asked.

Reiter nodded.

"I do. I want us to double up our training time," he said. "More sims, more walkthroughs, introduce one-on-one sims as well as company-level ones. We need to increase individual proficiency as well as our company cohesion." He looked at Starnes. "For all sims, I'd like you in the training room so we can get used to your updates and interactions with the rest of us." He looked at Adamski, Mo,

Bartonova, and Steele. "I'd also like all four of you to get qualified on the Lowe. When we get more, I want a seamless transition from your current machines to the new ones." *And in case I go down, I don't want the Lowe to just sit around.*

Mo grinned.

"I was annoyed with 'double up on training,' but you had me with 'get Lowe qualified,'" he said.

Reiter looked at Comidus.

"We have something for Gold Platoon as well."

The infantry officer raised an eyebrow.

"Really? And here I was thinking pilots got all the cool toys," he said.

"Well, you got more Orias missiles for your Cstalios, and the Iglasios are going to get a new turret courtesy of the Lowe team," Reiter replied. Starnes brought the image up on the projector.

"Glad I don't have to do that anymore," Bartonova said.

Reiter ignored her as the Iglasio turret resolved itself.

"Based on their plans for a magnetic point-defense system, the 35-mm cannon is going to be swapped for a magnetized version. This will allow it to beat other armored vehicles and older Panzerters," he said. "This is going to come with a power plant upgrade of course. Oh, and the Cstalios are going to be coated in the same heat-resistant coating as the Lowe."

"Well, damn, yeah, that's a lot of cool toys," Comidus said.

Reiter rose from his seat.

"We'll start training at 1000 tomorrow. Until then, we're on ready status three for QRF," he said. "Any questions?" When he saw no one raise their hands, he dismissed them. His stomach protested as he left the ready room, and he felt woozy. *Shit, I forgot to eat dinner. Fuck it, I'll get something from the cafe before bed.*

After making his way to the second floor, he stumbled into the cafeteria as the staff were cleaning tables. He walked over to the sandwich bar, and a cook got his attention.

"Hey sir, would you like some soup with your sandwich?" the man asked.

Reiter nodded.

"What kind is it?"

"Beef noodle."

Eh, sometimes it's good, sometimes it isn't. As he put together a sandwich and the cook reheated soup, he realized he wasn't the only one in here to eat. One of his pilots sat in the corner, eating a sandwich while watching the evening news. *Huh, maybe he comes here to be left alone? Or he's just also hungry.*

The young man made eye contact with Reiter as he retrieved his soup. *Shit, this is awkward. If I don't sit with him, he might think I don't like him. What's this kid's name again?* Reiter's head swam until he found an answer. *Merlin.* Despite his exhaustion, Reiter sat across from him.

"Good evening, Merlin," he said. "I'm not bothering you, am I?"

Merlin shook his head.

"No, sir, not at all," he replied. "Though, to be honest, I came here for some quiet."

Reiter gave him an understanding smile.

"People tend to wear on you? Don't they?"

Merlin blinked, an action his large round glasses emphasized.

"Yes, sir. It's not that I don't like my teammates, I just need to be left alone sometimes," he replied.

Reiter nodded.

"Trust me, after answering questions, planning, video conferences, training, I get tired of dealing with people too sometimes," he replied. "How is Corporal Steele? Like, as a leader?"

Merlin shrugged.

"She reminds me of my English teacher. She's not what I expected at all, to be honest." He sipped his drink. "Although, lately we've been training with Black a lot. I kinda wish we still did our own thing."

"And why is that?"

"Well, besides more people, Corporal Mo has us walk around with brooms and pretend to be Panzerters! And I thought we were grown men and women!" Reiter chuckled. "Sir?"

"That whole stick was our old platoon sergeant's idea, and let me tell you, we out-simmed anyone in the regiment after doing walkthroughs," he said. "If I'm correct, your next walkthrough is a hand-to-hand class. Make sure you pay attention to what Corporal Mo and Steele say; it's a critical skill to have."

"With all due respect, sir, I don't see the point if seventy-five percent of decisive engagements are decided by weapons fire," Merlin replied.

Reiter smiled.

"Corporal Mo became an ace after a fierce hand-to-hand melee at the first battle of Riverside," he replied before finishing his soup. "Ah, that hit the spot. Good night, Merlin. I hope your attitude improves." He left the young man slack-jawed as he went back to his room. *Time for bed.*

"I DON'T REALLY THINK OF THE JUPITER AS SUITED FOR A RAID," Kennedy said. He stood around the planning table with Meyer and his two lieutenants. Splayed before them was a map of an airbase north of a medium Tharcian settlement—Garden City, according to local maps.

Meyer pointed to a bend in the river.

"It's more about overselling the amount of force we're bringing to the fight," she said. "We want them to think this is the tip of a major offensive, instead of a mere raid."

Kennedy held up a hand.

"Wait a minute, you want us to plunge through a seam in the Tharcian defenses, hit this airbase, and destroy anything on the ground? Then raiders are going to come land, secure the buildings, take anything valuable, and cover us as we bail?" He shook his head. "There's way too much about this I don't like."

"There's also the issue of a recon team that went missing near this town here," Ballard said. "Riverside, it says."

Meyer and Kennedy exchanged a look.

Briefly, an image of the animalistic Tharcian who killed Blake came to the forefront of Kennedy's mind.

"My primary concern is getting cut off. The Jupiter is tough, but it can be overwhelmed," he said. "And I think this airbase is too far for us to be supported."

"I hear you, and again, this is necessary," Meyer repeated. "Because besides destroying local airpower, gathering intelligence is the other objective of this raid."

Kennedy sighed.

"Again, support. How do we know a larger force won't consolidate and attack us?" he asked.

Meyer gave him a wry smile.

"Because they'd have to choose which attack to head off," she said. She pointed to a physical map on the wall. "Wake will be heading up a raid on a Tharcian supply center at the same time."

"I see, so they'll have to pick their poison." Kennedy tried imagining spearheads along his and Wake's routes. "And to the Tharcians, it'll look like they're getting enveloped in the center there."

Meyer nodded.

"Are you in a more agreeable position now?" she asked.

Kennedy nodded.

"Yeah, I appreciate the subterfuge here." He looked at his lieutenants. "Have the company assembled in"—he checked his watch—"two hours." They saluted him and left. He looked at Meyer. "I don't even think the new paint has dried on the Jupiter yet."

"You'll get another coat of paint when you get back," she said. "And while you're out, I'm going to confront Guard Colonel Chaney. I'm going to get to the bottom of this whole thing with you and Wake. Unless there's a new ace policy the MAG put forward that your lieutenants are somehow exempt from, it's suspicious."

Kennedy nodded.

"Thank you for doing that. I would enjoy peace of mind about this whole thing. I have a vision, and I'd hate to be lied to." He left the command tent. After eating, he made his way to the field hangar and mounted his Panzerter.

With his company marshaled, he led them out the gate. He caught sight of Manticore Company leaving in the opposite direction. Reaper Company turned south, heading towards the front. Artillery shells passed overhead, no doubt heading for Tharcian positions.

"We're approaching the front. Prepare for forward passage of lines," Kennedy said.

He received a string of acknowledgments and hailed the frontline units ahead of him. The units ahead of him directed them to lanes which they used to pass into hostile territory. Just like that, they were in Tharcian lands again.

Crossing a river, they made their way towards the first waypoint. Ballard took point, leading them towards a T-intersection. Orienting his map on the intersection, Kennedy directed them to follow the lower part of the T. He guided them through the darkness until he saw runway lights in the distance.

"Fan out, stick to your teams," Kennedy said. "Leave the buildings as intact as possible. When everyone is in position, we advance on my mark." He waited. Reaper Company had been reinforced to near full strength at eleven machines. Two went with Ballard to the left, two followed Fletcher right, with the final four staying with Kennedy.

He kept a close eye on the command matrix. Slowly, the dots moved toward their predesignated positions. *If we weren't slow about this, we would have been detected a while ago.* Suddenly, Fletcher's team stopped. Kennedy narrowed his eyes.

Then a dot vanished.

"Reaper 6, Reaper 5, we're under Panzerter attack!" The normally eager Fletcher's voice rang with fear.

"Roger, we're on our way," Kennedy replied. He brought the Jupiter up to a run, but the Martian troopers overtook him. One fell as its head exploded. *Sniper.* Then two more fell, a silvery blur piercing both of them. "What the hell!"

Kennedy and his remaining wingman closed with the Panzerters attacking Fletcher's group. They had engaged her team in hand-to-hand combat, negating his ability to provide supporting fire. Fletcher whirled about, her mace smashing a Tharcian sword to glowing bits. Another rushed her, eager to protect its comrade. She knocked off its head as Kennedy poured his strobe laser into its back.

A high-caliber shell struck him. The Jupiter staggered, but it was only a glancing hit. One Panzerter, the one who'd lost its sword, attempted to drag its smoking friend out of the fight. *How noble.* His wingman took aim. And its rifle, arm, and torso disintegrated in a flash.

Kennedy looked up to see five more Panzerters bearing down on them. Three dumped automatic fire into them while another helped drag the smoking one away. The fifth took a knee and blasted him with a high-velocity shell. *There's the sniper.* He retaliated with shoulder cannon and strobe laser fire as Fletcher fought her opponent hand to hand.

One went down from a shoulder cannon hit. Fletcher smashed her opponent's shoulder, rendering the limb useless. To their shock, the pilot pulled their own arm off. Swinging it like a club, they struck Fletcher's machine across the face. She spun away before recovering. She slammed her opponent across the chest, knocking them flat.

While Kennedy kept two of them suppressed, he noticed the sniper discard their rifle and draw their sword. Fletcher noticed too, clashing with the new opponent as Kennedy moved to support her. He was going to draw his mace when he noticed something on the ground. A sword from a fallen Panzerter. *I can parry much better with this.*

Grasping the Tharcian weapon, he ignited the blade. Turning towards the melee, one of the Tharcians he'd suppressed leaped toward him, sword drawn. Fletcher had come within weapons range, pummeling the other Panzerter as it tried to drag another fallen comrade. Kennedy clashed blades with the Tharcian Panzerter. It spun away, switching opponents with the sniper and drawing another sword.

I've seen this animalistic fighting style once before.

"You!" Kennedy said over an open channel. "You're the one who killed Comrade Blake!"

The sniper blocked his path. He used wide forceful swings to steer them aside before knocking them over.

"Oh, so you're the one that got away, huh?" The Tharcian pilot caught Fletcher's mace with both blades, severing its head. His follow-up stroke cut her arms off at the shoulders before kicking her over. He rounded on his opponent. "By the way, it was your boss's fault—he threatened my sisters!"

Kennedy took a step before he noticed Fletcher's earlier opponent start moving again.

"Well, you'll pay for the deaths of my comrades with your own," Kennedy said. "Starting with this one." He prepared to impale the hapless Panzerter when an alarm went off. Proximity alert. He spun and stabbed out.

He caught the sniper center of mass, its own sword raised high. The Panzerter slouched, their sword cutting off the tip of the shoulder cannon before deactivating.

Kennedy yanked his sword free of the dead Panzerter.

"Or that one would do."

The Tharcian kept at him. A burst from the strobe laser brought him back down to the ground.

"Of all the obstacles between me and a better Mars, you're the most persistent, the most personal." Kennedy readied his sword. "Enjoy watching your friends die like I had to watch mine!"

"Fuck you!"

Well, he's not eloquent. Malevolent instinct reared its ugly head in Kennedy's mind. *I'm enjoying this way more than I should, but that's a problem for later.* He lifted the sword. A burst of rifle fire struck him. *What?*

The Panzerter before him seemed as if it was made from the dark night itself. The only lit feature on it was the blue glow of its sensors. It was about a head taller than the Jupiter. Kennedy shivered. *What the fuck?*

"Union pilot, my name is Captain Paul Reiter. I'm your opponent."

21

I *should have been here sooner.* While providing supporting fire earlier, a jam in the railgun had created enough electrical feedback to stall the Lowe. The time wasted restarting the machine and all its systems had cost them dearly. Most of his company had been injured, and Bartonova was most certainly dead.

Now he stood face to face with the Union's knock-off Lowe. He didn't think the rifle would do much, but with the open channel, it had been enough to distract him from killing Steele. Now, he just had to defeat this guy and his cronies and he'd be clear. The fake Lowe hunched over, looking ready to leap into the melee. Instead, it raised its laser and opened fire.

The weird laser machine gun it used would have melted through any other machine. The Lowe shrugged off the repeated hits as he charged forward. Discarding his rifle, he bashed the Unionist with his shield. The Unionist staggered but recovered. When it swung its sword, Reiter's Tesla sword met it in a shower of sparks.

"Captain Reiter, you're in my way," the enemy pilot said as he hopped backwards. His wingmen had broken off and were retreating. Reiter pressed his attack. "I have a vision for Mars, and besides that, revenge on that young pilot."

"Whatever vision you have, it's an existential threat to my home," Reiter replied. *He's trying to stall me. If the railgun wasn't still jammed, I'd be able to end this fight a lot quicker.* Reiter rounded on his opponent, the Lowe's fluid movements exposing flaws in the Union machine.

"I assure you, my vision goes beyond Mars," his opponent said. "I seek to benefit all mankind."

Reiter clenched his teeth. The Lowe was faster and stronger than this knock-off. It was clear with every wavering parry his opponent made.

"Really? I doubt that," Reiter replied. *I need to keep him off balance, prevent him from focusing.* The Tesla sword flashed back and forth. Every impact cast sparks into the night.

"Why is that, Captain Reiter?"

They got caught in a blade lock. Static flashed about both machines. Reiter's arms tensed as if he was trying to overpower the Panzerter with his own muscles.

"Because in my normal life, I teach history," Reiter said. "People who claim to be pure benefactors rarely are." He broke the lock and slashed horizontally.

The fake Lowe stepped out of the way.

"You're not a soldier?" The laser flashed before him.

Reiter brought his blade through the weapon as it presented itself.

"Only part-time," he replied.

The fake Lowe lowered its shoulder and tackled him. The real Lowe crashed to the dirt, slamming Reiter's head against the back of his chair.

"Humph, should have sent a real one," said the Union pilot.

The sword filled Reiter's vision. He fired his head-mounted

machine guns. The anti-infantry weapons pinged off the fake Lowe's face. It staggered back before driving the sword down.

Only for it to shatter against the Lowe's raised shield. The Unionist recoiled, allowing Reiter to toss him off. His sword hummed as he spun around wide. His erratic swings caught the fake Lowe's arm, cutting the limb clean off.

The Union machine staggered away. It was clear the Unionist had taken a severe beating. Multiple places sparked or leaked static. Its own shoulder canon was severed along with its arm.

"For a part-timer, I sure kicked your ass good," Reiter said. He tried to ignore the wail of alarms as several support systems cut offline. His sword and shield at the ready, he tried not to give away that his machine was in no better shape. Shells smashed into his armor. The remaining Unionists covered their retreating leader.

"This isn't over, Captain Reiter," the man said.

Really? No 'you've won this time, Tharcian scum, but I will have my revenge' nonsense from this guy? He sighed. *Of course, a real Unionist isn't a cartoon villain.*

"As long as you threaten my home, I'll stay in your way," Reiter replied.

The fire let up as the Unionists put more ground between them. They disappeared into the night. As soon as the area was cleared, Reiter sighed and removed his helmet.

That was way closer than it should have been. He carefully grasped the control sticks. *I need to get better. We're past the point where I could just steamroll whatever we came up against.* He looked over at the fallen form of Bartonova's Panzerter.

"Viola, I'm sorry," he said quietly. *If I didn't jam the railgun . . .* Reiter shook his head. He couldn't afford to grieve or be emotional, not now, anyway. Fox Company needed him to be stoic, to be the eye of the storm.

Gold Platoon rolled up with the salvage team. Reiter stayed to help them as well as deter any more Union Panzerters. He assisted the recovery vehicles drag away Bartonova's machine and collect heavier pieces of debris. As he worked, he noticed soldiers and techs being drawn to one of the fallen tinhats.

The machine in question bore hideous colors. It took Reiter a second to realize they were the colors of the Union flag. *An ace, probably a Union fanatic too.* He noticed its missing arms and vaguely recalled Mo doing that.

"Gold 1, what's going on down there?" he asked.

After a short delay, Comidus came over the net.

"One of the techs said they heard banging. Now my boys are saying they hear it too," he replied. "The hatch looks jammed. They're going to try cutting into it."

"Roger, keep me updated," Reiter said. He kept an eye on the tinhat as they brought heavy tools forward to cut into the hatch. He saw drones racing off west. *Maybe they seek the fake Lowe.* Reiter grinned at the thought of that Unionist, for all his talk, getting killed by drones.

"They're most of the way through the hatch," Comidus said. "It'll be open any second now."

Reiter turned his attention back to the fallen tinhat. *I hope we can get valuable intel out of this one.*

The pilot burst out of the hatch. Reiter couldn't make them out in the darkness, but he saw them strike a tech. He flipped on his floodlights. Only one of them remained intact and powered, but it had the desired effect.

The pilot froze, blinded by the intense white light. Infantry rushed forward, and the Unionist put their hands behind their head. Reiter could see the pilot was a young woman as they put cuffs on her. *I wonder, what should we ask her first?*

"WE PULLED HER OUT OF MOTHBALLS FOR THIS," CHANEY SAID. "Tharcian ships we took more or less intact in the last war are kept for target practice and weapons tests." He stood in a cozy lounge space located on the Phobian North Pole. A jazz band played relaxing music for the attendees. From the outside looking in, he was attending a formal party rather than a weapons test.

This champagne doesn't hurt the image. He took a sip from his glass and glanced sideways at the fleet admiral.

"I hope you're satisfied by our target today," he said.

The older man smiled as the target was towed into view on the monitor. The heavy cruiser on screen now was a much older design, still taking after an ocean-going vessel in shape. At roughly a kilometer and a half in length, the TNV *Anchorage* had once stood at the pinnacle of naval design. Now, it was merely a target.

"I remember the action that captured her well. I was the gunnery officer aboard the *Popovich* at the time," the admiral said. He scowled. "Right before we surrendered."

Chaney nodded. He was just a kid then, but he remembered his parents' reaction to the news. He gripped his champagne a little tighter.

"Well, Comrade, would you like to do the honors?" Chaney offered. The older man nodded, and Chaney gestured to an attendant. The woman approached the fleet admiral with a microphone while Chaney tapped his glass. "Attention, comrades, the test is about to begin."

The fleet admiral beamed. The PFS *Metro* loomed onto the screen. Built during the arms race between wars, the *Metro* was one of the first heavy cruisers to be designed keel-up by the Union. Her boxy hull, lined with bulbous weapon emplacements, contrasted the antiquated *Anchorage.*

"We decided the Metro class would be first in line for particle-cannon refits," Chaney said. "They were state-of-the art immediately after the last war, but they're showing their age now."

"Oh do I know. Feedback I gave influenced the design," the older man said. "The weapon blisters? An improvement over turrets, so we could have omnidirectional fields of fire."

Chaney nodded and looked at the man.

"So I take it you're ready?"

"I've been ready twenty years, Comrade Colonel," the fleet admiral replied. "Metro, you may fire when ready."

The *Metro* moved in front of the Tharcian vessel. Nothing happened. The *Metro*'s engines sputtered and died.

"Metro, what's your status?" Chaney asked as the fleet admiral fixed him with an icy glare. "I assure you, Comrade, the Metro's power plant is well within the requirements to field these weapons."

After a brief moment, the ship's captain replied.

"Sorry about that, some of our circuit boards were past due for maintenance. We're disciplining the personnel responsible right now."

Chaney relaxed slightly as the older man's anger was redirected into space.

"If we send a shuttle with parts, could you fix it and continue with the test?" Chaney asked.

"Roger, Comrade. It should take twenty minutes once the parts get here," the captain responded.

With the shuttle flight time, it will probably be an hour. Chaney informed the fleet admiral, and the older man nodded.

"I'm glad to hear it was a circuit board and not your weapon system," the admiral said. "These Metro-class vessels suffer from burning through minor components like circuit boards. It should be addressed when the line gets refitted in general."

Chaney nodded as an attendant approached him.

"Excuse me, Comrade Colonel," she said, "Guard Colonel

Meyer is on the line, and she's demanding to speak with you. She says it's about her Jupiter pilots."

A smile crept onto Chaney's face. *Ah, yes, my greatest project.*

"Tell her I'll be right with her," he said. "Comrade Fleet Admiral, if you'll excuse me during our intermission, I need to attend to another project for just a moment."

The older man nodded, and Chaney took his leave of them. Entering a private booth, he took a fresh glass of champagne and answered the call.

"Good evening, Comrade Colonel. I hope your night is going well?" Meyer asked. The image of the battalion commander grew hazy before him.

He nodded.

"We have a few technical issues, but they're being worked out," he said. "What is it you need?"

"Answers," she replied. "Specifically, what are you doing with Kennedy and Wake?" Her eyes narrowed. "I know you're up to something beyond just collecting combat data."

Chaney smiled coyly.

"Well, Comrade Meyer, I'll have to return to the surface to discuss this with you," he said. "I can't discuss the matter over a video call."

Meyer scowled.

"Very well then, Comrade," she said. "I'll try to find time during the ground war I'm actively fighting to accommodate your visit. Meyer out." Her image vanished from the screen.

Chaney merely sipped his Champagne and smiled. *If only you knew, Meyer, then you wouldn't be able to make enough time for me.*

He returned to the lounge. His attendant informed him that the Metro had made its repairs and was ready to resume operations. As he walked to the fleet admiral's side, he smiled.

"Now, Comrade, without further ado," Chaney said as he made a grand gesture towards the derelict *Anchorage.*

The older man nodded. The *Metro*, which was burning back toward the test site, came back into view and prepared to cross the T again.

"*Metro,* you may fire when ready," the fleet admiral said.

The Union heavy cruiser came about. After the crew confirmed their firing arc clear, a single double-barreled weapon blister closer to the bow swung onto their target.

Blue light flashed. Then again. The *Anchorage* was lost in a cloud of gas and debris as its decks decompressed. Chaney glanced at the fleet admiral. The older man's face was drawn into a real grin.

"Are you suitably impressed, Comrade Fleet Admiral?" he asked.

The older man nodded.

"Yes. I want production of these weapons to begin immediately," he replied. "The entire Metro-class will replace their railgun with them. Your project has the full backing of the admiralty."

Chaney nodded.

"Thank you, Fleet Admiral. I will begin talks with shipyards immediately."

KENNEDY SCOWLED. THE FIELD HANGAR BUZZED AS TECHS RAN parts and ordnance here and there. What parts and ordnance they could find, anyway.

He turned to the senior technician.

"You said it'll take how long to repair the Jupiter?"

"Well Comrade Major, and it'll take three weeks before they're fully combat-effective," the woman replied.

Kennedy sighed and walked away. He paused and spun around.

"Prioritize only the systems absolutely critical to moving, shooting, and communicating," he said. "How long would that take?"

The technician frowned as she tapped on her tablet.

"About a week," she replied. "Then the main hold-up is that all the joints in your legs need to be serviced or outright replaced. We're also facing a shortage of ammo for your shoulder cannon."

"Bullshit," he said. "I just saw a truck drop off four pallets of 155-mm shells. There's no way we're facing a shortage."

"Those shells are earmarked for artillery," she said. "We simply don't have enough to feed our big guns and your magazines."

Kennedy looked back at his Jupiter. The powerful machine seemed naked in the field hangar, multiple tarps covering the exposed sections where armor had been stripped away. He shook his head as he looked back at the technician. "Are we at least able to get another strobe laser in a week?"

"No," she replied, not even looking at him anymore.

Kennedy grabbed his hat to throw it but halted and took another look at the Jupiter.

"Do we have enough spare parts to convert the shoulder cannon to a laser and equip a rifle?" The technician continued to ignore him. He looked at her rank and coughed. "Excuse me, *Guard-Sergeant*, can you answer my question?"

She blinked and after hearing his request again, she scrolled through her tablet.

"Yes, Comrade Major, we can swing that in a week," she said.

Kennedy nodded.

"Good, thank you," he replied. *Even if it's just an impertinence, Comrade, you got in my way.*

He headed back towards the barracks, stopping next to Fletcher's old tent. Snow was sticking to the ground and the structures. He kicked a pile of snow, scattering it to the wind.

Captain Reiter. He threw tent flaps aside and entered his own barracks. *Fake soldier.* He tossed another flap aside and kicked his boots off into the wall. *He's in my way.* He dragged his socked feet across the wooden floor and dropped into bed. *Bastard.*

Closing his eyes, all he could see was the black silhouette and bright sword of his enemy. *How could he best me? He's a part-time soldier. I was born and bred for battle. My body was rebuilt to be even better.* He punched the tent wall next to him.

His machine, that has to be it. Yeah, that's it. He shrugged off multiple hits from the strobe laser and just kept coming. He shook his head. *Except the Jupiter was based on data from that machine, so mine should be better.*

The tent wall rustled.

"Hey, Comrade Major, are you doing alright?" It was Ballard.

Kennedy sighed.

"No. I could use a smoke, though." He sat up to let his subordinate in. Ballard ducked into the room. After handing Kennedy a cigarette, he bent over to light his own.

"Mind if I sit here?" Ballard motioned to Kennedy's camp chair.

Kennedy waved him on.

"It's not like I'll be sitting there." He leaned over to have his own cigarette lit.

"Have you heard Captain Wake talk?" Ballard asked. "As in since we came to this front?"

Kennedy shook his head.

"He's always been a party hardliner," he replied. "I honestly don't think there's much he can say that'll shock me at this point."

Ballard exhaled a great cloud of smoke.

"What about genocide?" he asked.

Kennedy choked.

"What?"

Ballard nodded.

"I heard him talking to his pilots about it in the barracks not long after they got back. He said the only way for lasting peace was to dismantle Tharsis as a country, but the Tharcian people would never tolerate that and would resist the Union forever." He took another drag on his cigarette. "Anyway, he finished by saying that, as long as Tharcians existed, there would be no post-scarcity, because they would constantly consume resources we need, so it would be better to completely eliminate them as a culture."

Kennedy fiddled with the cigarette in his fingers.

"I don't like it. Not that I care for Tharcians. If they don't think we should exist, then I don't think they should exist, fuck 'em," he replied. "That being said, his rhetoric justifies that Reiter bastard fighting as hard as he does. I'll get with Meyer and talk to him." He exhaled hard. "Do you think she survived?"

"Fletcher?" Ballard asked. He nodded. "Yeah, I do. She's a feisty one, she is." He took a drag from his cigarette. "In a lot of ways, she's as implacable about having children as you are about building a better future."

Kennedy nodded.

"I see," he said. He shook his head. "I need to calm down. I got overly emotional during that last battle with Reiter, and I'm positive that's what cost me."

Ballard was quiet for a moment.

"I don't like that Wake guy," he finally said.

Kennedy raised an eyebrow.

"I thought we were done talking about him," he replied. "What's your issue with him?"

"Not to sound defeatist, but if things go sideways, his words and attitudes have sealed our fate and our legacy," Ballard said. "Again, I don't want my daughter to remember me as a monster."

"She was how old when your wife died?" Kennedy asked.

Ballard sighed, clouding the air.

"She was seven," he replied.

Kennedy stepped across the barracks room and set a hand on Ballard's shoulder.

"And she was a toddler when you got married?" he asked. Ballard nodded. "Then, no matter what the history books say, no matter what the party line is, she will always remember that her father was a good man."

Kennedy may have been mistaken, but he was almost certain he saw the other man's eyes glisten.

"Huh, so that's a Unionist?" Mo asked. They had repurposed a study hall into a makeshift cell. Reiter, Starnes, Steele, Adamski, and Comidus stood on one side of the one-way mirror with him.

Steele folded her arms.

"I don't know why we haven't put a bullet in her head," she said.

I swear the temperature just dropped. Mo reached out and took her hand. She didn't react at first, but then she grasped his hand tightly.

"Easy, Steele, no matter what this pilot has done, she's entitled to the same protections as another POW," Reiter said. "Although, she's barely eating or drinking. Maybe she's worried about getting drugged?"

Starnes shook his head.

"If she was worried about being drugged, she would have just refused food and drink," he said. "She may be depressed."

"Well, boo hoo, I feel so bad for her," Steele said. Mo shivered.

"I mean, to some extent, it's just ungrateful," Adamski said. "It's not like we're feeding her some field kitchen slop. She's getting quality food from the cafeteria."

"Is it possible she has a tracking implant in her body?" Comidus said. "I mean, that would hurt if they knew where to find us."

"Even if she doesn't, once she sees outside, she'll know where this base is located. Is that a risk we're willing to take?" Adamski asked.

"We don't have POW facilities for pilots or MAGs set up on this front," Reiter said. "You all heard the RCO same as I did."

"Yeah, but does the Union know we have her?" Steele asked. "Because if not . . ."

"We are not the Unionists, and we will not start acting like them!" Reiter said, raising his voice.

Mo and the others stared at him. *I haven't heard him talk like that in forever.*

Reiter sighed and looked back into the room. "Get Merlin up here, I got a job for him."

"Why do you want Merlin?" Mo asked. "He doesn't strike me as the interrogator type. He's more like an accountant."

"That's it," Starnes said. "He's soft-spoken and non-threatening. A female is more likely to speak to him."

Adamski raised an eyebrow.

"You two are talking about sending him in there?" he asked. "We do not know how dangerous she is!"

"Then I'll have Stovepipe pull security for him," Comidus said. "No rifle, just a sidearm."

Reiter nodded.

"Bring them both up here," he said.

Merlin and the rifleman known as Stovepipe didn't take long to get to the improvised cell. Stovepipe's nickname became clear as he approached with a cigar in his hand.

"You realize this is a smoke-free floor?" said Reiter.

The man put out his cigar and tossed it in the trash.

"My bad, sir," he said.

Captain Reiter looked at Mo.

"Mo, Adamski, Comidus, and myself are about to go sit in on a conference call with the regiment," he said. "I'm leaving you and Starnes in charge of gathering intelligence from this pilot."

Starnes clapped Mo on the shoulder.

"It's alright, Corporal Mo, I'll take good care of you," the major said.

Reiter nodded and left with the first sergeant and XO.

Merlin looked incredulous.

"What are you guys about to make me do?" he asked.

"Nothing crazy," Starnes said. "You're just going to go in there and have a conversation with that young woman."

Merlin adjusted his glasses and looked at her. *At least she's easy on the eyes, dude.* Her hair was blonde to the point of being white, and it came down to her shoulders. *It's almost unearthly.*

"Uh, is there doctrine for this? Or protocol? Or something?" Merlin asked.

Starnes nodded.

"You can answer her questions, but don't give away any operational or technical knowledge," he replied. "And you won't be alone. Stovepipe here will be keeping watch with a handgun."

Merlin shook his head.

"I mean, what am I supposed to ask? How do I even know she speaks English?"

Starnes shook his head.

"Most former colonies speak English and use other languages for formal events," he said. "Besides, they've talked to our pilots in English before, so odds are she'll understand you."

Mo put his hand on the kid's shoulder.

"Hey, we're all going to be alright here," he said. "You got this."

Still looking stressed, Merlin entered the room with Stovepipe right behind him.

"You think he'll get anything out of her?" Mo asked.

Starnes shrugged.

"Doubtful. If they're anything like us, their pilots have been trained to resist interrogation and will try to escape at the first opportunity," he replied.

"Then why hasn't she tried escaping?" Steele asked. "It's not like we're keeping her in a high-security cell. She's in a study hall, for God's sake."

"Maybe it's about opportunity," Starnes said before gesturing at Merlin. "Let's just watch."

The study hall featured a table, a bunk they had dragged down there, and a small monitor. Merlin sat awkwardly at the table while Stovepipe stayed near the door. The prisoner lay in her bed in a fetal position.

"Um, good evening, uh . . . My name is PFC Merlin, and I'm going to be, uh, interviewing you." The prisoner refused to move. Merlin adjusted his glasses and looked at his notes. "Uh, let's start with something simple. What is your name?"

No answer.

"Do you think they're trained to not give up anything?" Mo asked. "She's not even reacting to him."

Starnes shook his head.

"No, there's more at play here," he replied. "I'm just not sure what exactly." He typed a note on his tablet and sent a message to Merlin.

The young man uncomfortably checked his own tablet.

"So, I'm going to read you your rights in accordance with the 2047 Geneva Convention," he said. "You're going to be fed three times a day on sustainable rations. Your quarters will meet acceptable living standards. As an officer, you're exempt from physical labor. As a lawful combatant, you will not be subject to experimentation or enhanced interrogation techniques. Your healthcare needs will be attended to as if you were a regular Tharcian soldier. Do you have any questions?" Merlin adjusted his glasses and looked up. "Any questions at all?"

"I don't think we'll get anything out of her," Mo said. "Let's get ready to—" Starnes shushed him.

The prisoner sat up slowly.

"My name is Claire Fletcher. I carry the rank of Guard Lieutenant."

Mo blinked. *Wow, maybe we'll get something out of her after all.*

22

"The weather reports say we're expecting heavy fog on the eighth of November," the regimental commander said. "Because of that, we're initiating Operation Flashflood that morning." On the screen before Reiter and his staff, a map of the area came to life and zoomed in. "All company commanders, take note of your positions." The regiment followed a northwest-flowing branch of the river toward Objective Mauler.

"It looks like we got the south side of the river with Early Company," Adamski said. "I hope they're in much better fighting shape than the last time we saw them."

Comidus shook his head.

"If they have more than one man, then I'm fine with that."

The regimental commander's voice returned to the call.

"We'll coordinate bounding movements across the formation," he said. "When Early and Gamble move, they will be supported by attack boats. Fox and Hollywood will guard the assault barge. When the advancing companies get set, the companies with the barge will move up with it, hand off the barge, and advance with the boats until they reach their target."

"So there's going to be long periods where we're not moving," Reiter said. He looked at Adamski. "We need to be sure no one gets complacent." Adamski nodded.

"Once we're in sight of Mauler," the RCO continued. "We'll take this southern area while another regiment takes the northern area opposite, then two fresh regiments will attack Mauler itself while we hold the flanks." The map shifted to show the projected movement of various units getting into position. "Any questions?"

"How will we coordinate air and artillery support in the fog?" Early Company's new commander asked. "It'll be hard to get positive ID."

"That's why it's paramount your soldiers get positive ID before requesting fire support or CAS," the RCO replied. "It's going to be chaotic out there, but remind your soldiers to take that tactical pause."

"How soon can we expect our next wave of reinforcements?" asked Hollywood's commander. "And will they be more children?"

Reiter shook his head.

"The academy kids have been good," he said. "But they had no business fighting in this war."

"You'll receive another wave of veterans and some colonists," the RCO said. "The new marshal is trying to curtail enlisting military academy cadets unless our back is really against the ropes." With no further questions, the man dismissed them.

Reiter sighed and leaned back in his chair.

"If Starnes and Mo are done with that pilot, we need them and Steele up here for planning," he said.

Adamski brought up the map data they had for the region.

"Here we are," he said. "Northwest-flowing branch of the river terminates in Crater Lake, the feature that mostly surrounds Mauler."

Reiter took in the image. The intersection of multiple rivers and Crater Lake effectively made the core of Mauler an island. *It'll be hard to attack, no matter the angle.*

"Highlight the area we'll be holding," Reiter asked. Adamski highlighted a strip of land to the south of Mauler. *Sparse trees, mostly flat ground.* Reiter shook his head. "I'd hate for us to sit there too long."

Starnes, Mo, and Steele entered the room and took their seats.

Reiter's gaze hovered on the empty chair between Adamski and Steele. Where Bartonova should have been. "Find out anything useful?" he asked.

"More or less," Starnes said. "Corporal Mondragon?"

"Well, we found out a few things," Mo said. "Some of questionable usefulness." He brought up an image of the heavy Panzerter Reiter had fought before. "This machine, which we codenamed 'Fatman', is called the Jupiter. It mounts an artillery piece on its back, and it's got a machine-laser."

"So, it really is a Lowe knock-off," Reiter said. "Anything else?"

"Yeah, that guy you fought is a Guard Major Kennedy," Mo replied. "His company butted heads with ours, and well, she had some weird things to say about her company."

Reiter raised an eyebrow.

"Like?" he asked.

Starnes held up a hand.

"To be clear, I'm about ninety percent sure this is some kind of misinformation," the major said. "Corporal?"

"Well, she claims her company are all designer babies," Mo said. "Made specifically to pilot Panzerters into battle."

Reiter whistled.

"If that's remotely true, then that Kennedy guy just took a serious blow to his ego." He raised an eyebrow at Starnes. "You said ninety percent. I assume you have an alternative explanation?"

Starnes nodded.

"I think it's more probable they took orphans and conditioned them to be perfect soldiers over creating them in a lab," he said. "Although, when Foundation found itself on the verge of starving, they created farmers to handle their agricultural needs."

"And you don't think they would see the military applications for that practice?" Reiter asked.

Starnes shrugged.

"We have similar technology," he said. "We use it to cure birth defects and health problems. It's one of the reasons our infant mortality rate is essentially zero." He sighed. "And designer babies aren't always stable. Sometimes the genetic material doesn't properly bond. In the United States, designer babies have a forty-five percent mortality rate, and they pioneered the technology."

Reiter leaned forward in his chair.

"So you're saying what, exactly?" he asked. "That they have some kind of factory churning them out?"

Starnes nodded slowly.

"It's worth mentioning we have a cultural bias against taking what she said at face value," Starnes said. "To treat human life so cheaply—it's unthinkable."

"Is there any value from a psy-ops perspective?" Adamski asked. "Like looking more monstrous to intimidate us?"

Starnes shook his head.

"I don't think she meant it that way," he said. "It would require a cultural understanding of us we haven't seen from the Unionists yet."

Reiter rubbed his chin.

"I want a word with the pilot myself," he said.

"I wouldn't advise that," Starnes said. "What if she attacks you and you're out of the fight?"

"I don't think she will," Reiter said. "Just a hunch, but it seems like there's more at play here."

The meeting went on. They discussed their incoming reinforcements, formations, and movement plan. Reiter eventually settled on splitting the new bodies evenly between his two platoons and dispersing the infantry between the Panzerter teams.

So, the Union might be growing soldiers, huh? He shook his head. Better not to think about it at the moment.

———

THE JUPITERS GLARED AT EACH OTHER ACROSS THE ENTRANCE TO the field hangar. Their stance and stoic gaze made them seem far more ancient, like statues at the entrance of a tomb. *These aren't ancient statues, though, they're cutting edge war machines.*

"Good afternoon, Comrade Kennedy," Wake called out to him. "I assume you're here for inspections?"

Kennedy nodded. He stood near the foot of his own Jupiter with Ballard. Smoking, he looked at Wake as the other man approached. Like him and the lieutenant, Wake wore a wind breaker with a thermal lining. Snow flitted about the field hangar.

"Comrade Wake, since you're more familiar with Manticore's Panzerters, maybe you could lend a hand," Kennedy said.

Reaper and Manticore were consolidating for the immediate future until enough pilots and Panzerters were available for both companies to return to three-quarters strength. With a mere seven machines between the two of them, it would be a while. *But we have two Jupiters. That makes up for lower numbers.*

They walked to the far end of the field hangar. Kennedy looked up at the first machine he had to inspect and shook his head.

"Not ready," he said. "Some armor panels still need to be replaced and there's unrepaired damage to the sensor ring." He walked over to the next one.

"This one will look better tomorrow," Wake said. Pointing to the tarp covering the right arm, he continued. "The parts to overhaul the arm just arrived this morning."

Kennedy shook his head.

"Still not ready," he said. "Besides the arm, it doesn't have a rifle." They walked over to the next machine. After going around the outside of it, he nodded. "This one's ready." They walked over to Wake's machine.

"As you're aware, the leg joints are in the middle of an overhaul," Wake said.

Kennedy nodded. Both Jupiters stood with tarps covering their legs to protect their bare structure. A broad, slightly curved metal shape caught his eye.

"Is that a new weapon?"

Wake grinned.

"It is, somewhere between a sword and an axe with a heated edge," he said. "Eggheads are calling it a shield breaker."

"I see," Kennedy said. *One of those would have been helpful against Reiter.* He paused on the way to his own machine. *Reiter.* Unlike everyone else in his way, the Tharcian captain refused to budge. *He let Blake's killer go unpunished; he took one of my best soldiers.* Kennedy looked east.

"Comrade Major, are we just going to skip your machine?" Ballard asked.

Kennedy shook himself before nodding.

"Yes, I already know it's not ready," he said. *Sorry, Ballard, you probably want to get this over with and get away from Wake.* "Let's get over to your machine."

"What are those hideous personal colors?" Wake asked.

Ballard took a long drag before answering.

"I was in the regular forces, Comrade," he replied. "I'm just remembering my roots. That's why the legs are painted the way they are."

Wake whirled on the other man.

"I don't know what kind of outfit you belonged to, Guard Lieutenant," he said, "but the Mobile Assault Guards don't do things in half-measures."

Unblinking, Ballard took another pull on his cigarette.

"Does that include genocide, Guard Major?" he replied.

Wake sneered at the other man.

"You're using some harsh language there, Comrade," he said. "I prefer cultural reduction."

Ballard flicked the butt of his cigarette into the cold gravel.

"Use whatever words you please," he said. "But I'll have you know that we are better people than you've been proposing."

Wake's sneer didn't waver.

"Why, Comrade, us being better people is precisely why we need to enlighten the children of Tharsis," he said. "Toss out the rotting husk of their class traitor society and educate their youngest members into being productive citizens of a Martian community."

Kennedy stepped between the two men.

"I'm going to have to stop you two right there," he said. "Ballard, you may not agree with Wake, but you *will* respect his rank." He looked at Wake. "Don't talk about your ideas around my people, especially the kid stuff. It's a sensitive subject for a lot of them." He glanced at the final machine on the row. "And that last machine isn't ready." Kennedy began to leave the field hangar, Ballard right behind him.

"Sorry about that, Comrade Major," Ballard said. "I shouldn't have let him get under my skin."

"Your contribution to Reaper Company is level-headed leadership," Kennedy said. "It helps that you don't lose your shit in public." He sighed. "Although, were I in your place, I'd put some stock in what he says."

"Why do you say that?" Ballard asked.

"What do you think the Tharcians will do if they win?" Kennedy asked. "They'll take your daughter and teach her to exploit people for personal gain." They cut between the barracks on the way to their own. Kennedy felt a hand on his shoulder.

"Honest question, and please don't report me for asking," Ballard said.

"Shoot," Kennedy replied.

Glancing at the surrounding barracks, Ballard kept his voice low.

"The Union exploits us, no question about it," he whispered. "Is it really any better that we're exploited for the good of the community?" He sighed. "To some extent, I honestly don't see how we're any better."

Kennedy echoed his sigh.

"I'm not going to say anything about that treasonous statement," he said, "but I will point out to you that everyone in the Union is 'exploited' for the common good, even our leaders." He formed an O with his thumb and forefinger. "It's a circle of commitment."

"If you say so, Comrade," Ballard replied. "And thank you for not reporting me."

"You're a good man," Kennedy said. "Even if your ideological loyalty isn't all there, you've shown outstanding loyalty to the rest of us. Besides, I made a promise, didn't I?"

Ballard grinned.

"I nearly forgot," he replied. "Which actually reminds me." He reached into his uniform pocket and pulled out a physical photo. "That's Penny."

Kennedy looked at the photo. A young girl smiled brightly despite missing her two front teeth. An auburn-haired woman, who looked like a grown version of her child, sat next to Ballard in his dress uniform.

"I'll try to get you some face time before the next battle," Kennedy replied. "And when this is all over, well, we'll figure it out then."

"So, she's still not eating much, huh?" Reiter asked.

Mo nodded.

"I think she's trying to resist being drugged," he replied, "but Starnes thinks she's just depressed."

"Well, he is the intel guy." Reiter glanced at Stovepipe.

"Ready?"

The infantryman nodded.

"This pistol isn't really my speed, but it'll be a bad day if she tries anything funny," Stovepipe said.

Reiter nodded and entered the room, Stovepipe in tow.

"Good afternoon, Lieutenant Fletcher," he said. "My name is Captain Reiter, and I'll be conducting your interview."

Fletcher had been lying on her bed when he entered. When Reiter announced himself, she perked up. Slowly, she rose from her bunk and drifted over to the table. Reiter pulled a chair out for her, and she looked at him curiously as she sat. Reiter walked to the other side of the table for his own seat. Stovepipe's hand never left his pistol.

"A private interviewed me yesterday," she said. "Why the change?"

"I had my own questions," Reiter replied. "I figured they'd be best communicated if I asked myself." He motioned to the stack of half-eaten meals in her small garbage can. "Are you being fed adequately? Is there some dietary supplement you need?"

She looked at the stack of trays.

"Your people keep giving me too much," she said. "And the meat upsets my stomach."

He raised an eyebrow.

"Do you not normally eat meat?" he asked.

She shook her head.

"Other than fish and meat-substitutes, no," she replied.

Reiter glanced back at the glass.

"Make a note, add a fiber supplement to her drinking water," he said. As he looked back at her, he explained himself. "That should help your system digest food better."

She looked away.

"My body is supposed to be more efficient than yours, anyway," she said.

"That actually leads me to my next question," Reiter replied. "Are you really a designer baby?"

She smiled coyly.

"For people that don't think I should exist, you sure have a more polite term for what I am."

"What do other Unionists call you?" he asked.

"Tubers," she said. "Because of the shape of the nurseries."

I can't tell if she's acknowledging this to mess with me or not. Reiter thought of his grandmother clutching her prayer beads and telling him how precious he was. *Cultural understanding.*

"You said we don't think you should exist," Reiter said. "Why is that?"

She sneered.

"Because your people are class traitors," she said. "You'll

undermine a united mankind at every opportunity, and you'd throw me and other tubers in camps." She rose from her seat. "Because the fact we exist disgusts you."

Reiter looked back at Stovepipe.

"Relax, Stovepipe," he said, then returned his attention to Fletcher. "Sit down, Lieutenant. Class is in session." She returned to her chair, treating Reiter to an icy look the whole way. "Are you in a camp right now?"

"No," she said.

"Then you'll be relieved to know we have no intentions of sending you to a camp at the moment, as POW facilities for pilots haven't been established yet." He cleared his throat. "Furthermore, we still don't believe you."

"What do you mean you don't believe me?" she asked.

Reiter sighed.

"Well, life is precious. As a people who were once nearly wiped out, we'd know," he said. "To just manufacture people en masse . . . Well, that cheapens it, considerably." He sighed. "As terrible as we think the Union is, we don't think they're so cartoonishly evil as to do that to you."

Fletcher seemed to stare through Reiter in that moment.

"What do you mean, 'do that to' me?" she asked.

"Well, they would have deprived you of any choice in the course of your life," he said. "If they bred you for the purpose of fighting and dying, well, to be frank, that's messed up. I mean, why would you be motivated to fight beyond the fact that they told you to?" He sighed. "Anyway, we think it's more probable you were orphaned young and brainwashed into believing you were bred solely to fight."

"Wow," she said. "You're really trying to make me doubt my own lived experience."

"Well, do you have a serial number or something?" Reiter

asked. "Some way to prove you were born in a tube rather than from a woman?"

Fletcher looked away, clutching the bottom of the sweatshirt she wore.

"Did I ask something too personal?" Her continued silence answered the question. Reiter rose from his chair. "If you need some time alone, I'll grant you that." He turned towards the door.

"Why?" Fletcher asked. "Why do you care if I need to be left alone?" Reiter looked back at her. "I am your enemy, after all, aren't I?"

"Even if you are our enemy or were born in a tube, you're still a young woman with dignity," Reiter said. "You're not an active threat and thus entitled to the same respect we would grant anyone else." He turned back. "Come on, Stovepipe, let's leave her alone." He left the room quietly with the infantryman.

"Well, sir, what do you think?" Mo asked.

Reiter shrugged.

"I don't think she's blustering," he said. "She's too unfamiliar with our culture to come up with something like that."

Mo looked back through the glass.

"Asking whether she was marked made her uncomfortable," he said.

Reiter nodded.

"She wouldn't have had a visceral reaction like that if she was lying," he said. "And the way she freely offers up information, she hasn't been trained to resist interrogation."

Mo looked at him.

"So the Union doesn't think they'd allow themselves to be captured," he said.

"Or they don't believe we'd take prisoners," Reiter replied. "We did learn something else valuable about the Union."

"What's that?" Mo asked.

"They ration their food," Reiter said. "She's not used to eating the portions we've given her, or meat." He folded his arms. "Instead, they eat meat substitutes and fish. But if they have colonies, why would they need to ration food?"

Mo shrugged.

"I don't know. Aquaculture is pretty efficient," Mo said. "Unless their population is a lot bigger than we think."

Reiter looked at Lieutenant Fletcher.

"What if," he began, "they face a food crisis because they inflated their population past what they could comfortably sustain?"

Mo looked back at Fletcher.

"Do you really think?"

"I think the pieces are all coming together."

BALLARD'S MARTIAN STALKED THROUGH THE FOREST. TWO wingmen followed him in a wedge. He put a hand on the picture of his family. *Soon, Penny.* Somewhere ahead of him lay a downed dropship under fire. Most of the combined company was unable to sortie, so they'd just sent what they had. He checked his map. Still three clicks out.

"Slow up, we're approaching the crash site," he said. Cutting his speed, he followed the nav markers to the objective. In the darkness, he saw the flash of automatic weapons in the tree line.

He raked his laser across the Tharcian position and darted right. High-caliber rounds tore through his former position. *They got Panzerters.*

He took a knee in a thicket as his wingmen came around his left. *I need to get ahold of the dropship crew, but their radio's probably out.* He glanced at his ammo count and laser charge cycle. 40/40. Fifty-five seconds to recharge.

"Hamilcar, do you have eyes?" he asked one of his wingmen.

"Roger, Comrade, two Panzerters and some infantry," Hamilcar replied.

"Type?" Ballard asked.

"Uh, looks like a Mark IV and a heavier model," Hamilcar said. "Not the Black Knight, though."

Two, eh, not that terrible.

Tracers raced past his position, searching for metal. Ballard sprang from his position and returned fire. It was the Mark IV. Despite a valiant effort, it was ultimately brought down by an ammo explosion, caught in the L formed by his and Hamilcar's fire. *One down.*

A red glare burned in the night. Ballard heard a rapid popping sound. *Rockets, lots of them.*

His other wingman took the brunt of the assault. Rockets pummeled his Martian like hail. At first the damage seemed mostly cosmetic, but then the Martian staggered. The warheads buried themselves deeper and deeper into its metal skin. The Panzerter collapsed in a flaming wreck. Smoke poured from gaping holes in its armor.

"Hamilcar, where is he?" Ballard asked.

"Off my 11," Hamilcar replied. "He's a *big* motherfucker."

"Run to your 9, across his front. I'll run to 12 so we can flank him." As Ballard pushed his machine to a run, he searched for his target.

It loomed out of the trees into a clearing to his left. It resembled a Mark IV, but it was broader. Thicker limbs moved the ponderous machine about as it carried a rocket pod on each shoulder. *The base model looks not too different from a Mark IV, but with a lot of extra armor bolted on.*

It caught sight of Ballard's Martian and opened fire.

Tracers spread from the barrel as Ballard rolled his machine to the right. *Some kind of shotgun?* He came up on a knee and returned fire.

A green flash left orange scars on its shoulder. *Damn, too thick for lasers?* It shifted back towards Hamilcar. Red rockets searched for the MAG pilot.

Ballard's shells had little visible effect on the heavy Panzerter. Most simply bounced off its thick armor panels. *How much punishment can it take?*

The Tharcian shifted to take another shot. *All that armor's weighing him down. His joints.*

Ballard rolled forward. The world around him spun, and his head smacked his chair. At point blank, he fired his laser. The green beam burned through a hip plate as the Tharcian turned.

Ballard hopped back as shells struck the Tharcian's rear armor. Its armor held. As Hamilcar surged forward while firing, the Tharcian turned towards him. Ballard drew his mace.

At close range, the shotgun ripped Hamilcar's Martian apart. Scattering the gray Panzerter meant turning his back on Ballard. He kicked the Tharcian's lower leg.

Its knee buckled, then snapped. The Tharcian fell onto its broken leg. Stuck in a kneeling position, it was wide open to Ballard's mace. Ballard swung and continued swinging.

When he finally stopped, coolant ran in rivers into the soil. The heavy Panzerter lay crumpled and smoking. For the Tharcian pilot, the armored husk became a tomb.

Ballard surveyed the surrounding scene. The dropship survivors huddled around the wreckage of their fallen aircraft. Bodies lay scattered across the forest floor. Four Panzerters lay smoking where they'd fallen. He shook his head.

I've seen this picture enough times I'm starting to lose count. With a sigh, he trudged over to the survivors. He ignored the blaring alarms. He knew his maneuvering had taken a toll on his Martian.

He guided the survivors back towards a firebase before departing towards his own. *Now we need reinforcements on top of reinforcements.* He imagined a nursery, full of new lives. As he recalled his own childhood, he imagined them being taught basic skills like math, reading, and writing alongside drill and ceremony. He'd learned the importance of saluting officers, rooting out class traitors, tactics, and practicing soldier skills.

He shook his head.

Might as well dump those newborns into a grinder. How many of us have died so far?

Morning light cast Firebase Blake in a murky haze. *I'm almost home.*

"Reaper 3, where are your wingmen?" asked Gate Control.

"Tower, we got dragged into a tougher fight than we thought we'd be getting. I'll debrief Guard Major Kennedy when I get settled."

"Roger, Comrade. He's expecting you," Gate Control replied.

Ballard eased his machine into the field hangar and removed his helmet. *What a shitty day.* He touched the photo of Penny again. *I'd be just like the rest, dying for nothing, if not for Major Kennedy.* He left his helmet in the cockpit and climbed up the ladder to the hatch.

Kennedy was waiting to help him out of his machine.

"Hamilcar? Barracka?" he asked.

Ballard shook his head.

"A heavy Panzerter got 'em, one we haven't seen before."

"Damn, they were good men," Kennedy replied. Ballard nodded. "So this heavy Panzerter—"

"It wasn't the Black Knight," Ballard said. "I wouldn't be here if it was." He looked at the Jupiters down the line. "Would have been easier if I was riding one of those."

Kennedy looked over his own machine.

"I should be ready to sortie tomorrow," he said. "We're getting reinforcements as well, so our combined company will be at full strength." He looked at Wake's machine. "Twelve Panzerters, including two Jupiters." He grinned.

"By the way," Ballard began, "after I shower and nap, I'd like a word with you about this better Mars."

23

M o leaned over the railing so he could get a better look at the incoming Panzerters. Occasionally, he'd look at the new sergeant rank on his shoulder. It still felt weird seeing it there.

Unger leaned over the railing next to him.

"So, we're getting more pilots?" she asked.

Mo nodded.

"Yeah, a couple veterans," he said. "Guys and gals who did their time and got out."

"So they're, like, older than us?"

Mo shrugged.

"Yeah, but they haven't seen combat, so don't let them disrespect you," he said. "That being said, act mature."

The new Panzerters docked in the hangar. Mo walked down the catwalk to greet his new pilots. One of them was a rather portly man who seemed to stretch his combat shirt. *He certainly hasn't missed any meals.*

The new pilot noticed Mo approach and walked over with a sense of self-importance.

"Hey, you must be those cadet pilots I heard about. I'm Corporal Novak, though I hope I'll be a Sergeant again soon," he said.

"Actually, Novak, I'm Sergeant Mondragon and I'm your team leader," Mo replied.

Novak folded his arms.

"What year were you born?" he asked.

"2116," Mo replied.

Novak smiled.

"I was in my third service year."

"Cool, how many Panzerters have you shot down?" Mo asked.

"Say again?" Novak asked.

"You heard me, how many kills do you have?"

Novak shrugged.

"None. We weren't at war then."

Mo pointed to a row of silhouettes painted on his own Panzerter.

"I have ten, and Unger, the cadet behind me, has three. Don't patronize me or my soldiers, are we clear?"

"Oh, I didn't mean to come off as patronizing, Sergeant, won't happen again," Novak replied.

"Good," Mo said. He could have sworn Novak muttered "Dick" as he walked past him to his other new soldier.

There was something familiar about this one. His sandy hair was cropped rather short, and a squared-off set of glasses framed his gray eyes. *He almost looks like . . .*

"I can't believe I'm stuck with that douche," the pilot said. "Hope he didn't give you too hard a time."

Mo shook his head.

"Trust me, after the initial invasion, nothing seems too hard," he replied. "Sergeant Mondragon, or Sergeant Mo, whichever makes you more comfortable." He held out his hand.

The other guy smiled and shook Mo's hand.

"Corporal Wes Merlin at your service."

Mo chuckled.

"No way, *that's* why you look familiar," he said.

"Oh, you must be Merlin's older brother!" Unger added.

Merlin Senior's smile wavered.

"So Ernie's out here, huh?" he said. "Mom'll be pissed to find out he got sucked into this, but she'll be glad we're together."

Mo nodded.

"Trust me, if my sisters got involved, I'd be pissed," he said. "Then again, they already got pretty close to the action." They began to walk towards the ready room.

"Really?" Merlin the elder asked. "How old are they?"

"Well, my twin sisters are twelve, and my youngest is five," Mo replied. "They were being evacuated and, well, had a front-row seat to the battle where I became an ace."

The older man shook his head.

"Damn, poor things must have been terrified."

"Dude, so was I," Mo said. "I was the only thing standing between them on a boat loaded with refugees and like three tinhats."

They collected Novak and gave the new pilots a grand tour of the facilities at Garden City Tech. They showed them the cafeteria, the dorms, the ready room, the war room, and Fletcher's cell.

"I've never seen a Unionist in person," Novak said. "I figured they'd be hairier."

Mo ignored him, but their prisoner stirred, as if realizing there were people outside her room.

"Mondragon, if you're out there, I'd like to speak to Captain Reiter again," she said.

Mo reached for the mic linked to the PA system in the cell.

"I'll see what I can do. We're going to have another interview prior to your medical exam, anyway."

She shifted in her bed.

"That's what I want to talk to him about," she replied.

That's interesting. Could it be related to proving she is what she says she is?

"I'll have a word with him,' Mo said and left it at that.

As they walked away, Merlin the elder had a few questions.

"You guys are comfortable letting your CO just sit down with a prisoner?" he asked. "Excuse me if I sound dumb, but isn't that a recipe for an assassination attempt?"

Novak nodded.

"He should let a skilled subordinate conduct interviews. I would be glad to volunteer."

"What, so you can drool over her?" Merlin asked.

Mo fought back a laugh.

"Actually, Merlin, your brother did the first interview."

Merlin looked alarmed.

"Tell me he didn't drool over her."

Mo shook his head.

"He actually got some solid info out of her," he said, "most of which we're still following up on, but so far it lines up with what we learned from pulling what's left of her machine apart."

"And that is?" Novak asked.

"The tinhats are deathtraps," Unger answered. "They have minimal standards for pilot safety. For example, if the head's damaged, then spalling will be channeled directly into the cockpit."

Merlin grimaced and waved a hand in front of him before mouthing "No thanks."

"So, Captain Reiter, what's he like?" he asked.

Why do I keep getting this?

"The first thing you'll notice is his voice," Unger said. "It's so deep and smooth, I could listen to him read the dictionary. He's tall too."

Mo shot a sideways glance at Unger.

"Well, he's a history TA on the civilian side," he said. "Most of the company's senior leadership died during the initial invasion. When we got here, he was the senior-most officer."

"We've got Major Starnes too," Unger added. "But he's more like an advisor. Reiter is definitely calling the shots in Fox."

Mo led them to the infirmary, where they met Smith in the late stages of having his burns from the previous battle treated. They returned to the cafeteria for a late lunch.

A voice rang out across the room.

"Wes?" Merlin the younger cried.

The older brother grinned.

"Hey Ernie, nice place you got here."

KENNEDY FROWNED AT THE WEATHER REPORT. FOG ROLLING IN early tomorrow morning gave the Tharcians an edge if they wanted to try anything funny. *And it's going to be thick too, so that'll really muck up our satellite mapping.* He brought this up with Meyer, and she shrugged.

"Best we can do is use short-range comms and relays," she said. "If the Tharcians want to fuck around, we'll find out quick."

He nodded.

"So we're being kept in reserve, then?"

Meyer nodded as she pointed to her map.

"Yes. North of us and even farther than that, we're massing combat power for another push into Tharsis. Here Goblin and Sandman will be spread in a screen in front of the firebase." She traced her finger in a rough triangle. "If the Tharcians attack, your company will move to crush them. We also have the 28th and 49th Panzerter Battalions supporting our northern and southern flanks, so we won't get overwhelmed if they concentrate their forces on us."

Kennedy nodded.

"I understand. I'll put my people to bed and have them on fifteen-minute ready status." *She knows they'll try something, and so do I. Those conniving Tharcians can't help themselves.*

He left the battalion commander to her devices and headed towards the barracks.

The icy, humid air outside the commander's tent stung Kennedy. After walking a few meters, his feet already felt cold and wet. *I'm running low on good socks.* Ballard waited for him near the entrance to the barracks. The old hat puffed on a cigarette under the overhang. Sleet began whipping at Kennedy as he approached. *Fuck this slush box.*

"Get our people together," he said through chattering teeth. "Tell them to get some sleep but be prepared to mount their Panzerters in fifteen minutes."

Ballard nodded and sheltered his cigarette.

"I don't know about you, but the Tharcians can keep their crummy weather," he said.

Kennedy passed him to enter the barracks.

"Comrade Ballard, I wouldn't be polite enough to call this weather crummy."

The older man laughed as Kennedy left him in the slush for the warmth of his own room. Out of his wet clothes, the pain began setting in. Kennedy wrapped himself in his blankets and shuddered, his skin more sensitive because of the temperature. He killed his light and tried to get some rest.

With the glowing heater his only light source, his wet clothes above it cast dancing shadows as they swayed on the clothesline. Occasionally, a gust of freezing wind penetrated the canvas walls, chilling him in his synthetic blankets. The chills only got worse when his blankets began making him sweat.

After hours of fitful sleep, Kennedy got up. He sauntered over to his canteen and gulped down some water. Satisfied, he lay back in his bed. *A better Mars.*

What would a better Mars look like? Ballard didn't want military tubers. "No more lambs to the slaughter," he'd told him after a mission. Part of Kennedy agreed. The regular Union citizen probably didn't realize the sacrifice of not just their lives, but their life. Their entire existence was predicated on killing and dying for the Union cause. That being said, they wouldn't have been granted their chance at life had the Union not created them.

There's another layer to people, and it's not something you can determine by genetics, training, or code. Kennedy stretched out a hand to the ceiling. *I wish I had a word to describe it, but the part of me that's, well, me.* He relaxed. *I'm sure the Tharcians have something like that too, and if that's the case, we can't just murder a bunch of them. No, there's got to be some Tharcians that would love to work for the common good. Yeah, they have a working class—surely those people would love to be liberated. If only they knew.*

Kennedy blinked as he looked at his watch. 0035.

0241.

0450.

In the distance, he heard a shrill scream.

Kennedy bolted awake and swung himself under his bunk. The ground trembled. He sprang to his feet and grabbed a dry uniform and jacket. Cold wind grasped at him through new holes in the outer barracks walls. Kennedy jumped into his boots and ran towards the field hangar.

Snow flurries whipped past him as he joined the stream of pilots running to the hangars. Shells rushed past overhead, some destined for Union positions farther back, others seeking payback for the damage done by the Tharcians. After scrambling up a ladder and racing down a catwalk, Kennedy found himself in front of the Jupiter.

He dropped down from the catwalk into the clavicle hatch. Turning and taking his seat, he closed the hatch. The monitors rose into position, and an armored shell locked into position over him.

Donning his helmet and strapping in, he brought the Jupiter online. The engine switched into active mode. Sensors painted his surroundings. His displays lit up, and the safeties disengaged.

"All units, radio check," he said. His company acknowledged him, but he received no feedback from Battalion. "Leviathan 6, respond." Silence. "Any Leviathan element, please respond!"

"This is Leviathan 6. Reaper, keep your company close to Firebase Blake. We've got two attacks coming upriver." Meyer's voice on the other end of the line softened the bad news.

Two attacks?

"Do you know anything else, 6?" Kennedy asked.

After a delay, Meyer came back.

"I'm getting our supporting elements to send what support they can," she said. "But they're reporting additional attacks on their positions. As of right now, we don't know which one is the main thrust."

Kennedy looked at his matrix.

If the main thrust was just north of them, they risked being cut off. If it was farther south of them, then the Tharcians could seize the main road back to their provincial capital, potentially rolling the entire flank. At the extreme north, the main thrust would meet the spear tip pointed at their heart, stalling any hope of advancing.

Kennedy grit his teeth as he led the company just outside the firebase. As they dug in on the shores of Crater Lake, all he could do was wait.

THE ASSAULT BARGE CONTINUED TO BLAST AWAY WITH ARTILLERY. Reiter was impressed with the sheer amount of firepower. In turrets toward the bow, the barge mounted twin 155-mm howitzers, with a bank of cruise missile platforms towards the stern. Autocannons lined her flanks and front, all the better to destroy aircraft, missiles, and IFVs.

Fox Company walked along her left flank, ensuring the autocannons would see little action on that side. Black took point, led by Mo. A section from Gold Platoon trailed them: four Iglasio IFVs and a Cstalio missile carrier. Reiter centered the formation in the Lowe, along with Adamski, Comidus in his Iglasio Commander, and Starnes in the tactical truck. Behind them came White, supported by the other half of Gold Platoon.

Eventually, we'll run into Early Company. The weather report hadn't been joking when it said the fog would be thick. Novak's Panzerter was less than 300 meters in front of him yet still nearly impossible to make out in the fog. *This fog is so dense, I doubt the railgun could penetrate it.*

The rhythmic pounding of the barge's guns threatened to dull his senses. To focus, he looked at the pictures of his fallen friends. *I started this war merely defending my homeland. It was my town the enemy rolled through, tinhats that tore up my streets. The longer this goes on, though, the more I feel like I see the Union for what it is.* His hand rested on a picture of Bartonova.

They took each of you from us, one or two at a time. I don't want your deaths to be for nothing. His mind wandered back to their prisoner. *Lieutenant Clarissa Fletcher, they robbed you of being the thing you wanted and made you fight for the right to have something you should have always had.*

Fletcher had, on the verge of tears, revealed what the Union did to the "tubers" to ensure they were easier to control. Her reproductive facilities had been butchered. From the way she had worded it, the medics expected her tubes to be tied or some other procedure that was easily reversible. What they discovered horrified them.

"She'll need major reconstructive surgery if she wants to have children," he remembered one saying. "What they did is reversible, but it's just so senselessly destructive." Fletcher was an enemy combatant. She'd killed Tharcians. Yet Reiter found himself pitying her the more he learned about "tubers" and how the Union treated them.

Equity and fraternity my ass. He scowled into the cold soup in front of him. *It's always a con. Some grifter brings nothing to the table and promises paradise to everyone. Then millions starve. Or in the Union's case, you create a servant class in your classless society.* He sighed. *If we survive, we might as well dismantle the Union. These tubers will eventually if we don't.*

"Heads up, Early is in contact. They're not much farther ahead," Mo said.

"Roger. Let's double-time it, Fox," Reiter said. They pushed their Panzerters into a run. Crashing through trees and bounding over rocks, they came upon the rear of Early's perimeter. Muzzle flashes perforated the fog ahead of him.

"Black, move around Early's perimeter," Reiter said. "Early 6, we have a team moving in front of your perimeter."

"Roger, we're tracking," came the reply. Within seconds, the shooting ceased. The Unionists in front of them were either dead or retreating.

Damn, it's a lot harder to track my people in this. Fox Company resumed their formation and pressed forward. The barge dropped anchor next to Early Company as attack boats sped alongside Fox.

"Black 1, the next phase line is going to be at a weather station," Reiter said.

"Roger 6, I'm tracking," Mo replied. The image of a fatman bursting through the fog alarmed Reiter as soon as he thought of it.

"Black 1, FRAGO: if a heavy Panzerter blocks your way, Aussie peel out of there," Reiter said.

"I would, but we haven't rehearsed that as a team so it'll be tricky," Mo said.

"Contact! Ten o'clock! Two tinhats!" Smith cried.

"Push through!" Mo replied.

Reiter smiled. Muzzle flashes ahead gave away the Unionists' positions. The IFVs sped by as the Panzerters opened fire and continued. By the time Reiter got to them, the tinhats were already doubled over. Black smoke mixed with gray fog.

They must not realize the scale of the attack here. The Unionists wouldn't stop them with a bunch of weak formations. Not while they had this much combat power rolling through. *There's either an intelligence failure here or a trap waiting.* He pushed the thought away. An entire plan shouldn't hinge on your enemy screwing up.

"Fox 6, Fox 3," Starnes said. "Just got a tight beam from Regiment. The fog's going to thin out over the next hour and lift ahead of schedule.

Guess a plan shouldn't hinge on the weather, either.

"Let's pick it up, Fox," Reiter said. "This weather won't hold up, and we still have a lot of ground to cover."

They resumed the breakneck pace from before. After 15 more minutes of crashing through the woodlands, Mo called for them to slow down.

"I think we're coming up on Phase Line Storm," he said. "Yep, I see it now, there's the weather station."

"Roger. Form it up, Fox," Reiter said.

Black settled into position from 9 o'clock to 1: Mo in the center, Unger and Merlin Senior to his left, Novak and Smith to his right. White took up 6 o'clock to 8:30. Steele anchored the middle, with the rookie Zorro and Merlin Junior to her right and new bodies Strauss and Tancred to her left. Reiter's group formed up in the middle with Gold Platoon remaining split between the teams. The attack boats patrolled ahead of them and to the rear. Reiter twisted in his seat to check his map when the radio blared.

"Aircraft at 3 o'clock! In attack formation!"

Shit.

"Gold Platoon! Engage with missiles and autocannons!" Comidus cried.

The attack boats added their own air defenses to the mix. Drones crashed to the ground near them. A few strafed blindly with autocannons.

"Friendlies! Friendlies!" Starnes cried.

"Cease fire!" Reiter ordered. *Great, just what we needed, a friendly fire incident. Can today get any worse?*

"Don't worry, Comrade Meyer," Chaney said. "I'll take my leave of you soon." The battalion commander snorted at him. *How unladylike.*

"Can't you see I'm in the middle of a battle?" she replied, barely looking up from her map table. "I need an update from Goblin 6, or anyone from Goblin. Same goes for Sandman." She looked at another operations officer. "Get the infantry companies pushed out. I need eyes out there."

"I would like to remind you, Comrade," Chaney said, "you're only getting this meeting once."

Meyer grit her teeth.

"Do we have to be alone?" she asked.

He looked over the staff in the command tent.

"It's a strong preference," he replied. "Though, I would hate to take you too far from your duties."

Meyer scowled as she looked back and forth.

"Wright, I'll be in the annex with Guard Colonel Chaney," she said. "Knock if there's any pressing developments."

She led the head of R&D back towards a wing of the command tent. The room was much smaller, with a narrow table and a few chairs. Meyer took a seat across from Chaney. He smiled under her icy gaze.

"Why are you playing games with two of my best pilots and leaders?" she asked. "I have a right to know."

Chaney shook his head.

"No," he said, "you don't, but I'm giving you the *privilege* of knowing." He smiled at her discomfort before continuing. "How many breeds of tubers are there?"

Meyer furrowed her brow.

"Breeds?" she asked.

Chaney chuckled.

"Templates, archetypes, classes, jobs," he said. "You know how much they carry the burdens of our society? The jobs they must do?"

Meyer shook her head.

"I've never thought about it," she admitted. "Not once."

Chaney sipped some water from his canteen.

"Well, then, dear Comrade," he said, "allow me to enlighten you." He leaned back in his chair. "Ever since we created them, we've had farmers, fishers, factory workers, construction workers, soldiers, and other templates for the hands and feet of our society."

"You want something more out of them?" Meyer asked. "Is that why they're getting the benefits they are?"

Chaney nodded.

"During their recovery, we activated some dormant genes within them," he said, "subliminally trained them to be greater than their peers."

Meyer scowled.

"Why?" she asked. "And for how long?" Chaney chuckled and rose from his chair. "How did you find out about this?"

"You know why many countries fall?" he asked. Meyer hesitated, prompting a chuckle from the guard colonel. "Of course not, you haven't really been cultured at a military academy." With a sweep of his arm, he went on. "Their leadership becomes decadent. Even in good socialist nations, the leaders become fat and sheltered." He paused for dramatic effect. "Chairman Nicholas saw this coming."

Meyer gasped.

"Chairman Nicholas died before the last war," she said.

Chaney waved a finger.

"He was a visionary, dear Comrade," he said. "He left a classified memoir, in which he detailed four predictions." He held up four fingers. "One: the Republic of Tharsis itself wasn't an existential threat to the UMR, but cyclic wars with them were." A finger went down. "Two: border friction and animosity generated by the intelligentsia would cause the Union to prosecute a war it was unprepared for, one it would lose, starting said cycle." He lowered another finger. "Three: decadent leaders would enable the cycle until either Tharsis destroyed the Union or tubers rose up and tore it apart themselves, and four: the Union could only survive if leaders forged by hardship took the reins."

Meyer folded her arms.

"What made him so sure the tubers would rise up?" she asked. "Most only know the bare minimum they need to function in society and do their job well."

Chaney waved his hands around him.

"It's the wars, Meyer," he said. "If they interact with occupied civilians, read materials that would be banned back home, they'll eventually find out they've got a raw deal." He sneered. "They'll learn how they fight for a nation of hypocrites."

Meyer looked uneasy.

"So let me get this straight," she said. "Kennedy and Wake are what? Prototypical congressmen?"

Chaney shook his head.

"With the rights they've earned," he said, "they could potentially be chairman."

Meyer shifted uneasily.

"I'm not sure how to frame this, Comrade Colonel," she said, "but I think you've made a mistake."

"The order to elevate Kennedy and Wake came directly from the First Minister," Chaney said. "If anyone made a mistake, it would be him. Now where exactly do you believe he made a mistake? *Comrade.*"

"I've heard disturbing things from Wake," she said. "The thought of him being chairman . . . It scares me."

Huh? This is unprecedented. Chaney returned to his seat. All the bluster and preening melted away. Pulling out a notepad, he looked at Meyer.

"I'm listening," he said. "What have you heard? What has he said?"

Meyer leaned forward.

"He believes that to truly end the threat of Tharsis," she said, "we need to *liquidate*—meaning kill—every Tharcian over the age of six and reeducate the rest."

Fuck, that's millions of people. Chaney sighed.

"Truly, this is a problematic development," he said. "Unfortunately, he's too valuable to the war effort to turn into the Review Service." He looked up from his notes. "Give him the most dangerous missions and assignments that come to your battalion, even if they're suicidal." He shook his head. "Scratch that, especially if they're suicidal." Making another note, he stood up. "Best-case scenario, he becomes a martyr while pushing us closer to victory."

"Are you trying to leave, Comrade Colonel?" Meyer asked.

"I have to. We need to activate another candidate," he said. "Ideally one without his disposition."

Meyer shook her head.

"I don't care for the Tharcians," she said, "but his ideas go too far."

Chaney shook his head.

"You don't get it, Comrade Meyer," he said. "This isn't about the Tharcians." As he walked to the exit, he looked at her. "If tuber resentment rises to the surface, he'll be looking at liquidating *us* and every other normal."

"There's another issue," Meyer said. "Kennedy and Wake are currently in the same company."

Damn it, he could have been a good one.

"If Kennedy dies but we remain unliquidated," he said, "then the price was worth it. I'll activate two more candidates." Chaney left the annex with Meyer not far behind him.

"Where is the closest Tharcian advance?" Meyer asked. "Call Reaper 6 and send his combined company there."

Chaney shook his head as he left. *What a waste.*

24

K ennedy's Jupiter knelt in a copse of trees. Through the thinning fog, he could just make out the silhouettes of Tharcian Panzerters. *Just a bit more, all the way into the kill box.* When the six Tharcians entered the kill box, he opened fire.

Most of his company joined him. The Tharcians staggered and fell. Kennedy pushed forward, followed by about half of his company. More Tharcians rushed them.

They didn't stand a chance. Trapped in a fatal L and firing blindly, the Tharcians were cut down before they could do any serious damage.

"All points, damage report," Kennedy said. None of his company's vehicles had been seriously damaged. "Wake, let's split here. There's bound to be more."

Shells stabbed through the fog, searching for them.

"There're boats on the water!" one of his soldiers cried. "They're coordinating fires from across the river!"

So there are more Panzerters over there.

"Ballard, take out those boats," Kennedy said. "We need—" A

Panzerter crashed to the ground. *What the hell? I didn't see her get hit.* Then he noticed an IFV racing away from the Panzerter, a wire leading back to the fallen machine. *Those crazy bastards.*

He attempted to engage them with his rifle, but the Tharcian evaded him.

"Watch out for IFVs. They're using tow cables to trip us," he said.

"I see them!" a pilot cried. He raced after the IFVs. Flame burst from the trees, and the pilot suddenly staggered and fell. Kennedy's forces scoured the tree line with weapons fire. Flames blossomed from the trees as the hidden missile carrier exploded.

"Reaper 6, attack boats are a wash," Ballard said.

"Roger, all units, enter the river," Kennedy said.

Wake came in on the command net. Isolated in the fog, it was essentially a private channel for the two of them.

"They've been telling us to avoid the rivers unless we absolutely have to," he said. "What are you after?"

"The brass's utter fear of the water has certainly been noticed by the Tharcians," Kennedy replied. "So I doubt they expect us to be there." In the distance, he heard the pounding of heavy artillery. "Besides, they have big gun positions not too far from here, and silencing them—"

"—could scare and confuse them," Wake finished. "Maybe even enough to disorient their attack."

Kennedy nodded in his cockpit.

"Right on the money, Comrade." He waded his machine into the river, focusing hard on not getting stuck. "All units, if you feel yourself getting stuck, don't slow down." The Jupiter seemed to bob in the black water. Ice floes scraped at the sides of his machine as it waded through the cold river. Occasionally, the drifting remains of an attack boat bumped into one of his Panzerters. This tended to result in spooked pilots, but so far they seemed to remain undetected.

"All points, make landfall on the opposite side of the river," Kennedy said. "There will probably be more Tharcians, only this time, we'll be behind them." He arranged the nine Panzerters assigned to him into three triangles led by himself, Ballard, and Wake. Ballard's wing made landfall to his left with Wake on his right. *With me and Wake strung out along either a supply line or reinforcement route, Ballard's most likely to make contact.*

"We're all clear," Ballard said. "But there's definite signs Panzerters moved through here."

Kennedy looked at his matrix. The analytics projected a 73.6% chance a company-sized element was to his north, closer to Ballard. *Those are pretty good odds.*

"Reaper 3, turn north and follow the trail," Kennedy said. "The other two wings will fall in, echelon right, and follow." The company moved into formation and advanced. To his left, he could see the rightmost Panzerter in Ballard's wing. If they received contact, Kennedy's wing would push forward and flank while Wake went the long way to cut them off.

Just like that, Kennedy was in the slowest pursuit he'd ever been a part of. Each Panzerter took cautious measured steps. *How far did these guys go?* Kennedy shifted in his seat, struggling to find the most comfortable way to stretch while at the same time controlling the machine and keeping watch.

"Reaper 6, we got eyes on enemy Panzerters," Ballard said.

Finally!

"Maintain your distance. Try not to tip them off while the rest of us move into position," Kennedy replied. The Panzerters continued their cautious march but at a greater pace. Cringing every time they knocked over a tree or stepped on a hidden structure, Kennedy kept his eyes towards the enemy.

Shells raced past his Jupiter. *Shit.*

"We're in contact!" Kennedy said. "Ballard, Wake, maneuver. I'll establish fire." He unleashed his rifle on the nearest muzzle flash. An orange glow told him his aim had been true.

Kennedy's eyes danced to the superlaser's readout. The weapon was ready to fire, but still Kennedy hesitated. *It's not that it isn't an impressive weapon, but will it overcome the thermal blooming in the fog? And even if it does, I'm giving away my exact position.* He fired another burst at a shadow and sighed. *It's not like I'm not already doing that, anyway.*

The super-laser swung over the Jupiter's shoulder. Kennedy planted his crosshairs on a shadow in the fog. He squeezed the trigger.

Green light lanced out from the shoulder cannon. The shadow burned a bright orange before falling. *Okay, thermal bloom isn't that bad.*

The Tharcians stood little chance. Strung out and surprised by an attack from the rear, they fell quickly to the Unionists' attack. Surveying smoldering wrecks along the edge of the river, Kennedy nodded in approval.

"Area secured, Comrade," one pilot reported. "What now?"

Kennedy cast his gaze south.

"Simple," he said. "We go hunting."

"I don't like the sound of this," Mo said over the command net. "Early reported being in contact, then nothing. Now Hollywood is saying they haven't heard from Gamble in a minute either."

After a long pause, Captain Reiter finally replied to him.

"I'm getting on Regiment. I'll have answers soon," he said. "Hopefully."

Mo sighed and stretched in his seat. He switched back to his team network.

"Hey everyone, be sure to stretch while we have some down-time," he said. "We might have to move soon."

"I never thought I'd have so much downtime during an offensive," Merlin Senior said.

"This whole war has honestly been underwhelming," Novak added. Mo rolled his eyes.

"Trust me," Unger said, "this is way better than QRF."

"Agreed," Smith said. "This beats rushing off to stop an attack from turning into a breakthrough."

Mo smiled.

"Enjoy this time while you can," he said. "During the initial invasion, it felt like whenever we turned around the Union was there." He peered out into the thinning fog and shuddered. *I can't imagine anything making me want to go back to that.* He thought of Legousi's laugh, Bartonova's smile, Varga's words, and shook his head.

I think I'm getting numb to it all, and just like that I get a little of the feeling back. Will it stay like this forever? Or will it just go away? I want to remember them forever, but every day puts me further from our last conversation. He caught a glimpse of his reflection and smirked at the man staring back. *I hardly recognize the nearly thoughtless teenager I was a month ago.*

"Black 1, please respond," Reiter said.

Mo blinked back to the present and switched his mic channel.

"Go for Black 1?" he replied.

"Higher wants us to forge ahead," Reiter said. "We'll advance on the south bank until we hit the next waypoint. From there we hold until Hollywood approaches with the barge and passes us. You're tracking?"

"Roger, Fox 6, I got you Lima Charlie," Mo replied. "When are we pushing off?"

"In another thirty mikes," Reiter replied. "This fog's thinning and not helping as much as it should."

Mo set a timer and sighed.

"Roger, 6, standing by," he said. "Heads up, Black, we're moving in thirty. Enjoy your downtime while you can."

"What happened to Early Company?" Smith asked.

"Unknown," Mo replied. "I believe part of our FRAGO will be reestablishing contact with them or whoever's left." *I'd feel bad if Early was killed down to the same guy as before.* He shook his head. *No, there's no way they got wiped out again. It's more likely they just lost comms.*

"How do you want us to move, 1?" Smith asked.

"You are just full of questions today, 3," Mo replied. "We'll start in a file and go to a wedge as the fog thins, just like rehearsals." *They all know their positions, it's been pounded into their heads.*

"Think we'll see fatmen?" Unger asked.

"Don't jinx us," Merlin Senior said.

Mo checked his timer. Six minutes left.

"Alright, people, start stepping in," he said. "The plan may be coming apart, but that's why we have our training." The timer clicked down the minutes and seconds. *It's always weird how the minutes before a movement seem longer than the preceding hour.*

Before the timer hit zero, Black was already in formation. Smith taking point, Novak his wingman, Mo himself in the middle, Merlin Senior behind him, and Unger bringing up the rear.

"Fox 6, Black 1. We're ready, status 1," Mo said over the command net.

"Roger, Black 1. Step off on your mark," Reiter responded. "We'll be five minutes behind you."

"Roger, 6. Stepping off." Mo switched back to his platoon net. "Black, move out!"

"Such a manly tone," Merlin Senior said. "I can hear the muscles in his voice."

Mo chuckled.

"Quiet, 4," Smith said. "You only want him for his body."

"What's the matter, 3?" Novak asked. "Jealous?"

"Negative, 5," Smith replied. "I'm exotic around here—I could have whoever. But 1 is White 1's."

"Wait what?" Mo asked. His face burned a bit. Laughter filled the net.

"If it's any consolation, 1," Unger said, "3 didn't figure that out on his own—I helped him."

Mo shook his head as his team tried to talk through their laughter. In spite of the embarrassment, he found himself smiling. *It actually reminds me of the old days.*

Their Panzerters walked at a deliberate pace. Their rifles swung through their assigned sectors, searching for targets. The only sounds were the hum of their engines and their heavy footfalls.

Smith's machine signaled a halt.

"I got contacts across the river," he said. "Panzerters, three of them, unknown type."

Mo furrowed his brow.

"Could be friendlies," he said. "Try hailing them on Regiment."

"Attention Republic machines," Smith said. "This is Black 3 of Fox Company, identify yourselves."

The three machines started towards them.

"Oh thank God," said one of the pilots. "This is White 1, Early Company. We've been about torn apart."

That voice. Mo switched to the net.

"I remember you," he said. "You were at the Battle for Airport Road."

"No fucking way," the survivor said. "You made it here too? I guess my odds are slightly better."

"They've got this big ugly machine," one of the other pilots said. "It had this shoulder laser that worked in spite of the fog."

Mo swore.

"Sounds like they upgraded their fatman," he said. "Fall in on us. We're retaking your objective."

"Are you serious?" the survivor asked. "That 'fatman' chewed through us like we were nothing. What are you going to do?"

"We've got a new machine rolling in behind us," Mo replied. "It's more than a match for the fatman." He took a swig from his canteen as his team resumed moving. "Besides, I have a score to settle with that pilot."

"A score?"

"I apparently killed his old commander," Mo said. "He tried to kill my best friend and ended up killing my old crush. On top of that, I captured one of his officers."

"Why do you insist on fucking with these people?" the survivor asked.

"They threatened my sisters," Mo replied. "Now shut up and fall in."

"KEEP YOUR EYES OPEN, PEOPLE," KENNEDY SAID. THOUGH THE fog was lifting, snow was starting to fall. *This will probably be their last chance before the rivers freeze.* He narrowed his eyes as they approached a bend in the river. He glanced at his matrix: 7% chance of an ambush. The computer system believed that two more companies would be near an armored barge downriver from them. *Well, it hasn't been wrong yet.*

Kennedy paused. *That sound.* Through the gray clouds, drones dove on them. One of the sleek aircraft dropped a pair of bombs directly on one of his wingmen. Another failed to pull up and simply crashed into a Martian Trooper. Two drones remained, swinging around for another pass. Lasers reached for them. The drones managed to savage them with cannon fire before succumbing to the lasers.

Desperate for a status report, he looked at the matrix. Seven units remained operational, although a few had been damaged. *We still got some fight left in us.*

"Comrade Kennedy, do you want us to keep moving?" Ballard asked. "It might be wiser to head back to Blake or get comms with Battalion."

"Of course we should keep moving," Wake said. "We have the potential to cut the offensive heart right out of the Tharcians!"

We just lost two Panzerters, but the Jupiters have enough fire-power to equal three to five machines. Again he consulted the matrix. To his surprise, the odds of ambush had gone down to 3%. *Huh, I wonder why that is?*

"Listen up," he said, "we're forging ahead. Today we reach Riverside, tomorrow the Gulf of Curiosity!" His company surged forward. Wake's wing led them, followed by Kennedy's and then Ballard's. They rounded the bend. And immediately came under fire.

A Martian collapsed into the black waters of the river. Another withered under repeated hits.

Wake rushed forward, shells glancing off his frontal armor.

"You can throw everything you have at me." His superlaser swung forward. "It won't be enough!" The green beam bisected a Tharcian Panzerter. Wake was lining up a second shot when a salvo struck his flank. The beam swept across the surface of the river before racing through trees and into the sky. Kennedy's wingman charged into the fray, only to be struck by a high-caliber round. The Panzerter's torso exploded.

"Captain Kennedy, I'm calling you out," said a voice on an open net.

Him.

"Well, if it isn't the boy who murdered Blake," Kennedy said. "I hope your sniper friend is well."

"Oh, just dandy," the boy replied. "Especially since Lieutenant Fletcher sang like a canary when we captured her."

What? He's lying. There's no way they'd take her prisoner. Then again, how the hell would he know her name? He's lying about the singing part, though. She doesn't know how to sing.

"Since we've softened your armor to roughly the same protection as mine, why don't you draw your mace and we can settle this like men?"

He thinks I'm Wake. It's dark tonight. He smiled. *Oh, he's about to be shocked.*

The fire had lifted from the stunned Wake. A Tharcian Panzerter emerged from the wood line and drew a sword.

Kennedy moved to where the other soldier could see him.

"Except I didn't fall into your trap, Mondragon," he said. "I'm fresh as I can be."

"That's not saying much," Mondragon replied. "Especially if you were born in a soup can."

Kennedy grit his teeth and drew his mace. *He's trying to get under your skin. Don't let him. Nobody fights well when angered.*

"Wake, fall back with the others," Kennedy said. "Come back around behind them. I'll hold their attention here." As he returned to the open net, he focused on Mondragon.

"You're a foolish tactician if you're preventing your forces from simply swarming me."

"First of all, I tried to weaken you first," Mondragon said. "And secondly, you're indulging me, which confirms something I suspected." They began circling each other, weapons drawn.

"And that is?" Kennedy asked.

"That for you, this is personal," Mondragon answered. "What I'm not sure of is why, but there's about six different ways I figure."

Kennedy swung first. It quickly became clear that for the moment, neither of them held a distinct advantage. The Tharcian easily dodged Kennedy's slow swings and ponderous movements. In exchange, the Tharcian was unable to deal more than a few glancing blows.

"You're up to something," the young man finally said.

"What makes you say that?" Kennedy asked.

"Your machine was a lot faster the last time we fought," he said. "You're stalling."

Kennedy easily parried the incoming blow.

"What makes you think I'm stalling?"

"Because I'm also stalling," Mondragon replied.

Weapons fire erupted from the position behind Kennedy.

"Kennedy, they got us in the flank," Ballard said. "Wake's trying to fight his way to you."

Fires ignited behind Mondragon.

"I'm not going to let you pass," he said as he lunged at Kennedy. Kennedy met his blade with his mace. He forced the Panzerter back toward dry ground. Sparks flew from its joints as the Mark IV struggled to hold the Jupiter back.

"It really doesn't look like you have a lot of choices." Kennedy forced the Tharcian farther into the wood line with each blow. After knocking his opponent through a tree, he swung his superlaser into action. "Sayonara, boy soldier."

The laser seared into the Panzerter's shoulder. Its sword bounced away as the arm melted and burst. Gases from inside the machine began igniting, and the face began to melt. The Tharcian staggered and fell to a knee.

Kennedy staggered forward and kicked the stricken machine's head.

"Good effort," he said. "Lousy execution."

Another Tharcian machine ran into the clearing, then another, then another. Kennedy sighed and leveled his rifle at them. One by one, each machine fell as 100-mm shells tore through their armor at close range.

"Comrade Kennedy, coming over a hill! It's—" The soldier's line went dead suddenly.

Damn he's here. Kennedy broke into a run. As fast as his machine could carry itself. Unfortunately, it was not fast enough.

"WHITE, PUSH FORWARD," REITER SAID. "RELIEVE BLACK, THEY'VE been in contact too long. Gold, get eyes on and do your thing."

Zeroed in on another Unionist, he fired the railgun. The Lowe bucked with recoil. Another tinhat was shattered. The railgun's capacitors whined as they recharged.

"6, White 1. You have a fatman bearing down on your position!" Steele cried.

Must be Kennedy.

"All forces, let him through," Reiter said. "I'll deal with him myself."

"It's not who you're thinking," Starnes said. "That Kennedy guy was a team player. This guy couldn't give a damn about his subordinates."

"Roger, Fox 3," Reiter said. "Gold Platoon, focus on recovering any pilots you can. We have a lot of downed machines in the area." He focused on the fatman bursting through the trees ahead of him.

Reiter took aim with his railgun. The fatman staggered, its shoulder-weapon torn to scrap. *Too high. My next shot will be the end of him.*

The fatman returned fire. Shells pummeled the Lowe. Reiter backpedaled down the slope into cover.

"Adamski, head around with White," he said. "I'm going to try drawing the fatman away from the main battle." He dropped his rifle and grabbed a sword.

The fatman crested the hill. Reiter's shot grazed the hill, flinging dirt and debris into the air. As it emerged from the cloud, the fatman swung at him. Reiter's blade met the Unionist's in a shower of sparks. *This guy is pretty damn determined.*

The Union Panzerter was just fast enough that Reiter had to focus fully on defense. *Wear him down. He'll start making mistakes, he'll get tired. Let him.*

Parry after parry, blow after blow, Reiter kept the fatman at bay. Though the machine itself couldn't tire, the pilot controlling it was a different story. A feint with his sword allowed him to drive his shield into the fatman's chest.

The Unionist staggered, allowing Reiter to follow up with a swing through the machine's knees. For good measure, Reiter pried the fatman's head off with his sword.

"Fox 6, Gold 1," Comidus said. "They got reinforcements sporadically showing up."

"How's recovery efforts going?" Reiter asked.

"We got a couple back, but a few didn't make it," Comidus replied.

Reiter grit his teeth and checked his map.

"Fox Company, begin bounding back," he said. "Cover Gold while they displace. I'll provide covering fire." He took up a hull-down position on the hill. As the railgun swung over his shoulder, Reiter grabbed his targeting computer.

Before him lay sparse woodlands with intermittent fighting between Panzerters. Muzzle flashes along the ground told him infantry were duking it out on the ground. *The barge.*

"Hollywood 6, Fox 6. We need supporting fire from Barge!" he said.

"Roger, Fox 6. Be advised we have supporting units throwing their weight into this fight," the other commander replied. *Good, that should turn things around.*

Shells soared overhead as they raced toward Union positions. Tucked away on his hilltop, Reiter attempted to direct the course of the battle. Panzerters from Hollywood were fording the river to reach his side. Drones screamed down onto Union forces, dealing out bombs and cannon fire generously.

"Fox 3, sitrep?" Reiter asked. He plugged another tinhat with his railgun. The Union machine disappeared in a shower of metal and flame.

"Our most damaged units have been ditched or pulled back," Starnes answered. "Most of our downed pilots have been recovered, but some of them need immediate medical attention."

"Coordinate a medevac with Fox 5 and Gold 1," Reiter replied. He put another tinhat down. "Do we have units in contact?"

"White Platoon and Fox 5 just broke contact," Starnes replied. "They're trying to avoid becoming decisively engaged."

"Hollywood is entering combat," Reiter said. "As long as they're absorbing contact, we should be able to displace." He scanned the plain for targets, but none presented themselves. *I could have sworn White was in front of me. Did they get lost to my left?* He glanced at his map and sighed. *Some kind of battle tracker is a must. I'll have to bring it up with the Lowe team.*

"Fox 3, do you know where they are?" he asked.

"Well, Gold Platoon is taking the long way around," Starnes

said. "They should make contact with Hollywood's rear in five mikes."

"And White Platoon?" Reiter asked.

"They should be in front of you to your left," he replied. "Fox 5 might be using the wood line to conceal their approach."

Reiter nodded. *I figured they'd be out that way.*

A scream filled Reiter's ears. He looked up to see a Union drone bearing down on him. The shark-like craft unleashed a burst of cannon fire. Reiter responded with his point defenses. Then the bomb came.

Reiter blasted away with his point defenses, but the bomb still detonated meters from the Lowe. The blast tossed the Lowe like a rag doll. Reiter's head slammed against the bulkhead behind him. Stars exploded behind his eyes, but he soldiered on.

25

"All Leviathan forces, this is Reaper 6," Kennedy said. "The enemy is on the ropes. Scatter to avoid their artillery fire." He looked at his command matrix. Another battalion had taken the fight north of Firebase Blake, allowing his own battalion to concentrate on this battle. In all, seventeen Panzerters and two companies of infantry came under his field command. Meyer's orders were clear. Win.

"Make every shot count. Try to thin their numbers," Kennedy said. "I'll take care of the barge." He pushed the Jupiter to a run. *They haven't noticed me yet. I need to be careful. This machine is more vulnerable to artillery than a standard Martian.*

Kennedy took his machine through a winding path back towards the river. *When they asked me what I wanted my personal colors to be, I wanted to make a statement.* The Jupiter scraped past trees in a low crouch. *Now I wish I picked olive drab and mud brown.*

He brought his machine to the edge of the river and took a knee. He could make out shells leaping into the air upriver. *It'll have point defenses, most likely autocannons. If those big guns can direct fire, I'll be in trouble.* He eased his machine into the river.

Kennedy crouch-walked while doing his best to hold his rifle out of the water. His superlaser hung right above the black water. Icy chunks bumped into his head and shoulders.

The Jupiter swayed in the current. He witnessed cruise missiles streak overhead towards Firebase Blake. *I need to double-time it— those missiles could be enough to knock down the base by themselves.*

He struggled to make the Jupiter move faster. The muddy river bottom clung to the Jupiter's feet. The current pushed against the massive machine, and his crouch limited his speed. The rush of the river and squeal of the engine were the only things he could hear.

Kennedy gasped. His mouth felt like cotton. He fumbled under his seat before finding a water bag. He gulped down the salty fluid and felt his body cool slightly. Then water splashed into his lap.

He looked for the seam where the hatch lowered and spotted condensation. After a couple more steps, more water splashed into the cockpit. *Shit, above the waist isn't sealed. I can't afford to get water in the engine.* He cursed. He still couldn't see the barge. *Well, I guess I'll make myself a target.*

Kennedy brought the Jupiter into a standing position. He unleashed his rifle in the general direction of the barge. And ran.

The water behind him burst, rising high into the air. *That didn't take them long.* Kennedy took the Jupiter through a series of random zigs and zags. His maneuvering shook whatever water remained in the hatch loose, causing it to drip into his lap.

Autocannon rounds pummeled the Jupiter's armor. Kennedy grit his teeth. Their aim wasn't wild like before. Rather, the barge's gunners focused on his joints and his sensors.

His super-laser whirred to life. The barge's guns swung toward him. Kennedy closed his eyes and squeezed the trigger.

The Jupiter lurched backwards. With a resounding splash, it fell into the water. Kennedy's head slammed against the bulkhead behind him. Water splashed across his cameras and poured onto his face through the seam in the hatch.

Through spots and water, Kennedy saw a mushroom cloud rising into the air. He struggled to bring the Jupiter to its feet. He couldn't tell if alarms were going off or if his ears were still ringing. Turned out that water had leaked into his auxiliary batteries. *Damn, can't fire the superlaser at full power again.*

Kennedy staggered ashore. Tharcian Panzerters rushed towards him. He blasted them with his rifle and shoulder laser. Pushing his way towards the base of a hill, he found himself on his last magazine.

The Tharcians were in disarray. Two here, one there. He dropped them quickly. *They're not overtaking the Jupiter in drips and drabs, not unless Reiter's here.* After emptying his magazine into a Panzerter V, he spotted something next to a fallen Martian. A laser rifle. *Lucky me.*

Wielding the laser left-handed, he continued his drive towards the hill. *It's the most prominent terrain feature here. We take it, we'll be able to rout the Tharcians.*

"Captain Kennedy!" a female voice growled over the net. A Tharcian Panzerter approached him, sword drawn. "You're the one who hurt Mo."

What? Mondragon survived? He surveyed the Tharcian machine. It had already seen an intense battle. It wouldn't survive a duel with the Jupiter.

Kennedy fired his laser and shoulder laser. His opponent flirted between the beams. *She anticipated my move?* He parried her sword with his mace. He stepped back, angling himself up the hill. The power draw from firing both lasers delayed his riposte.

"Well, next time I kill a Tharcian, I'll be more thorough," he said.

"Come near him again, and I'll kill you," the woman replied. She forced him back farther, even scoring a glancing blow on his leg.

"No, young woman," Kennedy said. "I meant you." He swung his mace at just the angle to shatter her sword's ceramic core. His follow-up brought his mace across the Panzerter's face, knocking it back down the hill. He took aim with his laser rifle. "Not bad. I'm just better."

His proximity alarm went off, and Kennedy noticed a shadow. He swung his mace hard behind him and looked. There was the Black Knight, sword raised.

"WHITE 1, ARE YOU OKAY?" REITER ASKED. HE WAS JUST ABLE TO hold the fatman at bay. "White 1! Respond!"

"I'm okay, 6," she finally answered. "I'm just rattled."

"Fall back now!" Reiter said. He was able to stagger his opponent. With a moment to breathe, he glanced around.

"Fox 3, how's the retreat going?" he asked.

"There you are," Starnes replied. "Regiment has ordered a fighting withdrawal."

Reiter clashed with the fatman. He grit his teeth.

"Keep updates urgent," he said. "Need to focus. 6 out." With broad swings, he kept out of the fatman's reach. *You're not getting close, not against me, Kennedy.* For a moment, it looked like one of his blows knocked Kennedy off his feet, only for the tuber to regain his composure just beyond Reiter's reach.

"Captain Reiter," he said. "You're in my way again."

Reiter steadied himself.

"I'm always going to be in your way," he replied. "As long as you keep attacking us."

"You declared war on us," said Kennedy. "Your people are guilty of escalating this war." The fatman paced just out of reach, searching for an opening. "Your bourgeoisie oppressors dragged your lot into this fight. Why do you fight so hard for them?"

"Seriously?" Reiter asked. "You invaded our country, killed our people, trashed our cities, and you didn't expect us to fight back?" He resumed his attack on the Union machine.

"To be honest, I expected the whole rotten structure to fall apart," Kennedy said.

"Why don't you answer your own question?" Reiter asked. "They bred you to be slaughtered—why the hell would you fight so hard for them?" He locked weapons with the fatman, sending sparks and static everywhere.

"You answered the question yourself," Kennedy replied. "I was born for this." He broke the lock, maneuvering and lunging in an attempt to get inside Reiter's guard.

"They bred you to die," Rciter said.

Kennedy rolled inside his guard and swung his shoulder cannon to bear. Reiter's point defenses peppered the gun barrel, venting gas into his face. Kennedy lunged back, shield high.

"From my perspective," said Reiter, "it's horribly ironic that a classless society without property created a servant class that they could treat like state property."

Kennedy lunged out of the gas cloud. Reiter fell for a feint as Kennedy rolled left, blasting the Lowe's head with his laser. The sensors on the left side of Reiter's head died. He grit his teeth. He was looking away from the screen when his map caught his eye.

"I fight for them because they gave me a chance," Kennedy replied. He tried to stay on Reiter's left, but he was having none of that. Reiter swung to keep Kennedy on his right, glancing at his map again. "I have a chance to change my own destiny and that of my people!" He raised his laser, but Reiter anticipated the move, cutting through the barrel of the weapon. "That's something you would never understand!"

"I understand better than you think," Reiter replied. He knocked the mace aside and slashed at the fatman's shoulder. "Before shit hit the fan, I spent every day in front of young adults, teaching them history."

"I don't see how that changes anything." The fatman grabbed its disabled arm and tore the limb free. Reiter pivoted, but it became more difficult to keep the Unionist where he could see him.

"It's simple," Reiter said. "Think of it like a vaccine: they're not going to make the mistakes of us or our predecessors." The limb obscured his vision, and the Lowe lurched sideways. *I might have to lose this fight to win the battle.* Desperate, Reiter squared up on the fatman and lunged forward. The fatman lunged as well. The two machines met with a resounding crash. Reiter drove the point of his sword into the fatman's leg. The Lowe rocked with the impact of the severed arm. *We're stuck together. Good.*

Reiter reached for his targeting computer, and the railgun swung forward over his shoulder.

"What are you doing?" Kennedy cried.

"I'm going to wreck your base," Reiter replied. He felt the fatman struggle to stop him and free itself.

"Impossible. Firebase Blake is out of your range," Kennedy said.

Reiter grinned.

"Maybe for some cheap Union piece," he said, "but not for good old Tharcian engineering." He opened the bailout panel. *I'll only get one shot at this.* He adjusted the railgun's angel as much as he could.

"Fire that thing at this range and you'll destroy both machines!"

"I know." Reiter squeezed the trigger and jerked the lever downward. The seat slid backwards as shrapnel filled the space the cockpit used to occupy. The recoil of the railgun and the force of the exploding Panzerters tossed the armored cockpit away from the hill. Reiter's head slammed against the walls of the cockpit as it bounced and rolled across the terrain.

When the cockpit finally came to rest, it lay on its side. Reiter shook his head to clear the ringing and went to work. Once he freed himself from his restraints, he opened a hatch on the floor and removed a go bag as well as a thermite grenade. The bag had a day's worth of rations and room for a few more things.

He tore his map and pictures off the cockpit walls and stuffed them into the bag. He unhooked the targeting computer from its mount and removed the radio hub. Kicking open the hatch, he pulled a pistol out of the compartment and crawled out of the pod.

He looked over his shoulder at the Lowe. The powerful machine and the fatman in its embrace had been reduced to a burning heap. *Sorry it had to be like this.* He tossed the thermite grenade in the cockpit and made for his own lines. As the adrenaline wore off, he shivered. *Damn, I've got a long shitty walk ahead of me.*

MEYER GRIMACED AS THE RINGING IN HER EARS DIED DOWN. *WHAT kind of shell just hit us?* The command tent lay in tatters around her. Tables, files, and computers were scattered across the area. Light snow had already covered the surrounding equipment. Shivering, she pulled her hood over her head.

"Hey, we found Comrade Colonel Meyer," called a voice. A group of soldiers staggered over to her. "Comrade Colonel, are you hurt? Do you need medical attention?"

Meyer patted herself and shook her head.

"No, but I need a radio," she said. "And a sitrep, and a map."

The young soldier looked about.

"We're still assessing the damage to the firebase," he finally said. "Most of the damage is between the command tents and the radar arrays. Counterbattery radar didn't even pick up the incoming round, it was so fast."

Meyer furrowed her brow.

"They splashed our perimeter just this morning," she said. "How were they able to get a gun close enough to hurt us without escort?"

The soldier shrugged.

"I don't have an answer for you, Comrade," he replied. "I'll see if we can scrounge some long-range comms for you."

Meyer walked toward the field hangar, overstep filled with purpose.

"Are our air defenses intact?" she asked.

The other soldier started after her.

"Mostly," he replied. "The Tharcians hit us pretty hard."

"I want all our battalion's forces pulled under our air defense umbrella," she said. "Get Kennedy, Wake, or anyone who can fight on the line and bring them in." The soldier nodded as he struggled to keep up with her. "Is my Panzerter ready?"

He shrugged.

"I don't know, Comrade," he said. "I'm not a mechanic."

Meyer shook her head.

"All I really need are the radios and the matrix," she replied. She hurried through the field hangar. Her Martian Commander had become something of a hangar queen. The Panzerter had been cursed with substandard joints at some point during repairs and needed a bracing tower to remain upright.

Meyer climbed up the access ladder to her machine. With a groan, she turned the wheel that opened the hatch to the cockpit door. After scrambling down the ladder, she dropped into the pilot's seat. She took the Panzerter through its startup sequence as quickly as she could. As her radio filled with static, she immediately attempted to raise her companies.

"Reaper, Goblin, any units out there," she said. "This is Leviathan 6. I need a sitrep now." It took her a few minutes of talking into the void before she got a response.

"This is Reaper 3," the voice on the other end said. "We're dragging some of our wrecks with us."

"Sitrep, Reaper 3," Meyer replied. "I need it now."

"Roger, Comrade," Reaper 3 said. "We managed a localized counterattack, but the Tharcians had just enough reinforcements to beat us back." He paused. Meyer didn't dare risk keying the mic and missing a piece of the report. "The Tharcians gained ground, but they stalled, and the rivers will freeze before they can move like this again."

Meyer flexed her shoulders and lay back in the seat.

"How many losses?" she asked.

"Well, we're dragging back the Jupiters," he replied. "We've got four walking machines remaining, including some stragglers from Sandman. We've got infantry in tracks ahead of and behind us."

Four machines out of 21. Meyer shook her head.

"Get under our air defense umbrella as quick as you can," she replied. "We're going to need to rush repairs to our remaining machines." She switched over to Division Net. "Problematic X-Ray, Leviathan 6, I have a sitrep." She had to tolerate about an hour of silence before she got a response.

"Apologies, Comrade, we had to move most of our command post farther west," the voice on the other end of the line said.

Meyer relayed the status and disposition of her battalion.

The other voice sighed.

"The offensive from up north made some gains, but they

stalled." He coughed before continuing. "The whole division is going to be pulled to the second line. We need to rebuild."

Meyer sighed.

"Can I expect a timeline to turn over Firebase Blake?" she asked.

"That is still being determined," the man replied. "But expect it to happen in the next week."

Meyer nodded.

"Roger, I'll begin making arrangements immediately," she replied. "Anything else I need to know?"

"The line is stiffening," the voice replied. "Your position is secure, and we don't believe any more Tharcian attacks will reach your location."

Really? You don't? Even after it became clear we don't know their full bombardment capabilities?

"How good is this intel?" she asked.

"Solid. Both sides of the frontline are worn to the nub," he said. "Our advances stalled early and neither side will be capable of anything major in this theater soon."

Meyer looked at her command matrix. Her units had all entered their air defense umbrella.

As a sigh escaped her lips, she slumped in her chair. *Soon, soon I'll be doing paperwork again. After all of this, going back to that for a month or two will feel like a vacation.*

26

Reiter approached Fletcher's cell. He sighed and braced himself for the conversation ahead.

"Ready, Stovepipe?" he asked.

The infantryman nodded.

"After you, sir," he replied.

Reiter faced the door to her cell and knocked.

"Lieutenant Fletcher, may I come in?" He shifted uncomfortably. *I can barge in if I wanted to. Hell, the one-way mirror lets us see her every action.* He shook his head. *I should have curtains put up for her.*

"You can come in, Captain Reiter," Fletcher said.

Remember, strong enough to be gentle. Reiter entered the room.

Fletcher sat at the head of her bed wearing GCT sweats. "What are you going to ask me today?"

Reiter cleared his throat and sat at the table.

"My superiors have a proposal for you."

She scowled at him and looked away.

"I've already told you, I don't know anything your people don't already know."

Reiter shook his head.

"It's not like that," he replied. "They would like you to submit to a series of medical exams. They want to know how much the Union government meddled with your genes."

Fletcher didn't look at him.

"They want to find out how human I'm not?" she asked.

Reiter shook his head.

"It's not like that. We're going to have more prisoners like you, and we just want to be sure our ignorance doesn't lead to neglect." He steadied himself. "Besides, they're offering you an incentive."

"Why?" she asked. "It's not like I'd have a choice if you just took me."

"Our doctors can repair your . . . lady parts," Reiter replied.

Fletcher blinked and leaned towards Reiter.

"Say again?"

"Whatever the Union did to keep you sterile," he replied, "our doctors can undo it."

"But how do they know that?" she asked. "Don't I have to go through a bunch of tests?"

Reiter waved her off.

"Our medical science is pretty advanced," he said, "and depending on the details, it won't hardly cost anything." She gave him a questioning look, and he held up his hands. "Not that you're paying for it. The military is covering the financial cost of the treatment."

"I'll do it," she said quickly.

Huh, wow, that was easier than I thought. Reiter stood from the table.

"Well, that was all I had for you today," he said. Fletcher stood and looked him over. "Can I help you?"

She shook her head as she approached him.

"No, Captain Reiter," she said, "you've helped more than enough."

Stovepipe shifted in his corner, but Reiter held up a hand to steady him.

Fletcher got within a hands' width of him. "You couldn't be more different from who I thought you'd be."

Reiter nodded.

"That's what happens when you talk to someone," he replied.

Fletcher's next action surprised him. The young woman stepped forward and wrapped him in a tight hug.

"Thank you," she said. She smelled faintly of sweat and strawberries.

Reiter broke her warm embrace and stepped back. He smiled.

"Fletcher, when this all ends, choose your own path." Smiling still, he walked out of the room and back into the hallway. His smile faded when he saw his guests. "She agreed to the terms," he said. "You better hold up your end of the deal."

The man in front of him tossed his hair.

"Why, Captain Reiter, I'm hurt," he said.

"I know the kind of people you work for," Reiter replied. "Starnes told me enough."

The Secretary for the Speaker of the house scoffed.

"Oh, trust me, Captain," he said, "that brute Skara was far more indulgent than my superiors."

Reiter gave him a stern gaze. The man in front of him folded his manicured hands in front of his body and smiled at Reiter with some of the whitest teeth he'd ever seen. *This guy probably never worked a day in his life.* His gaze crept over to Fletcher through the one-way mirror. *He keeps addressing me as "Captain." All he sees is my title and authority. Must be the only thing that matters to him.*

"You can stop ogling her now," Reiter said. "She may be a prisoner, but you will treat her with dignity."

The secretary scoffed.

"First of all," he began, "they grew her in a lab. You really think she has dignity?" He turned his expression back to Reiter. "And for the record, Captain, I outrank you."

Reiter clenched his fists.

"You serve, Secretary?" he asked. "Because your haircut is out of regs, as are those streaks in your hair, and you're out of uniform."

The other man laughed.

"No, Captain," he said. "I'm a public servant in the sense that I help our representatives. I could never wear a uniform."

Reiter folded his arms.

"Good," he said. "Let me be clear: you don't wear a uniform, you don't have rank, you don't outrank anyone, and you certainly don't call shots five miles from the front." Reiter's voice remained even and measured through his whole tirade, but the representative reacted to each statement as if the captain had struck him.

"Are you questioning my authority?" the secretary asked, his voice rising. "Because I can rescind the deal!"

Reiter shook his head.

"No, you can't," he replied. "Your boss can, and she will likely keep it to keep the military lobbyists content." Reiter remained calm in spite of the growing impotent fury of the secretary.

"I think you're overestimating your position, Captain Reiter!" he bellowed.

"And I think you're underestimating the bad press your boss would get if she slighted the Black Lion," Reiter said. "Getting up and working for a living has its benefits, you know."

"Don't let that title go to your head, Captain," the secretary replied. "I'd hate to see you fall to an accident once the war's over, assuming you live."

Reiter stepped into the other man's space.

"And you listen here, you little shit," he said. "You're a bureaucrat. You don't get to come in here, make a bunch of demands, ogle my soldiers and my prisoners, or otherwise make an ass of yourself, are we clear?"

The secretary growled and stormed off.

Reiter sighed and turned around to see the Merlin brothers slack-jawed with a puzzle in their hands. "What's up, guys?"

"Did you just tell that dude to eat shit?" the older one asked.

"More or less," Reiter replied. "What are you doing with that puzzle?"

"Seeing if Fletcher wants to help us put it together," the younger one replied.

"That bored, huh?" Reiter asked. The brothers nodded. "Well, maybe you can find out if they have hobbies in the Union or teach her about siblings. Anyway, go ahead."

As Stovepipe let them in, Reiter caught a faint whiff of strawberries. *Must be an air freshener or something.* Shaking his head, he went to medical.

"AMY, CAN YOU CHANGE THE CHANNEL, PLEASE?" MO ASKED. "I'D rather watch another nature doc."

Amy rolled her eyes as she sat in the chair next to his hospital bed.

"Haven't you learned everything there is to know about Earth's oceans?" she asked.

Mo rolled his eyes.

"No, Amy, we know more about the surface of our planet than

Earth knows about the bottom of their oceans," he replied. "It could really inform us what our own oceans might look like thousands or even millions of years from now." He motioned to the TV. "Hell, a number of species are diverging from their imported ancestors already in ways—"

"You're cute when you're nerdy," she interjected.

Mo rolled his eyes, but he smiled. His broken ribs had already been healed, and most of his burned skin had been replaced. The only thing that remained to be healed were his arms and legs. *A week or so of physical therapy and I'll be ready to go.*

The door to the infirmary swung open.

"Am I interrupting anything?" Adamski asked.

Mo shook his head.

"Nah, Top. I was just asking Steele to change the channel for me."

Adamski nodded.

"Steele, could you give us a few?" he asked. Steele nodded and left. Adamski took her chair and sat next to Mo. "How are you holding up?"

Mo shrugged.

"As well as I can be," he replied. "Losing good people is never easy, especially the kids."

Adamski sighed.

"It's not going to stop, Mo," he replied. "This has the potential to be a long war."

Mo shrugged.

"There's no getting used to this. But what else am I going to do?" He looked up at Adamski. "I can't mope every time we lose someone, or we'll lose more people. I need to keep my head clear and focus on the mission."

Adamski folded his arms.

"Was your head clear when you challenged Kennedy?" he asked. "Or were you thinking of Bartonova?"

Mo grit his teeth.

"He's different," he replied. "That battle's personal."

"How?" Adamski asked. "Because he killed your old flame? Or because he knows who you are?"

Mo looked away.

"That one has ideas," he said. "And he's a hero to them. Killing him would be a PR nightmare for the Union."

"He's an ace piloting an advanced machine," Adamski replied. "You're lucky he got sloppy and didn't kill you." Mo sighed. "Luckily, things should be different next time."

"Yeah, because I'll be a better pilot," Mo said.

Adamski smiled.

"Not only that, but your Panzerter will be better."

Mo looked at him quizzically.

"No way."

Adamski grinned.

"The first of the new models is on its way," he said. "You'll pilot it once your injuries heal."

"I'd pump my fists"—Mo nodded at his arms, wrapped in bandages with sections in regen-gel—"but they're unavailable."

Adamski shook his head.

"Kid, some days you remind me of Gos." Sighing, he stood up. "You've come a long way since you joined Fox, Mo. For what it's worth, we're all proud of you."

Mo tossed his head back onto the pillow. His body felt like a lead weight, but in spite of the circumstances, he smiled.

Guard Colonel Chaney held his chin as he mulled over his choices. Guard Captain Wake floated in a healing tank before him. Chaney paced around the black tile room, his only light coming from Wake's tank. He paused briefly to consult a readout detailing the man's mental state.

"Are you sure about this?" he asked. "He's less stable than the last time I had him in the tank. At this rate, the 'great man' project will face a severe drop in candidate success rate."

The other man in the room merely watched Wake float in the tank.

"Then activate more," he said.

"What?" Chaney asked. "Why?"

"We're not only trying to cultivate the next great leader," the man said. "We're searching for techniques that will allow us to usher in an endless golden age. We'll need more than two subjects."

Chaney dismissively waved his hand.

"It's easier to monitor and control two," he replied before motioning to the tank. "Possibly one."

The other man shook his head.

"You can't terminate this one," he said. "There's a finite number of candidates. We can't afford to lose even one."

"This one *is defective*," Chaney spat. "We can't allow him to develop into a leader."

"I think we should," the other man replied. "Trying to create a morally flawless leader is more likely to result in psychotic breaks."

"We have a pool of millions of candidates," Chaney replied. "We can handle thousands of psychotic breaks before it affects the sustainability of our program."

The other man shook his head.

"At that point, we'd be suffocating the most talented members of our military," he said. "That would cost us the war."

"Comrade First Minister," Chaney said, "if a tuber rises from their ranks with Wake's tendencies and realizes what we've done to them for a hundred years, they will turn that genocidal anger on *us!"* He collected himself and cleared his throat. "I apologize for my outburst, but the only thing keeping us from becoming obsolete is our control over their numbers and education."

The First Minister of the Union of Martian Republics clicked his tonge as he approached Wake's tank.

"You said it yourself, Chaney, we're obsolete. Essentially, I'm building my successors."

Inside the tank, Wake's eyes opened.

27

Guard Lieutenant Colonel Meyer leaned back in the lounge chair. *This recovery center is amazing.* As they advanced southwest during the initial invasion, MAG forces had seized a mountain resort town without resistance. Though some of the residents had fled, most were more than willing to work with the MAG forces for labors.

After a massage and a dip in a Jacuzzi, Meyer felt the best she had in years. The cozy wooden cabin she stayed in was unlike anything she'd seen before. Though the styling was incredibly old, the materials and processes used to make them were modern. A fire cackled in a stone fireplace, and snow blanketed the ground outside.

Picking up her tablet, she began going over the latest reports. The front had stiffened, but the rivers were already freezing. *So the Tharcians have lost their advantage on that front.* Her battalion was being reorganized. For each full Panzerter company, she would also have an infantry company. Her support companies were being refitted with newer equipment.

Shoulder-fired lasers, new rifles, and upgrade kits for the IFVs?

The infantry are getting spoiled. She smiled more when she saw the new organization of her Panzerter companies. Each commander would receive a Jupiter, along with their second-in-command. *Now that they're hitting mass-production, we'll be getting even more of those machines.* Meyer paused and looked out the massive window to her view of the snowy mountain side.

Soon Kennedy's going to wake up and we'll be much closer to winning this war. She smiled at her view. *Maybe when this is all over, I can retire somewhere like out here.* She set her tablet down and closed her eyes. Her head started hurting, and the end of the war suddenly seemed an eternity away.

KENNEDY OPENED HIS EYES. THE FLUID IN THE HEALING TANK didn't sting them. *Here I am again, floating in a tank, recovering from injuries inflicted by Tharcians.* He grit his teeth and grimaced; his replacement molars weren't quite set. *The same group of Tharcians, both times.* He took a deep breath through his mask. The sweet, cool air filled his lungs and relaxed his body.

We beat them on the battlefield, but as long as there's Tharcians like Reiter, this war could go on forever. The thick liquid bubbled around him as more circulated in. Kennedy looked at his hands. *I was made for this?* He clenched his fists. *I'm barely more than a Panzerter. Am I just going to end up like one? Scrapped and recycled when I can no longer perform?* He shook his head. *No, they wouldn't offer me everything they did if I was a mere tool.*

But what if they would? What if it's all a ploy to make me fight harder? He closed his eyes and took a deep breath. *I'll sleep soon. Maybe I'll be able to learn more of our history. That will make the path forward clear to me.*

"Did you lose your cold-weather gear?" Reiter asked. He stood by Mo's bed.

The younger soldier flexed his healing hands.

"I may have loaned it out to my sisters while they fled," he replied.

Reiter shrugged.

"That's fine. I'll just report it as combat losses. We'll need your sizes later, though." Relaxing slightly in his chair, Reiter looked at the TV. "The railgun was a total loss. They're using the components they can salvage to create new weapons for the Lowe line."

Mo sighed.

"And here I was hoping to use one myself."

"Well, cheer up," Reiter replied. "French said the magnetic weapons under construction are going to be overall more effective: more ammo, less recoil, and a higher rate of fire."

"So, like regular rifles?" Mo asked.

Reiter gave him the more-or-less gesture.

"It'll be an overall upgrade," he said. "But we're going to see the Union get tougher too." *Especially Kennedy.*

Mo looked over at the TV.

"I heard you went to bat for Fletcher," he said.

Reiter sighed and put his hands in his pockets.

"What the Union did to her is unthinkable. I would like to think, if the situation was reversed, they would do the same."

Mo shook his head.

"You damn well know that isn't the case, sir."

Reiter didn't look at him.

"Mo, in the long sad history of the human race, the cycle of war has continuously spun," he replied.

"What are you talking about?" Mo asked.

Reiter locked eyes with the young soldier.

"The seeds of this conflict were planted in the War of 2112, the seeds of that one in World War 3, World War 3 in the Cold War, and so on," he said. "I hope that, in some small way, our actions here can prevent another bloody harvest in twenty years."

Mo shuddered.

"That Union commander I fought at Riverside, he said something similar, how my role would be his in twenty years, fighting a young Unionist."

Reiter furrowed his brow.

"We need to be careful to prevent that future," he said.

Quietly, they looked at the TV.

A WORD FROM THE AUTHOR

Dear Reader,

Amazon lists millions of books, and I'm glad you discovered this one. But if you'd like to know when I release a new book, instead of leaving it to chance, Please, subscribe to my Substack. You'll get free short stories as well as updates on my work.
Yes please-Sign me up!
No Thanks-I'll take my chances.
I've also included bonus materials for you my incredible backers, I enjoyed writing them and I hope you enjoy them.

For Paperback reader's, I've included a QR code so you won't be left out.

PREVIEW OF EVE OF BATTLE

He staggered through a snowbank. Bitter winds whipped at the young man's face as he soldiered on. A machine gun chattered in the distance. In response, a Panzerter's rifle roared. The trees that still stood lacked leaves. With the young man coming closer, Captain Paul Reiter noticed something on his back. Another soldier.

From the jagged green and gray lines over off-white, Reiter could tell the young man was a Tharcian, likely a pilot due to his lack of heavy clothing. As the snowstorm howled outside, Reiter pressed his own machine forward. His Lowe, perhaps the most advanced panzerter the Tharcians had produced, stomped through the frozen woods like a giant out of fairy tales.

"Fox 7, do you have ID?" he asked. His 1st Sergeant, Master Sergeant Adamski, followed in a Panzerter IV. The venerable machine had seen two refits since the start of the war, and at the moment could go toe-to-toe with any Union Machine.

"That's Merlin Jr, and it looks like he's carrying Zorro," he replied. "Gold 3, get them inside, I'll call up the MEDEVAC."

Reiter looked ahead. Panzerter rifles intermixed with auto-cannon and machine gun fire. *Somewhere White Team is taking a beating.*

"Stovepipe, on me," Reiter said. "We're going to relive White team and the scouts, Fox 5, fall back to Landfall, and prepare to receive more wounded."

"Roger Fox 6," Stovepipe replied. "I'll be on your 5." Despite the temptation to run, Reiter kept the Lowe at a brisk walk so he didn't leave Stovepipe's tracked Iglaiso behind. "Are you going to commit Black Platoon?" Reiter shook his head despite the other man's inability to see him.

"No, if we commit more forces to this skirmish, we risk escalating it, and that could turn into a battle," he replied. "And we know what our orders are."

"Yeah yeah, defend your positions, but don't get decisively engaged," Stovepipe growled. "Biggest crock of shit I ever heard. Some Uni fuckstick is sitting in my easy chair in your home, but don't bother trying to go fight them." Reiter sighed. Their regiment had been part of the Gallacian Provincial Watch before that province had been overrun by Union forces during their initial offensive. Now they'd been integrated into the regular army's chain of command, but the long retreat to their current position still stung.

Switching to thermals didn't do a lot of good in an active snowstorm, so Reiter was surprised when his passive thermals picked up a hit. Another Iglaiso, a recon type, plowed through the snow towards them. The IFV's tracks squeezed over the howl of the wind as it rushed past them.

"Nomad element. Fox 6, report," Reiter snapped. The Iglaiso ignored him and continued running away. Another Iglaiso followed it, this one with a split turret.

"I don't think the nomads are doing to well," Stovepipe replied, but Reiter ignored him. Instead he broke into a run, crashing through trees as he went. Up ahead he could see the battle. A lone

Panzerter IV just barely held off three tinhats. She was belching smoke and already down an arm. Wrecks littered the snow covered forest. Some Panzerter IVs, a pair of Iglasios, and a tinhat. *Steele.*

Reiter charged the nearest tinhat. In one hand he raised his shield, while the other took aim with his new rifle. With a high-pitched ping, a 90-mm heavy metal slug punched right into the Union machine. The ugly thing crashed to the ground.

Its companions opened fire. Reiter grunted as shells hammered his shield. Firing a second time, he smashed a shoulder off one. To his surprise, the first one began struggling to stand back up. *I must have hit nothing vital.*

"White 4, fall back," Reiter barked. "You did your job, the Reece platoon lives."

"Can't do 6," She replied. "Nomad 3's stuck." Reiter put another round into the first tinhat. This time its hips shattered. *Damn it, she's right, we can't leave them.*

"Gold 2 can tow them," he snapped. "You fall back, I'll cover you." The final intact tinhat backpedaled, unleashing a furious barrage as it did. Reiter returned fire. A hammering auto-cannon signaled Stovepipe catching up to him.

While the lighter weapon could do little against a panzerter's thicker armor, it proved more than capable of smashing a tint's sensor ring. Blind and down an arm, the second tinhat lay still. By now the last one had given them the slip. Reiter looked at the tinhats he'd knocked out.

"Union pilots," he called over the external speakers. "Surrender, you'll be treated with all the respect according to the Geneva convention of 1995." Sure enough, the pilots crawled out of their downed machines. "Stovepipe, you got room for two more?"

"We'll have to have some of my guys ride in the scout track, but yeah we should," the infantryman replied. "When do we get a fancy magnetic gun system?" Reiter chuckled. With Steele limping back to base, Stovepipe's riflemen dismounted. After a few minutes of shouting and bribes, they had the scouts and POWs helping them hook tow cables and dig out the recon vehicle.

Reiter focused on the surroundings, ever wary of a follow-up attack. When none came, and the scout vehicle had been freed, he gave the order to mount up and move out. He let Stovepipe's Iglaiso precede him as they made their way back to base.

"Raptor X-Ray, Fox 6, our screen revived contact," he said. "Inform Early company of the changeover." He never wore gloves in the cockpit, as he'd always preferred the greater sensation of his bare hands. With the Lowe's sensitive controls, it made sense, but the weather made his hands numb. *That's what I need to recommend next, heated controls. At least my bum warmer works.*

"Hey 6," Stovepipe called. "You're not obligated too, but do you mind explaining why you came out here instead of sending Black Platoon?" Reiter grinned as he switched his mic back to the company net.

"A few mark IVs could be any Tharcian armored company," he said. "But the Lowe? That's us, and it freaks out their rookies." Even though his machine traded the all black paint job that'd made it infamous among the union for added splotches of green, gray, and white, captured soldiers still identified it as "the Black Knight."

After an hour slogging through snow and mud, they arrived at the town of Landfall. The municipality still had people living there somehow, despite about of the building being damaged or knocked down. Once he'd parked the Lowe in a kneeling pose in an empty lot with the rest of Fox company, he donned his gloves, killed the engine, and climbed out.

As the frigid wind met his face, he shuddered and pulled his jacket on. Gray clouds hung overhead, casting snow on the town. Landfall itself consisted of a couple blocks stretched along the main road, a provincial highway that led to the city of Grunbeck.

While dismounting his panzerter, Reiter noticed some of his soldiers hard at work with snow shovels and sandbags. *This ought to be good.*

"Hey gents, what's going on here?" he asked. At the start of the war, he'd been Black Platoon's leader, but the ferocity of the initial Union Offensive saw him take over the company during the desperate scramble to stem the tide. At Twenty Seven, he was not much older than most of his soldiers.

"A little something I cooked up," Sergeant Mondragon said with a grin. "The laser weapons the Union tends to favor don't mix well with water, you know, dispersing the beam in all." He pointed at his platoon mates, Corporal Merlin the elder, and PFC Smith. The two held sandbags high so Reiter could see they'd been packed with snow.

"Union laser hits our handy snowbag," Corporal Merlin began.

"And the snow turns to steam, scattering the beam," Smith finished while demonstrating the scatter with his hands. Merlin glanced towards the area where white platoon's machines normally parked.

"Hey, sir, is White still out?" he asked. Reiter hadn't given Col. Hawke his After Action Review and Battle Damage Assessment yet, but he could see the other man's concern for his brother.

"No, they're back," he replied. "None of their machines have been recovered, but Invincible is working on that." He held up a hand before Merlin could get a word in. "Ernie is ok, we had to MEDEVAC him and Zorro, but she needed it way more than he did."

"What happened?" Merlin asked. Reiter clapped him on the shoulder.

"You should be proud of him," he said. "Unis shot them both down, Ernest was able to bailout, Zorro couldn't. When we picked him up, he'd carried Zorro ten clicks in the snow." Merlin sighed in relief.

"So he's not too bad?"

"He's being treated for early stages of hypothermia and frost-bite," Reiter replied. "But he'll be biting at your heels before too long." Mo grabbed the taller man's shoulder.

"Hey man, if you need to take a walk, we got this," he said. Merlin shook his head and retrieved his shovel.

"Thanks Mo, but nah," he said as he returned to work. "If Ernie comes back and I'm slacking, that's hardly the example a brother should set." Reiter turned to leave, but stopped himself. *One more thing.*

"Before I leave, you stooges should be getting a new LT before long," he said. The pilots of Black Platoon shrugged. Their last LT had been killed during a patrol along one of the highways north of Landfall. As his soldiers went about their work, Reiter made his way towards a mom and pop diner centered on main street. With the regimental command post in sight, he took a deep breath and entered the building.

THANK YOU FOR READING! IF YOU'VE ENJOYED THE STORY SO FAR, you can find Eve of Battle available for Kindle here and Audible here.